FATAL

ETERNAL NIGHT SHIFT SERIES

CURSE

BOOK THREE

LENA NAZAREI

Design and distribution by Bublish

ISBN: 978-1-647047-05-4 (paperback)
ISBN: 978-1-647047-04-7 (eBook)

For the real "Tank": thank you for the snuggles. Thank you for staying with me in bed when I didn't want to get out - even if it was 12 hours or more. Thank you for sleeping at my feet while I write and letting me wipe my tears on your fur.

For the real "Olivia" & "Ellie": I know that I'm not always easy to be around. Thank you for cleaning the house when I'm too busy writing, putting up with me and my crazy mood swings, letting me be your mom and never telling me I'm dumb to follow my dreams.

For Emily: thank you for the Starbucks deliveries, listening to my emotional phone calls and then telling me to shut up, stop crying and start seeing how awesome I am.

For Andrew: thank you for taking my calls and texts when I'm at my lowest and always responding with love and understanding. You've gone into murky places - facing your own darkness – to be with me in the abyss 'til I'm ready for the light again. I hope we always go in and help each other out of those caves.

For Jeremy and Logan: thank you for the dinners, the crazy texts, the edits and the ideas. Thank you for always keeping it real and never holding back. Thank you for accepting me just as I am and being a safe space. Most of all, thank you for letting me pull you into this insane, vampire world and trusting me when your alter egos.

For my real fellow nurses, doctors, case managers, social workers, chaplains and nurses' aides: there is *no way* I would've survived the pandemic in one piece without you all by my side, holding me together. I'm coming out of this nightmare better than I was before. The world will never truly know what we went through – and still go through - in the darkest days. But I wouldn't fight this battle with any warriors but you.

For my Fans, Street Team and Fanged Family: When I sent my first book into publishing, I never could've foreseen the journey I was beginning or the blessings it would bring. I now have friends from all over the world. I'll forever be grateful that you choose to read my books and ask for more. Thank you for the supportive messages you send me.

I love you all.

JUNE 2020

I have to admit that writing all this stuff out really does help. The first month of my vampire life was, to say the least, traumatic. Being able to journal it all and then turn it into a book makes it feel like a cool story instead of something I had to survive. When you read this next one, you'll see why I need a way to deal. I'm not sure if this is a healthy coping strategy but it works. Since you all seem to love it, why not keep it going?

I know the first two journals made it seem like my life is a non-stop action movie full of danger. It really isn't like that all the time. After that initial month, people stopped trying to kill me for a little while. It was a much-needed break from fighting for my after-life. For a good six months, I got to be kind of boring.

First, I split my time between my house with the girls and the manor with Sorin. My daughters and I would watch movies, hang out with Rhys and plan my wedding. That last part is the girls' most favorite thing to talk about. They were living their best lives looking through magazines and Pinterest. They're my own little, private wedding planners. Sarah, their step-mom and my ex-husband's wife, also got involved in the planning. At first, she didn't want to "over-step" but eventually she couldn't help herself. It got to the point where the mere mention of floral arrangements resulted in Rhys and Tom going for a walk to escape the squealing. Sarah, Olivia, Ellie and I are having so much fun that I almost don't want the wedding to ever happen.

Next, I focused on being able to defend myself and control my magic. Tamela was training me in martial arts while Sorin was training me in my powers. She had this long, thin Japanese sword with ruby red tape around the hilt. I'd watched her practice with it, like a dancer, fluid and deadly. I'd begged her to train me but she kept telling me that she would know when I was ready to handle it. Until then, that cool sword was off limits.

Lilias had planned to visit me again to work on my farseeing when the world shut down to travel. I've been practicing on my own. I feel like I have a good handle on it but what do I know? And, Sorin doesn't know much about it so he can't help. It's pretty useful for scaring him in the shower though.

In March, I started my journaling. Monica had mentioned it and then so did Alex. He said he writes everything down to get through his tougher times. I knew about his sister's disappearance and her undead visit at his window but he's alluded to things that were a lot worse. He didn't offer details and I didn't push. He did say that writing it out helped it "make sense." So, I wrote out my first couple weeks as a vampire. Eventually, it was published and well – you guys know the rest. In April, I wrote the next one.

I also set aside time to support the wolves. When Diana first became pack leader and wanted to unite us all - vampire and wolf - she had a lot of work to do. She needed to break down the old ways and build up a new normal for them. She was meeting with Sorin for "leadership lessons" and I was an encouraging ear when she just needed to vent. The werewolves aren't happy about her leaning on vampires for advice but they love that she's bringing order to the chaos so they're forgiving her "new ways." I barely heard from Monica from October of 2019 until this last month. I missed her so much and wanted desperately to know she was okay but I knew she needed space. What's that old saying? Let it go and if it comes back to you it was meant to be. That's what I did with my best friend.

Last of all, I knew deep down, I had to leave the hospital. I want to stay a nurse but I can't stay there forever. So, I came up with my plan to go back to school. Eventually I'll be able to teach nursing students online. Jeremy was so supportive of my academic endeavors. When I told him my plan he actually said "I wish it was an option before I had to leave teaching." Sorin is also supportive since he hates when I go to work. I can't blame him – I mean the hospital is the place where I was attacked, hunted, kidnapped and almost murdered by three different people. Teaching seems like a good way to keep being a nurse but get out of the hospital and spend more time with the people I love.

You know, work-death balance is so important.

After Evelyn kidnapped the girls, and a hunter was literally touring the building, I had to think long and hard about what I wanted for my life. I was holding onto being a bedside nurse so hard that I was losing sight of what it meant. The reality was that I put everyone at risk. I used to think that being a nurse and a mom was all I was. But being turned and falling in love changed all of that. And even though the possibility of centuries was before me, nothing was really promised. I wanted to use my time to its fullest potential. Which meant I needed less time in scrubs and more time with the people who matter. I've spent so much time telling Olivia and Ellie that it's okay to put themselves first sometimes. The truth is, I stopped putting myself first a long time ago.

I think it's time I do.

Okay, I'm getting ahead of myself. Let me go back one month to May of 2020. I know it's six months after the last story you read but I promise you aren't missing anything exciting. Let's recap and set up the timeline, shall we?

March 13, 2020 my daughters were told to take their books and instruments home from school. We knew they might not be back to school the following Monday while government officials determined if this new COVID-19 virus would be an issue for us. I thought they'd be out of school for a week or two. Now, it's June and they just finished out their year completely online. Thankfully, Sarah took over as the full time everything while Tom and I care for the public on the frontlines.

My precious time off was quickly taken from me as nurses either fled the hospital or worked 70 hours a week and patients rushed into the emergency room every time they sneezed or coughed. All activities were shut down. Movie theaters, skating rinks, gyms…. they all closed their doors. While most people were told to work from home, public service workers were told to prepare for the worst. Our city talked about turning local college dorms into homes for the frontline workers so doctors, nurses and aides could work insane hours without exposing our families or the public.

In the midst of this Rhys, myself and other vampires who worked the frontlines knew we couldn't contract the virus or wear out from too much stress on our bodies. We've been signing up for any night shift we could to spare our human counterparts from unnecessary exposures or becoming fodder.

Even while I'm writing this in my journal, I'm in the breakroom of the unit. Rhys is downstairs in the blood bank. We can only work nights but we work pretty much every night. Before I get into the latest saga of my vampire life, I urge you to find a nurse or doctor or cop or ambulance worker …. buy them a meal and give them a hug. They are not okay.

I

May 2020

The man beside me was sound asleep. For all intents and purposes, he was actually dead to the world. Whether or not we die when we sleep is a philosophical debate that I don't have the time or energy to get into. All I know is that watching Sorin sleep peacefully next to me is a rare occurrence. Because he's so much older than me, he needs a lot less rest and frequently is MIA when I arise for the evening. I still don't completely understand the massive "To Do" list that a master of a city walks around with but I know that my fiancé always has a crushing weight of tasks to complete. For the hundredth time that week, I felt guilty going to work instead of helping him. We still didn't have a new assistant to replace Will. Sorin would never complain or refuse to help someone so I had no real clue how overwhelmed he was. Jeremy came over a lot to help Sorin with anything he could do. I know Sorin appreciated it while also wishing it was me. Every once in a while, he mentioned how nice it would be when I was done in the hospital and we could be a team. I actually had a resignation letter in my locker at work. I was so close to quitting when the virus hit our country. Then I was too guilty to walk away from my peers.

Don't get me wrong. He understood how important it was for me to be on the frontlines while the humans figured out how to handle the new virus. Contrary to popular belief, we value your lives. We don't want to see you all wiped out. But on top of that, we didn't want the pandemic to continue for selfish reasons too. Eventually, someone was going to notice a group of people that never got sick in a world that was majorly ill. As masses of humans died, the supernaturals like werewolves and vampires we're getting closer to being exposed for the "not-normals" that we are. COVID-19 was a problem for all species. So, Sorin supported me going back to the hospital to help. He knew what it would cost me spiritually to sit on the bench while my friends were at war.

We were getting through each night as it happened. I picked up every shift I could but made a point to take some nights off so no one noticed how energetic I still was when everyone else was exhausted. We put our wedding ceremony on the back burner until we knew everyone could come together to celebrate safely – human or not. We did have something to look forward to though. Our mating ritual was coming up soon. Since it was supernatural guests only, we didn't have to worry about social distancing or masking or the venue being closed. It was happening in the little grove where Sorin and I met. In two short weeks we were due to declare ourselves mates in front of those that we cared about. Once mated, we would be together until the end. Rhys would give me away. Monica, Diana, Alex, Jeremy and Logan would be witnesses. As much as I wished the girls would be there, I knew they couldn't be. They would be at the wedding and that was good enough for me.

Sorin stirred and I felt him wake. It was a rush in my body like warm water sliding through my veins. It happened when he walked into the room or when he woke. It took a little bit to get used to it but became a welcomed sensation over time. It was like the smell of the ocean when you pull into your vacation town and know you're about to have a great week off. After a few weeks of it, I'd asked if Sorin had the same thing happen when I get home or wake up. He smiled and answered "I was worried that I didn't have the same effect on you that you have on me. Nice to know it's equal."

That's Sorin. He never really answers a question outright. I think he likes being mysterious. He's always saying things like *we have an eternity to find out about each other* or *I would not have you become bored with me*. Like that would ever happen.

Before opening his eyes, his arm was already snaking out from the covers to wrap around my waist. He pulled me into him and I giggled. "Well, good evening."

"Good evening, my love." His eyes opened and the grey of them still made me catch my breath. He had this way of looking at me like I was the only person in the room - even when I wasn't. He locked his gaze on mine anytime I spoke to him. For him it was an issue of respect. He thought that not looking people in the eyes showed you were hiding something or not valuing that person's time. I'd spent my human life fighting for attention. Tom was always too busy to really listen. The kids, like most kids, never listened. Co-workers were always talking to you as they moved from one task to another. Patients had trouble really focusing in on what you were saying. Even Rhys had the habit of talking from behind his computer at work or multi-tasking while listening to me. So, it took some time to become accustomed to Sorin's rapt attention when I spoke. It was one of my most favorite things that he did. He looked into my eyes when I was talking to him and listened when I spoke. I'd made a point to try to do that more often with people – look them in the eyes and really hear them.

Attempting a chaste kiss, I softly laid my lips on his. He answered me by pulling me even closer and turning the kiss into something much less innocent. As desperately as I wanted to lie in bed with him all night, we both had a busy schedule. After a few minutes, I found the willpower to end the embrace and wiggle from his grasp to sit on the side of the bed. "Sorry sire but there's too much to do and not much night to do it."

He groaned "You are right, as always. Just wait until your first summer. The nights get even shorter. I do miss the winter."

"Say that the next time you slide down the steps again."

The pillow thrown at my back told me he wasn't thrilled with my quip. "One time in 500 years I lose my balance and it is a frequent joke. I was distracted by your dress so it is actually your fault I fell."

I laughed. "I'm just so glad I got to see it. I was starting to believe you were perfect which is exhausting for those of us who are not. It's just a shame I wasn't recording you. I'd love to see it again."

"Katherine, you promised you would tell no one."

I stood and raised both hands in the air. "I swear I didn't."

His left eyebrow arched high and he looked unsure what to say. He was achingly sexy but I fought the urge to jump on top of him. "I am glad you find joy in my fault. While I am far from perfect, I assure you that I will never fall again. It was a fluke."

"Whatever you say," I made my way to the wardrobe for a robe. Wrapping it around me, I turned to face him. "I don't need to see it again. I can play it in my head over and over for the rest of my life."

He groaned and threw himself back against the pillows to look at the ceiling. It was rare to see Sorin mope but that was definitely moping. The joke wasn't funny anymore and I wanted to see powerful, unstoppable Sorin again.

"Join me in the shower," I said over my shoulder as I left the room.

Yep, that worked.

2

The BMW was already on when I walked into the garage. I didn't know who started it every night for me but I loved the little gesture. Vampires don't get cold so we don't need to get the heater warm before we get in but someone still warmed it up every night.

I shed a tear when we sold the van to the used car dealer. It wasn't because I loved the Odyssey; I actually hated that van. But when I'd pulled the thing off the lot ten years ago, it had booster seats in the back. It'd been on road trips. It had French fries in the seat crevices and crayons melted onto the upholstery. Now, Olivia was fifteen and Ellie was thirteen. They were talking about the cars they would buy soon and the colleges they wanted to go to. I didn't need a minivan or booster seats or room for strollers. Pulling away from the van had been like closing the lid on a box full of memories.

The girls loved the BMW, of course. In true teen fashion, they'd asked no questions about where it came from, only if they could film TikToks in it and if they could show their friends. Olivia wanted to learn to drive with it and I knew she was hoping to use it when she got her license.

Since Tom knew the truth, he knew exactly where the car had come from. It'd taken him some time to really come to grips with what I was. I think it's hardest for him because he knew me for twenty years as a human, had children with me, shared a bed with me but never really knew me. Now, he was having to learn who I really was and deal with my new condition all at the same time. I didn't have any anger for him anymore. We were both young and still had a lot of growing and learning to do when we got married. Life got hectic and the bills piled up. We always thought we would have more time to fix things but time wasn't on our side. When we divorced, it was a wakeup call for both of us.

Plus, poor Tom has to go out and patrol the streets knowing that supernatural creatures exist. He knows they're hard to kill and even harder to recognize. I can't imagine the fear and vulnerability he feels. He can't talk to anyone about it either. He comes over to the manor every once in a while, just to be able to get things off his chest. We tell him to call first so we know the manor won't be full of vamps but he's welcome when it's safe for him.

Thinking of Tom prompted me to call the girls. They picked up on the second ring. When the squealing and screams hit my ears, I was reminded that they had a sleepover tonight to celebrate Addison's birthday. "Mom," one of them chirped at a pitch that would be uncomfortable for any ears but was excruciating for vampire hearing. I pulled the phone away and connected it to the car system.

"Hey Olivia. Sorry. I forgot about the party. Just checking in. Have fun. I'll text when I go to bed in the morning, okay?"

"Okay, love you."

"Love you too." The line went dead leaving me in the silence of the car. I missed them so much sometimes that it hurt. Being trapped in a night-only existence really made it hard for me to be with them full time. Their lives were in the sun and that's what I wanted for them. We could rearrange everything – put them in home schooling for good, flip them to a night life. I knew that they, Sarah, and Tom would do it for me. But that was seriously unfair. They deserved warm days at the park and normality.

Experiencing the girls being kidnapped and almost killed because of me told me exactly what the right thing for them was. I had to be more of a part-time parent. Letting Sarah and Tom have them full time was the hardest thing I've ever done. At first, I felt like garbage. Then I saw how happy and safe they all were. I see them on weekends when I'm not working and we have a lot of fun. We catch up on their lives and talk about the wedding. Someday I'll sell the house and the girls will visit me at the manor but that day is far off. For now, this arrangement works.

Is it awful of me to wish that they were a little less well-adjusted without me around? Yeah, it is but I'm just being real with you. I wished they needed me more.

Pulling into the parking garage, I found my usual spot open. It wasn't far from the walkway entrance and gave me a chance to see Alex before heading up to work. At every entrance was someone checking temperatures and handing you masks. The first few times they checked my temp it read low – like really low. They thought it was their thermometer. Then Alex assured them that some people run low and not to worry. No one questions a doctor. Now, they all joke about how "cold-blooded" I am. Then I quip that you have to be to survive as a nurse. They laugh.

Same exchange every night.

And tonight, was no different. Afterwards, I made my way to the office of Dr. Alex Kitchner – hematologist, human friend, my fake doctor for my fake condition, and researcher for the werewolf and vampire cure. He's a busy man.

I tapped my knuckle against the door. Before he called "come in" I already knew he was there. I could hear his heartbeat and smell him. Alex smells like fresh laundry and some kind of spice. It perfectly fits him – clean with a hint of something exciting underneath.

Opening the door, I stepped in, pulled off my mask, put it in my pocket and closed the door behind me. He knew I couldn't carry or contract COVID so he stopped looking for his mask when he saw it was me. "Good evening, Kate." He was writing something in his journal so I let him finish. While he did, I moved some books off his second chair and plopped down to wait. A few minutes later, he closed the book and turned his seat to face me. "What can I do for you?"

"Nothing Kitchner, I'm here to check on you. We've all been so busy I haven't seen you in a week." He looked tired. His jaw was covered in the stubble that drove the female staff crazy. His brown hair was getting a little long and I saw that it was curly when left to its own devices. The blue eyes I was used to seeing seemed dull and a fair amount of green had come into them. Instead of the Caribbean waters they used to mimic, they now looked like the ocean water closer to the east coast. I knew that some people had eyes that looked like different colors under different circumstances but seeing it was different.

I leaned towards him and took his hand. "Alex, are you sleeping? Eating? Taking days off? You look terrible."

He smiled and looked down. "Thank you but I promise I'm fine. It's all hands-on deck right now. I'll take a break when this is all over."

"Do you mean COVID or the cure or Monica?" I knew I'd hit a nerve because he pulled back, took his hand from mine and ran it through that mass of hair. "Sorry, Alex. I just want to look out for you. Has she called?"

"No," he said and dropped his face to his hands. "She said she needed space and time. I get that. But when you were turned you didn't shut everyone out. You still came to work."

My heart ached for him, like literal chest pain. In the last six months, Alex had quickly become one the most important people in my life. He'd protected me when I was turned, got me on straight nights and fought for the hospital to accommodate me. He'd been abducted and drugged because he'd helped me. He'd sat by Monica's side when she was in the hospital and didn't want to see me. And he'd started to have feelings for her. It was perfect because Monica had loved him for half a decade so she was over the moon. I thought they'd be happily ever after.

Then she'd been scratched by a werewolf and become post-human. After the night of the fashion show, she'd quit her job and retreated to her pack's place an hour from here. Her maker, Diana, was teaching her how to be a lycanthrope. Monica had asked everyone to respect her need for time. We did and she'd cut ties. But, while I had Sorin and Rhys and the girls, Alex had no one. Just like that, he'd been cut off from the one piece of happiness and hope in his life. So, he'd buried himself in work and finding the cure for Monica's condition. I didn't think she knew about it. Diana was donating blood to help him research. Knowing Alex, he didn't want to give Monica the promise of a cure unless he knew he could do it. While I was rooting for him to succeed, I was worried about him. He'd put the cure for vampirism on hold – and that was fine. We had plenty of time. But he'd also stopped looking for his sister. He didn't even talk about her anymore. It might be a good thing since he'd needed to move on for a while but it also might be a seriously unhealthy way of not dealing with things. Since I wasn't trained in mental health, I left it alone. Plus, who was I to judge? I was far from mentally sound.

"Alex," I said. "It was different. I had to push forward. I have kids to provide for. Plus, Sorin wanted me to help find the person who attacked me. I had to come to work and figure it out. But I was not okay. It took months for me to adjust and stop wishing I was never turned. And remember, I had Rhys and Sorin. Monica needs to be with her kind for a little while. She doesn't have to work so she's taking a much-needed break. But I know one thing. She cares about you more than you probably know."

He looked up. "I knew she liked me the whole time. I knew she had a crush on me. But I hardly thought of her. Then, I saw her – really saw her. My feelings changed. Just as they did, she did. Human Monica liked human Alex. But, how do we know that the new Monica will feel the same? Maybe she's moving on from her old life. She's dropped whatever reminded her – you and me. And, let's be honest Kate – Monica and I never started. We had one nice night with a limo and champagne. That's hardly a relationship. Maybe she's realized that I'm not really who she thought I was. She had a crush on a man she hardly knew."

That sent my chest pain from a five out of ten to a ten out of ten. I knew exactly what that felt like. I stood, stepped towards him and lifted him up for a hug. Even if he didn't want it, he couldn't fight me off. I was too strong. But he didn't resist. He melted into the hug and I felt his arms encircle my back. He used to feel so big to me. In that moment, he felt smaller – weaker. He rested his head on my shoulder and sighed, sounding exhausted. It made me miss the tough man that I used to believe didn't care about anything or anyone. The person in my arms was utterly fragile and close to breaking.

"Alex" I said into his hair. "I don't believe that but let's say it's true. Let's prepare for Monica falling out of love with you, whether it's because she never really knew you or because she's changed too much. It's her loss. Because I have gotten to know you, the real you and I think you are the smartest, bravest, most loyal person I know. You are selfless and brilliant. And, all your little broken parts make you who you are. So, she may not like you that way anymore but I promise you it's not because you are not worthy of love."

I felt him shutter and knew he was holding back tears. I could smell the salt of them just inside his body. I rubbed my hand up and down his back. "Please," I whispered. "Please don't stop taking care of yourself. Get sleep, eat something hot, take a shower that's longer than it needs to be and watch some TV. If not for you, do it for everyone that's depending on you. You can't save the world if you collapse."

He pulled back, showing that he hadn't let the tears spill out. He nodded his head and wordlessly picked up a backpack that looked like it had seen college with him. He slid off his white coat, laid it on his chair, dropped his journal into the bag and zipped it up. I took his elbow and led him out of his office. A white board graced the wall left to his door with a marker dangling from some string. He grabbed it, wrote OFF TOMORROW. The pen fell, bouncing up as the string stopped its descent.

"Good job, doc." I led him to the garage and then to his car. When we reached it, he fumbled through his bag for keys.

"You didn't have to walk me to the car."

I smiled. "Consider me your bodyguard. Want to make sure you go home safely and don't double back to work."

He laughed and unlocked the door. "Scout's honor. I'm going home and won't be in tomorrow."

Opening the door, he hesitated. Turning to face me, he leaned down and kissed my cheek. "Thank you, Kate."

"You're welcome, Alex. You're stuck with me and I don't let my people hurt alone. Call me later, okay?"

With that, he climbed into his car, shut the door and started the engine. As he pulled away, I felt a strange ache. He seemed so bruised and isolated and it killed me. I wanted to call Monica and rip her a new one but that wouldn't help anything.

That man deserved so much better and I was going to lay a serious beat down on the next person that caused him pain.

Before I reached the door, the dreaded mask was back in place. It was annoying, especially since I couldn't get sick. But no one knew that so I had to play by the rules. The one nice thing about the mask was that I didn't have to worry about my fangs anymore. For the most part, I had them under control. However, a blood spill or a bout of rage could still bring them to life. Before the mask mandate I would have to hide them. Now, the mask did it for me.

Bet you humans didn't think about the masks making it easy for monsters to walk among you.

The fifth floor was hectic as usual. The sounds of monitors, IV pumps and call bells flooded the unit. I found the board, wrote down my assignment and proceeded to get report on each patient. Tonight, I was working with Jackson and two nurses I didn't know. The hospital was having to hire more travel nurses to keep up with the patients. I figured these two new faces were travelers. I used to hate having agency nurses on the unit but that was how I met Diana so I was trying to greet each one with an open mind.

Diana was the one who turned Monica into a lycanthrope. It wasn't her fault. She was in wolf form and fighting to protect my children but Monica had been thrown into her. Diana still felt horrible. The last time I talked to her she was still saying that she wished it never happened. I had to keep reminding her that my kids were alive because of her. Whatever Monica was going through I knew that she would have died for my daughters. She never would have traded them being dead so she wouldn't be a werewolf. Diana was being harder on herself than any of us ever could be.

She was also the new leader of her pack. I didn't totally know what that meant but I knew that she had to kill three of her cousins to get the role. I also had a good idea of what Sorin went through every day as the head vampire and he'd been doing it a long time. I couldn't fathom the stress poor Diana was under. Last week she was talking to Sorin and I heard her ask how to deal with resistance among her pack so things aren't perfect yet.

Plus, she was dating my maker so that was awesome and weird at the same time.

A couple times I'd planned to go out and see Monica. I'd even gotten to the car once before I changed my mind. It wasn't my place and I had to let her come to me when she was ready. So, I went back inside and punched the punching bag for an hour.

The two travel nurses were practically hopping while waiting to give me report. It was hard to really introduce myself so I just wrote furiously and moved on. I followed the smell of cologne and metal to find Jackson in the lounge, shoving a hoagie in his mouth. "Sit down, hot stuff," he said around his giant bite.

I pulled out the chair next to him and tried ignore the smell of onions and Italian dressing. I honestly don't know how I used to eat human food. I still liked certain food smells but the idea of actually eating it makes me want to gag. It looks completely unpalatable to me now. I know it's ironic for me to be telling you all how gross meat is when I drink blood but again, being totally honest.

Jackson swallowed and washed it down with a Pepsi. Rubbing his hands on his pants he winkled at me. "When are you going to let me take you out?"

I rolled my eyes. "For the hundredth time I'll tell you that I'm engaged, that you are too young for me and that you could never handle what I offer."

He wiggled his eyebrows. "Girlie, you'd be surprised what I can handle. And, I'm calling BS. I saw your boyfriend, remember. He's younger than me."

"Drop it, muscles. It's not going to happen. And, if you keep this up and Sorin catches wind, they'll never find your body."

He flexed his arm to show me his biceps. The scrub top strained under the swell. "I could bench press your fiancé and then snap him in half. Date a real man."

I laughed and slapped his bicep. I didn't mean for it to be hard but he winced. "Put that away, Tarzan. No need to fight over me. I'm all his. Give me report so you can finish your feast."

After hearing about the two patients he was handing over, I left him to his meal and the belief that he could someday win me over. All six of my patients were sleeping. I hated to wake them up but I knew I had to assess them and ensure they were okay. Most of them understood. One guy called me some choice words before allowing me to listen to his lungs, bowels and heart. When I was done, he flipped me the bird and rolled away from me. He was pissed but he'd get over it.

When I was done passing meds, I focused on filling up all the PPE holders with gowns, gloves and masks so the staff would have what they needed. I took some time to read the doctor's notes so I could pass anything important on to the next shift. I knew that it was hard to have time to look in the chart on the busy, daylight shift so I liked to learn what I could when we had downtime. I know that the nurses around me were stressed and scared of what was coming. But I was grateful that no one was trying to kill me and my kids were safe. So, the hospital just didn't seem that awful to me.

Alongside us this shift was one of my favorite nurse's aides, Lacey. To all the nurses out there, be nice to your aides. They work really hard and our shifts are made or broken by them. For those of you not in the hospital, the nurse's aides get drinks and snacks, change patients, get them to the bathroom or on the bedpan, wash them up, get vitals and blood sugars and a ton of other things. I've had an aide save my butt more than once. They are freaking hard workers. A good aide is one of the best things we could ask for and Lacey was one of the good ones. Her hair was streaked with blonde tonight and it made her look like she belonged on a sunny beach, not on a night shift in a hospital. She smiled when I took a break and joined her at the nurse's station. "Kate," she said. "I hate nights but I love when you're here."

"Thanks, Lace. How's your night going?"

"Good," she chirped. "I was just down on four trying to find out what's going on with Dr. Kitchner."

Lacey was great at her job and I loved working with her. That being said, you had to be careful around her. She knew everyone's business and was very good at finding out things that you wanted hidden. The mention of my friend's name perked up my ears and made me defensive. I had to be good at hiding my feelings. If Lacey found out that Alex and I were close, the whole hospital would know by the end of the night.

"What do you mean?" I asked, trying to sound nonchalant.

"He's looking rough. Something's up. I'm thinking break up, which means he's available. I know you don't like him but a lot of girls here would love to be his rebound."

I shrugged my shoulders. "Maybe. I don't know. He's not my type." I hoped I wasn't laying it on too thick.

She didn't seem to be suspicious, just kept going. "Well, no one so far knows. Guess he doesn't really talk to anyone. But I'll find out."

I needed to change the subject or get away so I pulled out my phone. "Okay, let me know. I love some gossip. Sorry, Lace. I gotta text someone."

I stood, walked away and texted Jeremy. I didn't know what he was up to but I pretty much talked to him every night. He and I were so alike in so many ways. It made him easy to talk to since I didn't have to explain very much. He always seemed to know what I was feeling or how I would react to things. Sometimes when we hung out, he'd use his power on me and fill me with a feeling of peace. I think it was part of the reason I wasn't stressed out at work anymore and why I was able to deal with the girls being with Tom and Monica not talking to me. Jeremy helped me have more good emotions than bad. It made things easier to accept.

It also helped that the whole "time is fleeting" thing was no longer part of my reality. I think a lot of human stress comes from the feeling of time being limited. When your time on Earth switches from a hundred years max to thousands – a lot of pressure comes off your shoulders.

ME: What are you up to?

JEREMY: At your place. Helping S make calls.

ME: That's nice of you.

JEREMY: Had nothing to do + love looking at him.

ME: Ha. I get it. Enjoy the view ;) I'll be home soon. Still be there?

JEREMY: I'll wait to see you then go.

ME: Stay.

JEREMY: Nah. L is off tomorrow. Spending time with him.

ME: Good. C U soon.

I dropped the phone into my pocket and made my final rounds. Then, made the patient assignments for the morning and reported off to the nurses. Everything was done so they just needed to watch them until daylight shift showed up.

When I reached my car, the mask came off. Before COVID, taking off my bra used to be the best part of the day. Now, I didn't have to wear a bra thanks to the vampire makeover and taking off my mask was the best part of the night.

I pulled out of the garage and thought about how nice my last six months had been. I was in love and about to be mated and married to a dream man. My kids were doing great. Tom was more supportive than ever. My maker was in a relationship for the first time in centuries.

Alex was taking tomorrow off for some self-care. Jeremy was quickly replacing Monica as my best friend. Also, there was always a chance I'd get her back too. Plus, there was hope she'd be cured.

I wish I'd known that was the last normal night I'd have for a while. I would have enjoyed the fresh air on the way home before it all fell apart.

4

I pulled up behind Jeremy's car and bounced into the manor. I was still running on the high of the nice night and the victory of getting Alex to go home. As soon as I crossed the threshold, I smelled Jeremy and Sorin. The smells were tangled so I knew they were in the same room. Sorin smelled like a cabin in the woods after a summer rainstorm. I don't know how else to explain it. Jeremy was different, he smelled like fresh cedar and citrus. I wondered what I smelled like and made a mental note to ask.

I found them in the office, heads together and reading something. "Hello boys," I said from the doorway.

They both looked up, flashing brilliant smiles. "A frontline hero," Jeremy quipped. Sorin rose and crossed the room to meet me. After a kiss, we walked back to Jeremy. I saw the appointment book on the table and realized that was what they'd been studying. They had been talking about plans for the next few days and when Jeremy could be available to help. I saw the chaos of the book and knew that Sorin had a great deal on his plate. Again, I felt horrible for not being able to help the last few weeks.

"If you take tomorrow night with Logan, I can be here with Sorin to help. I'm off tomorrow and the girls are going to Virginia to visit Tom's parents."

Sorin's eyebrows raised. "Really?"

"Sure," I said laying my hand on his back. "Tell me what you need and I'll happily oblige. I want to help."

"I will take that assistance. What is your rate?"

I smiled "A back massage and a hot bubble bath with you."

Jeremy stood. "With that, I'll excuse myself. I need to get home." He came to give me a hug before whispering "jealous" in my ear. I laughed and playfully slapped his back.

"Go home and see your husband. I'm sure he'll enjoy a night with you. Thank him for being so patient while you helped out here. I can't thank you enough."

He shrugged. "That's what friends are for, Kate. Text me tomorrow."

"Drive safe," I said.

When I heard the front door open and shut, I turned to Sorin. "What do I smell like?"

He stopped drinking the glass of blood in his hand and laughed. "What?"

"I'm getting really good at being able to recognize everyone's smell and find them that way. Just wondered what I smell like."

He set down his glass and wrapped his arms around my waist, starting to sway. I knew this move. He loved to dance with me. I didn't know if he'd been like this before me but since we'd been together, we'd shared a lot of dances. We danced to music, no music, inside and outside. Tonight, he was dancing with me while lightly brushing his nose over my neck and into my hair. Something about it was so sensual. He whispered into my ear "you smell like an apple orchard, roses in the moonlight and honey."

"Oh really," I purred. "I sound delicious."

He slid his soft lips down the side of my throat and kissed my clavicle. "Yes, delicious." My body came to life, reacting to the kiss and his words. The feel of his breath against my skin was like a light electrical charge.

I rose onto my toes to brush the tip of my nose over his hair. "You smell like the air just before a storm breaks and lightening fills the sky."

"I sound dangerous," he said.

I pulled back to look into his eyes. "Very," I answered.

He spun me and pulled the back of me into the front of him, continuing to sway. His hands slid under my scrub top and up to grasp the weight of my breasts. "I think we have time before the sun comes up to continue to investigate. I want to be thorough in answering your questions about scent. It's possible that different parts of your body carry different smells."

"Well," I responded breathlessly. "I do appreciate your attention to detail. Shall we head to the bedroom?"

He didn't answer, just scooped me up and had me in our bed before I could say anything else. When we finally fell asleep, I wasn't able to speak anymore. And, he was very certain that he'd thoroughly explored every inch of me.

5

After rising for the night, it took me a minute to remember that I
didn't have to work. I checked my phone. There was a text from
Rhys telling me he was coming over, a text from the girls telling me they
were safe in VA and a text from Jeremy telling me to enjoy my bubble
bath. A missed call from an area code I didn't recognize didn't have a
voicemail attached to it so I assumed it was a telemarketer.

Sorin wasn't next to me.

I headed to my bedroom and found a sundress to wear. I hadn't slept
in this room in months but all my stuff was in there. The full closet was
a testament to how much Tamela and I loved to shop. I never thought
I'd have so many clothes that weren't scrubs.

The dress I chose for the night was thin strapped with buttons up
the center. It was soft to the touch, almost reached the floor and flowed
when I walked. Large purple flowers spotted the white fabric. I preferred
to be barefoot when I could be so I didn't slide any shoes on. When I
was human, being shoeless meant hearing the slap of my feet against
the floor. Now, with vampiric grace, my walk to the kitchen was silent
as I ran a brush through my dark hair.

I found Tamela, Sorin, Edwin and Rhys around the island and checked the clock. I'd slept in a little bit and was famished. Guess our escapades the night before wiped me out harder than I'd realized. Rhys poured blood into a glass and handed it to me when I approached him. I kissed the top of his head, took the drink and crossed to my fiancé. The chairs were full so I stood next to him. He didn't skip a beat, just stood, gently pushed me towards the seat and kept talking about the plans for the evening. One of the things I loved about him was the very old customs he still held onto. He never sat while I stood. He also opened doors for me, wouldn't allow me to step in puddles or mud, bowed whenever he saw me dressed up for an event and led every dance.

Anyone who thinks chivalry is dead has never dated a 500-year-old Romanian vampire.

"The doors will open soon," Sorin said. "It's been a while since we allowed visitors and I know my people are missing the gatherings so let them come together. Naseem is already checking the grounds. Edwin, please station at the door. Tamela, please be at the solarium bar. I will be around as much as I can but we do have a lot to get done this evening. Kate, you can be my witness for grievances. Rhys, can you be in the office to take notes for the record?"

Rhys nodded, "Whatever you need."

I spoke up. "What exactly am I doing?"

"Our people bring any issues to my attention. For example, it may be a property dispute or a perceived wrong-doing. They stand before me and plead their case. Along with my witness, I decide how to handle it best and give my judgement. We will talk through each one but most are very minor. Tamela has been filling in but she is truly needed as a guard. This way she can be utilized in her best way and you can learn what it means to be my partner. We may not be mated yet but it's important they start to see you as the Lady of the city. I'm afraid to say it's not all glamorous."

I looked back at him and winked. "I'm here to help, boss and I'm a quick learner. I'm sure I can handle the whole package."

His eyes sparkled and a smirk crossed his face. "Remember you said that."

Edwin stood, finished his drink and placed his glass in the sink. "I'm going to walk the house before I open the doors. Summon me if you need me."

"Same here," Tamela added and followed Edwin out.

I looked over at my maker. Tonight, he looked especially young. His hair had more red than brown that evening. It was probably the forest green shirt he was wearing. Certain colors brought out the red in his hair and the green in his eyes. He had dropped the masking like he usually did when he wasn't at work and was around other vampires. When he was using his power, his eyes were a muted brownish-green like river water. When we were away from humans, I didn't need the makeup or dry shampoo to hide my looks and Rhys didn't need the masking. I loved when there were no illusions between us.

"How are you, Rhys? I feel like I haven't seen you in a while." He'd been just as busy as me at the hospital but since we didn't work on the same floor we didn't cross paths much. Plus, he spent his nights off with Diana.

"I'm good, Katie. Not too much you don't know."

"How's Diana?" I asked.

A smile crossed his face that told me they were still going strong. "She'll be coming by soon. You can see her and ask her but I think it's going well."

"Have you met the family yet?" I immediately wished I hadn't asked when I saw that smile falter. "Sorry."

"It's fine," he waved his hand in the air. "It's just that they aren't ready, you know? They're still mad that she's friends with vampires. They need more time before they find out their pack leader is dating one."

I decided we should change the subject. "Have you seen Alex recently?"

"No," Rhys answered. "It's been too crazy."

"I saw him last night," I continued. "He looks awful, Rhys. I sent him home to take a day off. I don't think he's eating and he's definitely not sleeping. He's at the hospital 24/7. I'm seriously worried about him. Have you heard anything about Monica?"

Rhys shrugged. "Diana just says that she's doing well and thriving. She's shifting much easier every month. Everyone in the pack loves her."

"Is she coming back?" I hated being so blunt but I wanted to find out before the manor was full. Sorin had made it clear that no other vampires were to know how close we were with the werewolves. A lot of vamps still didn't like lycanthropes. When we started to bring the two groups together, it wasn't going to be just the wolves that threw up resistance.

"I don't know, Katie. Diana's very protective of Monica. She doesn't tell me any personal stuff."

I sighed. "Poor Alex." The rest of my thought was cut off by the sound of people talking in the foyer. Vampires were arriving for the night. Sorin laid his hand on my back and I knew it was time to move.

"Let us adjourn to the office to prepare," he gestured to the kitchen door. Rhys and I followed our cue, standing and walking out of the room.

We were met with a group of four vampires talking to Edwin. Everyone was speaking at once so it was hard to pick out the words. The foursome was made up of what I can only describe as "punk rockers." Their hair was a mix of florescent colors and ranged from mohawk to mullet. Silver lined each of the four sets of ears. Ripped jeans, concert tees and jean jackets completed the look. One guy even had two drumsticks in a back pocket. If they were a vampire garage band, I was going to have to hear them play some day. It was too unique not to experience.

Sorin reached the group and they all turned. One by one they shared a high five with him and greeted him with genuine joy. He said hello to each one using their names so I discovered that the four vamps were Ryan, Seth, Joy and Gary. They thanked Sorin for opening up the manor to guests again and asked if they could play at the next "shindig." He agreed and they rejoiced.

So, I was right – vampire rock band. As we headed up the stairs to the office, I was filled with excitement from the prospect of hearing them play at the next party and curious about what their band name was.

6

I spent the next half hour seated next to Sorin on his evergreen couch. Rhys was in a merlot chair, off to the side of the room and typing away on a laptop as each vampire spoke. The planned routine for each grievance was the same – Naseem would bring in the next vampire or two, introduce them to us and give a brief explanation as to why they wanted to see Sorin. Then Naseem stood by the closed office door while we heard the story from the vampire or vampires, asked them questions and gathered information. Next, Naseem led them out while we talked amongst ourselves and reached a verdict. Lastly, the bodyguard would bring them back to hear our answer.

The first round was a female who wanted to move into the city. She was from Florida and hated all the sunshine. She did some research, discovered how few sunny days Pittsburgh has and wanted to move. But, before she could settle, she had to present to Sorin for approval and to swear allegiance. Sorin approved the move and took her through the oath. As I listened to the words, I flashed back to the night I met him.

"Will you pledge to me your loyalty? Will you follow our laws, my judgement and submit to my authority?"

The girl in front of me agreed without hesitation to those words but I vividly remember my own reservations. If my recollection was accurate, I'd wanted to tell him to fuck off while also wanting to offer up my body at the same time. It was amazing how quickly everything can change and how different my life had become in six months.

She happily strolled out of the room to go plan her new life in the steel city.

The second issue had been vampire neighbors, a man and woman. The man was convinced that his neighbor had eaten his cat. The woman insisted that, while yes - she hated the cat - she would never consume another vampire's animal. The man was so sure that the pet was his neighbor's meal that he'd made her existence pure hell. The man was asking Sorin to make the woman pay him reparations of $1,000. The woman was asking for a restraining order against her neighbor.

Sorin listened quietly. When they were done, he stayed quiet. When he turned to me, I knew he was thinking something I may not like. While looking at me, he spoke to the room. "Please leave and I will bring you in when I am ready."

I heard Naseem take the two out, while keeping my eyes on Sorin. "What are you thinking?"

He spoke carefully. "I think it is time for our people to start to learn some of the things you can do." He held up his hand to stop my protests. "Not all of it but they know you have some kind of power. We all have magic. Let us use this opportunity to show off one. It will end this feud while also starting the word among the city that the new Lady can see into minds. It will allow them time to begin respecting and slightly fear you."

"Fear me?"

"To rule thousands of powerful creatures, you must be respected and feared. This is what holds them accountable and keeps them in line. If they do not obey our laws, everything falls apart. Knowing that you can see into their minds and that I can feel lies, will make it very hard for them to get away with disobedience."

I drew in a breath and let it out. If I was being honest with myself, Sorin was right 99% of the time. I really should argue with him less.

"Okay," I relented. "How dramatic would you like this?"

"Contrary to popular belief, the less dramatic the more impact it has."

I nodded at him and felt his power fill the room. He called his vampires back into the room with just a thought. Even I could feel the pull from his call. The two neighbors returned with looks of hope in their eyes. They stopped side by side in front of us.

I stood, walking slowly up to them. Their looks transitioned from hope to confusion. Sorin's voice rang out from behind me. "My companion will look into your minds. The truth will be known soon."

Looking into the woman's eyes, I faced disbelief. I had the suspicion that she didn't think I could do it. "Think of the last time you saw the cat," I said and continued to stare into those eyes.

When I go into someone's mind, it's not always a visual first. Memories and thoughts come to me the same way they come to you. Sometimes it's a smell first or a sound. Sometimes it's a visual without any sound at all. That night in front of the woman, I heard the cat first. I could understand why she didn't like the animal. His "yowling" was awful on the eardrums. It sounded like his voice box has been damaged at some point. As the sound filled my ears, the vision joined it. I saw the cat through her eyes. They were on the back deck of her house. She had been sitting outside, enjoying the night and reading when the pathetic looking animal walked up.

"Hello, stinky," she said to the thin, black and white tabby. I could sense her feelings about the cat. She was slightly annoyed but didn't really hate the cat. She pulled over a small bowl with dry cat food and I shared with her the wave of nausea from the smell of the animal's dinner. Despite the fact that the odor of the kibble made her sick, she kept it around for the hungry kitty. Smiling, she watched the cat run up to eat. "Does he ever feed you?" Her answer was the cat gratefully chowing down. Running her hand down the animal's matted fur, she returned to her book.

I pulled back from her vision, turning to Sorin. "It wasn't her," I said. "She actually felt fondness towards the cat."

The woman sighed and I turned my attention to the man. "Never mind, I heard what I needed. It wasn't her. We can go now. I am retracting my complaint."

"Too late, Boris." Sorin spoke from behind me. His voice filled the room with heat; I was guessing he had sensed something off the male vamp. He wouldn't have been mad for no reason.

"Think of the last time you saw the cat," I said, locking my blue gaze into his brown one. I felt his resistance and my ears filled with humming. He was humming in his mind, an attempt to fight off any memories. "Just tell me the cat's name." He continued to fill his thoughts with humming and refused to answer the question.

From beside us, the girl vampire spoke. "Tiger."

With the mention of the cat's name, the man was no longer able to lock the thoughts out. The cat filled his mind. It laid on a dirty couch, its tail flopping up and down with a thump. Boris was at a table with bills stacked up next to him. A few of those bills said FINAL NOTICE. He really didn't want to go back to work and was brainstorming ways to make some money quickly. He knew the cat had to go since he couldn't afford the food. There was no reason he couldn't make money off of the loss of the cat, too. He didn't hate the thing but sacrifices would need to be made. As I saw him stand, approach the kitty and wrap his hands around the tiny neck, I pulled out of his head.

"Bastard," I whispered and his face filled with fear. I saw his muscles tense but Naseem had his arms around the man before he could move to attack or flee. I turned to Sorin. "He snapped the cat's neck to blame on her. He thought he'd made some easy money to pay off some bills and no one would ever know."

"You prick," the woman screamed. "I would have taken him. Why?"

"It was my cat. I can do whatever I want with it," he growled. Naseem was behind the angry man, holding each of Boris' arms before anything could happen.

Sorin laid his hand on my knee when I sat down next to him. He was scarily still, watching the man fight against the bodyguard's grip. "Stop," he spoke and his power filled the room again. This time the bulk of it was directed at Boris and I saw the impact like a punch to his gut. He sagged in the bodyguard's arms. Naseem let go, as the man slid down to his knees on the floor.

"Look at me," Sorin said. The man looked up to see his ruler and face his sentence. Sorin stood. "Anyone who can snap the neck of a defenseless animal for the purpose of greed is someone I worry about around my people. You will leave this city. I will show you mercy, give you two weeks to pack and find another city that will take you. In those two weeks, you will stay away from your neighbor. You will not speak to her, cross your land into hers or seek retribution. Do you understand?"

The man found his strength and stood. He was a few inches shorter than Sorin's 6'2" but didn't let that slow him down. I wasn't good at pinpointing age yet but I'd wager my paycheck he was about 450 years younger than his Lord, yet he appeared to be ready to make the stupid mistake of resisting Sorin. "I want the second judgement," he groaned.

I didn't know what that meant but when all eyes turned to me, I had a pretty good idea.

"You are the second judgement," Sorin said to me.

I wasn't exactly prepared or coached for this but I had a solid grasp of the weight on my shoulders. As the "back up" judge in these proceedings, the man was asking if I agreed. I was pretty sure that vampire law required a second opinion to agree and a witness to write it down before it was the "end-all-be-all." I gathered up all the knowledge and experience I'd had as a nurse among the public for over a decade and put on my game face.

I walked slowly into the direction of the shaking Boris and made a point to hold my head high, never breaking contact with his gaze. "You took in a living thing, a helpless thing and cared for it. You made it trust you and rely on you for sustenance and life. Then, when it benefited you, you made the decision to take its life for a thousand lousy dollars.

You played God with a helpless creature, then tried to pin your crime on another of your kind. What's to stop you from doing that with a human or vampire in our territory? I want you out of our city."

His face filled with rage. I saw the struggle in his eyes. He wanted to lash out at me but knew he'd face Sorin, Rhys and Naseem in the process. He also feared me, didn't know exactly what powers I possessed and worried I knew more. I didn't know anymore and was scared of what I would find in his mind. I had spoken the truth; I just wanted him out of my city.

I saw the resolution cross his eyes and he made the safe choice. He squared his shoulders, gave a bow to Sorin and said, "I'll be gone in two weeks." Then he turned to the door and left the office.

"Make sure he leaves the manor," Sorin addressed Naseem who followed the angry vamp out. Sorin then turned to the woman. "I apologize for what he put you though. He will be gone soon. If he says or does anything to you, call me immediately."

She let out a breath that I think she'd been holding for a while, then nodded her head in approval and left the room.

Sorin's gaze found me and he gave me a respectful nod. "You will make debates much easier. I have always been able to feel lies but for you to be able to see what really happened - it will change things for the better. I am in awe of you."

Rhys stood, coming to my side and pulling me into hug. "Same, kid. I'm so proud of what I just saw you do. Almost brought a tear to my eye."

I returned the hug, then pulled out of it. "I'm glad you two are so happy. I'm a little worried about the messed-up stuff I'm gonna see in people's noggins." I returned to the couch and plopped down. As much as I loved helping Sorin and catching bad guys, I was starting to understand the seriously sick individuals we may encounter. If I was going to start looking into the heads of vampires, I may need to put together some kind of cleansing ritual to help me deal with the icky bits.

Sorin and Rhys came to sit on each side of me. Each man laid a hand on the knee on their side. "You're not in this alone," Rhys said.

"We will be with you and you will do much good for our city," Sorin added.

I looked to my maker's emerald greens, so full of love and admiration. Then I turned to face the grey irises of the man I loved. Both of them would likely lay down their lives for me. They'd die before they'd ever see me in danger.

But they wouldn't be the ones seeing the terrible things people hid in their minds. Only I would.

7

I laid each of my hands on the hands of the two most important men in my life and squeezed. "I'm good," I said. "It was a shock but we did the right thing. Let's get through the rest of the grievances so we can enjoy our evening off, please. I'd like to go down and mingle a little."

Rhys stood, returning to his chair and laptop. Sorin laid a kiss on my cheek. "Are you certain? You could rest between each."

"Let's just do this," I answered.

I felt Sorin's power shoot out of him and into the hallway. He was calling in the next round of issues for his review.

Naseem came into the room without another vampire. The concern on his face made me immediately nervous. Standing at an impressive 6'8", I'd begun to believe that nothing would ever worry the bodyguard. I'd seen him break up fights like he was dusting the mantle. He rarely spoke so I didn't know much about him but I knew he was not tolerant of drama. To see him upset was a shock to everyone in the room.

"What is it?" Sorin questioned, rising to his feet and instinctually standing in front of me to shield me.

Naseem didn't offer much. He just said "She's bringing her now."

Before we could ask his meaning, Tamela led a girl into the room. When I say girl, I don't mean "girl" in the broad sense. The female that came in with Tamela looked to be in her teens. Tamela was six feet tall with no shoes on, so she made many women look small but the girl next to her was tiny. I don't think that poor female had eaten in a long time. Tamela's dark hand holding onto the girl's thin arm showed us just how pale she was. I mean, as a Caucasian, Irish-blooded vampire – I'm pretty pale. However, this young lady before me made me look flushed. Her skin was almost paper white.

She was barely over five feet with stringy, dirty brown hair that fell to her waist in waves. Her eyes wildly moved around the room. A mix of fear, anxiety, confusion and optimism filled her blue eyes and made her very hard to read. Her bare feet peeked out from a dress that had been worn so long the skirt had collapsed into strips.

Sorin took a step towards the girl and she shrank into Tamela, away from him. He froze, slowly reversing his steps. You didn't need to have empathy to know that something horrible had happened to this female.

"Is she a vampire?" I asked the room.

"She is," Sorin said quietly like he was afraid to upset her. "She doesn't feel new but she does at the same time. I've never felt anything like it."

Tamela had wrapped her arms around the small girl in a gesture of protection we didn't see often in the Amazonian bodyguard. As her friend, I knew Tamela was full of tenderness. I also knew she took great pride in hiding her softer side from the majority. She especially didn't want Sorin to see her be anything but tough. As her maker, Sorin had raised Tamela up into the self-sufficient bad-ass that she was. She would rather die than look weak in front of him. Something about this female had made her drop her pride and become almost motherly.

I slowly rose from the couch and stepped towards the cowering teen. She glanced at me fleetingly and returned her gaze to the floor but didn't pull back. I took that as a good sign. Laying my hand on Sorin as I passed him, I sent thought from my mind to his to let him know I was approaching her but to be ready in case it went bad. While we all saw a harmless little girl, I'd been through enough in the last six months to know not to trust people right away.

Cautiously moving to my friend and the stranger in her arms, I was grateful for the choice to not wear shoes. Maybe this girl would see my bare feet and find comfort in our mutual lack of shoes. I know that's a stupid thought but I was grasping for commonalities.

When I reached the two women, I laid my hand on the girl's back. I could feel her bones under the thin skin. If she was a vampire like Sorin said, she didn't feed well. Her shoulder blade lifted off her back and was prominent next to the thin strap of her dress. I ran my hand tentatively down her hair, in the same gesture I would use to comfort my own teenaged daughters. My touch made her freeze but I didn't stop. I stroked down the knotted tresses and then returned to the top of her head to begin again. As I continued the reassuring touch, I found Tamela's eyes.

"Who is she?" I whispered.

"I don't know," she answered. "A couple brought her in. They found her in the woods near their home. That's all I know. They are downstairs to answer questions."

Sorin rose and moved slowly towards us. "Tamela," he spoke just above a whisper. "Take her into Kate's room. We will come find you after we speak to the couple. Naseem, bring them up, please."

Naseem left the room followed by Tamela, leading the little vampire out of the office. I felt tightness in my chest. That young girl had obviously gone through something awful. All I could think of was my daughters and how vulnerable they were in this world. Sorin wrapped an arm around me just before I thought my knees would give way. "She's so small," I said turning into him.

"I know," he said. "We will find out what happened, I promise you that."

My imagination didn't have time to spiral down into all the possibilities of what could have left that girl a shaking, scared skeleton. It was stopped by the arrival of the vampires who had brought her to us.

8

The man and woman walked into the office holding hands so I assumed they were a couple. I'd been trying to get to know all the vampires that came by Sorin's house. I didn't think I'd seen them before but it was hard to tell. There are more vampires in the city than you probably realize.

"Justin and Beth," Sorin said when they were in the room and the door was shut. He crossed to shake their hands. "It has been a long time. Please, come in and sit."

Justin stayed standing next to Sorin but Beth did cross to sit in the merlot chair that Rhys wasn't occupying. Her brown hair was cut short, showing off her big, brown eyes. She reminded me of what fairies might look like if they chose to be human - dainty and soft. She reminded me of Lilias in that way. Justin was also on the small side. He was half a foot shorter then Sorin. His blonde hair was almost white, making his blue eyes pop out from the fair skin and hair. Beth looked close to tears but made the point to acknowledge my maker and glance at me.

Sorin addressed both of them when he introduced us. "This is Rhys. He is a confidant and will take notes of everything we say in here. On the couch is Katherine. She is my soon to be mate and Lady of this city."

Justin and Beth both looked at me in surprise. I was getting used to it. So many of Sorin's people believed he would never choose a mate. He was well known for being "hard to pin down." I knew he had many lovers before me; we were very honest with each other. But what I had learned over time was that most didn't get a second night with him. They all thought they'd be the one he fell for. He was basically the most eligible undead bachelor within a 200-mile radius for centuries. Now that he was declaring a mate, everyone wanted to see who finally got him to promise monogamy. And, 95% of them were disappointed when they saw it was me.

I stopped taking it personally months ago.

Beth was one of the few. Her eyes showed a little curiosity and confusion but then it was all happiness. Most vamps were all about free love. They slept with each other, didn't care about gender or labels and loved not being attached. But some, like us, the couple before us or Jeremy and Logan, chose mates to be loyal to. Beth seemed like someone who loved who she was with and wanted everyone to have that. It was rare but I did encounter that response every once in a while.

Sorin led Justin to the couch and they both sat with my fiancé in the middle and Justin facing his partner. "Please tell me how you came to find this girl and bring her to me," Sorin said to both of them. "Any detail may be helpful so be thorough."

Rhys was clearly ready to type everything. No one needed to tell him how important it was. I was on the edge on my seat, bursting with questions. But I knew I had to let them tell the story organically and trust Sorin to ask the right questions.

Justin looked at Beth so she started. "We were walking in the woods. We do it almost every night. Mostly we look for animals and mushrooms and things like that, you know? We like to take pictures of different species and catalog them. We've seen some very rare things but we almost never see people out there. It's why we live there."

Sorin interrupted her. "I'm sorry, for everyone, please tell them where you live."

"Oh," she said. "Sorry. We live not far from Johnstown. It's rural where we are, mostly woods." She looked to Sorin for approval and he nodded, so she continued. "Three nights ago, we were walking and heard something coming. Usually, it's a deer but sometimes it's something you don't want to necessarily encounter. We see wolves out there. This sounded big so we pulled back to hide behind a fallen tree. When the smell hit us, we knew it was another vamp. Like I said, we never see anyone else out there so we were surprised. Justin stood up first."

She nodded to her partner and he took over the story. "I'm not a fighter," he started. "I wanted to see who the vamp was before I decided if we should run or introduce ourselves. I mean, we don't own that land, others can move in but no one has in so long. I think it's because it's hard to get blood out there. We have to come into the city every week or so to stockpile."

"You're getting distracted," Beth prodded gently.

"Sorry," he said. "I stood up and saw this girl. At first, I thought it was a kid because she's so small but as I focused in, I saw she was more like a college student, you know? Still young but at least not a kid."

I looked at Sorin and Rhys. To me they were so old but I also knew they'd both been turned in their twenties. They'd really had so much more life to live as humans when it happened. At least I'd had forty mortal years to have a family and see the beach at sunrise and all those human things. My maker and lover had really been so young. I had the sudden urge to hug them both but controlled myself. Sorin turned to me. I knew he was trying to never use his power on me but also knew that sometimes, if the feeling was strong enough, he'd get a taste of it. He must have felt my sympathy for them because he turned, gave me a small smile and a small kiss on the cheek. He might not know exactly why I was wanting to hug him but he was still assuring me he was okay. We turned our attention back to Justin.

"She had this dirty dress on and looked like a scared animal. I didn't even think, I just grabbed Beth and we rushed to her. She held onto Beth and wouldn't let go. She was so scared of me. The closer I got to her the more she freaked. So, I backed off and Beth talked to her. She won't say anything. She's totally mute. All I know is that she drank a liter of blood when we took her back to our place. Then, she slept all day and half the next night."

Beth picked up the story from there. "I tried to give her some of my clothes, tried to give her a shower. She wouldn't let me take off her dress. I even left the clothes in the bathroom and made the bath, then left the room. So she could have privacy, you know? When I went back in thirty minutes later, she was curled up in the corner on the floor. She never got in the tub or changed."

Justin spoke next. "So, we called and Tamela told us that you were opening the manor for a gathering tonight. We figure that you were the best person for this." Justin gulped and let out a breath. "I don't know what happened to this girl but I think it was bad, Sorin. Like, really bad."

Rhys stopped typing. Beth wrapped her arms around herself like she was trying to protect herself from the harm that girl had experienced. It sent a chill down my spine. Sorin laid his hand on my leg like he was trying to remind himself that I was next to him and safe. We were all thinking of the hundred ways young girls can be used and abused.

"You did the right thing," Sorin said. "She is safe here. We will care for her and find out what we can. May I contact you with more questions later? I may need to come out there to see where you found her."

Sorin stood and we all followed. "Of course," Justin said, crossing to Beth and sliding his arm around her waist. It was hard to imagine anyone being scared of Justin. He looked like someone who'd be more into comic books than horror. I'd have to ask Sorin what he knew about the couple. I'd been through enough to know not to rule anyone out.

They shook Sorin's hand and he told them to be sure to get blood from his stock to replace what the girl had drunk. They left the room, leaving just the three of us again. I don't think any of us knew what to say. I knew I was going to need a hot shower to feel clean after seeing the kitten murder and hearing about abuse. Then I needed to facetime the girls to know they were safe. Plus, a seriously long time in Sorin's arms.

But first, I needed to go see this broken vampire. "I'm going to go talk to the girl," I told Sorin and Rhys. "I don't think you two should approach her until we know more. She clearly doesn't like men. We already saw how she reacted to you, Sorin."

Sorin nodded. "You're right. She needs females right now. Rhys and I will finish the final grievances for the night. I don't think there are many left. Please, find me once you've seen her."

I crossed to Rhys and pulled him into a hug. "Love you."

He returned the hug and spoke into my ear. "Are you okay? Are you sure you want to do this? Tamela is with her."

Pulling back to look at him, I answered. "Yeah. I'm okay. I'll find you after."

I found Sorin and kissed him. He smiled, knowing what I was thinking and feeling without me having to say it. He knew there was no point in asking if I wanted to do this. He knew I would.

Even if I wished that I didn't need to.

9

The girl looked so small and frail on my big bed. She was across the bed, on her side, facing the headboard and looking at the naked birch tree wallpaper that graced the walls. Tamela sat next to her. As she rubbed her hand up and down the girl's back, she hummed something I didn't know. It sounded old and had a soothing effect that contrasted the toughness of the bodyguard who sang it.

When Tamela saw me walk in, her eyes said it all. She was heartbroken, worried, angry and confused. Many people looked at her and saw a tall, strong warrior. They thought nothing would upset, scare, hurt or break her. She had spent a long time building that character and refining the presence she put off around others. But I'd gotten to know her. Over countless nights of talking while she styled my hair or we looked at clothes online, I'd learned the woman inside, the one that Sorin had rescued, raised, trained and turned. She had a heart bigger than any other being on this planet. Her personal mission called her to look out for the little guys in the world. She was a fighter for all of those who couldn't fight.

And, this was exactly the kind of thing that hurt her the most.

I slowly approached the bed but the girl didn't even look over at me. She didn't tense. She didn't acknowledge my presence at all. I whispered to Tamela. "Has she said anything?" The bodyguard shook her head.

I sat gingerly on the bed, lying myself down between her and the top of the bed. My face rested just in front of hers. She continued to look up at the trees on the wall so I took her in for a second. The blue of her pupils seemed dull but that could be malnourishment. I doubted she knew how to mask. I was sure we'd have to cut out some of the tangles in her light brown hair. It had fallen over one of those aquamarine eyes but she made no moves to brush it away.

I just started to talk. "I have two daughters. One is thirteen and one is fifteen. Olivia and Ellie. They love to play soccer and Olivia plays the flute. They have a dog that they love but they want hamsters too. Last night they went to a slumber party so I can only guess they ate their weight in pizza and cake. They're probably asleep now but I'll talk to them when they wake up and I go to bed. They live with their Dad because they're all still human. I miss them so much."

While I spoke, her gaze had slowly fallen to look into mine. She was still cautious but some curiosity had crept up. I kept going. "I've only been a vampire for six months so I still remember what it was like to be human, to be a real mom. I remember picnics and the pool. I remember Christmas mornings, coffee and French toast. I remember how it felt to be pregnant and what it felt like to hold them for the first time. But, it's different now. I want them to grow up, to have families and to be human."

I don't know what part of that got to her but she scooted into me and laid her face against my chest. The subtle shaking of her muscles proceeded the hot tears against me. The sobbing was the first sound to actually come out of her. It wasn't talking but it was progress.

I kept talking while I let her cry. "Olivia thinks she wants to be a doctor. Could you imagine wanting to be a doctor right now? If she's still thinking that when she's a junior, I want to set up some time for her to actually come to the hospital and see what it's really like. It's not like the TV shows she watches, that's for sure. Ellie doesn't know what she wants to do but they both have time. I just want them to be happy. If they can pay their bills and love going to work then they'll have the dream that most people don't."

"She could be a secretary." Her voice was muffled against my chest but I could hear how hoarse it was. It sounded painful for her to talk. The sobbing had subsided so it was possible her throat was raw from the crying. But it sounded more like someone who didn't talk often. Tamela and I froze. We were both afraid that if we moved, she'd get spooked and stop.

I gingerly started to run my hand over her hair. I cautiously spoke. "Why a secretary?"

For a minute she was silent and I was afraid I'd ruined it or it was fluke but then she spoke again. "Girls can only be moms, nurses, teachers or secretaries."

I met Tamela's eyes and we both thought the same thing but didn't speak. It wasn't the time for a feminist rant and it wasn't about us. We just stayed quiet and let her talk but she didn't continue. I was going to have to keep the conversation going without pushing too hard. "I'm a nurse."

She slowly broke away from my arms and wiped at her bloodstained face. "You are?"

"Yes, I am."

She glanced backwards. "Are you a nurse?"

Tamela smiled but the girl couldn't see it. I think Tamela was just happy that the girl thought she was "safe" enough to talk to. "I am not," Tamela answered. It was probably not the right time to explain how females could be bodyguards.

The girl looked back at me. "Can you help me?"

"With what?" I asked.

"To wash myself," she said, looking embarrassed. "I feel dirty. Can I wash, please?"

I fought back tears. She was asking for permission to bathe and sounded like she was expecting me to say no. "Of course," I said. "Can Tamela help? I want to make sure we're all safe."

That reasoning seemed to make sense to her and she nodded. "Yes, let's stay together. Is the bathroom in here?"

"No," I answered. "It's just down the hall." Fear filled her eyes and I had to work fast to not ruin the little momentum we had started. "The men are downstairs and we'll be together."

She seemed to calm down. I sent a thought to Rhys and Sorin. *Don't come out of the office. We're walking her down to the bathroom.* I didn't need a response to come back. I knew it made it to them and they wouldn't question it. They'd do what I asked and we'd talk about it later.

"Would you like some of my clothes?" I was much taller and fuller than her but Tamela's clothes weren't an option. I slid off the bed, went to my dresser and opened my drawers. "Anything you want."

She didn't move for a minute or so. She was gathering courage, energy or both. When she wiggled off the bed and stood, she wavered a little but centered herself and slowly stepped to the offered clothing. Her eyes were wide and I could see she was overwhelmed. I pulled some flannel pajama shorts from one drawer. They would probably go to her knees but they had a drawstring and could be cinched to fit her tiny waist. Then, I retrieved the matching button-up top. "These are very comfy. How about these?"

She didn't say anything, just pulled them into her chest and dropped her face to look down. She was preparing herself for the walk down the hall. The fact that something so small was filling her with such distress shattered my heart. Someone had really messed this young girl up and I was enraged that anyone could hurt something so defenseless. I leaned in and whispered into her ear. "I won't leave your side and Tamela will stop anyone who comes near you."

Tamela heard me and reacted, going right into protection mode. She stood, towering over the girl and went to the door. She laid her ear on it before pulling it open, then turned to us and nodded. I wrapped my arm around her tiny frame and we began the walk. The hallway seemed so unimposing that evening but I could remember how long it felt the night Sorin led me to his bedroom for the first time. I'd been overwhelmed by my turn and afraid that Rhys wasn't who I thought he was. I hadn't even been sure if I could trust Sorin. Glancing at the girl, I thought that must be what she was feeling now – *who can I trust and am I safe?*

Walking her down that hallway, I felt more protective than I'd ever felt over anyone but my children. I would've laid down my life for her and I knew Tamela was feeling the same. I felt Sorin and Rhys in the office as we approached but they were silent. I breathed a sigh of relief. If this girl had known they were in there, she'd never trust me again.

Once in the bathroom, we locked the door and didn't turn on the lights. We didn't need them to see and I was afraid to overwhelm any of her senses. Tamela plugged the bathtub and slowly turned the faucet to start filling the tub. The roaring of the water did make the girl jump but then she settled down again. I gingerly pulled the clothes from her grasp and laid them on the counter, turning to her. "I'm going to take off your dress. Are you okay with that?"

It took everything inside me not to cry when she started to tremble and nodded. I didn't move yet. "You're allowed to say no and I won't touch you. You also can take the dress off yourself. We can turn away if you'd like."

"It's okay," she said. "I don't think I can. You have to take it off."

I didn't know what that meant but I slid the straps off her shoulders, noticing again how her bones stuck out just below the surface. Her white skin seemed impossibly thin, like those bones may rip through at any second. When the dress was on the floor, I picked it up. The tag on the inside was filthy and had faded over the years. I hoped for a name of the girl or a store but couldn't make out any of the letters on it. It smelled like dust and reminded me of an attic that no one had entered in years. "Do you want me to wash this and give it back to you?"

Again, she looked afraid to answer.

"It's okay either way," I said sweetly, using my nurse voice.

"I want to keep it but not wear it again, if that's all right." She approached the full tub and Tamela stopped the water. She reached out a hand to the girl, who took it and stepped into the giant bath. Once in the water, she seemed to relax slightly. I wondered how long it had been since she was in hot water. Tamela knelt onto the floor behind the girl and I didn't need to hear anything to know Tamela would be in charge of hair. If anyone could save those strands, it was Tamela. I knelt onto the floor at the girl's side, grabbing the loofah from the side of the tub.

"I'm going to wash you. Is that okay?" The girl nodded and actually closed her eyes. That was a good sign. "Do you like flowers or fruit?" She opened her eyes, revealing utter confusion. I chuckled. "The body wash," I explained. "We have a flowery one or one that smells like lemons and orange."

The confusion continued. I don't think anyone had asked this girl anything for a long time. Between the clothes and the soaps, I think she was overwhelmed by choices and unable to make decisions. "How about the fruits? The smell always makes me happy." She nodded, relieved and laid back to close her eyes again.

Citrus filled the room when I snapped open the bodywash and poured it over the loofah. The girl pulled back. "Not that. I don't like the smell." I froze and pulled the sponge away. She looked terrified and I couldn't tell if it was the smell or that fact that she'd spoken up.

"That's okay." I threw the sudsy loofah into the shower and pulled out another one. This time I opened the other body wash and let the smell of orchids and lavender fill the room. Once the new loofah was sudsy, I cautiously reached for her. "Is this good?"

She nodded and rested back. Lifting up a thin arm, I rubbed the loofah down it and saw the white suds mixing with the dirt on her skin. I had thought she was pale without realizing there was a layer of dusty dirt on her. As I washed her, she became even fairer. I didn't think it was possible for skin to be so porcelain but it was in front of me. She didn't resist as I washed her arms, her legs and her chest. I handed the loofah to Tamela, who gently urged the girl to lean forward. She did and Tamela washed her back. As we washed, we looked for signs of abuse but the skin was pristine.

Once washed, the girl leaned back again. Tamela rubbed something through her hair and started to work at the knots with a big, plastic comb. While she did this, the girl relaxed and I stayed silent. If she needed rest or quiet or whatever, I was giving it to her. We would have plenty of time to talk to her. For now, she deserved hot water and to be pampered.

Twenty minutes later, Tamela was able to run the comb through the hair, top to bottom. I would never get over how good she was with any hair you handed her. I was also honored to be one of the few people that knew about Tamela's secret hobbies.

Tamela broke the silence. "I should probably trim off a few inches. The ends aren't worth trying to save. Is that okay?"

"A haircut?" The girl looked excited and I was struck by how innocent she looked. It was such a young reaction. "Okay."

Tamela nodded her head towards the sink and the drawers underneath. I rose, crossed to open a few drawers and find the scissors. Bringing them back to Tamela, I watched her trim the girl's ends like a pro. Once done, she handed them to me and I returned them to the drawer. I heard the girl rise out of the bath and looked in the mirror. Her reflection was so pale in the darkness. She was achingly slim. I brought a towel, wrapping it around her when she was out of the water.

After drying her off, we helped her into the pajamas. "There are a lot of vampires still downstairs. My fiancé is back in his office with my maker. They're very nice and there's blood in there. Would you like to go get something to drink? I promise Tamela and I will stay with you."

She nodded. "Okay. What is your name?"

I smiled. In all of this I didn't think to introduce myself. "Kate. What's yours?"

She looked at Tamela and back to me. "I don't know. I can't remember. I can't remember anything."

IO

After two large glasses of blood, the freshly clean young vampire was looking settled on the long green couch. Tamela stood at the door, appearing to guard us against intruders, but I knew it was all about that little girl right now. The girl had her legs tucked under her and a blanket around her. We don't get cold so I knew the blanket was more about feeling safe than keeping out a chill. It had been Rhys' idea and the girl did look less scared within the yellow throw. I'd never seen it but someone had found it in the house and brought it to her. I had a feeling we were never getting it back from her and doubted that Sorin cared.

I was next to her on the couch. Sorin and Rhys sat in the chairs across from us, careful to maintain distance. Sorin voice was soft and gentle. "Tell us what you remember."

He'd used that soft voice on me before: once after the barn and once after we'd rescued the girls from their kidnappers. One of his powers was how he used that voice to affect you. He could fill you with terror, cause you to fall in love or soothe you just by speaking with power.

I wished Jeremy was there. He was able to fill you with the emotion you needed the most. It's called waking dream. If you needed peace or happiness or courage, he could literally give it to you. He'd be able to take all her fear away and give her courage. But it was too late in the night to call him and I knew he needed a night with his husband so I didn't text him. If we couldn't get anywhere with this girl between the four of us, we could always bring Jeremy in later.

"Nothing," she said, a voice from the blanket. "I remember finding the people in the woods. I don't know how I got there."

"What's the last thing you remember before the people in the woods?" Sorin asked.

"Nothing," she repeated. "It's all blackness."

"How old are you?" I asked her.

"I don't know," she answered.

Rhys leaned forward. "Do you know why you drink blood?"

The question made me shutter. What if this poor girl didn't even know what she was?

"I'm a vampire," she said matter-of-factly. "Aren't you guys?"

"Yes," Sorin said. "We are. Do you know how long you've been a vampire?"

She looked confused when she turned to me. "I've always been a vampire."

I laid my hand on her cheek. "No, honey. We all start as human. All of us were people first and then someone turned us into vampires." I pointed to Rhys. "He made me a vampire."

Tamela stepped up to Sorin and laid her hand on his shoulder. "Sorin made me a vampire."

"How?" the girl asked.

I took in a breath. "Well, we drank their blood when we were human and it made us vampires."

She looked at Tamela, to me and then at both men. "Why would you drink blood if you didn't have to?"

"I was dying and Rhys saved me," I answered.

"Sorin also saved me," Tamela joined. "These are good men. They will protect you and never hurt you."

The girl looked at the men again. "How are men made vampires?"

Sorin smiled. "The same way. I was made a very, very long time ago. A woman turned me into a vampire." It was the first time I'd heard anything about his turning. We never really talked about it. I thought it was off limits so I never asked. I realized now that I needed to spend more time asking him about himself.

I looked at Rhys as the girl did. "I was made by a man. It was not to save me. But I was made the same way we all are, by drinking their blood."

She turned to me with eyes wide. "I was a human?"

"You were, sweetie. At some point, you were a human and someone made you into a vampire. We don't know why, though. It happens for all different reasons. But it's always done the same way. You drank a vampire's blood and became like us; you stopped being human."

She dropped her gaze down to her lap. I saw her trying to think about what it all meant and remember anything. She shook her head to clear away the darkness but when she looked up, I knew it hadn't worked. "What if I don't want to be this way? Can I go back to human?"

"No," I whispered and fought back tears. "You can't."

She leaned into me and I hugged her. Tamela came to sit on the other side of her and wrapped her arms around her too. When the girl began to shake, I knew she was crying again. It could be frustration or grief or God knows what else but she was sobbing for the second time in one night. I just let her cry. The men sat quietly. I knew them and felt the anger coming off of them. They were furious at whatever person or circumstance had led to this helpless creature crying on our couch. But, without knowing anything there was no one to direct that rage at.

When the sounds died down to whimpering, I lifted her head to look at me. "I'm tired," she said in that little voice. "Please can I go to bed?" There it was again. She was asking permission to do something so simple, something that anyone should be able to do and she was afraid we would say no.

Sorin stood. "Tamela, please take her into Kate's room for the night. Tuck her in and stay until she sleeps." He looked to me and I nodded to show him that was okay. We all wanted her close.

Tamela lifted the girl into her arms like a child and carried her from the room. I heard her begin to hum when they hit the hallway. We relaxed, dropping our guards when the girl was safely in my room.

"What do we do?" I was asking Sorin but would have taken any plan from anyone. I felt so useless to help that little girl.

"I will start to send everyone home for the night so the manor is secure again. Rhys, are you staying?"

"Sure," he said. "I already told Diana not to come by tonight so there's no reason to go home."

"When you have time," Sorin addressed Rhys. "Please search for missing persons reports that match her description. Start with Cambria County and work out."

Rhys grabbed the laptop. "I'll start ASAP and work until I fall asleep. I'll have some leads by nightfall."

"What can I do?" I asked Sorin.

"You've already gotten her cleaned, talking and trusting you. That's more than the two of us could have done. Please, rest. Check in on the girls. See if Jeremy can come by tomorrow night. We may need him to help calm her so we can push a little harder. If we can recover any memories, we'd be better able to help."

"I'm supposed to work tomorrow night."

"That's fine," he answered. "Tamela will be here with her. I will keep my distance until she trusts me but if Jeremy can help, maybe she'll be okay around us. You need to go help your peers on the frontline. I'll call you back if necessary."

"Promise?"

"Promise," he responded. "Go shower and call your kids. It's about time for them to awake. I can't imagine there are many left downstairs. It's getting close to sunrise. I will be holding you in thirty minutes."

Shower, kids and being held. He always knew exactly what I needed.

11

My hair was still damp and steam was still pouring out of the bathroom into the hallway when I peeked in on the girl. She was sound asleep and Tamela lay next to her. I knew my friend wasn't sleeping yet, she was just staying still to not upset the resting female. She turned to see me and winked.

"Staying next to her 'til she wakes?" I asked and wasn't surprised when Tamela nodded yes.

"If she wakes," the bodyguard said. "I don't want her to be alone and scared or wander into the sun."

I smiled. "She's lucky to have you."

"Get some sleep," Tamela said and I shut the door to let them rest.

When I called the girls, it was Olivia who answered. "Hi, Mom."

"Hi, kiddo." I was so relieved to hear her voice. After the night I'd had, I was afraid that every young girl was in imminent danger, even though I logically knew that was crazy.

"Where's your sister?" I asked.

"Sleeping," she answered. "You okay?"

"Yeah," I said. "I just miss you so much."

"Me too," my daughter responded. "When can we see you again?"

"Soon. The hospital's so busy. There's a lot of sick people to take care of. And, I wouldn't ever want to risk bringing it to you." I knew I couldn't catch COVID but we didn't know yet if I could carry it on my scrubs or shoes. Ever since the kidnapping, I never wanted to be the reason my kids got hurt or sick every again.

"I know, Mom. Are you going to be okay? What if you get sick?"

"I'm being extra safe," I explained. I couldn't tell them that vampires couldn't get the virus but I could allay their fears. "When Ellie wakes up, give her a big hug and kiss from me. I love you two so much. When you get back from Virginia, maybe we can try those cake samples. That is if you aren't sick of cake."

"I'll never be sick of cake. Love you too, Mom. Good night." The phone went dead and I laid it on the bedside table just as Sorin came in.

The sight of him still sucked the air out of my lungs sometimes. It's hard to believe that in the midst of this awful night, I could still be filled with love and happiness. But that's what happened when he pulled his shirt over his head, tossed it onto the couch, kicked off his shoes and headed for the bed. He looked troubled and I think he was just as desperate for an embrace as I was. It was terrible of me to think that only women would feel bad for this girl. All of us had bad things in our pasts, traumas to overcome. For me to assume it wouldn't dredge up issues for Sorin or Rhys was unfair. Looking into Sorin's eyes, I knew he was dealing with some things and needed to feel safe, too.

I pulled back the covers and patted the space next to me. He slid in, up to me and I let the covers fall on top of him. Pulling pillows behind his back, he rested against the headboard so I could settle into my favorite spot, his chest. As I laid my face against his pec, he wrapped his arm around me. We lay there, silently, not sure what to say or what subject to broach.

"How old do you think she is?" Sorin asked. I think, since I was human the most recent and a mother of girls, he was relying on me to judge. I've heard from vampires that the longer you've been on the Earth, the harder it is to judge human age.

"Nineteen or 20," I guessed. "Young but not a minor."

He let out a sigh of relief. "I couldn't tell. She looks so young."

"I know. At first, I thought she was a child. But I had to think of my daughters and remember Rhys was mid-twenties when he was turned. You were twenty-nine. She's younger than you guys but older than my daughters."

"Yes," he said. "But when I was turned, I was considered middle aged. I look older than what a human of the same age looks like now. Same with Rhys. We lived hard lives in our short time as mortals."

"I'm sorry I've never asked more about your life. I don't know anything about you and I should."

He kissed the top of my head. "We have centuries to learn about each other. But I will tell you, I will never lie to you. As hard as it may be to hear, I will tell you anything you ask."

I didn't like how that sounded. I wondered how bad his backstory was, what he had survived. I knew we didn't have the time to even start to unpack it and I didn't think I could handle anything else on top of seeing that thin girl gulp down blood. It reminded me. "She is so thin. How is that possible? Was she that malnourished when she was turned?"

"I doubt it," he said. "She was likely slim but the state she is in now makes me suspect that she's been living off animal blood."

"We can do that?"

"We can," he answered. "For a short while. But over great spans of time, we start to look like that. We aren't nourished properly. It is a miracle she hasn't turned into a ravenous beast. Most would have lost control by now."

"I saw her naked. She looks like someone stretched skin over a skeleton. But there are no signs of abuse, thankfully."

"Kate," the way he said my name told me I was about to hear something I wouldn't like. "She is a vampire. Any signs of abuse would be healed the next night. Even if she's sustained years of torture, we wouldn't see it. She'd heal each time."

"Oh, God," I whispered. It hadn't occurred to me that we'd never see any scars or injuries or bruises. I was examining her the way a nurse would examine a human victim of abuse or assault. But she was a supernatural creature. She wouldn't show physical signs only psychological or emotional.

He squeezed me tighter, showing me that I was safe and with him. I knew he was feeling my emotions. Or, he was just thinking the same thing I was. Either way, we were both disturbed by the possibilities of what that girl went through. The idea that someone could torture us for centuries and we'd just heal, never succumbing to death, was unthinkable. I knew the man under me would die for me but I'd been a victim before – locked in a box – and I knew the fear I felt. And, my captor had never actually been able to do the things he'd wanted to.

"We don't know yet what she went through. She may just've been out in the woods for a long time, living off animals and sleeping out of the sun. Just because she's thin and has amnesia, doesn't mean she was victimized." I was hoping it was true but even as I said it, it didn't line up. She was afraid of men and had blocked out all memories. That didn't usually come from being a recluse.

"You're right," Sorin agreed. "Let's find out more before we head down these dark paths."

I kissed his chest and looked up at him. "Thank you," I said.

"For what?" he asked.

"For being a good man. For coming to the barn to save me. For coming to the school to save the girls. For saving Tamela in that basement. For killing the men that hurt her." I kissed his lips. "For choosing me even though I'm flawed and broken and come with baggage."

He ran his hand down my cheek to rest over my heart. "Thank you for making me believe that I am a good man and worthy of love. I didn't believe either of those before you. We saved each other."

12

When my eyes opened, I was still lying on his chest. It rose and fell so rarely. When we sleep our breathing slows to almost nothing. It was weird at first but I'd gotten used to it and stopped counting his respirations when he was asleep. He stirred when I laid a kiss on his sternum.

"I need to eat and get ready for work. I want to check on the girl, too."

He nodded. "Do what you must, I will handle things this evening. If you do not hear from me, please be sure that all is well. Would you ask Jeremy to come over tonight? Just in case he is needed. But, please ask him to let me know when he is coming. I don't want her to see a strange man without warning."

"You got it." With that I was up, pulling on scrubs and texting while I headed for my room.

ME: Hope you had a good night with L. Can you come by tonight?

I peeked in on our guest. She was still sleeping. Tamela was awake and texting. She winked at me. "Telling Edwin he's in charge for the night. I'm not letting her out of my sight. She's my priority."

I put my hands up. "No argument from me. Her hair looks amazing. You really missed your calling." It was fanned around her and looked healthy. Now that it was cleaned, brushed and dry, you could see it was blonder with less brown. With her pale skin, she looked like a sleeping fairy tale princess, waiting for a prince to wake her with a kiss. The yellow blanket was still wrapped around her. My motherly instincts were screaming to stay home and care for her but I knew Tamela had it under control. I needed to save calling off for real emergencies.

I slipped out of the room and checked my phone. I had a response.

JEREMY: Called to a friend emergency. Can't explain now. Won't be around tonight or maybe tomorrow night. I'll stay in touch and keep you updated. Tell S I'm sorry.

ME: No worries. Please let me know if I can do anything to help.

JEREMY: Thanks, doll. Got it covered. See you soon. Xoxox

I ran down the stairs for a thermos of blood to-go and hoped to see Rhys. I wasn't disappointed. He was at the island with a half-full glass and his laptop. The furious typing didn't stop when I came in. I slid up to his side and kissed his cheek. Then he took a break and made eye contact.

"Hi."

"Hi," I answered then hesitated, not saying what I wanted to.

He saw it. "What's up?"

I sighed. "Thank you for saving me and being a good man. I'm sorry I've never asked more about you or your life. And, I'm sorry you were so young when you were turned."

He smiled and pulled me into him. "Oh, Katie. It's okay. I let go of all that a long time ago. And, you're welcome. Please don't worry about not asking. We have so much time to talk and get to know each other."

"That's what Sorin said."

"Well, it's true." Tonight, for whatever reason, his Scottish accent was more present. Maybe it was me talking about the past. It's like it made him regress. Or, maybe I just don't notice it as much anymore. "We don't have to rush learning all about each other like humans do.

Time isn't forcing us to hurry things. I promise you'll learn all about me." He let me go and kissed me quickly. "And, I'd save you a thousand times again. The same way you've saved me. That's what family does."

There was no way to follow that so I didn't try. Some things just didn't need to be said. He went back to the computer and I prepped my thermos. When I left the room, I gave a last glance back to my maker. Then, I said a silent prayer that he would find someone that loved him and treated him the way Sorin treated me.

The Beemer was warming up when I walked out. My phantom car starter could be Rhys since he was in the kitchen nearby. Did Sorin come down to start the car while I was talking to Rhys?

I pulled out of the driveway, fighting this sick feeling that I shouldn't be going in. A feeling of dread sat in my stomach. Had I forgotten something? Was I missing something? I hadn't had any visions in months. As far as I knew everyone was okay.

Didn't change the fact that I knew this was going to be a bad night but I didn't know why.

13

My spot was open so I pulled in, cutting the engine and finishing off the B positive in my thermos. Grabbing my bag, I stepped out, locked the car and headed for the walkway. I wasn't sure if Alex would be in but I was going to stop by. I needed to know he was okay and try to shake this dread.

I heard him inside his office and knocked. The door swung open and he was on the phone waving me in. "As soon as the tests are back, I will let you know." Whoever was on the phone, it was obviously a work call so I stayed quiet. It was clear from my conversation with Lacey the other night that no one knew we were actually friends and there was no reason to let the cat out of the bag now. The last thing I needed was rumors about Dr. Kitchner and Nurse Kate. If Lacey caught wind of that, it would be in the Pittsburgh Post-Gazette by morning. I could not face 100 nurses asking if I was dating Alex.

When he hung up and turned to me, I had to admit he looked better. He'd clearly slept and showered. The clothes were fresh also. I was hoping that meant he'd eaten as well. "You look so much better, Alex."

He cocked his head. "I looked that bad, huh?"

"And smelled bad too."

"Ouch," he responded, putting his hand to his heart.

"Just being honest, like any good friend would. I don't know if the humans could smell you but I could. I can also tell you that there is too much sodium in your diet. Your skin smells salty."

He arched both eyebrows in response. "You can tell that?"

"Yep," I answered. "I can smell when someone has too much sodium in their system or sugar or acid, even. Plus, infection. I can also smell cancer. It smells like rot."

"Kate," he shook his head. "It's killing me that we can't tell everyone about vampires. We could save so much time, just walk you around so you could tell doctors what's wrong with the patient."

My expression must have been clear because he raised both hands. "Whoa. I'd never tell. I'm just saying, what a waste of abilities."

"I get it," I said. "I feel the same. I wish I could just call a doctor and say 'Hey, check for cancer, I can smell it.'"

"You can always let me know. I'll listen."

"True," I said. "How's your work going?" I was referring to the wolf cure and he knew it.

"Slow but steady. The vampire one started the same way but I think I can use what I know about that cure and tweak it for lycanthropy."

"Great," I answered. "You know, if you ever need anything, you can tell me, right?"

"Of course, Kate. What's going on with you tonight? You seem really upset."

I was trying to clear away this sick feeling in the pit of my stomach but I couldn't figure out what it was or how to make it go away. Usually, there's a vision to figure out or we know something horrible is happening. But other than the girl at Sorin's house, I didn't know why I'd be so upset. Maybe it really was just that. I mean seeing that starved girl and the thoughts of what she may have endured was enough to upset anyone. I was sure that was what was making me so unsettled.

"I'm fine, Alex. I was just really worried about you. That's all." It wasn't exactly a lie but it was close to one and I didn't like it.

"Why? Because I was tired? I slept and I'm fine." Clearly, I wasn't the only one omitting some truths. I could see in his eyes that he was far from okay. Yes, he'd eaten, showered, changed his clothes and slept. But that didn't address any of the real issues. He was still unsure what was going on between him and Monica. He was still desperate to cure her so she wouldn't live as a slave to the moon. He wanted her back to human and back in Pittsburgh. He may not be saying it out loud, but I knew it's what was in his broken heart. He was also feeling the pressure of the pandemic so he wanted to give the patients and staff his time, too.

"Are you reading my mind?" he asked.

"No," I raised my hands. "I promise. But I'm still feeling some of what you're feeling. I can't help it. It's coming off of you pretty strong."

"Wait," he said. "Since when are you an empath? When did that power show up?"

I had to think about it. Was that what was going on? Was I developing a new power? "I don't know," I answered, honestly.

"Tell me what you think I'm feeling."

I really didn't want to do that but I also respected him too much to lie anymore. "You feel guilty that you aren't on the frontlines, on the unit, carrying for patients more than you are now. You hate that you can't be up there helping us. You feel guilty that you haven't figured out how to cure Monica. You blame yourself for the relationship not being able to start. You think you did something wrong the night of the fashion show and that's why she left. You want her to come back and be human but not for selfish reasons, because you want to help her."

His eyes were wide but I saw the effort he was putting into hiding his response to what I had said. "Yes." That was all I got.

"I'm so sorry, Alex. I didn't know I could do that. I swear. I wouldn't have felt those things if I could control it. I'll tell Sorin and he can train me."

"I believe you, Kate. I've seen how quickly you gain a power but I thought you were done acquiring powers."

"So did I," I answered.

"I'll say," he started. "It's unnerving to hear your feelings put into words when even you can't understand what you're feeling."

"Trust me," I assured him. "I know. Sorin's done it to me a few times. Now that I know what it's like, I feel bad for getting mad at him. Sometimes the feelings really are so strong you can't help but feel it. Are you mad?"

"I don't think I'm mad but you'd be able to feel if I was. I know you didn't do it on purpose. Doesn't make me feel less vulnerable, though."

I stood to apologize and beg him for forgiveness again but the words were sucked out of me along with all the air in my lungs. I almost fell over but caught myself. Something on his bulletin board caught my attention and changed everything. Suddenly, I didn't care if he was mad at me, I just wanted to get out of that office immediately. I took a couple seconds to think about what to do with the single piece of knowledge that had just shook up my entire world.

Do I tell him? Do I keep it to myself for now? What would it mean for him to find out?

He turned to face me. I pulled my eyes away from what I was looking at so he wouldn't know. "Kate?" he asked and stood to face me. "Kate, what's wrong?"

"Nothing," I lied again. "I think I got bad blood." I didn't even know if that was a thing but I knew I had to get away from Alex and talk to Sorin. "I have to go. I'm calling off upstairs. Please back me up if they ask."

He put his hand on my shoulder. "Of course, don't even call. I'll go tell Jerry but Kate, tell me what's wrong. I know you're lying. You're scaring me. Did I do something wrong? Say something wrong?"

"No," I assured him and tried to fill my eyes with kindness. I hoped he believed it. I didn't want to hurt him anymore but I had to get out of there. "Please, Alex I have to go. I promise I'll tell you as soon as I can. Please, trust me."

"I trust you. Go."

I fled the room, speed walking back to my car and making the conscious effort to not use vampire speed. I wasn't calling anyone until I was out of the hospital and knew that no one could hear me.

I flashed back to the picture tacked on his bulletin board as I climbed into the car and dialed Sorin. When he answered I was 100% sure of what I'd seen.

"The girl where is she?"

Sorin didn't hesitate or ask why. "Out in the garden with Tamela. I'm standing at the window looking at them now. Why?"

"It's Alex's sister."

14

It felt like an eternity to get from the hospital to the manor. It took all my willpower not to speed to the house. The dread in my stomach was gone but it was replaced with a dozen other feelings. I had so many questions. Where had she been? Who had turned her? Had she been this close the whole time? Without her remembering anything, we would need to rely on Alex for information but I was not telling him we found his sister until we knew more.

I slammed the brakes when I was in front of the door of the manor. Throwing the car into park and cutting the engine, I sent a thought to Tamela. *Keep her outside and away from the office until we call you.*

Done. She sent it back instantly. I was grateful for her unquestioning loyalty in that moment. We didn't want the girl to hear what we were saying until we knew what it all meant. Sorin met me in the doorway. "Rhys is on his way too."

I was hit with concern and frustration. He was angry that the girl was possibly being mistreated in his territory and he was unaware. He was scared that I was so close to this again, that I had been in danger too many times and he didn't know if this girl put me in danger again.

He didn't want me to ever go back to the hospital. I used what energy I could to muster a psychic wall between us, to block out his emotions. I was afraid he'd feel me blocking but he seemed to be too distracted to catch it.

I focused on the issue at hand. I had left the hospital and forgot to tell Rhys. Thankfully, Sorin had taken care of it. "What about duties for the night? Anyone coming," I asked him.

"No. Is Jeremy coming?"

"No," I answered and was grateful. I loved Jeremy but I didn't want anyone seeing her until we knew more. I also didn't want Jeremy to mess with her feelings without knowing what she'd locked away. "Some kind of emergency. It's good timing."

Rhys pulled in behind me and was at the manor door in a flash. "Is it true?" His disbelief washed over me. He wanted so desperately for me to be wrong. I blocked his emotion, trying to maintain my sanity and focus with this new power.

"Yes," I said, looking out into the yard. I didn't see her or Tamela but I smelled the bodywash I'd used on her in the air. She was walking around out there and I was grateful for whatever minutes of peace she had tonight. "Come inside."

We waited until the heavy office door was shut before saying anything else. I started, "Thirty years. She's been missing since the late 80s and can't remember anything?"

"It's hard to imagine," Sorin said. "Where has she been?"

I dropped into one of the chairs. "Oh, Sorin. She was only seventeen. We were off. She was a kid. I always pictured her jet-setting in Europe or something. I can't believe she was here. How would you not know? Shouldn't she have been brought to you by her maker?"

"Yes," he answered. "And, I have been in power since before she was born. If she was made here or moved into the territory, I should have been notified. Sadly, we know that just because there are laws doesn't mean everyone obeys them. If they did, my position would be unnecessary."

Rhys paced the room. "We have to tell Alex."

"No," Sorin and I both responded in tandem. "We can't," I continued. "Not until we know what happened to her and where she's been. He's so fragile right now, Rhys. One more thing and he'll break."

That brought on a different issue. "I might as well tell both of you while I have you together. I have a new power, empathy."

Sorin cocked his head. "When did this arise?"

"Tonight, I think. If it's been longer, I haven't noticed but tonight it was obvious. I knew exactly what Alex was feeling, all of it. I could describe it in detail that he wasn't even aware of. He's not doing well and this is going to destroy him. Forget that we don't know what she's been through. She was this close and he had no idea. When he sees how frail and uncared for she is, he'll crumble."

Rhys shook his head. "We can't keep this from him. It's wrong."

Sorin ran his hand through his hair. "A few nights. Just a few nights to figure this all out and we tell him, I promise. But we need to try and find out more before we bring him in. Ultimately, we may need him to fill in some questions and try to break through her amnesia."

He looked up at me. "As for your new power, it's not unheard of for powers to develop after months of nothing but as I've said, it's not normal for a vampire to have almost a dozen powers. We cannot lose sight of training you. As for the empathy, at least this is something I can train you in quickly. You will find that feeling what everyone around you is feeling will wear thin quickly."

"Please," I said. "It's bad enough to see things, I don't need to feel them, too."

Sorin's expression changed, he had an idea. "Let's bring her up and call her by name. See if it brings anything back."

It felt risky but we didn't have much else to work with so it was worth a try. This little girl wasn't some lost, broken thing anymore. She was the cherished sister of someone I cared for deeply. If I could get her back to him, it would be worth trying anything.

Bring her up, I sent to Tamela. Sorin arched his eyebrow. "Sorry," I said. "Should have let you do that."

"No," he relented. "It's good that you are taking charge."

I didn't have time to see if he really meant that or not when the girl came in with Tamela. She had a flower tucked behind her ear and looked a lot less like the frightened mouse we'd seen the night before.

"Hi, Sheena," I said and we all held our breath. Tamela looked confused but just watched the girl for a response. All eyes were on the teen.

"Who is Sheena?" she asked with genuine interest.

We all let out the air we were holding. Hearing her name didn't jog anything.

That would have been way too easy.

15

Sheena stood next to Tamela, looking at each of us. She was waiting for us to explain what was going on and one of us was eventually going to have to say something. She was still wearing my pajamas, which only made her look younger. I hated the idea that I may say something that would take away the little joy she'd found in the garden. I approached her, took her arm and gently walked her to the couch. We sat. I felt that Tamela was worried about what I was about to say but trusted I would do it the right way.

"You are Sheena, honey. That's your name." I spoke as kindly as I could while keeping my voice clear. I didn't want her to think there was a chance I wasn't sure.

"I am?" she asked. "How do you know?"

I looked over to Sorin and he held up his hand, indicating I should wait. "I just do," I answered. "I saw a picture of you with your name on it. I was hoping it would help you remember."

"No," she said. "I'm sorry. But, it's a nice name. I like it."

Sorin waved me over to him and I stood to cross to him. He addressed the room, "please excuse us. We will be right back. I ask you to stay here."

Tamela went to sit next to Sheena. Rhys found his place in one of the merlot chairs as Sorin and I left the room. He led me back to our bedroom, not speaking until we were in the room with the door shut. "You need to go into her head, Kate."

"What?" I asked. "No."

"Yes," he answered. "But, carefully. We don't know what she's blocked out but we cannot tell Alex until we know something about where she's been. We can be gentle with her but it will take too long. Or, we can use your power to start to look, find out what is still inside her brain and let her brother know where she is. Imagine if this were your daughter? Would you rather wait months for therapy or want to know where she was, broken or not?"

That was a low blow but he had a point. I'd rather have them in rough shape than not at all. And poor Alex had waited thirty-plus years to see his sister, wondering the whole time if she was dead or alive, happy or miserable. I didn't want imagine the things he'd thought over the last three decades. We had a chance to end his misery.

"Okay," I relented. "How do we do it?"

"Just like you did with the man and his cat. You mention something, then look into her head to see what it conjures." He appeared confident but I felt his fear. He was afraid to put me in harm's way, even psychological harm. He wished he could do it, he wanted to protect me from what I may see. But he knew I'd hate it if he tried to take this off of me. He was right.

"I love you, Sorin. More than I can say." I blew out a breath. "I'll do it and see what I see. I'll be okay and you'll be there when I come out. Whatever I see, it can't hurt me, not really. I won't be in danger."

He ran his hands through his hair, which I knew meant he was uncomfortable. "I don't think I like you having empathy. Now, I know how it feels to have someone know your emotions."

I kissed the tip of his nose. "Just puts us on an even playing field, that's all."

He shook his head. "Katherine, when you're in the game, there is no equal playing field. You are much better than all of us but I'd prefer if you didn't let people know. It may ruin my image of ultimate power."

Once the moment of levity was over, we remembered I was about to go mess around in a teen girl's head. The glee was sucked out the room instantly. "Are you sure?" he asked.

"Let's just do it. The more we think about it and talk about it, the longer it takes for Alex to get Sheena back."

Opening the door and walking back to the office was both difficult and easy. It was difficult because of what I was about to do but it was the right thing and we knew it. We'd find out once and for all what had taken the girl away from her family. We would give peace to a dear friend and reunite siblings. Alex deserved a happy moment and I wanted to give it to him.

I knew they'd both have some healing to do but they'd have each other.

16

Everyone was where we'd left them a few minutes ago. Sheena was now twirling the flower around in her fingers while Rhys told her a story about picking flowers in Scotland. His accent was musical whenever he talked about his home. I loved hearing stories about his country and wanted to sit down to listen but we had a mission.

The room fell silent when I crossed to the couch and stood in front of the girl. I dropped to my knees, kneeling on the floor and adjusting until my eyes lined up with hers. The blue had brightened up after all the blood she'd drunk. Looking into them, I couldn't believe I hadn't seen it before. They were Alex's eyes. I'd looked into them for years. Even when we were just co-workers and not friends, I'd been affected by his eyes. Now, they faced me again in a small face.

She'd lost the fear she'd come with and looked more like a child, curious about a new experience. I took a deep breath and prepared myself. What I was about to do could change her and I for life. And, our lives were a hell of a long time.

"Sheena, I want you to remember Alex. He's your brother. He was ten and you'd left home. You were gone for two weeks but you came back to visit him. You knocked on his bedroom window …"

I stopped talking, letting her take it in. Throwing myself into her head, I saw utter darkness. It wasn't the black of night but the complete absence of anything. I looked around the emptiness and saw a speck of light, a small orb. Then, two orbs. Then, three. Then, thousands. It was a night sky. She was looking up at the sky and naming the constellations. When she knew the adults were asleep, she jumped down off the hood of the car she'd stolen and started the walk to the house she'd never live in again. She shouldn't be there but she had to see Alex. He was way too little to turn now. In eight years, she'd come back. They'd be vampires together, travelling the world and free from this prison.

The house came into view. The speed that accompanied her new condition came in handy. She'd walked a mile in a minute. Just the sight of the white, two-story home made her sick to her stomach. She hated leaving Alex in this place but what could she do with a kid on the run? The light was off in his bedroom so it was easy for her to walk up unseen. She was thankful that her parents had given him a bed on the first floor. It was the one right thing they'd done.

She thought about going up to their room and scaring the shit out of them. She was super strong now. Wouldn't it be great for them to be the ones getting the beating this time? For them to be the weaker ones, the scared ones? But there was no point. She had to keep a low profile. They had to think she'd run away or none of this would work. It would be worth it when she changed Alex and got him away from them.

Tapping on the window, she saw him sit up and smile when he saw her. He lifted the window and threw his arms around her. Shocked, he pulled back and yanked the cover off his bed. "You're cold," his little voice rang out.

I was seeing Alex as a fourth grader. His hair was the lighter than what I would see on the man 30 years later. But those blue eyes were brilliant, even bluer and brighter as a boy. The years would dull them some. I had thought his eyes were pretty in 2019. I had no idea how mesmerizing they'd been in 1988. His cheeks were still rounded with baby fat and his skin was soft and untouched by sun or age. No wonder his sister had been so protective. He looked like a cherub.

"I'll never be cold again, buddy." I heard her say.

"Come inside," he begged. "I'll tell Mom and Dad you're home. They won't be mad, I promise."

"I shouldn't have even come," she answered. "I have to go but I promise I'll come back for you. I have to say goodbye but it's just for now. I'm going to see the world and never grow old or get sick. When you're eighteen, I'll come back and make you like me. Then we'll do all the things we talked about. We'll be free."

He cried, "No, don't go. Don't leave me with them. Take me." He reached for her and she jumped back. He rubbed his arm across the stupid nail that her dad kept promising he'd fix. The smell of the blood hit her nose before it welled out of the gash. The fangs snapped into place painfully and she was ravenous. She had to get away from him.

He saw her and screamed. The terror in that sound ripped into her heart. She'd scared him and she had to go. Her parents were coming. She could hear them.

"I'm sorry," she cried out as she rushed away from her sobbing little brother.

I pulled out of her brain with a snap and fell backwards. Rhys rushed to catch me and lifted me to my feet. "What did you see?"

I glanced down at the girl. She met my gaze with expectation. "What happened?"

"I looked into your mind and pulled out a memory. Did you see it?" I asked her.

"I see it," she answered slowly. "But it doesn't feel real. It doesn't feel like it was me."

"What did you see?" Rhys repeated.

"She's Sheena. There's no doubt. Rhys, do you remember the story that Alex told us about the night he last saw her?"

"Yes," he answered. "At the bar, the night after you turned."

"I saw it," I said. "From her perspective. I saw the house, him, everything. It's her."

Sorin stepped into us. "This will work then. We can do it small pieces at a time. Pull her memories in like putting a puzzle together."

I shook my head. "It'll only work for a little while. We need to tell her things to bring those memories out and we don't know that much."

"Let's work with what we have," Sorin explained. "Then, bring in Alex. He may be able to tell us more to help."

Sheena jumped up and startled us all. "He's here, my brother? That's the little boy in the memory? My brother, Alex. Where is he? Is he still with my mom and dad?"

Sorin, Rhys, Tamela and I exchanged glances. It was Tamela that asked her. "What year do you think it is?"

"Well, how much time has gone by? Like a year?"

We exchanged the same glances and it was Rhys who found the courage this time. He stepped towards her and to our collective relief, she didn't shrink back. "Darling, it's 2020. You've been missing for over thirty years. Alex is an adult, a doctor actually. We're his friends. He's been looking for you for a long time."

I saw all her muscles let go as she fell back to the couch. We all moved to help her but Tamela was fastest. "Sheena? Are you still with us?"

"Yes," the girl answered. "Just a little dizzy. Can I get something to drink please?"

Rhys quickly filled a glass with blood and brought it to her. She gulped it down and laid the glass on the coffee table. We waited to see what she'd say.

"How can I not remember thirty years?" she asked the room.

"We don't know," I answered. "That's why I went into your head. I should have asked, I'm sorry. But we don't know how else to help you remember."

She met my gaze. "Can I see my brother?"

I needed to be careful here. We didn't want to lose her trust but we didn't want to promise anything yet, either. "The same way we're protecting you, we're protecting Alex, too. Until we know more about where you've been, we don't want him to know yet. He's human, Sheena. And, he's been through a lot."

"But," she thought about her question. "Why are you friends with a human? Does he know about vampires? Wouldn't he want to see me? Why didn't you turn him?"

I raised my hands. "Oh boy, that's a lot. I mean, yes, he knows about us. And, we never turned him because he doesn't want it."

"Will you tell him I'm a vampire?"

"He knows," I told her. "He didn't know that night that you saw him but he knew something was different. He told your parents but no one believed him. Then, when he was in high school, he figured it out. He hasn't told me much more than that." I didn't think it was my place to tell her that he'd made it his life's work to try and find a cure. I didn't want to give her any hope of a way back to human.

"Doesn't he want to see me?" I didn't need to hear the pain in her voice to know what she was feeling. I felt the uncertainty coming off her in waves. She was afraid he didn't want anything to do with her. Not much had come back to her but she was remembering how much she loved her little brother.

"He does, he will," I assured her. "I'll bring him here, I swear. But, can we just find out a little more before we do? I want to be able to answer some questions for him, help him deal."

I expected her to insist, to beg, to push back but she didn't. "Okay. Can we do one more? Try to remember more?"

I looked to Sorin for his thoughts. He hesitated, "How do you feel?"

"Fine," I responded. "Not as bad as I expected actually."

"If you want to -" the doorbell ripped through the air and cut off Sorin's words. Normally, we'd hear someone pulling up but we were all so distracted by the girl that we'd dropped the ball.

"I thought you'd cancelled everything," I said.

"I did," Sorin responded.

He indicated for Tamela to stay with the girl. "What's going on?" Sheena asked.

"Nothing to worry about," Tamela assured her. "People stop by all the time. I'm sure it's no big deal.

17

Sorin, Rhys and I went to see who the surprise guest was but Naseem beat us to it. He was in the foyer with the visitor as we turned the corner to walk down the stairs.

Logan looked up and relief washed over him. "Thank the stars, Kate. I've been texting you and nothing. I thought you were in trouble."

Only then did I realize my phone was tossed on our bed and too far for me to hear the buzzing of the texts. "I'm sorry, Logan. I don't have my phone on me. What's wrong? Why do you need me? Is Jeremy okay?"

I reached the bottom of the stairs and gave Logan a hug. "Yes," he said. "He's away helping a close friend. He told me that you'd asked him to come by and he couldn't. Then, when you didn't answer your phone, he got worried and asked me to check on you. When you didn't answer my texts, I thought certain he was right." I felt annoyance off of Logan. Now that he knew I was alive - he was mad that I scared them both. "So, he begged me to come over. When I tell him you're okay, he'll be so relieved. But I've been with him long enough to know you'll be in trouble. He hates surprises and being scared." Logan didn't add that he was also upset and he didn't know I had empathy so I kept my mouth shut.

"Geez," I said. "I'll have to do some damage control. Thanks for the heads up and thanks for stopping by. I'd rather you do it and didn't need to than not and we could've used some saving." I paused, then added. "I'm so sorry I scared you, Logan." I felt his irritation replaced with calm.

We saw Logan out with a round of thank-yous and good-nights. We took advantage of the moment away from Sheena to plan for the next round of psychic interrogation. "Are you okay with one more memory tonight?" Rhys asked.

"I am," I promised them. "What do we want to try to figure out?"

"Who came before her," Sorin said. When he saw my confusion, he clarified. "The vampire who made her."

"Oh, got it. How?"

Rhys chimed in. "Just ask her to remember before the night with Alex. Anything that comes to the front will have some kind of clue, right?"

I shrugged and looked to Sorin. He didn't seem to have an argument. "It's all we have for now."

Sheena was curled up on the couch; the yellow blanket was back. Tamela answered the question before we could ask. "I got it from the bedroom. She started to panic when she sensed a male she didn't know was here."

"I'm sorry," the girl whispered.

"It's totally understandable," I explained. "But you're safe here, okay? People stop by all the time and we have lots of protection. You have nothing to worry about." When I saw her accept what I said, I moved on. "I want to look in your head again. Is that all right?"

"Yes," she said.

I returned to my position, kneeling on the floor in front of her. This time she knew what I was doing so I didn't need to be sneaky about how to trigger a memory. "Think of the time not long before you saw your brother." I tried to recall the story Alex had told me. "You went to a concert, I think. It was the last time that Alex saw you as a human."

I slid into her mind, finding that complete darkness again. Looking around, I searched for any signs of light, color, anything. For a minute, I walked around this black space, searching for the tiniest hope of life. But there was nothing to see. However, there was a smell – the smell of a school. First it was the lemon cleaner for the floor, then the faint smells of the cafeteria and paper products. I looked down to see white sneakers on my feet. Big, purple socks erupted from the tops of the shoes and met leg warmers. Following the sight, up my legs, I saw a jean skirt and a notebook on my lap. The letters GED were scratched into the notebook.

Glancing around, Sheena saw other teens around her age and then some that were older, like old enough to buy booze. It was her first day so she didn't really know anyone but she had no problem making friends. If her parents were going to force her to do this, she might as well get something out of it. Befriending someone old enough to buy her liquor would be a hell of a lot easier than stealing it. She may even let one of the guys feel her up if it meant free alcohol. It didn't matter to her. She'd already gone to third base and it wasn't that bad. It would be worth it to get drunk and escape her life for a few hours.

She zeroed in on one of the boys. His hair was strawberry blonde and cut the same way Bowie had his hair. The t-shirt sleeves had been cut off to reveal some very nice biceps. She saw a pack of cigarettes in his back pocket. He was awesome and she'd decided that he was the one she'd talk to first. He was in a group of four: him, one other boy and two girls. As she approached, she heard the cute boy talking animatedly.

"I'm telling you this guy has some seriously rad ideas. A bunch of kids from here go to these gatherings and listen to him talk. He has all this food and alcohol and he doesn't care if you take some. He's cool, man."

The four of them turned to see the girl walking up to the table. The cute boy was interested immediately. "I haven't seen you before," he said to her and she felt heat rise up her body into her face. "You new?"

"Today's the first day. I'm Sheena."

"Bobby," the boy answered. "This is Brian, Heather and Amanda. We're in psych together. You?"

"GED," Sheena answered and was mortified. She'd learned that once everyone found out you'd dropped out of high school, they all looked at you different. She definitely wasn't telling them that she'd been expelled, not dropped out voluntarily.

She prepared herself for the laughter or for them to call her lame or her least favorite – for them to ask her age. Instead, Bobby said, "Yeah, I got my GED. Wasn't even going to take college classes but I kinda like psych."

One of the girls spoke up, "Me too. Got my GED."

Joy washed over Sheena. She felt ten pounds lighter.

Bobby moved over to give her space to sit. She did and flushed when her leg touched his. "Want to go to a party after class?" he asked her.

She looked around the group to see if they were rolling their eyes but they weren't. They all looked at her expectingly, hoping she'd say yes.

"Sure," Sheena answered and the world went blank.

I pulled out of her mind and met her eyes. "Did you see it all?" I asked her. She nodded, eyes wide. "Do you know those kids?"

"No," she said and crumbled. "I'm not helping at all. I see these things but they don't feel real. And, all I see is what you see, nothing else."

I tried to hide my disappointment. "Hey, we already know more about you then we did ten minutes ago, right?" I patted her leg. "That's enough for tonight."

I stood, making eye contact with everyone else. "She was a GED student at some little community college or annex or something. I couldn't see much about the place. But she met a group of kids there. They took her to a party. I don't think she'd been turned yet. Her parents made her go to classes after she was expelled from school. I don't think she would have listened to her mom and dad if she'd been a vampire."

Sorin spoke first. "Could one of those kids have turned her? Was it night or day in the memory?"

I shook my head. "I don't know, I'm sorry. I'm pretty sure there were no windows. They were in like a student lounge area. It's possible that anyone of those kids were vampires. I mean they did take her right in without hesitation and invite her to a party. Seems like trouble, right?"

Like me, everyone was trying to get discouragement out of their eyes or voice. No one wanted to make Sheena feel bad.

"We have some leads and that's something to celebrate," Sorin said. When he moved towards Sheena, again she didn't pull back or look afraid. So, we really were making progress. He reached her and held out his hand, patiently waiting. She stared at it for minutes. I'd seen him stand stock-still for much longer so I knew he'd wait for however long it took. Finally, she placed her hand in his. He bent his knees to meet her gaze. "We will not stop until we learn what happened to you. I can promise you that everyone in the room will be loyal to you. Please go rest and we will learn more tomorrow night. I thank you for trusting us."

She did something I never thought I'd see. She smiled at Sorin.

18

I'd missed so many calls and texts while my phone was in the bedroom. Most of them we're from Jeremy and Logan so I deleted those. I responded to Jeremy's last one.

ME: SO SORRY! Didn't mean to scare you. Phone was away. L came by. All is well. Just lots going on. Hope you're ok, too.

I missed a call from Diana early in the night and returned the call. I hated waking people but when you can only talk sundown to sun-up, it was inevitable. She answered on the third ring and I'd definitely interrupted her rest.

"Hey," she slurred.

"It's me. Returning your call before I'm down for the day. Sorry."

"It's cool," she sounded clearer. "All part of getting into bed with nocturnals, right?"

I wasn't sure how to take that but Diana had a weird sense of humor so I figured it was a joke. As far as I knew, there were no issues between us and Diana didn't hide her feelings, so I let it go.

"What's up?" I asked.

"Can I come by tonight? I know you guys cancelled last night or whatever, but I really need to touch base with you all. I don't want you out of the loop for too long." I knew Sorin could hear so I looked to him. He nodded.

"Sure, sundown?"

"On the dot," she quipped. "Don't have to work?"

I groaned. I hated calling off but I was going to have to do it again. There was no way to not be here to see all this through. They needed me to see into Sheena's head, Diana wanted us and I couldn't face Alex until I was able to tell him.

"I do but I'm calling off. They'll have to get over it."

"Cool," she said before the call went silent. I hung up. Before calling the hospital, I checked my other missed calls. One was from Alex and one was from the medical center. Each had a voicemail attached.

"Kate," it was Jerry, my Director of Nursing. I prepared myself for him asking why I missed my shift. I was surprised by the rest of the call. "Dr. Kitchner contacted me. Take whatever time you need. We took you off the rest of the week. If you need more, let me know."

Holy crap, I thought. I don't know what Alex had said but he was freaking Goddess-sent. He'd gotten me the week off without even knowing what was going on. I owed him dinner or something.

I listened to his voicemail. "Hey Kate. I don't know what happened but obviously you're going through something. Listen. You've been here for months, working and helping, which is great. But the same way you sent me home, I'm sending you home. Take the week and try to enjoy it. The hospital will be here when you get back. Doctor's orders."

When the message ended, I think my heart swelled a little. He'd jumped in and told work to give me time – literally the thing I needed the most.

It solved one problem, got me the nights I needed to deal with our little "situation" but didn't fix the big one – telling Alex.

I threw myself onto the bed, back first, throwing out my arms and letting out a grunt of frustration. Sorin stepped up, grabbed my legs and flipped me over onto my stomach. I don't know if it was his strength or the promise of something to come, but it caused an electric thrill to run up my spine. I felt him straddle me and lower his weight onto the tops of my thighs. His hand slid under my shirt and up, pulling the shirt to the top of my back. I lifted to allow him to slide it off of me and toss it to the floor. When he started to knead my back muscles, I groaned in pleasure.

Vampires don't get sore muscles, everyone. No aches and pains. No arthritis. But that doesn't mean it doesn't feel great for someone to massage us. Tension is real, even for the undead. And, when you carry around some stress for a few nights or weeks, some TLC doesn't hurt.

Tonight, I gave into the provided TLC and let the man above me work his magic. His fingers dug into muscle fibers and along my spine. I sighed when he started to show some attention to my neck.

"Try to let go for a little while," he said and his voice caressed down my back. It relaxed the places that his hands hadn't.

But my brain had other ideas and the worry rolled around in my head. After fifteen minutes of trying to shut it down, I relented and rolled over. Sorin stayed straddling me, lifting so I could turn, then settling back down.

"What is it, *regina mea*?" he asked.

"Can you use your empathy this time? I don't know how to even explain it." I saw something cross his eyes before he found focus again.

"Don't feel guilty for missing work or making Jeremy scared. Everyone knows your intentions are always good. And, Alex will forgive you. He'll be upset, of course. But he will understand that we are protecting he and his sister. The same way he protected you this evening by telling your employer you needed time off." He paused and thought something over. "If I had done that, you would have been furious. Why did you allow Alex?"

That was a good question. I wasn't sure. Maybe because he was a doctor and was looking out for me. But, so was Sorin. Maybe it was because I didn't want Sorin crossing over into work stuff. "I don't know," I answered, honestly. "It just didn't make me mad."

"You are complex, Katherine. I think it will take me the rest of time to fully understand you."

The rest of time, I thought. We'd be together the rest of time. The idea had terrified me at first. Then it felt romantic, like destiny. What did it feel like now? Thinking about the rest of time with one man?

Before I could head too far down that line of thinking, his hands began to trail down the front of me, over my chest, down each arm and back. It was so calming. Now, that I'd been able to share my worries over Alex, I was able to truly let go and be in the moment. Sorin's touch was just strong enough to elicit some relaxation from my muscles but was light enough to not be stimulating.

I closed my eyes and enjoyed the rare moments of peace. I wasn't sure how many more we would get.

19

I was up early the next night. I wasn't like me to awake when the sun hadn't fully set but walking down the hallway to the bathroom, I could still smell it in the air, still feel it. I turned on the shower and stepped in. The hot water on my back after the amazing massage was perfect. I feel lighter, looser and ready to take on the night.

Sorin hadn't been next to me so he must have risen even earlier – perks of being old, I guess. I stayed in the shower longer than I needed to, hoping he'd show up but no luck. After the water was off, I found a towel and made my way back to my room. Opening the door, I remember that a girl was sleeping in there. I figured we may need to move my clothes into Sorin's room if she was going to stay for a while. Or, we could give her one of the many other bedrooms in the manor.

Seeing her curled up in that yellow blanket made my decision for me. If she wanted the birch room, she could have it.

I was able to pull a dress from my drawers and slip out without waking her up. In Sorin's room, I toweled my hair a little more and slid on the black dress. It was simple cotton and the kind of comforting outfit I needed. Returning the towel to the bathroom, I peeked my head into the office to see that the sun was down and my fiancé was not in there. Nor, was he in the kitchen but I heard some talking and followed it down one more level to Tamela's room.

She had set up a TV and had a handful of wires. Sorin was reading from a small white book. It didn't take long for me to realize they were trying to hook up a video game system to this new television. I laughed, came in and looked into the Amazon box.

The original Nintendo console was recognizable and a blast from the past.

"What are you two up to?"

Tamela disappeared behind the TV, returning with only one side of the wires still in hand. "It was Rhys' idea. He said that since she still thinks it's the 80s, let's find a couple ways to remind her of the time. Make her feel at home. He had this thing delivered."

I lifted the game system from the box and handed it to her. Sorin tossed the directions backwards. "I think she's got it figured out," he said.

When the Nintendo symbol flashed across the screen, we applauded. Tamela pulled two games out of the box and laid them on the shelf of the TV stand. "Did you build that stand?" I asked her."

"I did," she admired her handiwork. "I'm more than a pretty face, you know?"

The doorbell rung through the house and I remembered that Diana was due. Sorin and I excused ourselves, heading for the front door. Rhys had appeared out of nowhere, likely having stayed the night. We watched the two embrace in the doorway and share a kiss. Hanging back, Sorin and I allowed them to have their moment. Seeing the way they looked at each other filled me with some serious joy. I liked Diana a lot but Rhys was my family and I wanted him happy. I'd been afraid Diana would hurt him in some way. Like, she wouldn't reciprocate the feelings or would use him and dump him. Witnessing them adore each other put my heart at ease.

They turned to see us and showed no embarrassment. One of the many things I was starting to love about this supernatural life was everyone's utter ease with their own sexuality. At first I'd struggled big time, but now I loved it and could never go back to being ashamed.

"Sorin," Diana said.

He crossed to her to kiss each cheek and welcome her into the manor. "Please, enter. We can talk down here or up in the office. Is this confidential?"

"Not confidential but sensitive. Office?"

He gestured up the stairs. She started up with Sorin behind her. Rhys and I hung back. Diana reached the top and looked down. "You two are welcome. Might as well hear it. I know we'd just end up telling you anyway."

Rhys repeated Sorin's gesture up and I led.

Inside the office, Sorin sat behind his desk. Diana and Rhys found the couch. I angled one of the chairs to face everyone and sat. I didn't usually see Sorin behind the desk so he must assume this is official business. When he was sat there, he looked all "Lord of the city".

Diana started, "I need you to come address the wolves."

That got everyone's complete attention. I didn't know about the men but that was the last thing I'd expected her to say. I knew she'd planned on us all coming together eventually but I didn't think it'd be that soon.

Sorin leaned back in his chair. "I will need more information."

Diana rubbed her hands up and down her thighs. "I've built a council. Myself, Monica and four of our oldest and strongest wolves. They're sort-of informal leaders in the pack so I knew I had to get them on my side for this to work. We've talked long hours about a new treaty with the vampires but I want more than a piece of paper. I want us truly united. None of us wants to continue to worry about the next uprising. If we can do this here, maybe other territories and packs will follow. This is very delicate. It has to be done right. So, after months of us talking about it, of me meeting with you, I think it's time for you to visit."

She paused to let us take it all in and then continued. "If they meet you and listen to your ideas - if they see how well we work together, I think they'll see what we see."

Sorin steepled his fingers and rested his chin on them. He was listening and thinking, examining all the possibilities. We knew how tenuous this new alliance was with the werewolves but we all saw how good it could be for the future.

Rhys laid his hand on one of hers to stop her from rubbing her thighs nervously. She calmed with his touch and patiently waited. She'd learned that pushing Sorin was a bad approach. We all sat in silence.

He stood and came to stand at my side. He looked at me and then at the couple on the couch. "I think you are right, Diana. We can no longer just theorize and hope for peace. We need to make it happen."

She let out a breath and visibly relaxed.

Sorin laid his hand on my shoulder, still looking at Diana. "For any of us to have the real peace and hope for the future we want, we need to bring my people and yours together. I am honored to be a part of this. When shall I come?"

"Tomorrow night," she responded. "Let me prepare them. We all knew this was the next step. But I need to ask something and hope to not offend anyone."

"Go ahead," Sorin allowed.

"Please, just you." We started to object and she lifted her hands. "Listen, he can have a bodyguard in the car or outside. But it'll freak everyone out to have a vampire among us. A lot of them are still very scared of you guys. As much as I'd love to have everyone over, for the first visit, can we start with one?"

I stood, wrapping my arm around Sorin's waist. "How can we know he'll be safe? I trust you Diana but what's to stop a dozen werewolves from ripping him apart?"

"You'll have to trust me. No one will attack," Diana insisted. "The worst that may happen are some mean words, I swear. And, I think Sorin can handle that."

I looked at Rhys, then Sorin.

"I trust Diana but I also don't like this idea," Rhys said. It bought a side-glance from his girlfriend that told me he was in trouble for saying that and would pay later.

"I will be safe," Sorin said. "She's right. If the three of us walk in, it will look like a threat. Remember that we all played a part in killing wolves only six months ago. Seeing us together again, in their land, will not help our cause."

"Thank you," Diana said. "At least he gets it."

"It's settled then," Sorin continued, ignoring the glares from me and my maker. "I will leave after sundown and arrive an hour later. Any other business?"

Diana started to rub her thighs again and I realized that she had more. "Actually, yes."

Rhys patted her leg. "Just tell them," he counseled her. "Better to just say it."

I saw her eyes grow wet and smelled the salt of tears. I knew I wasn't going to like whatever she said. I thought of all the bad news she could have: cancer, death, poverty.

"Monica has asked me to pass on to you that she will not be coming back, ever. She's staying out with us. She's ending all things from her past for good."

My legs went weak and I sat down again. I think part of me knew this was coming but hoped it wouldn't. I could deal with it. We'd both changed and grown apart. We'd been friends for a long time but nothing is forever, right? Considering what she'd gone through because of me – I knew she'd probably be over our friendship and couldn't blame her.

There was one big problem with this plan, though. "Alex?" I asked but knew the answer.

She pulled a folded note from her pocket and stared at it. When she handed it to me. I thought about ripping it up but that wouldn't solve anything. So, I gripped it in my closed hand. It wasn't my place to stand in the way of whatever Monica had to say to Alex. But I was damn well going to be by his side when he read it.

"I'm really sorry," Diana said as a single tear escaped her eye and ran down her cheek. She swiped it away.

"I know," I said. Standing, I headed for the couch and leaned down to hug her. "It's not your fault, okay?"

"Okay," she whispered.

I just hoped she believed it.

20

After seeing Diana off, Rhys left for work. Sorin and I decided to walk around the property for a few minutes to gather our thoughts. It was a nice night and we hadn't done this in a while, just walk and talk. Life had gotten chaotic and busy and too many people needed something from us all the time. Finding minutes where we could enjoy being together was something we'd been making a point to prioritize.

Again, being undead doesn't mean you don't get stressed.

The land surrounding the manor was so much bigger than I'd originally realized. Those first few weeks, I'd never made it past our little grove. But over time, I'd explored and I'd grown to love walking through the trees that lay on the edge of what you saw from the windows. The forest was dense and it was like stepping back in time. Tonight, we walked hand in hand to the sounds of scampering squirrels and crickets.

"I wish you didn't have to go alone," I said.

"I did many things alone before I met you," he answered. "And, I will take Edwin."

"I know you know what you're doing. I just wish I could be with you."

"You're needed here. I would like you to continue to work with Sheena. She responds well to you and Tamela. I believe you can help her."

That brought up a different issue. "We need to tell Alex."

"Yes, we do," he admitted. "I think we need to tread carefully. I believe that he is about to have his heart broken so I don't think we should tell him about Sheena at the same time. We need to space the two out. But he will be angry that we held anything back from him."

"Exactly," I stopped and faced him. "Damned if we do, damned if we don't."

"Give him the letter when you see him next. Console him and allow him to grieve."

I interrupted, "You didn't feel him. He's hanging on by a thread. This will destroy him. His world will fall apart."

Sorin nodded and finished the thought I had interrupted. "Meanwhile, work to retrieve his sister's memories. I hope that when we reunite them, it will be with answers and offer them healing. It may help him cope with his lost love. He will lose Monica yet gain his sister."

I smiled. "How do you make everything sound so romantic?"

Sorin pulled me into him. "Speaking of you being able to feel others and romance. Let us start your training. Have you been able to shut the empathy on and off?"

I realized that I hadn't been feeling other people's emotions. My blocking had worked and I hadn't had to make the effort to maintain it. I was getting good at controlling my powers without even knowing I was. "It's off now. I'm treating it like I do my psychic magic and it's working."

"Good," he said. "There will be some things you will feel no matter what. They are too strong to block. But you should be able to only feel what you want. It will protect you from being overwhelmed."

He looked down at me, staring into my eyes and heat washed over me. My heart swelled, filling my chest to the point I felt breathless. It was his love for me, so strong that it couldn't be blocked. I swayed and he pulled me close to steady me. "Whoa," I sighed.

"Much better than words, isn't it?"

"So is this," I answered and lifted to my toes to brush my lips over his, then pulled back to admire him in the moonlight. The paleness of him almost glowed in the darkness around him. The grey of his irises made him appear unreal, only a fantasy. Yet, the hardness of him around me assured me he was real. Leaning in again to repeat the kiss, he took over. The love I was feeling rippled off of him, beginning to fade. It wasn't completely gone, just engulfed by something with more heat. A low thrum started in my core. The ache was underscored by a desperation for something. Looking into his eyes, I knew it was his desire.

"It's like the air you need to breathe."

"That's what you are to me," he whispered. "The oxygen that gives me life."

Before I could raise back up on my toes to bring our lips together, he brought his down to mine. The tickle of his power poured over his kiss and into my mouth, finding its way down to my core. It'd been too long since we had mixed our powers and they'd missed each other. When his electricity found the heat of my magic, it caused a reaction between us. Instead of the force pushing us apart, it pulled us together. The length of my body pressed against his, like I was trying to be a part of him. His arms around me were impossibly strong.

Without words, we dropped to our knees in tandem and I laid back onto the ground. He never broke that kiss, moving with me like we'd rehearsed this. Something about being away from the manor, away from everyone, made it feel like we were the only two beings on Earth. The worries of work, lost friends, wolves and painful memories were too far away from this moment to even seem real. I realized that while we were together often, we hadn't really let go in months. We were so busy meeting the needs of those who counted on us. And, I think we were always scared that something bad would happen again; we'd been holding back. We'd been a little lost from each other in the chaos.

On that ground, with the trees as our protectors, we let go and found each other again.

His hand slid from my face and found the side of my skirt, starting to bunch it up to raise it and bare my thigh. Once he felt flesh, he glided his hand up my leg to grasp my hip. I wrapped that leg around the back of him, trying to get my body even closer to his and showing him, I was all in. His slacks were thin tonight but it felt like way too much barrier between us. I held back my impatience, wanting desperately for this moment to last forever. I clutched the bottom of his shirt and pulled it over his head. It brought our lips apart. I expected him to go right back but he stopped and looked down at me. With the night sky above him, he looked like a dream. For the hundredth time I struggled to believe he was really mine. I was sure it would take centuries to believe it.

"You are so beautiful," he said. My power reached for his in the space he'd created between us and his power answered. I slid the straps of my dress down to expose my breasts to him. I wanted to feel my skin against his. He knew and granted me the sensation, continuing the play of our tongues. His hand on my hip found the side of my panties. The fabric didn't stand a chance as he tore them off of me. He broke our kiss again, long enough to get his pants off and onto the ground next to us.

My hands played on the muscles of his back but he had other plans. His hands found mine and pulled my arms above my head to be held against the ground. The control he had now sent my need into overdrive. I wrapped both legs around him to urge him into me and when he finally enter me, it brought on the first wave of pleasure.

He held my arms in place while he moved in and out of me. My first release was quickly replaced with the start of another clenching need in my core. He raised up enough to be able to look into my eyes. I hadn't seen the dance of lights between us in months but in those woods, the lightshow was back – the breathtaking waltz of our combined magic. His eyes were all I saw as I tried to focus my dizzying mix of sensations and clenching need.

When the ache turned into ecstasy and ripped through my body, his did as well. With my new empathy, I felt his orgasm along with mine. It was all-encompassing and overwhelming – our pleasures entwined.

I saw his expression in the dying light of our powers and knew he'd needed this as much I had. We'd missed each other even though we saw each other nightly.

We were suddenly ripped from our fantasy by the sound of tires on gravel. No one should've been coming up the driveway. We leapt to our feet and Sorin was pulling on his pants. I ran, breaking through the tree line, with Sorin on my heels. The driver must've had the window down because his smell hit my nose before I could see him.

"No," I cried out, turning to Sorin. "It's Alex."

21

I n seconds, we reached the edge of the driveway and ran for the front door. When the car came to a stop, we stood side by side before the entrance, putting us between the doctor and the vampires inside.

As Alex killed the engine and opened the driver's door, I made a valiant effort to calm my nerves. If I was frantic, he'd worry. I had to be calm to keep him calm. Slowly stepping down the stairs to meet him at the car, I plastered what I hoped was a friendly smile on my face.

"Alex," I said when he was out of the car. Even to me it sounded too sweet and definitely suspicious. "What are you doing here?"

He answered my smile with one of his own and his eyebrows arched high. He looked at Sorin and I, probably taking in the fact that Sorin was shirtless and I was clearly flustered. "Hey, I was worried about you. You okay?"

"Yeah, why?" I walked up to him and gave him a hug. He squeezed harder than I think he would have for a human, holding on a little longer than usual before letting go.

He scoffed. "Well, let's see. Last time I was with you, you looked like you'd seen a ghost – which is saying a lot for someone as pale as you. Then, you rushed out of my office, called off from work – which you only do in an actual emergency - and I haven't spoken to you since. I had the strong and very realistic concern that someone was trying to kill you again."

I forced a laugh but knew I wasn't fooling anyone. Sorin came up behind me and shook Alex's hand. "Doctor. It's good to see you. I hope you are well."

"I am," Alex answered. "Thankfully, Kate forced me to spend a day sleeping and eating. Otherwise, I don't think I'd be standing in front of you. I just needed to see she was fine."

Sorin laid his hand on my back. "As you see, she is well. I do thank you, however, for getting her the week off. I think she was also overworking herself."

My friend looked back and forth between myself and the man at my side several times. I didn't think he was going to buy what we were trying to sell. Normally, I'd invite him into the manor but there was no way I could do that. I didn't know where they were. I sent Tamela a mental plea to stay wherever they were. I had to think fast. I knew what I was about to do and knew it was worth it but I wished I didn't need to do it.

"Sorin," I took a breath and let it out. "Would you go get the note, please?" I didn't need to explain. He was gone in a silent blur. We heard the door open and shut without seeing it.

"Alex," I started. "I need to give you something." I took him by the arm and led him away from the door. We were only a few feet away when the sound of the door was at our backs and Sorin was walking next to us. I paused, taking the paper wordlessly and Sorin left our sides with the same grace he always showed. I continued leading Alex towards the grove. I wanted a peaceful and beautiful place for his heartbreak. It killed me to add an unpleasant memory to my special spot but he deserved this.

Sitting on the bench side by side, I gripped the page tight. All around us, the Christmas lights that decorated this part of the grounds shone warm white. They gave the air a fairytale-feel and made Alex look more handsome than usual. But sadness slowly appeared on that face. It was clear he knew what was coming. I didn't know if it was better to give him some time to prepare or to do it quickly without ceremony.

I lifted my hand, still locking away the painful message in my grasp. He looked down at it like it may be tarantula not a simple page. I spoke but it came out so low I was worried he may not hear. "Diana brought this. I haven't spoken to Monica but she told Diana she's not coming back. She left this for you. I don't know what it says. Just give me the word and I'll destroy it."

He heard me. I saw it cross his face. "No," he whispered. "I need to know." He laid his hand on top of my fist lightly, afraid for me to let the thing in my hand go. I slowly unfurled my fingers, half expecting to see the letter was shredded from the force of my squeeze. But the awful white paper was still intact. For a moment, it sat in my flat palm with this hand hovering over top of it.

When he took it from me, I let my hand fall onto his thigh to reassure him I was there. My gaze was on his face when he unfolded the note and began to read. It may have been a minute or thirty, I'm not sure because everything around us seemed to stop while his eyes slid over the words. His expression gave nothing away. She could be saying that it wasn't him, it was her. Or, she could have been calling him profanities. There was no way to know from his face. Doctors are like nurses, they can hide their feelings and separate from the pain of what they're doing, hearing or saying.

Pain was exuding off him and breaking through my wall. I couldn't stop from feeling his heartache. It felt like someone was sticking a knife into my chest and turning it. I could feel the words on the page rolling in his head. She said that she had changed too much and it was too painful to come back. She said that the Monica he'd known, the one that had loved him, was gone and that he should let go of her for his own good. I wanted to vomit, cry and run all at once. I knew he was questioning everything he knew. He didn't feel like he was a

LENA NAZAREI

good doctor, a good friend, a good anything. He felt like a failure. Underneath it all, he didn't love Monica but he thought he might have. He had believed he was destined to be alone for a long time and she'd given him hope of something different. But this note proved he'd been right all along. I forced the wall back up to stop the influx of his feelings. It felt so wrong to know.

I reached out for his face and rested my hand under his chin, turning his head towards me. He didn't look up but had stopped reading the page for the third time. "Look at me," I said. The eyes lifted centimeter by centimeter until they met mine. "People are put into our lives for a reason: to teach us something, show us something or provide us something and vice versa. Sometimes they only need to be in our lives for an hour to serve that purpose, sometimes it's decades. Monica was only meant to be in your life for a short time. She showed you that you can love and can be loved. But she's not meant to be your forever, only to show you the possibility is out there so you don't give up." I leaned in close to make sure he was listening. "Don't you give up."

He was silent and his eyes showed nothing, just continued to stare into mine. I held his chin, afraid that if I broke contact with him, he'd lose his anchor and fall apart. I made sure to keep his gaze, working to show in my eyes how important he was. "You've never let me down, Alex. You've protected me, fought for me and been by my side even before I knew I needed you. You will never let me down."

Before I knew what was happening, his lips were on mine. His hand found my hair and took it in his grip. My muscles responded instinctually, relaxing and leaning further into him. The hand that had been on his chin moments before was behind his neck and kneading. I couldn't think. An unquenchable need filled me and wanted Alex. His smell enveloped me, making it hard to breath. The kiss warmed when his tongue urged my mouth open for him, which it did. As it caressed my own tongue, it hit my fangs and I tasted his blood. The drops slid down my throat and a fire built in my stomach. I wanted more - more of the kiss and more of the blood. My desire for his body mixed with the hunger and snapped into my head.

I pushed him back. "Stop," I yelled, jumping up and backing away from him.

"Are you okay?" he asked.

"Me? Are you okay? I cut your tongue, tasted your blood. Jesus, Alex. I almost didn't stop."

He stood and tried to close the distance but I held up my hand. He took a step back. "I don't want you to stop, Kate."

I shook my head. "Alex, you're in shock. You just had bad news and you're looking to feel better, I get that, I do. I'm not the way, though."

"Why?" he asked. He looked so genuine, so confused.

"Because," I paused. I needed a second to think before I spoke. I didn't want to hurt him even more but it wasn't just that. I wasn't totally sure of what I was feeling, if I hadn't wanted this to happen.

"Because of Sorin?" he asked.

Sorin, I thought. *Oh God, Sorin.* I'd just been with him only half an hour ago, only feet from where we stood. What was I thinking?

"That," I said. "And other things. We're friends. You're human and I'm not. I respect you too much."

"Bullshit," he said, stepping towards me as I backed away. My back hit a tree and he didn't end until he was close enough for me to feel his heat. I looked up to meet his eyes, trying to show him I wasn't confused, trying to be confident in my refusal.

"You want me," he was close enough for his breath to warm on my cheeks. "I may not be an empath but I know that. Me being human means nothing. Nor does us being friends. And, Kate," his gaze dropped to my mouth and then back to my eyes. "I can respect you and still want you."

I was working to keep my breath steady. His gaze was too intense to break away from and my lips were still tingling from his. I felt my resolve weakening when his eyes broke away to focus on something behind me. He tilted his head to the side and gasped. Stumbling backwards quickly, he fell onto the ground and continued to crawl backwards, away from the sight at my back.

"Shit," I said and didn't need to turn.

I smelled the orchids already.

22

I had a second to choose my priority. He'd already seen her so I couldn't change anything by grabbing her and running. I had to focus on him. He'd just read a "Dear Alex" letter, kissed his friend and seen his missing sister in the span of fifteen minutes. If I didn't handle the shock correctly or quickly, his mind could snap for good.

I dropped to the ground and crawled towards him, putting a hand on each side of his face and forcing him to look in my eyes. "Alex, look at me. Look at me now."

I heard Tamela behind me. "I'm so sorry Kate, I looked away for a second."

I heard Sheena. "I wanted to go to the bench. I like it there."

"We're going inside, we'll come out later," Tamela said and I felt the two of them rush away behind me.

Alex was looking around wildly, his eyes too wide to be comfortable. All of the color was gone from his face. "Look at me, Alex," I commanded and he did.

His hands grabbed my arms, holding onto me. "She – she – she-" he babbled. "Why? How? When?"

"Alex," I used my nurse voice, the one that tells people to get the crash cart and call a code. "Focus on my eyes and listen to me. Sheena's okay. She's here at the manor and she's okay." He was starting to focus. "You're okay and she is okay but I need you to calm down so you can listen to me."

He was focused on me. The confusion was still there but it was less wild, more in control. Then the betrayal hit his gaze. "You knew? You had her here and you didn't tell me?" He pushed me away from him and stood, pacing. "How could you keep this from me? How long, Kate?"

I stood, watching him walk back and forth in the clearing. "Alex, listen."

He stopped and turned on me furiously. "How long, Kate?" he roared.

"Three nights."

"What?" he talked towards me. For a second, I forgot I was a vampire and just saw how big, strong and mad he was but I stood my ground. "You knew when you were in my office and didn't say a word?"

"I didn't know yet, not exactly. She showed up here and couldn't remember anything. I didn't know it was her until I saw the picture in your office."

"You've seen it a dozen times, Kate. How could you not know?"

I had to be careful but I couldn't lie anymore. "Because Alex, she didn't look like herself. She looked different enough from the picture that I didn't see it at first."

"But when she told you who she was. I should've been the first call." He was pacing again but was looking at me the whole time. I felt the anger coming off of him. He wanted to hit something but was still controlled enough that he was worried about scaring me.

"Alex," I took a cautious step towards him. "She doesn't know who she is. She has no memory of anything after you saw her at your bedroom window." I reached out for him to stop his pacing and pulled him down to the bench, sitting beside him. "She thought you were still a kid. We had to tell her what year it was and that not everyone is a vampire. Alex, she doesn't know where she's been, who turned her – nothing."

He stared at me, a mixture of confusion, pain, fear and hope was replacing the rage. "No more lies, Kate. You tell me everything and then take me to her."

I nodded my head in agreement. "It's going to hurt, Alex."

"I don't care. I can't take any more lies. I can't be left in the dark anymore. Do you understand?"

"I do," I said, grabbing his hand and holding it for the next part. "She came to us when some vamps found her in the woods. She's been kept alive on animal blood which makes us very thin and weak. She was filthy and wearing an old dress. She's scared of men she doesn't know and still shakes when she hears a new voice. She's blocked out the last thirty years. Tamela and I washed her, gave her something clean to wear. I've been -" I paused, preparing myself for how pissed he was about to be "- looking into her mind to pull out memories."

He didn't move. "And?"

"All I've seen so far was her memory of the last time she saw you and some kids she met one time. That's it."

"Why wouldn't you tell me, Kate? You're the one person I believed would never lie to me." It killed me to hear him say that but I deserved it.

I took a breath and let it out. "When you really see her, I hope you'll understand. I wanted to be able to tell you more about where she's been and what's happened to her before you knew she was back. I'm so sorry, Alex. I was trying to protect you."

He stood, pulling his hand from mine. "I don't need your protection, Kate. I need the truth. I need one person in my life who won't -" he stopped himself "-nevermind. Forget it. Just take me to my sister."

I rose. "Come with me."

23

Sorin was on the porch when we walked up. He'd thrown another shirt on. I knew from the look on his face, he was aware of what was going on. He approached to meet us at the bottom of the stairs. "I am sorry this is how you found out, Alex." Sorin extended his hand but Alex did not reciprocate.

"You of all people," Alex said "should've known. If Kate had been missing for thirty years and I found her – then held her from you."

"You are right," Sorin said. "We chose for you but I assure you we had good intentions. She is your sister but she is one of my vampires. I look out for mine and she was not ready for a reunion. However, it has happened so I welcome you inside."

Sorin was being very diplomatic which could be good or bad, I wasn't sure yet. Alex hesitated at the doorway then crossed inside. We followed behind him and Sorin gestured for us to go right. I heard a giggle in the solarium, so I took Alex's hand and led him in that direction. When we entered the room, Tamela and Sheena sat at the bar. Sheena had a large glass of blood in front of her and was laughing at something the bodyguard was saying. I looked over at Alex. His face was slack, tears rolling down his cheeks. I saw him sway and thought I may need to catch him, but he took a step forward to balance himself. The women at the bar turned to us. Tamela stood in a protective stance with Sheena just behind her.

"It's okay, T," I said and she stepped to the side.

Sheena stared at the human next to me. First, she was frightened but I saw a slow realization pass over her face. "Alex," she whispered. Then yelled, "Alex!"

Jumping to her feet, she ran towards Alex. He dropped my hand and ran to meet her. When he wrapped his arms around her and lifted her, she started to wail, letting out sobs of happiness. He cried harder and dropped to his knees, still holding her. She was so very small in his big embrace. He was a man and she was a child but for a brief moment, I could see the little brother holding his big sister.

I was overcome with emotion and turned into Sorin, who held onto me and whispered into my ear. "It's okay, Katherine. They're together. They're safe and we're safe and we did the right thing." I felt all the emotion in the room and Sorin rocked me while Alex rocked his lost sister. I felt Tamela leave the room and knew it was too much for her too but she liked to be alone when she was overwhelmed.

When the crying died down, we all met in the middle of the room. I looked at Sheena and knew the blood stains on her face were probably similar to mine. "Sheena, let's go wash up and we can meet the boys in the living room, okay?"

She found her brother's face. I could see he needed a minute to collect himself. I think she did, as well. "I'll be right back," she said. "I promise." He just nodded as she took my hand and we left the room.

Ten minutes later, we were fresh faced. Sheena sat on the couch next to her brother. Tamela was in one chair. Sorin was seated in another chair and I was on his lap. His arm rested around me. For a second, I was uncomfortable, remembering Alex's profession of feelings for me but then I saw that his eyes were all for Sheena. I relaxed and listened to them talk.

"You really can't remember anything?" he asked her.

"Just the two things Kate found in my head," Sheena answered. "When she sees them, I see them too. But it takes a while for them to feel like my memories, you know? Are you really a doctor?" she asked.

"Yes," he answered proudly. "A hematologist." When she squinted her eyes, he elaborated. "A blood doctor. I study blood diseases."

"Oh," she responded. "And you work with Kate? You're friends?"

That's when he looked at me. I didn't see forgiveness but at least he didn't look pissed anymore. "Yes," he said, turning back to Sheena. "I work with Kate." I noticed he didn't address the friend part.

"You don't care that she's a vampire? That I am?" Sheena questioned.

"No," he said, taking her hands. "Of course not. It's a condition like anything else. I wouldn't care if you had diabetes, so why would I care about this?"

"How come you don't want to be a vampire? You'll get older than you already are?" Man, Sheena had no filter. She asked anything.

"Ouch," he laughed. "I'm not that old."

"But," she kept down her line of questioning. "I thought we wanted to be vampires together? See the world and be free."

Alex nodded. "Yes, we did. But, Sheena, I didn't know then what you were saying, didn't understand what it meant. I like being human. I like the sun and eating food. It's the natural way."

I didn't know how to take that. Did he think we were unnatural? That the way I was, was wrong? I think Sheena wondered the same thing because she furrowed her brow. "But you said. It's a condition."

He squeezed her hand. "Yes, and if given the choice. I don't want it."

We all sat silently, each thinking over what he was saying and what that meant for us. Sheena broke the silence. "I don't want you to die, Alex."

He leaned forward to rest his forehead on hers. "I'm not dying for fifty years, kiddo. We have plenty of time. Now," he pulled back and was obviously about to change the subject. "Why don't you come stay with me?"

Tamela and I jumped up. "Alex," I said. "Can we talk in another room, please?" He hesitated and his expression told me he didn't want to talk to me for a while. I gave him a look that told him I would not let it go. He made the wise choice to stand and follow me out into the solarium.

I whispered loud enough for him to hear but low enough, hopefully, for the other vampires not to hear.. "You cannot take her out of here."

"Why?" he whispered at the same level but with way more anger in his voice. "She's my family and she's not a prisoner."

"Alex, think straight. She has no idea what's happened to her or where she's been. She needs to be around her kind and I need to keep working with her to extract memories."

He leaned in, dropping his voice even more. "Dammit Kate, I'm her family. I'll bring her by every night but I'll be damned if I'm leaving her with you. Her *kind* tried to kill me six months ago. Her *kind* took your kids. And her *kind* is why she went missing. So, I'm sorry if I don't exactly trust vampires right now."

"Listen, Kitchner." I handed the tone right back to him. "I get it. You're pissed at me. You've had a shitty night. But, fuck you if you think I wouldn't die to protect you and that means your sister. You don't want to hear this but you're going to anyway. You're my friend and I love you. But you're not a woman and you've never been victimized. If things happened to her that she's locked away, when they come out, you have no clue what it's going to do to her. Trust me, Alex, there are some things you can never wash away."

The rage left his face and I saw the horror of it cross his eyes. He'd been so lost in the excitement of finding her and his anger at me that he hadn't stopped to think about what she could've endured.

He straightened up and stared at me. The fear and sickness that filled his eyes made me miss the fury. That I could handle; this was much harder.

I felt and smelled Sorin before I saw him walk in from my periphery. "Stay here, Alex," he said. "We have rooms and clothes. I will get fresh food delivered. You can see her from the moment she awakes until she lies down each morning. You can witness all her sessions with Katherine. We will keep no more from you."

Alex's shoulders relaxed. I thought about what it meant to have Sorin and Alex under the same roof, for me to be living with both. I wasn't sure exactly what my feelings for Alex were but I knew I couldn't handle losing another friend in a matter of days.

This was going to get complicated.

24

It took half an hour for me to tell Rhys the whole story. I left out what Sorin and I had done in the woods and my kiss with Alex but told him all the rest. He was silent through the whole thing, probably in shock or waiting for me to tell him it was a joke. When I was done, he was quiet for so long I had to check to make sure the call hadn't died.

"We should have told him right away."

I sighed. "Not helpful, Rhys. We know that now but we were just trying to do the right thing."

"I know," he said. "Put him in the room I stay in. It's next to the birch room so he'll be close to her. There's plenty of other rooms for me to crash in. I can swing by his apartment for clothes and stuff."

"That's nice of you but he's got this bag in the back of his car. He always has extra clothes and toiletries in case he stays at the hospital. He's already brought it in and called the hospital for time off. He's determined to be here every second with her."

Rhys sighed, "Alright, well, I'll be there when I can. You okay?"

I shook my head no but said "Yep." I actually wanted to pack and run to Rhys' cottage where life was much simpler but that was cowardly and I'd hate myself. "Love you."

"Love you, Katie. Try to rest." When the line went dead, I missed him already.

Coming out of the bedroom, I ran into Alex. He had the massive duffel bag in hand. "Sorry. I was told to come to the end of the hall."

I ignored the heat rising in my face. "Almost. Follow me." I lead him away from the bed I shared with Sorin and to the room Rhys normally stayed in. Opening the door, I expected a messy bed – it was Rhys' style. However, someone had made it and the room looked freshly cleaned. I cleared my throat and looked anywhere but him. "Sheena's right next door so she'll be close. None of the bedrooms have windows so it's easy to sleep during the day. Bathroom is a few doors down the hall. Towels in the closet."

I was backing out when he grabbed my arm. Instinctually, I looked up to meet his eyes and the betrayal I fully deserved. Imagine my surprise when I saw what looked too much like love. "Kate, I owe you a very big apology."

I was actually speechless and, trust me, that's rare.

He laid his hand on my cheek. "She told me. You gave her shelter, blood. You washed her, gave her clean clothes and your room. You protected her from the men until she was ready. You protected me until I was ready. You're so strong that sometimes I think nothing can hurt you but I did, didn't I?"

"I know what you were feeling, Alex. I broke your trust and while I did it for what I thought was the right reason, I did it. You and I are so much alike. We don't want to be protected, we want to be told the truth, respected for our strength and capability. I would've been furious if you'd hidden anything this big from me."

He pulled me into him, my head resting on his chest. I heard his heartbeat and it was so unusual. I'd gotten used to sleeping and resting against a silent chest that I'd forgotten the feel of the thumping against my ear.

"Thank you for getting her back to me," I heard his voice through his chest in one ear and from his mouth in the other. "If you hadn't come into my life, met Sorin, she could've been brought here and I'd never known. We were meant to know each other, like you said in the grove. We were destined to be in each other's lives."

Before this could go any further, I pulled back and broke from his arms. One plus of being the undead is you're strong and fast enough to get away from an uncomfortable conversation without barriers. I playfully punched his shoulder. "No worries, Doc. Just glad were friends again. See you tomorrow night, sleep good."

And, with that moment of sheer awkwardness, I was out the door and down the hallway in a blink. Leaving a man standing in a very clean guest room, likely wondering what the hell just happened.

25

When Sorin came into the bedroom, I was already lying under the covers in the dark, feeling very twisted up inside. I silently asked the universe to please let him have a shield up and not be using his empathy on me. I didn't know yet what to say to him. He lost the shirt he was wearing for the second time that night, tossing it off to the couch. His pants followed after. When he got into his usual position, I wiggled over to lay my head on his strong, silent chest.

Should I tell him about the kiss in the grove? Should I tell him it wasn't mine and Alex's first kiss? After all, I'd made out with Alex a few days after I'd been turned. I hadn't been dating Sorin yet, not really, so it never came up. Sorin and I knew we'd had liaisons before each other and vampires were very sexual creatures so it wasn't even like he'd care but tonight – I mean, we were due to be mated. We'd bonded with blood months ago and I had a ring on my finger. Sorin was ready to say goodbye to any other person in his bed for eternity.

If the tables were turned, and he'd kissed someone, would I want to know? Would I rather know than find out another way later? How would I feel if he'd hadn't told me? How would I feel if he did?

When Alex had kissed me the first time, we'd been overjoyed about the possibility for a cure. He'd seen something in my blood that gave him a real hope, which he hadn't had in a long time. I'd only been a vampire for less than a week and to say I was horny was an understatement. I'd gone years without sex and the vampire blood had turned my sexuality from a simmer to a high boil overnight. Poor Alex had been a very good-looking, hot-blooded man. When he'd kissed me, I had been unable to control myself. But, when that need for sex had mixed in with a need for blood, I'd pushed him away – just like I had tonight.

Had tonight been the same thing? Just a crossed wire? I mean, he'd just had his heart ripped out by Monica and felt alone, I'd felt it with him. Maybe, he'd just needed to hold onto something and I'd been the one next to him. Maybe, he'd needed a connection to anything to stop him from falling and it wasn't even about me.

Now that he had his sister back, he wasn't alone and wouldn't need someone. He was probably lying in bed, regretting that kiss. Or, maybe he had already forgotten about it. I mean, we'd never talked about our make-out session in the conference room again. He'd chalked it up to physiological responses to the correct stimuli and so had I. He was a doctor for goodness' sake. He knew that the right stimuli could make humans do impulsive things. He'd been in the grips of grief, of course he'd needed to feel loved and wanted.

It was nothing more.

I started to calm down, recognizing that what had happened with Alex in the woods really was a fluke – it was a blip – not worth mentioning.

"Katherine?" Sorin spoke into the top of my head.

"Yeah."

"Talk to me, what's going on?"

I sighed, lifting off of his chest to look up at him. "Tonight, was a lot. Monica broke up with Alex, broke up with me. You're going to the wolves alone tomorrow night. Alex found out about Sheena in the worst way possible and is staying right down the hall. My head is spinning and I'm just trying to process."

He ran his fingers through my hair, comforting me. I laid my head back down on his chest, letting him continue. I'd told him once that my mom would brush my hair to make me feel better, before she'd gotten crazy and abusive. He'd never forgotten that and knew it would help. I was filled with shame for not telling him about Alex. But I couldn't bring myself to do it. I couldn't see one more person hurt tonight. I knew it was selfish but I kept it to myself.

"I love you, Katherine."

"I love you too, Sorin. So much sometimes that it scares me."

He chuckled, "I do understand the feeling. Try to rest. I will be here when you wake. I won't leave until you rise."

He was such a good man and I was keeping something from him. I told myself it was no big deal, it was for him, it was for Alex. But I knew the truth.

I was afraid I didn't deserve him. That this would be the thing that made him see it and I would lose him.

26

I was still on his chest when I woke and his hand was in my hair. He'd probably brushed his fingers through it until he'd fallen asleep. "Good evening," he said. I didn't feel him wake so it must have happened before I did.

"Good evening," I responded. Lifting my head, I found those grey eyes sparkling and smiled. "You look perfect all the time, it's really not fair."

He feigned humility. "I cannot help it. I was made this way."

I touched my finger to his lips. "Shhh, you'll ruin the moment." Then, I replaced my finger with my lips for a quick kiss and bounced out of bed. "C'mon, perfect. We have to get ready for the night. We have guests and commitments."

He stood and started for the door but I caught his arm, pulling him back. This time, I started the dance. He looked down at me, "You are only delaying the inevitable."

I laid my head against this sternum and sighed. "I know. Just promise me you'll come back in one piece."

"I promise," he kissed the top of my head. "And, Jeremy texted. He will be by soon. I filled him in on our visitor, explained why he must tell no one and asked him to stop by. Perhaps, he can help you relax the young doctor should he still be angry."

"Perhaps," I said. "But I don't like using powers on Alex when he doesn't know. Besides, I think he's chilled out. His temper flares hot and quick but he calms down just as quickly."

"I know someone like that," he quipped.

I slapped his bare butt and looked up. "Not nice."

"I didn't say it was you." But, the twinkle in his eye told me that I was correct in my assumption and the slap was deserved.

I put my dress back on, seeing the mud on the back of it from our outdoor lovemaking. It felt like days ago and far away. It also brought back the kiss I was trying to forget, bringing a fresh pang to my gut.

"Katherine, are you okay?"

"Yep," I said, throwing on a smile. "Just need a clean dress. Get ready and I'll meet you downstairs."

I found the birch room empty and quickly chose an outfit. I didn't really care at that point, just wanted the offending dress and its attachment to my shame gone. I thought about telling Jeremy later. I knew he'd keep my secret and be a good source for reason. If he told me to tell Sorin, I would. If he told me to let it go, I happily would. In the meantime, I had to get myself together. If Sorin was worried, he'd be distracted with the wolves – or cancel. Either option would be bad. So, I brushed my hair and went dowstairs to be a good partner and host.

I heard them all in the kitchen and was obviously the last one down. Tamela, Sheena, Alex and Sorin sat around the island. The vampires had glasses of blood. Alex had a bagel with cream cheese and coffee. Everyone seemed happy. They were listening to Alex tell a story about Sheena. Apparently, she'd babysat Alex one time and let him watch *The Exorcist* when he was way too young to have watched it. He'd been terrified but kept the secret when his parents got home. Then Sheena had slept on his floor every night for two weeks until he'd been okay to sleep alone again. "She'd come in after my parents went to bed with a sleeping bag and be gone before they woke up," he said. "I made her check my closet and under my bed about 100 times in those two weeks."

Sheena spoke up. "I don't remember that but it sounds like I was a brave as a human. I wouldn't have been able to fight off a demon but I still came to protect you."

Alex smiled at her. "Yes," he said. "You were very brave. You still are."

Edwin came into the kitchen to ruin the fun. "Sir, we must leave."

Sorin stood, finished his glass and placed it in the sink. Then he crossed to me, pulling me into him and the kiss was soft, reassuring. "I'll be back," he whispered.

"You better," I said.

When he was gone from the room, my heart hurt. I'd been so concerned with a stupid kiss in the yard, that I'd never really considered he might not return from this meeting. I tried to stop myself from even heading down that road of thought. I had to trust Rhys when he said this was a good thing. I had to trust Sorin when he said he could handle this. He'd been around a lot longer than me and survived much tougher things than a meeting.

I tried so hard to believe it but it didn't stop me from being filled with dread.

I heard the door open and Sorin exchanging conversation. Jeremy was here. I let out a breath and thanked a higher power for his excellent timing. I excused myself from the kitchen and met them in the foyer just as Sorin was walking out. Before I could formally greet my friend, I had to see Sorin one more time. I gave Jeremy the "one second" finger and ran after Sorin. He stopped just before getting into his car to turn to me with a question in his eyes. There was no time to ask me why I was coming out before I met him and wrapped my arms around him. He returned my embrace, giving me a few extra seconds of squeezing. When he pulled back, he smiled. "I promise," he mouthed silently. Then, he disappeared into the vehicle, shut the door and I watched the car disappear.

I felt Jeremy come up behind me. Turning to face him, I let him mirror the hug I'd just left. "I'm so happy to see you," I said into his shoulder.

He squeezed and let go. "Is it true? She came from nowhere and can't remember thirty years?"

"Yeah," I shook my head. "Wait 'til you see her. She's skin and bones. She actually looks better than she did a few days ago but it still breaks your heart to see how frail she is. I don't think she has any powers, at least none that I can see."

"Well," Jeremy rubbed his chin. "If she's been living off animal blood like we think, she'd have lost her power. We can't hold magic without intaking human blood. Don't ask me how it works because I don't know."

"How could someone do that to a kid?"

"I don't get it, doll." He wrapped his arm around my shoulders and we returned to the foyer. "But there are some sick people in this world. Where is she? What's the plan for the night?"

"She's in the kitchen with T and her brother, Alex. Plan is to look into her mind again, see what I can find out. I need you to be here to keep her or her brother calm if necessary. We don't know what we're going to find but I can't imagine she's been living it up in paradise this whole time."

He sighed. "Good point. Alright, let's get some sustenance and get this party started."

I turned and stopped him with a hand on his chest. "Listen, she's a little skittish around new men so go slow."

"Got it," he held up two fingers in the scout's honor sign.

Once back in the kitchen, I watched her face when she looked up. Her smile fell and she stopped whatever she was saying. "Who is this?" she asked. Alex stood, ready to defend her and I realized Jeremy and him had never met face to face.

"This is my friend, Jeremy. He's very nice and he's here to help. Jeremy, this is my friend Dr. Alex Kitchner and his sister, Sheena."

He went to Alex first, hand extended and Alex shook it. "I've heard so much about you," Jeremy said.

Alex nodded. "Me, too."

Next, Jeremy slowly moved towards Sheena. "I'm Jeremy. It's very nice to meet you." He held out his hand. She looked at it and mimicked what she'd seen her brother do, laying her small hand in Jeremy's larger one. When he pumped it up and down, she smiled.

"I'm Sheena, I guess. Did I do it right?"

Jeremy smiled. "Very good handshake."

"Thanks," she beamed. "It was my first."

"No way," he exclaimed, dramatically. "I never would've known." I forgot sometimes that he'd been a teacher for a long time. He had such a way with new people and I'd bet that was why. I couldn't imagine how much his students had loved him. It was sad that he'd had to leave teaching. It was going to break my heart to leave the hospital and I'd wager that Jeremy had felt the same way when he'd realized his time in the classroom had to come to an end.

"Are we ready?" It was Alex. His question pulled me out of my thoughts and I saw that everyone was looking at me. I guess I was in charge tonight.

"Oh," I said. "Um, yeah. I have an idea. Everyone grab a blanket and meet me out in the side yard, just outside the solarium door."

27

The group followed my instructions and I led them to a large area of grass off to the side of the house, away from the little grove and bench I loved. In this part of the yard, strings of white outside bulbs hung from tree to tree, forming a square. When we opened the manor to visitors and had music, this is where they would mingle and dance. Tonight, without the party-goers, that square of grass looked like it was waiting for something.

Laying my blanket down, the others laid theirs around me. When I sat on mine, they did the same. Sheena was in front of me on the rectangle of yellow fleece that had become her security item with her brother by her side. On their own blanket, Tamela and Jeremy sat to my right. I glanced around seeing the expectation in Sheena's eyes, the worry in Alex's, the curiosity in Jeremy's and the concern in Tamela's. We all knew we were out here to extract another memory but none of us could guess what it would be.

"Sheena," I said gently, extending my hands to her. "I want to look in your head again."

She reached out to take my hands and let them fall to the ground between us. "Okay."

I hoped my soft smile but her at ease. "Tamela and Alex will keep you safe. Depending on what we see, Jeremy can take away any bad feelings."

She nodded. "Okay."

"Do you remember the party that the kids at the school invited you to?"

She nodded. "Yes."

"Did you go?" I asked and jumped into her mind. After the first two times, I knew to expect the darkness, knew it was part of the process and likely not long lasting. Walking around in the black space, I searched for any sign: a smell, a sound, a dot of light – anything. I was starting to lose hope when the campfire hit my nostrils and the sounds of clinking glass bottles filled the cavern of her lost memory.

The flames danced off to my left so I turned to face them. The bonfire was big enough for the dozen or so teens to comfortably sit around. They all spoke at once, laughing and telling stories. Scanning the faces, I was sure they were the same age group as the ones from her previous memory. Looking up, I saw the night sky through barren tree limbs. Those naked branches combined with the puffs of breath coming from the excited mouths of the college students told me it was sometime between when the dead leaves fell off and the new leaves grew.

The giggle to my left was recognizable so I walked towards it and found the girl from the cafeteria. She saw me. "There you guys are!"

I felt the weight in my clenched grasp before I looked down and over to see I was holding the hand of Bobby, the cool boy from earlier. I still couldn't believe I almost didn't sneak out for this party. If I'd listened to my parents and stayed home, I never would've known that Bobby liked me. "Of course I'm here," I said in Sheena's voice. "This place is so cool."

"I know," the girl said – I think she was Amanda and the one next to her was Heather. And, Heather was sitting in Brian's lap so they must be going out. I'd only met them that evening but I knew we'd be friends and hoped they'd invite me to more parties. "He lets us come out like every night," Amanda continued. "He has like every type of booze you could want, too."

"Rad," I said. "No one calls the cops or anything?"

"Nah," Brian jumped in. "He owns all the land around us so no one even knows. We can be as loud as we want." As if on cue, someone turned up the boombox and Livin' on a Prayer filled the night.

"Awesome," I said. Bobby broke the hand hold, walking away and then returning with a beer. I saw my hand reach out for it and it looked so small, so young, as it grasped the alcohol. After a few deep gulps, Bobby started to pull me away from the group and into the trees. I was feeling light headed, giggling and asking "Where are we going?"

"I want to get away from the noise so we can talk and I can get to know you," he said. I knew he was cute but now I knew he was nice, too. He wanted to actually talk to me. I took some more sips while we looked for a good spot. The fallen log we came across was perfect, so we sat side by side on the dampness of the bark. I had to lean against him since the beer was making me a little dizzy. He kissed my head. "You're so pretty," he said. "You seem way older than 17."

Heat rose in my neck and up to my face. "A lot of people say that." Looking up to him, his face was so close. "I think I'm an old soul."

He brushed hair out of my eye. "I believe that – in reincarnation, I mean. I think some of us are new on this planet but most of us have been here before." He sounded so smart. I loved listening to him talk. "And, I think there are some of us that are meant to serve a higher purpose."

"Like what?" I asked. The dimple in his right cheek sunk in as he smiled and I thought I would die from how cute he was.

"Like," he paused and then glanced up to the sky. "Like some of us are meant to be in this life forever, to be better than others, to rule this planet and stop those who destroy it."

"Wow," I whispered. "Like heroes?"

Finding my eyes again, his smile deepened. "Yeah, kind of. But more like higher beings, a more evolved species."

"How do you know if you're one of those? One of the higher beings?"

He touched his finger to the tip of my nose. "You get recognized by one – chosen – and then brought in."

"Are you one?" I asked. I knew I sounded childish but the beer was making it hard to not talk and I had to know.

"Not yet," he said. "But I hope to be. I want to be."

I had so many more questions. How do you get to be one? Do you know one? What does it all mean? But all those questions died in my head when he put his lips to mine.

This time I didn't pull out of her head. Instead, it felt like being yanked out from my back. Sheena and I gasped in tandem, gripped each other's hands.

"What was that?" Alex asked, grabbing his sister's shoulders to steady her.

"I think she just blocked me," I said in awe and examined the disbelief in Sheena's face.

"I did," she questioned. "How?"

"I think," I said cautiously. "I think you may have some power coming back, Sheena. I think when you were turned you either had or were meant to have some kind of psychic power – like mind reading or empathy or something like that. With one of those powers comes the ability to block other psychic powers. You might not have your magic all the way back but you did just block me."

"I'm sorry," she winced like a kid who is afraid they're in trouble.

I rubbed my hands up her arms. "It's okay, sweetie. You didn't do it on purpose, it was instinct. But the real question is, why? What did you just instinctually stop me from seeing?"

28

Jeremy jumped in. "Let's start with this, Kate. What did you see?"

"A party," I answered. "A bonfire outside. It was on someone's land. The kids from the annex were there, the ones that invited her. Plus, there were more – all young adults." I tried to look back at capture details. "They were listening to Bon Jovi, drinking, normal kid stuff. She was with the boy named Bobby."

"That's something," Tamela said. "We have a name. What else?"

"There was also a Heather, a Brian and an Amanda. They were all in that friend group, the one from the previous memory. I don't know whose party it was but it sounded like they did it every night and it was his land. They said he had no neighbors to call the cops."

Alex interrupted. "One of the kids you just named? Or another student?"

"Maybe," I answered. "I can't be sure. She was too focused on Bobby for me to hear any of the other conversation. They walked away from the party, into the woods. They were kissing and then she pushed me out."

"Was he a vampire? Bobby?" This was from Alex.

"I don't know," I responded. "It was night so any of them could have been. But we didn't get that far. I don't know if he bit her or if they kissed and left the woods."

"I remember," Sheena said and we all stared. "I remember what happened after."

I left up to my knees. "What do you mean?"

"It came back to me," she said. "After you left my head, the part after, it came back to me."

Jeremy and Tamela both leaned forward expectedly. The hope that she was going to get her memories back was on everyone's minds.

"And," I pried. "Did he turn you?"

She looked to Alex. He laid his hand on her cheek. "Whatever it is, you can say it," he assured her.

Returning her gaze to me, she blushed. "We did it that night. It was my first time. I can remember the pain, how happy I was and how much trouble I was in when I got home. But I thought it was worth it."

My decorum told me not to pry but knew this was no time to be timid. "Did he bite you? Did you drink his blood?"

"I don't think so," she said. "I mean, not that night anyway. I can't remember anything else. That's all that came to me."

I dropped back down to my backside, Tamela and Jeremy leaned back. Our hope for a full recovery was dashed. She must have sensed our disappointment.

"I'm sorry," she said.

"Don't be, honey. It's okay." I let out a breath. "But, before we let this go, think hard. Do you know where you were? Where that party was or whose party it was?"

We remained silent as she closed her eyes and furrowed her brow. The swell of her eyeballs behind her lids rolled side to side like she was searching her head. "No," she sighed and her shoulders fell. "That's all I have – what you saw and a couple things after."

Defeat shadowed her eyes when the lids fluttered opened. I had to stop her from quitting. "Hey, every time we do this, we get clues and we get closer to answers. You're doing so good."

When she met my gaze, I was relieved to see some of the sorrow gone. "Really?" she questioned.

"Yeah," I answered.

Alex scooted up to her. "I'm so proud of you, sis. You're so strong."

"Can we do another one?" she asked. "I want to do more, see more."

"If you can, then I can," I assured her. "What should we try to find out?"

"I want more memories of Alex back, is that okay? Or do we need to get more clues?"

I knew what I should do; I should push her to learn more about where she had been and tell her we could get more happy memories later. However, I also knew that she'd been gone for thirty years and an extra hour of not knowing wouldn't hurt anyone. Searching her hopeful face, all I could see was one of my daughters in a few years and it made my chest ache.

"Sure," I answered. "I think we can make that happen. But we'll do it a little different. Alex," I found his eyes this time. "Tell her about one of your favorite memories with her."

This time, she lay down to rest her head on his thigh. I watched as he looked down at her, their matching blue eyes locked together and he began talk. "It was my eighth birthday. It was at McDonalds in the play place. I was so mad that Mom and Dad were giving me a kid party since I thought I was a cool teen like you….."

As I slid into her mind, I smelled the French fries and was blinded by the bright sun pouring through the large glass windows. The screams of children bounced off the walls of the small room and the rumbling of kids crawling through the plastic tubes was like thunder on my ears. I hated that I was stuck with these booger factories instead of out with friends. But if I was being honest, I'd rather be with Alex than anyone else in the whole wide world. It was his birthday and I'd be here for that no matter where it was.

When his red sneakers popped out from the bottom of the slide, I ran up, grabbed his feet and pulled him out. His squeals of delight were replaced with full belly laughter as I began the tickle assault that he pretended to hate. When I stopped, he was gasping for air and the ruby of his cheeks matched the ruby of his shoes.

"Got you something, twerp. But you have to hide it and open it at home. You can't tell mom and dad, capeesh?"

"Capeesh," he said, breathlessly.

I pulled the wrapped present from my back pocket. He and I both knew from the size, weight and sound it made that it was a cassette. But he wouldn't know until he got home and opened it that it was Aerosmith. Our parents would freak if they knew but he'd wanted it bad and I thought he should have it. I wished I could see his face when he saw the surprise I left him on his bed.

When he smiled, his two front teeth were absent from the show and I thought again about how much I loved his school picture from that year. I kinda didn't want the kid to grow up ever. But I also knew he was vulnerable and that I wouldn't always be around to protect him so he needed to get bigger. Especially if dad ever turned his punching habit onto the poor little guy. I hoped to God that Alex would get big and strong enough someday to knock our old man flat. He definitely deserved it.

He wrapped his scrawny arms around my waist. "Love you, butthole."

"Love you too, skunk breath."

I pulled out of her head to see a tear streaking down each sibling's face, one clear and one red. "...when I got home," Alex was finishing the story. "I opened the Walkman you left on the bed and then the tape you gave me. I must have listened to that album a thousand times. I still have the thing in a shoebox under my bed."

She opened her eyes to release more blood streams down her cheek. "You do?"

"Yep," he said, wiping at his eyes. "With a picture of you, some letters you wrote me and a Scrunchie. I found it in your room after they packed up your stuff, when they stopped looking."

Tamela and Jeremy looked as embarrassed as I felt. We were voyeurs, watching a special moment that no one should be a causal audience to. I knew we'd all felt loss and none of us could say we weren't moved by the exchange between brother and sister. When Jeremy caught my eyes, I nodded a signal that he thankfully understood. We rose up quietly, walking away from the tender moment and leaving them to reminisce. I assumed Tamela would also allow them some time together but didn't want to push.

All I knew is that the sight of Alex being so gentle with his sister had moved something in me. I had to talk to Jeremy and get some things off my chest before my heart exploded.

29

By the time Jeremy and I had slipped away and were seated on the couch in the living room, I could hardly breathe. Even if I could've spoken, I wouldn't have known where to start. Jeremy's concern was all over his expression.

"Kate, what's wrong? Was it the memories? Maybe this is too much. Maybe you should stop," he rubbed my back and I was still trying to suck in air but my throat felt tight with unspoken feelings.

"It's not that," I managed to begin despite feeling like my larynx was not being cooperative. "Oh, Jeremy. I don't know what to do. I don't think I can breathe."

"With what? You're freaking me out." I heard the panic slipping into his voice as his power rolled around my shoulders and down my back.

Calm washed over me, drenching my fear and shame with the feeling of peace. I suddenly knew everything would be okay and that it would all work out the way it should. "Thank you," I said to my friend.

"You're welcome," he said, flashing his dazzling smile. "Now, tell me what has you so upset."

Taking in full lungs of air and clearing my mind, I figured the best was to tell him outright and quickly. "Alex kissed me last night and it wasn't the first time. The first time was just after I turned and it was more than a kiss but stopped before it went too far. We never talked about it again and we're friends. I met Sorin and fell in love. Monica loved him and he liked her so it was nothing. Yesterday, she broke up with him and I was there. He kissed me – I mean like really kissed me..."

"Hold on," Jeremy grabbed my arm. "Monica broke up with him and he kissed you in front of her?"

"No," I clarified. "She sent it in a letter. He read it next to me. She's not coming back."

"Oh," he said. I'd told him everything so he knew that she'd been MIA and what it meant for me that she wasn't coming back. "I'm sorry. Continue."

"So, he read it and then he kissed me. But, that's not the thing, Jeremy. The thing is that I wanted him to. I mean I didn't stop him; not until I tasted his blood."

He made the "timeout" sign with his hands. "Pause. You bit him?"

"No. My fangs nicked his tongue. The blood hit my throat and it, I don't know, snapped me into my senses."

"Okay, so you didn't really want him to kiss you then. You ended it," he pushed. "And, he was just reacting to the breakup. It wasn't even real."

"Maybe," I said. "But, it's not that. He told me he wanted me. That he desired me and thought I desired him."

"Do you?" Jeremy challenged.

I dropped my head to my hands and rested my elbows on my thighs. "I don't know. I thought we were just friends but now, when I look at him, it's different. You should see him at work. He's brilliant and caring and selfless. And, watching him with his sister tonight - but I love Sorin. We're bonded and he's chosen me as mate."

"And," Jeremy pushed.

"And, I was happy when Monica ended things with Alex. He deserves better."

"And," he pushed harder.

"And," I shook my head. "I don't want to lose Sorin." I paused and said what I was thinking. "But I don't want to lose Alex, either." I looked up to my confidant, wanting to know his reaction. I wanted him to tell me what to do. He was just looking back at me in what resembled awe. "Say something," I begged.

"What do I say?" he asked rhetorically. "You've got two men wanting your attention. You've rescued this girl and gotten her to her brother. You're helping heal them both. I mean, it's not like your life is awful. Actually, it's basically a fantasy novel."

I slapped his arm. "Not helpful. I'm in real distress here." But I wasn't really. He was still using his power so I was nice and chill. "Do I tell Sorin? What would I even say?"

"Listen, doll." He laid his hand on my thigh and squeezed. "Being bonded doesn't mean you won't notice others. Neither does being married or mated. You can want Sorin while still feeling lust towards another. You can love Sorin with your whole heart and still have room for others."

"But you and Logan aren't like that," I challenged.

He chuckled. "We're not perfect, my friend. I notice good-looking people like any other walking, talking male. I'm sure Logan does too. But we had plenty of time to sow our oats before each other. When I met him, I knew I was done playing..." he held up his finger to stop my interjection. "Not done looking just done sampling. When you mate – you're telling each other that there will be no other vampire in your bed again. That's what I wanted with Logan. Is that what you want with Sorin?"

"I think so," I said, in a moment of honesty. Not *yes* but *I think so*.

"I'm going to give you some advice and then tell you to roll it around in your head before you take it or leave it," he continued. "Tell Sorin. Don't let it linger or fester. Don't let him find out another way. If you guys are the couple that I think you are, you'll work it out together. Don't try to figure it out alone or make his choice for him. And, Kate?"

"Yes?"

He repeated the reassuring squeeze of my leg. "You need to really know if you want Sorin as your one and only for eternity because I guarantee he'll ask that question."

"How will I know?" I asked.

"I'd do anything for Logan, anything to hold onto what we have. I'd kill for him, die for him. I wouldn't let anything come between us. If you can say that about you and Sorin, then that's your answer."

I laid my head back against the couch. "You make it sound so simple."

"It's not," he conceded. "But I'd be lying if I didn't admit that I'm a little jealous and dying to see who you pick."

"Subject change, please," I begged him.

"Okay," he relented. "What are you going to do with this poor girl? Will you keep digging into her head? What if you find something awful that she'd rather left forgotten?"

I sat up. I didn't like the questions but I'd rather deal with this than my love triangle. "We have to keep digging. She deserves to know what happened to her. Alex deserves to know why he lost her for most of his life."

"I'm staying," he reported.

"Why?" I questioned.

"Because, I can help. The same way I just helped you, I can do that for her or him depending on what you see. I can help Sorin with his work when he gets back."

"I can't ask that of you," I resisted. "It's too much."

He held up his hands in protest. "Listen. You'd be doing me a favor. I'm so bored at home. Logan works all the time now that he's running the company solo. Plus, I *have* to see how this plays out. I'm invested now." He folded his hands together in prayer. "Please."

"Fine," I relented. "Might as well. And honestly, I could use the buffer between me and Alex. You can keep me cooled off if I start to heat up."

"Deal," he said. "I still have my suitcase in the car from the trip. I'm already set."

"Oh yeah," I remembered. "What was the emergency? Everyone good?"

He waved his hand in dismissal. "It's nothing. A dear, old friend. Pipe burst while he was sleeping. By the time the sun went down, his whole basement was flooded. It took us forever to drain the water. We couldn't salvage anything."

"Yikes." A big downside to our schedule is that plumbers, electricians, HVAC guys ... they aren't exactly working when we're up. Any time you call them it's an "on call" rate and you have to explain why they can't do any work during the daylight. So, we have to lean on each other for those kinds of services. "You're a good friend."

"Shucks," he pretended to be embarrassed. "No big deal. Just sorry I missed all the excitement here. A girl with a mystery and your sexy problems are way more enticing than scooping toilet water."

30

"Kate?" Alex called from the foyer.

I stood and excused myself from Jeremy, meeting Alex at the bottom of the stairs. "Hey," I said.

"Can we talk?" he asked, looking at the way I came from. "In private."

I thought about asking Jeremy to chaperone but that was ridiculous. This was Alex and we weren't twelve. We'd spent way more hours alone and not kissing than we had locking lips. Plus, I didn't think after strolling down memory lane with his sister, he was in the mood for seduction. I was safe.

"Sure," I motioned for the kitchen, knowing that a bedroom wasn't a wise choice and that Sorin didn't want us in the office when he wasn't here. "What's up?" I said when we were seated at the island.

"My parents are dead." He said it like he was telling me the weather outside. "They moved to Florida after I graduated med school and died a few years ago. Dad from a stroke and mom a few months after from heart failure. I hadn't seen them in years." I stayed quiet and let him go at his own pace. "They were not perfect parents but they were all I had after Sheena disappeared."

He cleared his throat. "Anyways, they didn't tell me much. They didn't talk about her. I didn't know about her getting a GED. When she went missing, they told me she'd skipped school. I assumed it was high school. They never told me she'd dropped. So, I don't know where she was going to school."

So that was it. He was trying to give me information, working the clues we had to figure out what the memories were, where she'd been.

"They had a storage unit they didn't pay on. After they died, I refused to pay the bill. Told the storage place to auction it off. I didn't collect what was in their house either. Told the condo place to sell what they could and trash the rest. If they had anything we could've used, it's long gone."

Tonight, his eyes were the same bright blue that I'd seen in his sister's face, the blue I'd first met in the hospital five years ago. He was locked in on me, like he was willing me to hear each syllable and do something with the information. Or, punish him for not knowing we'd need his parent's junk someday. He stared, waiting for me to chastise him.

"We don't need your parents," I said, instead. The relief exploded from him and down my arms. "We have you, Alex."

The relief pulled back as quickly as it had it had come. He didn't believe me. I gripped his shoulder. "You know more than you realize. Where were you living when your sister left?"

"Near Bedford."

"Okay," I said, rubbing his upper arm. "So, we start there. Look at community colleges in the area that offered GED classes from 86 to 89, right?"

He shook his head. "Yes. And, look for a Bobby."

Even I knew that we were looking for a needle in a stack of needles but I wasn't telling him that. "Right," I assured him. "We find him. Even if he's human, he'd still be alive."

"He would," Alex agreed.

"I'll send all this to Rhys," I told him. "He'll be able to do the most with what we have."

"Right," he said. I stood and he grabbed the hand holding his arm. "Kate, my parents." I sat down again. "They were strict and abusive. Not my mom so much, she'd just stand by. But, him, he was abusive." Shame came off of him like heat - shame and anger. He was humiliated to tell me this.

"No judgement," I said to him.

"The memory," he cleared his throat. "My birthday party. She told me after you left, that she'd always hoped I'd grow up strong enough to give my father a taste of his own medicine." His gaze fell. "I never did. When I was little, I used to watch him hurt my mom, hurt my sister and I'd wished to be bigger, to have muscles. One day, I did. But then, he wasn't a monster anymore. He was just an old man." When he brought his gaze up again, he'd gathered himself, had his doctor face on. "I went to school and never looked back. They left and I let them wither."

I couldn't stand the pain in those blue irises. "My mom was abusive." I'd said it before I realized it was coming. "She'd hit us sometimes but it was the words that really hurt. When I went to college, I left my little brother and sister unprotected. I don't know how bad it got but they still don't speak to me and she's dead. I didn't go to her funeral just came to work like it was any other Thursday."

I didn't know if that was the right thing to do, tell him a story of my own. It could seem like I was making it all about me or it could feel ingenuine, like I was saying *hey, all parents suck, get over it*. I just wanted him to know that I didn't think less of him because he didn't knock out his pops or rush to their sides when they were sick.

I winked. "Some people haven't earned our tears when they go."

It must've been what he needed to hear because he smiled. "Don't let our patients hear that," he quipped.

"It'll be our little secret, Kitchner." As soon as it was out, I wish I hadn't said it. It brought everything rushing back: the kiss, the taste of his blood, the heat and his words of desire.

"With that," I said, standing and backing up. "I'll go call Rhys and tell him what we need. He can probably get you a workable list in 24 hours."

Then, I ran like the coward I am.

31

I found my phone in the solarium with the intention to call Rhys but saw a missed call from Sorin. I returned that, desperate to hear his voice. "My love," he answered and the syllables sent my blood rushing.

"I missed your call. Everything good?"

"Yes," he answered. "It was rocky in the beginning but things are progressing. In fact," he paused and I sensed I wouldn't like this. "I must stay here for the day."

For the second time that night I felt like I couldn't breathe. "Why?"

"I give you my word that I am safe. We are making great strides and walking away now may hurt our cause. Diana has a very nice room in the basement that she made up for Edwin and me. She has offered it to us so we may continue our work." He paused for my response but I was silent. "I sense your worry, Katherine."

"When you're sleeping," I started. "You're vulnerable."

"I am old. I can wake in the day if I sense a threat." His confidence allayed by fear of him being killed by a rogue wolf but it did nothing for other worry. I wanted to tell him about Alex but I couldn't do it over the phone. I wanted to do it face to face and I didn't want him distracted by this when he was surrounded by lycanthropes. I'd have to wait another day to get this off my chest.

"Katherine," he broke through my thoughts and pulled me back to the conversation. "Should I return? I have time before sunrise if I leave now. Nothing is more important to me than you."

"No," I assured him. "We've worked too hard to get to this point. Stay with Diana but please be careful."

"I will. And, what of the young girl? What did you learn this evening?" He was trying to distract me from my concern.

"Oh," I responded. "Nothing important. I can fill you in when you're back. I'm going to have Rhys follow up on some things. It's probably a dead end but it's worth a shot." I tried to keep the pessimism out of my voice. "And, Jeremy is staying tonight. He'll be here when we try again tomorrow night, in case she gets upset."

"Good," he sounded relieved and I wondered why. "I will sleep better knowing he is there." That seemed a little weird. Was Sorin worried about Alex and I in the manor without him? Did he know something?

I went with, "Agreed" and avoided questioning him about the statement. "Sorin," I said. "I love you."

"I love you too, *regina mea*. I will be holding you the next morning; I give my word." Then the line went dead and my heart shattered.

I wanted him here. I wanted the moment in the woods with Alex to never have happened and to be 100% sure about forever with Sorin. I wanted him holding me and telling me everything was okay. But he wasn't here and the moment in the woods *had* happened. For all of my magic and abilities, I couldn't turn back time.

Before I could completely fall apart, I called Rhys. He didn't answer so I left everything we needed on a voicemail. I knew he'd hear it before bed and get to work as soon as he could. I really did believe that if anyone could find Bobby, it was Rhys. At the end of the message, I hesitated. I wanted to tell him everything or beg him to come over. But he'd only worry. So, I ended the recording with the usual "love ya."

I wanted to go out into the yard but I knew the sun was close and didn't know where everyone was. I didn't want to run into Alex. I figured it was time to lock myself in Sorin's room until the next night. When I found Jeremy in the foyer with a small suitcase, I realized I hadn't exactly told him where to bunk down. "Follow me," I said to his lost puppy dog face as I started upstairs.

With the master bedroom at the end of the hall, Sheena in the birch room and Alex in the room next to that, the left side of the hall was booked. So, I led him into the guest room on the right side, the one that shared a wall with the office. I'd only seen it once, when I first explored the manor. It was rarely used and we hadn't had this many guests since I'd met Sorin. Listening to T tell stories, I knew there as a time when the house was full of over-day partiers. But, Sorin had less and less of those large get-togethers and vampires from faraway territories always wanted to stay in a hotel now. I realized how nice it was to have a house full of friends.

Not to mention how relieved I was to have Jeremy in the room across from Alex when Sorin wasn't here. It's not like I expected Alex to sneak into my room while I was sleeping or anything. He'd never do something like that. I just was glad to have Jeremy nearby – exactly the reason why – I didn't know.

This room was much more toned down that the others. It was so different from Sorin's Japanese themed room and the birch tree wallpaper in Sheena's current room. The crème walls were decorated with several framed paintings of castles. I didn't know where each castle was from but they all appeared to be centuries old. The comforter across the queen-sized bed matched the gold and burgundy of the pillow cases. All the furniture was a rich walnut and likely thousands of pounds.

"Perfect," Jeremy said, checking his watch. "Sorin's cutting it close."

I sighed. "He's not coming home tonight."

"Oh," he nodded his head, trying to look unconcerned. "Where do you sleep?"

"Master room, end of the hall." Even to me, I sounded distracted.

"And, Alex?" One thing you learned about Jeremy quickly was his directness.

"Room across from yours," I answered with an arch of an eyebrow.

"And, if I hear shuffling between rooms?"

"You won't," I said confidently. "Trust me."

His hands flew up in defense. "Just asking, not judging. My loyalty is to you, toots."

I rose to my toes and kissed his check, then looked him dead in the eyes. "I assure you it won't come to that."

32

I spent thirty minutes, legs tucked under me, on the couch in Sorin's room – no, *our* room. Because it was our room. We'd spent almost every night together since the girls went full-time at Tom's and all of them were in this room, in the huge bed across from me, in each other's arms. Staring at that empty bed, my chest ached. It was hard to believe that for close to a decade I'd slept without a man next to me.

Sure, I'd had nights with the knees and elbows of my children in my sides, face and back. But for so many nights, I'd had an empty space at my side and never really cared. I'd believed I was fine and that my days of lovemaking, whispering in the dark and falling asleep with someone were over. It hadn't been a big dramatic thing. I'd just accepted my fate.

Now, the idea of sleeping alone was unfathomable.

I could still recall the night after I'd turned, climbing into bed with Rhys and finding comfort in the presence of person beside me. I'd spent a couple nights with him, adjusting to my new existence and learning about safe love – a love that wanted nothing in return.

Then, I'd spent the first night with Sorin – after the barn. I'd fallen asleep in his arms with the feel of him still inside of me. I'd risen in the same embrace and been ruined for the rest of time. I'd learned about a passionate love - a love that made time around you stop.

Six months later, I had this amazing life surrounded by all kids of love: the love of friends, the love of family and the love of a mate. It was a life I could only have dreamed of before turning and belonging to the night.

And, if I was being honest with myself, I truly believed it wouldn't last. I believed that it would all be gone soon and was always half-waiting for it to happen.

As I stared at that lonely bed, I worried that after telling Sorin everything, I'd never be in that bed again.

I wanted Sorin to be here. I wanted Rhys to be here.

But neither were. And, I couldn't be in that bed alone. It was too much.

Making a decision, I stood and left the room to find comfort.

33

When I opened the door to the room, Jeremy was in bed reading a book. He didn't even look at me, just smiled and lifted up the cover next to him. Shutting the door, I jumped in and pulled it over me. "How did you know?"

"What can I say?" he responded. "I'm just smart."

"I can't be alone," I said.

"I know."

"Tell me a story," I asked, unable to sit in silence with my thoughts. "Tell me about meeting Logan."

He shut his book, laying on the nightstand. "I had only been a vampire a couple of decades. My maker taught me well but had moved on so I was a ship without a course, I guess. I'd had to leave the university and didn't know what to do next. As a human, I'd been forever searching for the right thing, the thing that got me excited. I moved from religion to religion. I hadn't really found myself, figured out who I was or what I wanted. I tried all these different lifestyles and cultures but felt – I don't know – not wholly me. I was no different as a vampire. You should have seen me during the hippie movement. I cringe to remember the bell bottoms. However, that was a great time for music."

I tried to picture Jeremy as a hippie but struggled. Since being turned, I was still getting accustomed to the fact that my friends had been around for so long. They'd talk about full decades as memories and casually mention things that I'd learned about in history classes. While I logically knew that I could live for hundreds of years, it still took me by surprise when the vampires around me said things like "Back then you had to write by candlelight."

"When Logan came into my life," Jeremy continued. "I was seriously spinning out of control. Teaching was behind me. I was thinking about leaving the country actually, starting over somewhere else. I had plenty of money but very few things tying me to the states. You have to remember there was no internet then and book stores weren't open in the evenings so research was more complicated. You had to rely on the knowledge or book collection of a fellow vampire. Once I decided I wanted to travel, I had to decide where and how to get there safely. One evening, I drove to a nearby town with a library that stayed open late. Other than the librarian, there was one other person in that library. He was looking at books about European fashion."

"Logan," I said.

"Logan" he repeated. "I knew he was like me as soon as I saw him. What I hadn't known is that he would change my life, become the anchor I needed."

"Was it love at first sight?" I asked.

"No," he answered. "At first, we were just excited to talk to another vampire. That night, we talked until the librarian kicked us out. Then, made plans to meet the next night. And, then the next and the next. Before you knew it, I was staying over at his house so we could have more time together. You'd have to ask Logan his side of things but after that first night, I couldn't wait to see him again. After the second night, I couldn't have pictured an existence without him in it."

"I love that part," I said. "The part where you're getting to know each other, telling stories and learning all the little things. It's my favorite thing in a new relationship. Now, as a vampire, there's so much to learn, you know? When humans meet, they only need to learn like a couple decades of backstory but now – Sorin has 500 years of experiences for me to hear about. He says something small and I think 'wow, there is a whole story there'. He's so interesting and ..." I stopped, not wanting to say what almost slipped out.

"What?" Jeremy asked.

"What if he realizes in a year or two how ordinary I am?" I rolled away from my friend, not wanting him to see my face.

I don't know what I expected him to say, maybe something like *don't be ridiculous* or *you're interesting, Kate.* What he said was "Maybe that's why you're drawn to Alex."

I rolled back to face him. "What do you mean?"

"I mean," he looked down at me. "You've got some confidence issues, sister. If you're feeling not good enough or too boring or whatever it is, as it gets closer to your time to mate, you're getting scared. Then, here comes a nice, normal, safe human. You feel like you're on an even level with him so you're drawn to him."

It was something to think about. Maybe he was right and that's all it was. Maybe my feelings for Alex were more about me and less about the actual man. It was definitely something to meditate on.

"When did you know Logan was the one that you wanted to give yourself completely to?" I asked, hoping to hear some kind of secret in the answer.

Jeremy was quiet for a minute and I let him come up with the right words. "I was so lost, Kate. And, after him – with him – I felt found. He made me want to be better, you know? I had done some pretty awful things before him. He totally got me and accepted me exactly how I was."

"I haven't told Sorin all the bad stuff, yet." I sighed. "That's part of my worry. What if he hears it all and it changes the way he feels about me? How did you tell Logan? Did you tell him before you were mated?"

Looking up at him, he turned from me and looked ahead. Something danced over his eyes but it was gone too quickly to understand. "None of us are perfect, Kate. We've all done bad things. The important thing is to grow from them."

"Yeah," I said. "I guess you're right. I know Sorin has some bad stuff in his past. He doesn't talk about it but I can tell. It's just that, I can't think of anything he could say to me that would make me stop loving him."

Jeremy returned his eyes back to mine. "See. So why do you think it would work any differently for him? I've seen him with you. He isn't going to look at you any differently when you tell him everything. All that will happen is those worries you have will be gone."

"I hope you're right," I said.

34

When I rose, Jeremy was still resting beside me. I slipped out of bed and went to retrieve an outfit from the birch room. I made a mental note to move some clothes to Sorin's room so I could stop bothering Sheena. When I opened the door, I almost tripped over Alex. He'd brought in a pillow and blanket, making a resting place on the floor by her bed. It was so similar to the story of her sleeping on Alex's floor to protect him from nightmares. Only this time, he was protecting her. I'm sure he knew that she was strong enough to throw a car but he still had the instinct to be by her side in case of danger.

I thought of my two daughters and how close they were. Then, flashed back to them tied up and wrapped around each other when Evelyn had them kidnapped. They'd been scared, in danger and their instinct had been to protect each other. I felt a tear in my eye as I imagined what it would do to one of them to lose the other. Then, realized that's what Alex had lived through these last 30 years.

I backed out of the room, deciding to just wear the same outfit. I didn't want to risk waking either of them.

After a hot shower, I looked for Tamela. It felt like I hadn't really talked to her in days and I wanted to connect before everyone was awake. I wished we could go back to when we spent our nights talking instead of digging through a traumatized girl's head. I followed her scent. She was sitting outside, on the front steps, staring into the new night.

"Good evening," I said.

"Are you well?" she asked.

"I am," I answered. "You?"

"Oh," she hesitated. "I've been better and I've been worse. I don't like that he's away without me."

"Same," I agreed. "He's very stubborn, that one."

She scoffed. "You have no idea. So, wanna tell me why you're really out here?"

I sat next to her and rested my head on her shoulder. "I wish we could go back a week. It was so much simpler then."

"True," she let out a breath. "But we'd just be postponing now. It was going to happen no matter what. What's meant to happen always will."

I thought about it. "Do you believe that? I mean, really?"

"I do," she didn't hesitate. "Think about it. You're turned by Rhys and brought to Sorin. Sorin and you bond, are mating. You know Alex, who had a sister missing. The sister is brought to your mate." She paused for effect. "Destiny."

I thought about it. That would mean that everything that'd happened from the moment Will saw me was destiny, that I was a pawn in some fated game. Could it all be that simple? Could it be that everything was meant to happen? It was too much on top of everything already filling my head. I had to change the subject and distract myself.

"He's back tonight." I wanted to focus on good things. "And, we'll work with Sheena some more tonight. Rhys is looking into what we know so far but it might be pointless. We might see something tonight to solve the mystery."

"That's all you," she said and patted my thigh. "More destiny. You have the abilities to help her."

The combined smells hit my nose as the door opened behind me. Alex and Sheena came out to join us. "It's so pretty here," Sheena said and the youth of her voice still took me off guard. She was older than me but she still sounded like a child.

"It is," Tamela said while standing. "Would you like to walk before we do any work tonight."

"Yes," the girl said excitedly.

Alex replaced T on the steps as we watched the two females walk into the garden. Without thinking, I turned to look at him. He was just Alex, my friend. The stubble on his jaw had grown thicker over the day. I realized he must have to shave every day to keep it in check. He looked like he'd aged years in the last 24 hours. The awkwardness I was expecting between us wasn't there. Instead, I felt protective and worried.

"Talk to me," I said.

"I slept next to her last night. I was so afraid that she'd disappear when I closed my eyes." He faced me. "I want so badly to know where she was but I'm so scared, too. I laid there thinking of all the things that the world can do to a teenaged girl. We've seen it in the hospital, Kate – the things people do to each other."

"I know," I said. There was no point in pretending awful things didn't go down on a daily basis. We'd both been on the frontlines for it. "I've already thought of it, too."

He kept going. "I thought of your daughters, too. When they were taken, what could've happened." He looked ahead again, out into nothing. "Why does the world have to be like this?"

"I don't know," I answered.

"Promise me something, Kate."

I didn't know what he was going to ask and I was afraid of the request. The truth is I would have given him anything. I hoped he wasn't asking for something too big.

He faced me again. "Don't hide anything from me. Whatever you see in her mind. You can't keep it to yourself, okay?"

I felt myself trembling; without thinking I laid my hand against his cheek. "Are you sure, Alex? We can just stop. We won't know where she was but she'll be happy. You'll be happy. She'll walk in the garden and you guys can get to know each other again."

He shook his head. "No," he didn't think twice. "We can't risk that it'll come out someday when she doesn't have all this support. It could be 100 years from now when I'm gone and you're..." he stopped, changing lanes. "It's better to know now so we can start to heal."

I nodded. "Okay, then. I promise to tell you whatever I see."

By the end of the night, we would regret that promise.

35

Sheena had put a fresh flower behind everyone's ears by the time we were gathered on our blankets in the yard for the next session. Jeremy and Tamela had white flowers, I had red and Alex's matched the pink bloom of his sister's. Her head was in my lap, her vision full of the night sky above us. My friends were around us, quietly waiting for what may come. Rhys would be by at some point but from the phone call, I didn't expect good news. Sorin was due by 4am and was eager to tell me about his progress with the lycans and hear any new information.

The pressure was on.

I tried to relax my shoulders and not feel everyone's eyes on me. Focusing on the face below mine, I thought back to the thrill of my first teen love. I remembered the complete infatuation and all-encompassing kind of love that comes before the world has ruined your heart. "Sheena," I whispered and her eyes met mine.

"When you were at the party with Bobby, the night you made love..." I watched her face flush. "You were human. Do you remember what it felt like? To be human."

She nodded. "A little."

"Can you remember after that? When you became a vampire? Like you are now? In the beginning?" I slid into her eyes, back into the darkness of lost memories. It was different this time, less like a lack of anything and more like actual darkness. Taking steps around the dark, I felt something under my bare feet, something soft and wet. The urge to sit became overwhelming, it pulled me to the ground. Dropping to my knees, then my butt, I felt the same damp earth below me. The smell was old – moldy and awful. Sounds joined the sensation of touch. Scurrying of some kind of rodent was behind me but I didn't turn, I was too scared. The wind howled, slamming against the sides of the room I was in. I closed my eyes, then opened them again to see something forming off to my right – rocks. No, not rocks, stones – a stone wall. At first it was hard to make out in the lack of light but eventually my sight adjusted and it was clearer. A stone wall to my left, my right, in front of me and at my back. Pain flared in my back when it hit the stones behind it. As soon as I acknowledged the pain in my back, the rest of the pain came to life. There was pain in my legs, my arms.

The beating, Sheena thought. *He beat me because I didn't listen. He told me the rules but I didn't listen and now I'm punished. Do what he says, Sheena. For once, obey the rules and be good. Then, he'll let you out.*

She was locked in the room. She'd already tried the door. Even with her new strength, she couldn't get through the door. And, she couldn't fight him. He was too strong, so much stronger than her. She needed to give him whatever he wanted, pretend to like it, be nice. Then, he'd let her out.

She brought her arms up in front of her face. She was sure her back looked the same. The bruises were already starting to fade but the cuts would take longer. They were deep this time. He'd wanted her to bleed so she'd be depleted, thirsty and weak. Dropping her arms, she laid her head gingerly back against the wall. She'd spent her whole life fighting and disobeying and this is where it'd landed her.

He won't stop until I give in. Even she knew when to give in and give up.

The small bowl next to her was empty. She'd drunk the blood too fast, even licked the bowl and had no idea when he'd be back with more. She was so hungry.

"Come back," she screamed into the void and heard it lost in the stone. She didn't want to see him again but she was so hungry. The only answer was the wind outside. For all she knew, he'd left. Without windows, she didn't know if it was day or night. She could only assume that her falling asleep meant the sun was up but given how weak she was, that might not be true either.

"I never should have taken the car," she said to the rats that moved about their business. "Never should have run away." Then one last thought escaped her mouth, barely above a whisper. "I wish I'd never met him."

She lifted her leg for the 20th time that night, examining the chain. It was way too strong for her to break when he'd first thrown her in here, the first time he'd punished her. And then, she'd been at full power. So now, after who knew how many days in the basement, she'd never be able to break it. She thought about cutting her foot off but there was nothing in here to do it with. Plus, he'd catch her before she was out of the house and she wasn't going to make it far with one foot.

Rolling up into a ball, she laid onto her side on the ground. She needed to hold onto whatever strength and consciousness she had. She needed to prepare herself in case this was one of those nights he came more than once.

When he does, I will be nice. I will follow the rules. This is my life now. The old Sheena is gone.

But all resolve was melted away when she heard him coming down the stairs. With each thump on the boards, she shook. When he was this loud, it was to scare her. That meant he wasn't coming with more blood or to apologize. The heaviness of his descent told her he was still mad and wasn't done making his point. Even the rats ran, abandoning her to the onslaught of his temper.

She was alone when the door opened.

As she screamed in her head, we both screamed out loud. I was thrown from her mind with such force that I fell back onto the blanket. All three vampires were scrambling for our sides, not sure what the issue was but knowing they had to help us.

I heard Sheena wailing but it sounded far from me. Righting myself, I saw Jeremy chasing after the girl as she ran for the trees. Alex was behind them but slower than the vampires. Tamela wrapped her arms around me. "What did you see?"

Shaking, I let her hold me while I tried to settle myself and let go of the memory. I had to remind myself it wasn't real; it wasn't my memory but hers. As the present moment began to overcome the past, I started to breathe again.

I looked up to see Sheena being walked back with a man on each side of her. Blood streaked her face but she wasn't crying. Both men looked worried but the girl between them was the picture of calm. Jeremy met my gaze and nodded. I thanked the universe for his power as I reached out for Sheena.

She knelt onto the grass in front of me. "Are you okay?" I asked.

"Yeah," she answered.

"Who was it, Sheena? Who did that to you?" I said cautiously as to not upset her again. Alex's head whipped away from his sister to face me. His eyes hot with questions. I held up my hand to stop him from saying anything.

"I don't know," she said. "It ended before I could see."

"And," I was careful with the next question. "You have no idea about who it could have been or where that was?"

"No," she responded, sounding like she was afraid I'd be upset with her answer. "I'm sorry."

"It's okay," I said, standing before she could see how much that little mind-meld had rocked me.

"Stay with her," I said to Tamela and Jeremy. "In case more comes back or she freaks again. Alex?" I reached out my hand and he took it. "We need to talk."

Jeremy stepped towards me. "I should be with you. I don't think you're okay. I can help."

"No," I shook my head. "She needs you more. I won't be far. I'll call out if I can't handle it." He reticently returned to the women. Alex and I walked towards the manor. I couldn't say anything for a few minutes. I needed to get myself together before I changed his life forever.

When we were back in our spots on the front steps, sitting side by side, I started to keep my promise. "She was held by someone." It was better to do it quickly and directly. "In a basement, chained by the ankle. He starved her to make her reliant on him. Beat her and bled her when she disobeyed."

I assessed him for a second, watching his expression closely. "She was in the dark, alone. She blamed herself for running away, for stealing his car to see you, for not following his rules."

I wanted to hold the last one back but I'd promised Alex. It was better to hear it than find out later and know I'd kept it from him.

"He forced himself on her over and over until she stopped resisting."

36

He roared into the night sending birds from the trees. Clenching his fists, he stood and walked into the driveway then dropped to his knees and punched the gravel. I raced after him, laying my body over his back. I trapped his arms with mine, stopping him from assaulting the ground while smelling the blood that left his wounded knuckles. He fought against my embrace but I was too strong. He collapsed, sobbing and turned to burying himself in my chest. I held onto him like I could protect him from the pain but nothing within my power could stop this kind of injury. I thought about calling for Jeremy but I knew Alex needed to experience this. I knew that healing would only come after the pain.

Rocking him, I listened to him release the years of not knowing and the agony of the truth. He cried for the little boy that'd been left with abusive parents, for the teen girl that'd never been able to grow up and the terrified victim in the basement. He raged over the inability to have saved her. He let it out in wordless screams and gutteral moans until whimpering was all he was capable of.

And, all that time, I held onto him because it was all I could do for him.

He shivered with spent adrenaline and emotional shock. I didn't know when he'd eaten last and had forgotten in all of this that he was human. In that moment, he felt too fragile, too easy to lose. I whispered in his ear, "Please let me take you inside and get you something. Please, Alex."

He was either too weak to fight or didn't have enough presence of mind to argue because he stood. Wavering and silent, he let me lead him inside and into the living room. Once on the couch, I begged him to stay there until I returned.

When I was in the kitchen, I grabbed the edge of the sink to stop myself from falling to the floor. I'd just destroyed Alex and I was seriously second-guessing the decision to tell him everything. In the years that I'd known him, worked with him, he'd always seemed so stoic and impenetrable. Then, Will had tied him up in the barn with a fatal head wound. I could never unsee him, dying and hypothermic on that dirty floor. I'd believed he'd never been more human than that moment – until now. I think he'd take kidnapping and assault over what I'd just put him through.

Between him, my kids and Monica, I was starting to see how dangerous it was to be mortal and in my life.

I shook my head to stop the self-pity party. It was about Alex, not me. I rallied my determination and shuffled around the room in search of people food. Thankfully, Sorin was always prepared for anything. Ten minutes later, I was delivering a hot bowl of chicken noodle soup, a peanut butter-jelly sandwich and Coke to the man I'd left on the couch. Even I knew it was a dinner for a child but that food was a psychical expression of my desperate need to comfort.

He hadn't moved at all.

Laying the tray on the coffee table, I sat next to him. Using his chin to turn him to me, I smiled as warmly as I could but used my stern, nurse voice. "You had your time. Now, you will be strong for her, to get her through this. You're her big brother now."

It worked. He snapped out of his daze and looked at the meal. A minute later, he began to slowly eat and the pace picked up after the first few bites. I let out a sigh of relief. One thing I knew about psychological shock was that you couldn't let them shut down. You had to keep them moving and focused on the next task.

Bring her in, I sent to Tamela when he dropped the spoon into the empty bowl and finished the soda. The last bite of sandwich was in his mouth when they came into the manor and into the living room. He'd calmed down as he'd eaten and the Alex I knew, the doctor, was back. He greeted her warmly. "Hey, Sheena."

"Hi, Alex," she beamed and bounced into the room. "I heard you crying. Tamela said to give you time. Are you okay?"

"I am," his smile wavered and his voice shook but then he regained his composure. "I'm sad because someone hurt you."

"I know," she said. "But it was then not now."

"You're right," he responded. Clearing his throat, his gaze fell to the floor. "Do you think it was Bobby or one of the other guys from the party?"

"I really don't know, Alex." She was so calm. I couldn't help but worry about what would happen when Jeremy stopped using his power. "I'm sorry."

Alex met her eyes again. "Don't be sorry. It's not your fault."

"Do you want to look in my head again, Kate?" She looked so hopeful asking the question but just the thought of it made me want to vomit.

"Not tonight," I answered and felt the relief come off of everyone else in the room but her. She felt disappointed. I reached my empathy out to her, fighting through the fake calm that Jeremy was washing over her, to reach the real emotion underneath. She was ashamed for upsetting everyone and wanted me to find the one magic clue to who took her so Alex could be happy. She believed it was her fault that she'd been locked up, that if she'd been better, she never would have ended up there. But, under it all, she was scared to learn anymore.

I pulled back. I didn't want to feel anymore tonight. Waving Jeremy to the foyer, I met him at the bottom of the stairs and led him away from the excellent hearing of the others. "You have to let her process," I whispered in case we weren't far enough away. Tamela came in, joining us in back of the solarium.

I told them what I'd seen in her mind.

They were both silent when I'd finished. I wasn't sure what they were thinking or feeling and I was done using my empathy that night. I almost never liked experiencing the emotions of others. But you didn't need magic to know they were both upset. Jeremy looked sick and Tamela looked like she wanted to hurt someone.

Jeremy broke the silence. "You're right," he said. "She has to process."

Tamela stayed silent and remained angry at whoever had put that shackle on a teenager's ankle. God help that man if she ever found out who it was.

"T," I held her hand. "She's going to need you. You can talk to her in a way none of us can."

I saw the confusion in Jeremy's eyes, not seeing the need to explain. If Tamela didn't want anyone else to know, that was her business. A slight nod of her head was all I needed. Without a word, we turned and walked back to the living room with Jeremy at our backs.

"Alex," I said as we entered. "I need you to trust me, okay?" Our eyes met and he didn't need to say anything. He trusted me. "Please, let T sit there."

Jeremy sat in one of the chairs and Alex took the other, leaving the couch for the women. I stayed in the doorway, muscles clenched, ready to go to whomever needed me. When Tamela was settled next to Sheena, she took the girl's hands in hers and waited for her gaze. When Sheena was ready, I felt Jeremy's power pull back as I watched the horror of her past hit her face.

"It's not the beatings that hurt the most," Tamela spoke before Sheena's shock could paralyze her. "It's the promise that each one is the last, only for him to leave you in the basement again. I could hear movement above me and knew that other people were free, walking and eating whenever they wanted to. I would pray for them to realize I was down there and save me. I would force myself to be nice to him, let him have me, tell him that I liked it – anything to make him set me free. But, he wouldn't. When he'd walk up those stairs, I die inside. I asked God to kill me so many times. Only he didn't listen or he didn't care."

As she spoke, Sheena's breathing was fast and I prepared myself for her to pass out. Tamela gripped her hands, keeping her locked into her, not letting her run, forcing her to listen and hear. "Hours were days and days were weeks and I didn't know if I was six months older or ten years. Every time he came for me, I thought it would hurt less, that I would be immune to the pain but he made sure it was painful. It didn't matter if I fought or gave in, he never would have stopped, Sheena. Do you know why?"

Tamela waited for the girl to respond. Sheena's breathing was the only movement for a minute but then she shook her head and T continued. "Because he was bad. I couldn't have done anything to stop the abuse because he just wanted to hurt someone. He wanted to dominate, to have power over something."

Sheena's breathing was slowing and she wasn't using her whole body to suck in and release air anymore. She was calming down.

"He was bad," Tamela repeated. "I didn't do anything to deserve it. If it hadn't been me, it would have been another girl. There were some before me and there would have been more after me if he hadn't been stopped. None of us deserved it."

I scanned the room. Alex was stone-still, his face unreadable. Jeremy was pale and hard to read. Sheena was breathing regularly, her eyes wide and blood tears rolling down her face for the second time that night. Tamela was done talking but didn't let go yet. When Sheena fell into her, she wrapped her arms around her and let her cry.

I was so on edge that I didn't hear Rhys open the door and enter the room. It wasn't until he put his arm around my waist that I knew he was there.

If he'd been an enemy, I'd been in big trouble.

Sheena filled the silence. "I named some of the rats. They we're my friends." She went silent but I think we all knew there was more to say. "The worst thing he'd do to me was be gone so long that I would – would," she gulped "would have to kill one of my friends to drink their blood."

I turned into Rhys, trying to hold back the shaking. He didn't know what was happening but he knew it was bad. I sent thoughts to him, images of what I'd seen. After telling Alex, I couldn't stand the idea of saying it out loud again. When he squeezed me into him, I knew he'd seen and understood. He held me tight and I think it was more for him than me.

37

After a few minutes of nothing, Sheena had changed the subject. She'd asked Alex to tell her another funny story from their childhood. The air in the room changed. Everyone had been relieved for a small break.

Rhys silently pulled me from the room into the kitchen. I found a stool and made it before my legs gave out. Rhys stood in front of me, letting me rest my face against his chest and hold onto him. His hands rubbed up and down my back. "I saw it all," I said into his shirt. "The basement, the bruises and cuts, the chain. I heard the rats. I felt her feelings. Then, I had to tell Alex." My words spilled out in a rush. "Please tell me you have something."

His hands stopped and he tensed. Pulling back, I looked up to see him. A single head shake was all I needed but he elaborated. "There were so many places offering GED classes within a 30-minute drive of Alex's hometown. The names you gave me were really common at that time, too. I need last names or a specific place that she was at but Katie -"

He trailed off so I knew I wouldn't like it. It was better to get it over with. "Say it."

"Even then," he said. "We could be way off. There's a chance that her classes or those kids have nothing to do with vampires. There's also a chance that what you're seeing in her head is her memory but it's not accurate. You know, the way we remember a car being blue and then find out later it was green but we wouldn't have sworn it was blue."

He was right. So far, we had some quick scenes that I'd extracted from a girl who'd been locked away for a long time. Her recollections could have been skewed over time. The faces or names could be different from what she'd really experienced. If the names were right, Rhys wasn't wrong about them being really common names. Without knowing exactly where the classes had been, we could be wasting time. Plus, what were the odds that the place was still open, let alone had records of GED attendees from the late 80s?

"We have to try, Rhys. It's better to keep trying and telling them that we're tracking down leads than to give up. Start searching each place with a GED class at that time. If they have transferred their records to electronic, see if you can find a Sheena Kitchner that was registered. I think they'd rather find out a year from now than quit trying. While you do that, I'll keep looking in her memories. Just, not tonight, okay?"

For a minute, I thought he was going to argue but he agreed. "Of course. I'll spend every night on the computer. But, can't we find another way to bring out her memories? I don't want you doing it anymore. I think Sorin will agree."

"No," I stood, squaring my shoulders. "I'm doing this for her. What good is this power if I don't use it to help people?"

That brought on his pride smile; he was proud of me. "Okay," he relented. "I know better than to fight you."

Laughter rolled out of the living room into the kitchen. We followed the sound and found everyone giggling. Alex was finishing a story. "So, I learned that I couldn't train bees."

"I'll need that story someday," I said to the room as we joined them.

Sheena was beaming at her brother. "I wish I'd seen you grow up, Alex."

The mood in the room dimmed for a second before Alex brought it back. "I'll tell you a story about me every morning before you go to sleep if you'd like. Every morning for the next 40 years."

She nodded happily, then seemed to think of something. "But, won't you get married some day?"

Alex looked at me quickly and my eyes met his. I saw curiosity, pain, frustration, sorrow and hope all fill his gaze then fall away. He turned back to Sheena. "I don't think I will, sissy. So, when you're ready, we'll find a house with a very nice, windowless room for you." She jumped up and down, clapping with glee. "You will have the biggest, softest bed I can find and I'll tell you stories until you tell me to shut up."

"I will never do that," she squealed.

Jeremy chimed in. "Can we all agree that the rest of tonight should be something fun? I hear there's a Nintendo downstairs. I'd love to play."

"Me too," Sheena exclaimed. "Tamela?"

Tamela stood up. "I think that's a great idea. Alex?"

"A Nintendo? I'm in. Kate? Rhys?"

We looked at each other and shrugged. "Sure."

And that's where Sorin found us, crushed into the little room downstairs, sprawled on beanbags, taking turns with Mario and trying desperately to forget the horrors of the world outside.

38

"Well," Sorin said as he entered the room to see his bodyguard's victory dance. She'd beaten a particularly difficult level and was celebrating. "I haven't seen you this excited in quite some time." She took a moment to compose herself then handed the rectangle controller to Rhys. "No," he continued. "Please have fun, Tamela. I was teasing you."

I leapt out of the beanbag and was in his arms before Rhys could begin the next quest. I'd never been so happy to see him. Feeling him was the only way I could believe he was okay and home. A human man would need to catch his balance and take the weight of me so we wouldn't tumble backwards. Whether it was because he was old or because he knew how I would react, Sorin didn't hesitate or need an extra moment to adjust. Once his arms were around me, he lifted me up. Wrapping my legs around him, I buried my face in his neck.

"Hi," he whispered.

"Hi," I said. "Please take me upstairs."

"We are heading upstairs," he said to the room. "I trust you all to lock the manor down for the day and make yourselves at home."

Noises in the room increased after he shut the door. Then, they died away as he carried me up the two floors to our room. I stayed silent, using the time to breathe and decide what to say first. When we were in our room and the door was shut, I let him sit me on the edge of the bed. He removed his necktie, the jacket and his shoes. Then, undid the top few buttons of his shirt. Last, and my favorite part, he removed the band in his hair to let it fall. I expected him to continue to undress, but instead he dropped to his knees on the floor in front me and aligned his eyes with mine. "What is it?"

He brushed my hair back to tuck it behind my ear and I thought about saying nothing. I didn't want him to know the horrible things that'd happened to Sheena or my possible feelings for Alex. Gazing into those eyes though, I knew I'd never hold anything back from him again. The good, the bad, the ugly – he deserved to know all of me.

I started with what I'd seen in the young vampire's head since he'd left. He listened quietly while I painted the pictures and described the pain, the hard floor, the wind, the thoughts and the reaction Alex had when I told him. I ended the story when we'd gone downstairs to play the video game. He stayed silent, moving only to run his hand up and down my thigh. I watched it as I spoke. A few times, it twitched – at the really bad moments – then it would start again. It only stopped when I did.

His voice was low. "When her captor is found, he will be killed." His tone was clear and I believed every word. As scared as I was, I needed to speak before I lost my nerve.

"I need to tell you something else," I stood and walked away to the other side of the room. I couldn't do this if he was rubbing my leg.

"Worse than what you've just said?" he sounded confused and worried.

"Alex kissed me." The rest came out in a rush. "The night he read the note from Monica, he kissed me. It wasn't the first time. Right after I was turned, he also kissed me then. Both times, I kissed him back but then stopped him." When I heard nothing, I forced my muscles to turn and lift my head to find his eyes. I expected fury or grief.

What I saw was curiosity.

"I need more than that," he said, his voice giving me no idea of how he felt. For a second, I thought about using empathy but it was an invasion and I knew it.

"What do you mean?" I asked, taking a few steps towards him. "We kissed. Twice."

He cocked his head to the side in a movement that I'd started to adore. It was like an animal trying to figure out a sound. The arching eyebrow that accompanied it was the most endearing part of the familiar motion. It made my heart hurt. "I heard that part," he said, still calm. "What lead to it and how did you fell about it? How *do* you feel about it?"

"Well, the first time, he'd realized that my blood may be the key to the cure. We were so happy and then we we're kissing. I had the urge to bite him and it made me stop. This time, he'd read the letter. I told him that he was worthy of love and that Monica wasn't the one if she didn't see that. Then, he kissed me. I stopped when he nicked my fang and I tasted his blood."

I'd stopped stepping towards him so he took the next step to keep closing the distance. "And, what did you feel for him?"

I had to think. Feelings are so complex. It's hard to put them into words when you're asking. And, it didn't help that I was so scared of his reaction. I knew this could be the last conversation we had as a couple. The worst thing I could do was lie so I tried to put the feelings into words. "Fondness. A connection. I wanted to comfort him."

He took another step. "And, what do you feel for him now?"

"I'm sad when I think of him leaving. I feel this need to be near him all the time. I want him to be happy and find someone who loves him, someone who deserves him. He's brave and selfless. I want to be around him and see him laugh. I…"

"Do you love him?" He stopped, closer than before. If I reached out my arm, I could just touch him. I didn't drop my gaze but met his fully.

"I do," I said.

"Like you love me?" he asked.

"No," I said without hesitation. "It's different. My love for you is like finding a missing piece, like I wasn't complete but now I am. I think of losing you and I want to die. You're the breath that brought me to life."

"And, with him?"

I didn't think, just let it come out. "He's like the solid ground I stand on."

As soon as it was out, I felt pain in my heart. Did I just say something that would break Sorin? End our love? Send me from him bed, his home and his life? What did it mean for Alex? Did I love him?

Sorin filled the space in front of me. "May I feel you?"

"Yes," I whispered. This time I sensed him use his empathy, felt his power slide into my chest and around.

"Now," he was so close, I felt his breath. "Feel me."

I did. I opened myself to a blast of warmth, certainty and love. He wasn't angry or hurt. He was pleased I had trusted him with my feelings, been honest and raw. He understood the confusion and conflict I was feeling. My eyes grew wide and I searched his face to find a soft smile.

"You are so young, my love. You have never been truly loved because you didn't love yourself for so long. Now, your confidence shines like a lighthouse in a storm and others are attracted to it. You have believed that you are supposed to be a certain way and if you are any other way, then you are bad. I've had centuries to understand the complexity of lust and desire, and to know that you can love in many different ways." He laid his hand on my cheek. "You have only been a vampire for half a year and I have selfishly asked you to be mine forever, before you have experienced any other."

I thought I knew what he was saying and started to panic. "I don't want any others. I want you."

"I know," he said. "I have felt your love for me and I believe that our love is destiny. I was drawn to you the moment I saw you. I knew after our first time together that I never wanted to be with another. I know you want forever with me. I worry, however, that it is because I am all you know."

"Please don't break up with me," I begged.

He slid his hands down my shoulders to grasp each hand, then led me to the couch so we could sit side by side. I felt a little unsteady so I focused on him and what he was saying. My heart was in my stomach and my body was clenched, ready to take a psychological trauma that I'd never recover from.

He held each side of my face with his hands, making sure I was looking into his eyes. "I am not breaking up with you, *regina mea*. I want to be mated to you. We are fated to be as one. But we have time and there is no rush. I have waited too long for you to ever let you go. While I would never wish to share you with another vampire, I do think you need to explore your feelings for Alex."

"I don't understand," I shook my head.

"Katherine, you have faced more than most should face in a lifetime. You've been abandoned by your parents, unloved by your husband and alone for too long. You wait for those around you to disappoint, hurt or leave you. All while you protect everyone but yourself and use all your energy to help others. You've been given eternal life and powers beyond most people's dreams yet your choice is to use those gifts to continue to be of service. It is only natural for Alex to love you, especially now that you have brought his sister home. Perhaps your empathy feels his love for you and you confuse it as your own feelings. Or, perhaps you truly love him and he you." He ran his finger through my hair. "We will exist for a very long time. You must know for sure how you feel for him so that you do not have regrets later or carry bitterness."

"Do you have regrets?" I asked but already knew the answer.

"One," he said. "Like you, I had not been a vampire long. Like Alex, it was a human. But, unlike you, I did not have courage. I walked away, making their choice for them. But I only regret how I hurt them not the loss of them. Everything I have done has brought me to you in this place and time so it was all worth it. However, I do not want you to look back and wonder."

"I want to be with you," I said.

"And, you will be," he answered. "I am not letting you go. We will continue as we have, prepare for our future and remain bonded. But you do not have to hide your feelings for Alex or worry that I will leave you. As long as you want to be with me, I will be with you."

I was unable to move, too scared that this was a dream and movement would shatter the tenuous thread I was resting on. Sorin was reading me and shook his head. "You worry I will find you undesirable now that Alex has kissed you, that I see you as ruined. I could never, Katherine. I see you as a being full of passion and capable of so much love."

Instead of continuing to convince me with words, he showed me. Pulling me into his lap, he forced me to spread my knees and straddle him as he used his hands on my waist to bring me down to him. Heat rolled off his chest and I was overcome by his need. Releasing my disbelief, I opened myself to his emotion and let it convince me that he meant what he said. The reality of it hit me; I knew he was not leaving me but instead allowing me to be 100% myself. That knowledge emboldened me. I grasped the shirt and pulled it open. Buttons flew out into the expanse of the room. Swiftly, he had the shirt off and repeated my actions by ripping open my dress which fluttered in two pieces onto the floor. He crushed his mouth onto mine, showing me with his kiss that he did not want me any less. The hardness of him against my naked flesh showed me that nothing would change between us. We had rushed in the woods last time, hungry for each other. Tonight, I wanted it to last.

I broke from the kiss and slid backwards to find my footing on the floor, then reached for him. He stood, taking my hand and allowing me to lead him to the bed. Not letting my eyes leave his, I undid the belt first, then the buttons to let his pants fall to the floor. My hand found the hard length and caressed it gently. I loved the feel of the soft satin skin stretched over such rigidness. Dropping to my knees, I ran that same gentle stroke down to the base and wrapped my hand around that thick flesh. He sucked in a breath as I reversed the path my fingers had just traced with my tongue. Licking slowly from my encircling hand up to the tip of him, I heard his breath quicken. My fangs had descended, triggered by the strong need. He was right, desire for blood and sex can sometimes be confused and confusing. But that night, I knew exactly what I desired. Thankfully, I had learned how to do a lot of things with my fangs so he either didn't care or didn't feel them when my mouth wrapped around him. He groaned, fighting the urge to drive himself into my mouth. He let me be in control but I could sense him battling to remain still. It'd been a while since I'd done this, run my lips over him. We so often were overwhelmed with the need to be joined that we'd not really worshipped each other in a few months. So, I took my time and enjoyed the taste of him, not allowing myself to rush.

After several minutes of running my lips and tongue over that tender flesh, I stood and crawled onto the bed. Rolling to my back, I laid down to face him, making myself an offering. He'd been so patient as I played; it only seemed fair to give him the same. He accepted the invitation, running his tongue up the inside of my thigh and to the core that throbbed for him. The time I'd taken to tease and taste him had brought me to the edge. Picking up on my desire to go slow, he continued the reverent pace with deliberate gliding licks. Groans escaped my mouth and I fought the urge to beg. As the release sent convulsions through my body, I let the scream rip from my lips. Before the waves of pleasure could subside, his hands gripped my thighs and flipped me onto my stomach. A hand around my waist urged me onto hands and knees as he entered the slickness of my still shaking body.

The feel of him started that clenching need again. As desperate as my craving was for another release, I had offered him control and he'd taken it. I allowed his slow, measured rhythm. I allowed him to show me the way he needed me in that moment. Gripping my hips, he edged in, pausing to enjoy the sensation of being sheathed and then withdrew just as steadily. Each time, I ached for the feel of him again. As the pace increased, I started to move with him. My movement pushed his control to its breaking point and one hand left my hips to take a handful of my hair. As he sped up, I arched back to find the angle that caressed deep inside of me. My breath caught when he found it and he slowed his movements again. "Please," I pleaded and we both lost control. He drove in and out with the need of a man at his most frantic until we both cried out from climax.

When our senses returned to us, we were on our sides with him hot against my back and his arm around my waist. I turned to face him. "I love you," I whispered.

"I love you," he silently mouthed.

We feel asleep as two people with no secrets between us.

39

The buzzing of the phone pulled me out of whatever state we're in when we aren't up and moving around. Groggily, I answered with no attempts to hide my annoyance. "What?"

"I'm so sorry, Kate." It was Tiffany O, chipper night nurse. "Did I wake you?"

"Yep, what's up?"

"Listen, I wouldn't call you if I wasn't desperate. I need to leave tonight at 9 but I can't unless I have a replacement. Tiff can come in at 4am but not before. Can you pleeeeeaaaassseee work 9p-4a for me? I asked everyone else and didn't want to bother you but I looked out for you once and now I'm asking you to look out for me" She made the please about 27 letters long and I knew exactly what she was referring to. Months ago, she'd been witness to me leaving the supply closet with Sorin and knew that we hadn't been doing inventory. She, the other Tiffany and Jackson had kept that secret, knowing that someday they could use it for a big ask later. This was her calling in the favor.

"Yep," I said, letting her know that I was fully aware this was blackmail but wasn't going to fight it.

Her squealing resulted in my pulling back the phone and Sorin grimacing. Guess he was awake now. "See you at 9," I spoke from 6 inches away and hung up.

"What was that?" he asked.

"That was you writing a check my ass has to cash. Remember our little rendezvous at work. That was one of the eye witnesses extorting me. Now, I get to work tonight." As the annoyance was wearing off, it was starting to occur to me what this meant. "Poor Sheena, I won't be able to help her tonight."

"It's okay to take the night off from that. I'm sure she won't mind a break. It will give her and her brother time to reunite." He smiled.

Alex, I thought. Sorin and Alex would be in the same house without me here. Would they fight? I'd seen hints of the master vampire that others feared. But I also knew that he was a man of his word. If he said he was okay with it, I believed him. He wouldn't go through all of that just to kill Alex when I walked away. And Alex didn't seem like a fighter either. He didn't know about the discussion Sorin and I had. He didn't even know I had feelings for him. It was highly possible he was so excited to be with his sister, that he'd forgotten all about me.

I shook my head to clear it. I couldn't head too far down that tunnel of thoughts. I'd end up driving myself crazy with "what ifs." Sorin smirked. "What is going on in that beautiful head?"

"Trust me, you don't want to know."

He sat up, fluffing a pillow to rest against. "We have several hours before you need to go in. I have plenty of work to do this night and Jeremy is here to help. What would you like to do before you go?"

I could sense the promise of something wonderful under his words. I leaned in, laying my lips gently on his, then drew back. "As much as I would love to never leave this bed with you, I need sustenance after last night."

He closed his eyes. "Ah, last night. I must admit it was one that I will carry with me for centuries." He took a moment to imply that he was replaying it in his mind then those pale lids fluttered open.

"I can promise you more where that came from…" I moved my lips to the edge of his ear and whispered "master."

He groaned and I bounced out of bed to leave him wondering if it was the vow for more to come or the word *master* that had elicited that response.

After I was showered and dressed, I headed for the kitchen and the fuel I needed to regain my strength. I expected the whole house to be gathered around the island. Instead, I found Jeremy laughing at something Alex must have just said. They turned to look at me when I came in. They'd seen me so I couldn't slink out like I wished I could.

Jeremy stood, offering me his seat. He was pouring me blood before I could protest. I took the glass and drank the warmth to postpone speaking. I didn't know what to say. Alex was examining his bowl of cereal like it was the most interesting thing he'd ever seen. Jeremy was looking back and forth between the two of us, curiosity clear on his face.

"I'm heading up to help Sorin," he said. "He wanted me to tell you to see him before you go." Without allowing me any time to come up with a way to keep him in the room, he was out the door. I silently cursed him for not staying as a barrier or distracting Alex with some stories so I could eat and leave. What do I even say?

Alex cleared his throat. "Kate," his voice sounded rougher than usual. It could be that my hearing was so much better now or that his vocal cords were tighter. "I want to thank you for being honest with me, you know, about Sheena. I know that couldn't have been easy. You're a good friend."

Friend. He said friend. That was good, right? Whatever he'd felt in the grove the other night, it'd probably been a reaction to the break up and not about me at all. When he'd said he wanted me, he'd been confused. He saw me as a friend.

Was that what I wanted?

"Alex," I said and tried to turn off the voice in my head telling me to shut up. "I want to talk about what happened the other night." When he didn't say anything, I looked up. He was still staring at the bowl but had stopped moving.

"I shouldn't have kissed you," he said. "That was wrong."

"Shouldn't or didn't want to?" I knew I was starting a ball rolling that I couldn't bring back. But, Sorin had told me to explore these feelings. He loved me enough to allow me to figure it all out and I was damn well going to honor that. I was a bad-ass, female vampire in a new century and I was going to own it.

He met my gaze. "What are you asking?"

I stood, walking around the island to face him. "I'm asking if you were caught up in the moment, in pain and looking to feel anything. I'm asking if someone else had been next to you, would you have kissed them? Did you just need to find comfort?" His eyes were wide with fear and excitement. "Or, did you mean what you said? Do you want me? Feel something for me? Something more than friendship?"

His lips parted and I laid a finger on them. "Before you say anything. I ask that you're honest with me like I was with you. There's no wrong answer or right answer. I'll be in your life whether you like it or not. What I'm asking is *how* do you want me in your life?"

I felt him trembling against my finger. The sound of his pounding heart was loud in my ears. I turned down the thumping so I could hear his response and slid my finger from his mouth. He gulped a few times before any words could come out. "I think," he gulped again. "I think about you all the time. I dream of you. When you walk into the room or I see you come around a corner, my heart races. When something happens, you're the first person I want to tell."

I didn't know if I was happy to hear him say all of that or if I was scared. I think it was a little bit of both. I'd asked him to be honest and he had been. The question was, what was I going to do with the information?

His ocean eyes were staring straight into mine, no longer full of excitement or fear but lit by hope. "Say something," he said.

"I told Sorin everything." My sentence had hit him hard so I followed up quickly. "He isn't angry. He told me to explore it, to figure out how I feel about you."

He audibly gulped. "And," he cleared his throat. "How do you feel about me?"

It was my turn to gulp. I let it all pour out quickly before I could second-guess anything. "I want to be around you as much as possible. I feel this sense of calm when you're around, like everything's going to be okay. I don't know what it means, not really. I was so relieved when Monica broke up with you but then I was shocked when you kissed me. I love Sorin," his face fell. "But I think I love you, too."

We stared at each other, neither one of us knowing what to say and what to do next. Finally, I filled the silence. "Listen, I have to go into the hospital. It's a long story. I'll be back before dawn. Spend the night with your sister. Let this all sink in. Tomorrow night, we can pick back up with investigating where Sheena has been." He nodded subtly, more like a reflex then actual agreement. I think he was still processing everything. "We don't have to figure anything out tonight but we do have to figure this out."

I let all the words linger in the air, allowing him to have the next words. When he spoke it was simple, in true Alex fashion. "Whatever happens, we'll work through it together."

My smile was all he needed. He returned to his soggy Cheerios and I left the kitchen to find Sorin.

40

Sorin was in his office, behind his desk and in full Master of the city mode. Jeremy sat in a merlot chair, phone pinned between his ear and shoulder, scribbling on a pad of paper. "I agree," he said into the receiver only to be cut off and stop whatever he was going to say next.

A smile crossed Sorin's face when I entered. Whatever frustrating task Jeremy was trying to accomplish, Sorin didn't seem to have any doubt it'd be completed. He waved me over to his side. "I am sorry you must go in because of my visit to your workplace," he whispered in an attempt to not hinder the phone conversation across the room. "While I do not regret the moment we shared, it is unfortunate that you must pay the price."

That was it, nothing major. He was feeling guilty about me having to go in. I couldn't stop the smirk that crept across my face. Whatever the smile was, it seemed to confuse Sorin. His head cocked to the side in curiosity. I answered his unspoken question by placing a hand on each side of face and planting my lips on his. He didn't hesitate, just kissed me back. When we broke apart, he laughed. "Not that I am complaining but, what was that?"

"I just love you so much," I responded. "You never play games. You just mean exactly what you say and say what you mean. It's so freaking appreciated, you don't even know."

Before he could comment, Jeremy hit the off button on the call and dropped the phone to the table. His dramatic sigh pulled our attention to him. It was obvious he was collecting himself before speaking so we did the correct thing and let him have his moment, waiting patiently. When he looked up, he faced two utterly still vampires. "How does anyone deal with these calls?"

Sorin crossed to the flustered man and patted him on the back. "You may feel defeated but you did very well. Talking to the assistants of other masters always involves red tape and sweet talking but I assume you we're able to get an appointment?" Jeremy nodded so Sorin continued. "Then you have completed this task quicker than any other and I am grateful."

I hadn't the faintest clue what just happened but Sorin's words seemed to re-inflate the deflated Jeremy and that's all I cared about. I crossed to both men. "Whatever this is, I'm proud of both of you." I hugged them into me, squeezed and let go. "But I need to go be a nurse. Please behave." That got me an arched eyebrow from each man. Each independently knew about my confused feelings for the human in the kitchen but neither knew I'd spoken to the other. Even to me it felt confusing so I just planted a kiss on each cheek and rushed out of the office before any questions could be thrown my way.

When I swung open the door to the birch room, I was fully intending to grab some scrubs from drawers and run, but the sight of Sheena froze my next move. She was sitting on the end of the bed rigidly staring into the mirror. The look on her face was more like something you'd give a stranger than your own reflection. Either she didn't know I'd walked in or didn't care. Every muscle in my body held at attention while my brain awaited an order.

When she turned to stare at my face instead of her own, I softened. The sadness in her eyes was drowning.

With only a thought, I was seated next to her on the bed and had my arms around her. "Honey, what's wrong?" Sheena's mane was softening with each shower and conditioning session. It brushed the underside of my chin when she laid her face against my chest and melted into my embrace. I gave her a few minutes to lay silent in my hug before I pulled her back to see her face. "What's wrong?" I repeated.

"I'm a child," she whispered. "You and Tamela, you're women. But me, I'm a girl. I'll always be a girl."

Her eyes were so similar to Alex's that it made it harder to face the raw emotion in them. I couldn't handle seeing that pain. My brain understood that she was chronologically older than me but the mother in me saw a teenager struggling with the realities of growing up and the harsh adjustment of trauma. So many voices in my head were fighting to give a response: the mother, the vampire, the nurse and the woman.

In the end, the woman won. "Sheena," I started with softness in my words while I turned her to face the mirror, took the space behind her and started to finger comb her hair. "You're right. You'll always look 17. You'll always have the body of a teenager." Pulling her hair into three parts, I watched her shoulders sag. "You'll never look like me or Tamela or any other vampire who was made later in her human life." I worked the thickness of the waves into a braid. "But, how boring would this world be if everyone looked the same?" I let the silence fill the room so she could think about what I'd said. Her locks gave off the smell of flowers while I twisted and bound them into submission, wrestling the end into a hair tie. "And, Sheena?"

She met the reflection of my eyes in the mirror. "Yes?"

"You will forever look like the big sister that Alex loves more than life itself."

She smiled before she turned her head to catch the braid in the glass. Looking down, she pulled it to the front to play with the end in a nervous gesture. "Kate?"

"Yes," I answered.

"I have nothing to offer."

That phrase took me aback. I could understand her trying to reconcile the idea that she'd look the same for eons but I wasn't sure how to process the latest statement. "What do you mean?"

She shifted to face me, her small body turned with her back to the mirror. "You're a nurse. You have powers. Jeremy has powers. Tamela is strong, she protects the Lord. Alex's a doctor, he saves people. What do I do?"

A few responses rushed through my head but I wanted to think for a second. She deserved more that simple platitudes. She'd survived a nightmare and was still unafraid to be vulnerable with me, a person she'd just met. Responding to her trust and honesty with a phrase like *You have lots to offer* was unhelpful.

"Well," I said. "First of, as far as I know, all vampires have powers so I know you do. We just have to be patient as they come out. You pushed me out of your mind so I would bet it's a psychic power like mine. Once we know what it is, Sorin can help train you and find a way for you to use it to help."

Hope was sliding into her eyes. "Like you're doing with my memories?"

"Yes," I answered. "You can use your magic for something good. And, there has to be something else you'd like to do. I mean, one of the upsides to you looking 18 is that we could enroll you in some night classes. What would you want to learn?"

Confusion replaced the glimmer of hope I'd seen. She looked down. "I can't. I didn't finish high school."

I chuckled and that pulled her attention back to me. "Listen, kiddo. Rhys can hack anything and make you an identity, high school diploma and get you enrolled in a community college while still having time left in his lunch break. Trust me, you don't need high school to go learn about something you're interested in."

The smile that crossed her face warmed my heart. "Really?" she asked.

"Yep," I rubbed each of her arms. "You have world smarts, which most people don't have. You've survived some tough times. You can definitely handle a few classes. What would you like to do? What did you dream of becoming when you grew up?" As soon as I said it, I wished I hadn't. She'd just told me how sad she was that she'd never look older and I'd said *when you grew up* like an idiot.

Thankfully, it didn't seem to upset her. "I wanted to be a secretary. Like, have my own desk and answer phones and type and help important people be organized. That would be so wonderful. How many classes would I need to take to be a secretary?"

When the idea hit me, I couldn't believe our luck. I checked my watch and decided to not say anything to her until I could talk to the others. "I think that's a wonderful job. Let me talk to Rhys and we'll look into some classes. Then I can let you know when they start and how many you have to take. Sound good?"

"Yes," she squealed and hugged me. It was so similar to the way Ellie and Olivia responded to good news that I couldn't help but squeeze her an extra second longer. She was so young and so full of life. How could anyone have robbed her of a full life? What kind of monster had thrown this beautiful soul into a basement for decades?

She broke the hug. "Can I tell Alex about school?"

I smiled. "Can we wait until I talk to Rhys and know we can make it happen?"

"Of course," she said and thankfully I didn't see any of the excitement dull. "That's smart. I'm going to go find Tamela." With that she bounced out of the room. I grabbed my scrubs and a few outfits to move into Sorin's room. I really needed to just move all my stuff out and give her the room. But I didn't know if she'd actually stay with us or move in with Alex.

Just thinking about Alex going back to his place sent a mix of emotions through me. I was relieved by the simplicity of his not being under this roof anymore. It would be less confusing if he wasn't so nearby. However, it also made me sad to think about not seeing him so often. I mean he'd be at work but that wouldn't be the same. It's not like we could talk about all of this in the hospital. We'd have to go back to pretending to be casual work acquaintances. As I unloaded my outfits into Sorin's closet, I decided it was best to throw on my scrubs and get to work. The more I thought about it all, the more I wanted to curl up in a ball and avoid everything.

41

Pulling into the hospital was getting harder to do each time. In my gut, I knew my days there were numbered. It was just too much to continue to hide what I was, balance work with my life and find the motivation to walk through those doors. The only thing keeping me from turning in my resignation was the immense guilt I'd feel leaving all my co-workers on the frontline while I was safely tucked away. Slapping on my mask, I pulled myself out of the car and forced my feet to walk me into the Pittsburgh Medical Center so someone could comment on how low my temperature was and I could head up to pay Tiffany back the favor I owed her.

The noises of the floor hit me when the elevator doors opened. As I stepped out, I almost crashed into Lacey. Her skin was getting that golden brown that only comes from being outside in the sun. I could still smell the tanning oil on her and a pang of grief hit me. Six months in the darkness and I was still missing the sunlight. This would be the first summer since I was turned, the first summer I wouldn't take the girls on a beach trip, to the zoo or cookouts. Before I could fall apart, Lacey broke into my thoughts.

"Hey, Kate! I heard you were coming. Tiff said you owed her a favor for not telling anyone a secret. What's the secret? I'm dying to know. I promise I won't tell and I won't make you owe me a favor, either." She had scented a juicy story and wanted a bite. Too bad I was *never* going to tell her.

"Hey Lace. It's nothing, really." I moved around her and started my search for Tiffany. I heard her footsteps behind me.

"Okay," she relented. "But you know you can always trust me. Have you seen Dr. Kitchner, by the way? He hasn't been here in days. I heard that he's taking a leave of absence. I'm telling you Kate, I smell a break up."

The mention of Alex and the idea of her sniffing around him unexpectedly filled me with something close to jealousy. I fought the urge to turn and snarl at her, which shocked me. I had no right to act like that but it was true. I paused in the hallway, taking a few deep breaths. She was continuing to talk behind me but I couldn't focus on the words for a few seconds. When I had calmed myself, I caught the tail end.

"-so I promised all the girls that I'd find out what's going on."

Turning to face her, I forced a smile. "Sounds good, Lace. I'm sorry but I honestly don't want to be here so I'd rather just get the assignment, get to work and get through the shift. I don't feel particularly chatty. You understand, right?"

Her shoulders dropped a touch but she kept smiling. "Yeah, I get it. I have those kinds of days, too. See ya later." She turned and bounced away, likely heading to wherever she'd been going when I had met her in the hallway.

I let out a breath and continued my search for Tiffany.

Once I'd gotten report on the patients, I found my med cart and riffled through to ensure I had everything I needed for the shift. She'd stocked the cart before she'd left so I headed to each patient's room to assess them and pass any nighttime meds. The universe had been shining down on me because none of the patients sounded bad. I just had to make it seven hours and I could get home to Sorin. I wanted to talk to him before we had to rest. The excitement at my idea was keeping me focused but also making the minutes feel like hours.

After I'd seen everyone, I peeked at my watch. It was nearing midnight so I figured I could take a little break, then start my charting. I found my pen in my bun, where I normally stuck it at work and started to make a list of the things I needed to do. With any luck, I'd have enough time to get everything ready for the daylight team. As much as I hated being at work, I was going to be happy to have one of the favors I owed off my list of things to do. It made me wonder what kind of favor Jackson and the other Tiffany were going to ask for. It was probably better not to worry about it until the time came. For now, I was just happy to have a quiet night.

I don't think I could've been more surprised than when I looked up from my to-do list to see the man standing in front of me.

"Can we talk?" Alex asked.

42

Without thinking, I'd grabbed his hand and pulled him into the breakroom. It was an absolute miracle that Lacey hadn't seen us. I don't know how I would've explained to her that Dr. Kitchner was visiting me on my floor, in his civilian clothes, when he was supposed to be on a leave of absence. I'd worked hard to make everyone think we barely knew each other.

Pulling off my mask, I hissed. "What are you doing here?"

He stepped into me and the room suddenly felt much smaller. "I had to see you. You just dropped this bomb on me in the kitchen and left. I couldn't wait until you got back and slept to talk about this. Plus, I don't know if I can handle running into Sorin right now. What do I even say to him?"

He did have a point. I had just told the man I loved him and that my fiancé not only knew but told me to explore my feelings. Then, I'd headed off to work like it was no big deal, leaving those two men in the house together. While Sorin is ancient and wise, Alex is just a man. I'd left him with this huge revelation and no real explanation or expectations for what was to come. I'm sure once the shock had worn off, he'd been filled with questions. Alex was like me, a scientist. At our core, we had to analyze and understand everything.

Sticking my crumpled mask into my pocket I laid my hands on his chest, looking up. His heart kicked rhythmically against his ribcage, dancing along my right palm. "I don't have all the answers right now but I'm happy to tell you what I can so ask away."

He laid each of his hands over mine. "Why would Sorin be okay with this?"

"He's 500 years old, Alex. With that comes a lot of understanding and patience." I didn't want to tell him about Sorin's regret and the human he'd alluded to. It didn't feel like my story to share. "He wants me to know exactly what I feel for you and be sure of him. To do that, I can't hide or pretend it's not happening."

He gulped and cleared his throat. "And what is happening?"

"Well," I licked my lips. "I feel like a part of you is connected to a part of me. Like we we're always supposed to meet. At first, I thought you were arrogant and cold but, after I turned – after meeting you in the bar that night – it was different. I didn't see you the same, you didn't feel the same. You felt like someone I'd known before." I moved my right hand from his chest to his cheek. His hand remained on top of mine but his eyes closed like he wanted to focus on the sensation of touch rather than sight. "When I saw you on that barn floor, Alex-" I had to pause for a moment to remember he was here with me and not back on the floor. "-when you were dying – I don't know how to describe it - I would have killed anyone to protect you."

He took in and released a shaking breath.

"Since that night, you've changed in my eyes. You've become more than a friend. I wish I had the right words to really describe it or that you had empathy and could just feel it but this will have to do for now, Alex. I don't have more time to explain and I need more time to really understand."

His eyes fluttered open. "I don't know when it happened for me, Kate. I've always noticed you. You've always been in my periphery.

But I was so focused on finding a cure." He let out a soft chuckle. "Then, you were turned. At first, you were a convenient way to keep studying. I mean you worked here and you were a nurse, so I knew you'd understand the reason for the experiments. Plus, you needed me to cook up paperwork to get you on nights, so it felt like a win-win."

I arched my eyebrow in response to his unemotional explanation of how he'd seen me. It was hard not to make some snarky quip but I told myself to shut up and let him finish.

He continued, either ignoring my arched eyebrow or knowing he needed to get to the point. "But after the barn, just like for you, it changed. Not right away exactly, or maybe right away, I don't know. I pushed it aside, knowing that you were with Sorin. Once Monica was in the picture and Sorin proposed, I tried to ignore anything that I felt for you that was more than friendship. For a while, it worked. We fell into a routine and it felt natural – nice. Now, this last week or two, I can't ignore it. It's so strong - my need to be with you – next to you." His hands left mine and gripped each of my biceps. "I feel like I'm pulled to you and when I'm not with you, it's almost like a dull ache."

His face lowered but he stopped before his lips touched mine, hesitated. I leaned in to close the space between us and the kiss was gentle. Each one before this had been fueled by a hunger, a desperation. But this kiss was soft and slow. My hands found his broad back, felt the muscles under his t-shirt bunch. His hands slid into my hair, pulling my face into his to deepen the kiss. This was so different from the frantic moment we'd shared in the woods. I was so close to being lost in it that I didn't hear the door open or shut, just the gasp behind me.

I turned to face the wide-eyed Lacey.

"Oh shit," I said.

She was turning to leave the room when I yelled "stop." I felt my power rip from my chest before I knew it was called. The aide froze in place. "Turn around." She did.

Alex whispered behind me, "What are you doing?"

I ignored him, too lost in my desperation to fix the giant mistake that we'd just made. We'd been so stupid and now Lacey had witnessed our stupidity. If she left the breakroom with this information, the whole hospital would know by morning. Not only would everyone know that I'd been smooching with the hottest bachelor in the house but he was supposedly my doctor and treating me for my condition, which called into question my diagnosis and his ethics. We'd both be in HR by morning.

My magic slithered up my throat as I spoke. "You came into the breakroom and no one was in here. You forgot what you came in for so you're going to go back out and back to work."

She nodded "I can't believe I walked in here and forgot why. I must be losing it." She turned and bounced out, leaving us alone again.

Turning to face Alex, I saw shock. "When were you going to tell me that you developed mind-control?" I think he was a little angry but when I started to shake, his anger was gone. He grabbed my arms. "What's going on?"

I let him lower me down into a chair. He dropped to his knees in front of me. "I've never done that before," I was trying to stop my muscles from quivering but they weren't obeying me. "It's called glamour. I've seen Rhys do it. And, I've seen Sorin use his voice like magic, even felt it myself. But, Alex, I swear, I didn't know I could." I wrapped my arms around his neck and buried my face into the base of it. "What's happening to me? How can I have any more powers? What if I can't control myself when the next power comes and someone gets hurt?"

"Whoa," Alex soothed. "You're not going to hurt anyone, Kate. We need to talk to Sorin, ASAP. Can you get out early?"

I pulled back suddenly. "Oh my god, I have to get back out there, Alex. We can't draw any attention to us. I have to finish this shift. I owe Tiffany and the last thing I need is her telling everyone what she knows. Please, go back to the manor. We can talk more when I get back. Where's Sheena?"

"Breathe, Kate. She's with Tamela. Apparently, Sheena wanted to bake me a cake so Tamela and Edwin are helping her. Did you know Edwin was a chef in his human life?" That brought an unexpected laugh out of me, which felt wonderful. "I know," Alex smiled. "I think we were all surprised. So, I'll go back. But, please promise me you won't pick up any more shifts until everything calms down?"

I nodded.

He laid a kiss on my forehead, holding there for a moment. Then, he pulled back and looked down at me. My muscles had stopped shaking so I was starting to believe I really could make it through the shift. "I do love you, nurse Kate."

"And, I love you Dr. Kitchner. It makes things very confusing but I do love you."

There. We'd both said it and whether we liked it or not, it changed things. There was no going back.

43

My relief showed up at 3:30am and I couldn't have been happier to see any human being more than her in that moment. She'd had the team the day before so she barely needed report and I almost cried with joy. Thankfully, the rest of the shift had been uneventful. I'd spoken to Lacey several times and she really didn't seem to remember anything she'd seen. I was a little worried about how erasing memories affected a human's brain but I was so relieved that it'd worked. I knew Lacey well enough to know that if she'd retained the image of Alex and I hot and heavy, she'd never been able to keep it to herself. She'd have asked me 1,000 questions. The lack of an interrogation assured me that our little rendezvous was safe. Considering that I'd been working that night because I'd gotten caught being lusty with Sorin in the supply closet, I should've learned my lesson. But, I obviously hadn't and had almost gotten into trouble again.

I was eager to get back to the manor. I wanted to see Sorin. I wanted to see Alex. I wanted to talk to everyone about my idea for Sheena. I wanted to find out what Rhys had been able to dig up on Bobby and ask him to create a high school transcript and ID for Sheena. I needed to tell Sorin about my new power and have him tell me what it all meant. How could I go half a year with nothing only for two more powers to show up? Why now? When would it stop?

I wished desperately that I wasn't always controlled by the sun and could just stay up to get all this done. I'd promised everyone that we'd look into Sheena's head again the next night so I really needed to get all this done before that.

Plus, I really wanted some time with Alex to figure out what we were feeling. The sooner I knew, the sooner I could tell Sorin so we could all decide how to handle it.

I was 100% sure on two things: I loved Sorin and I loved Alex. I didn't want to exist without either of them.

Would they be okay with me having them both in my life? Was that what I wanted?

It was quarter to four when I walked out of the hospital into the garage. My focus was on my car but I sensed the movement to my left as the smell hit my nostrils. Letting my attacker know that I was aware of them wouldn't help me so I pretended to be oblivious as I strode towards the Beemer. I knew the exact spot in the garage that the camera didn't see and wanted to reach it. The second I stepped into that blind spot, my fangs descended and I turned on the werewolf.

The snarl was out of my mouth before I saw the face and died as I realized who it was.

"Hi, Kate," Monica said.

44

"Holy shit," I slapped my hand over my sternum. "You nearly gave me a heart attack."

She laughed. "Don't think you need to worry about that anymore."

My fangs retracted and a sarcastic "Ha ha" escaped my lips. "What are you doing here?" It came out sounding a little harsher than I intended but I wasn't taking it back. She wasn't exactly my favorite person at the moment. She'd ditched us all and broken Alex's heart after months of silence. But to be fair, I was actually glad she had.

"Not the reaction I was expecting," she quipped. "But I don't blame you."

She was slowly walking towards me. I held my spot. Partly because I didn't feel like going to her and partly because I wanted to remain out of the camera in case something happened. Call me paranoid but I didn't really trust many people anymore. And, she wasn't a person, was she? She was a werewolf. I felt her energy rolling off of her and knew why humans naturally felt uneasy around lycanthropes. They didn't know it but humans were picking up on the wolves' auras.

I sighed. "You told us that you were done with us, moving on and leaving your old life behind. I believe that was how you put it."

She had the courtesy to look embarrassed at least. "I did," she shrugged. "And, I was – going to move on, I mean." When she stopped, she was only a few feet from me and the smell was overwhelming. She'd been in animal form recently. Rhys had explained to me that their smell is based on how recently they'd shifted. The longer it had been, the more human they smelled. My friend had always smelled like cookies. Now, she smelled like the zoo.

"But I've been thinking," she continued. When she met my eyes, they looked genuine. Tears trickled down her cheek. "I miss you, miss our friendship."

Something inside of me shifted. I didn't soften exactly, just became a smidge less angry. "I've had time to think, too." I took a small step towards her but was cognizant of my placement. I was still not in the camera's view. "I missed you. I played all our fun moments together in my head about a dozen or so times. I remembered the pain of trying to save you in the barn - watching Will sink his fangs into you, you being thrown to the ground. I can still feel the horrible ache when you were in that hospital bed and couldn't get over what I was." I knew what I was going to say and prepared myself. Tonight, was the night of being honest – honest with Alex, honest with Monica and honest with myself. "I remembered how loving and understanding I was when you were turned - which happened because you saved my daughters."

I squared my shoulders. "For that I will always be grateful to you. But I also remember that we all risked everything to save you and Diana. We gave you time and space." I let the anger return to my eyes. "And, you told us that you were moving on. After months of nothing, you didn't even do it to our faces. You sent Diana and made her do it. Because, ultimately you are a coward, Monica. You broke Alex's heart and mine."

The tears were no longer rolling down her cheeks but pouring. "I know," she said. "I'm so ashamed of myself, Kate. You have to believe me. I wish I could take it back."

"You can't," I said. "So, let's be adults. You're done with me and I'm done with you. We'll see each other for pack or vampire business and continue to work on bringing our kind together to protect the peace. None of us wants bloodshed or conflict." She was sobbing now but I didn't let it stop me. What I was going to say needed to be said. "I don't hate you Monica but I don't know you anymore. And, you don't know me. The women who were friends are both gone. Let's let them rest in peace."

Then, I turned and headed for my car. I heard her at my back. It was just whispers but she knew I would hear her. "Please, Kate. Let me fix this."

I'd said what I needed to. I climbed into the car and left her in my rearview without looking back.

45

I found everyone scattered around the kitchen. Jeremy, Tamela, Sorin, Rhys and Sheena all had glasses of blood. Alex had a piece of cake that looked big enough to feed several men. He was shoveling a fork full of it into his mouth. Some of the electric blue icing smeared his lips. His laugh was muffled by the bite and mixed in with the laughter of the rest.

"What's so funny?" Everyone turned to me. My chest was tight from the amount of love I felt for all the faces around that table.

"Katherine," Sorin stood and crossed to me. "Please come join us. How was your shift?" He led me back to the stool he had been sitting on and pushed his glass towards me. I sat, knowing he'd get himself a new glass and there was no point in arguing. It's just the way Sorin was. I gulped down the warm blood, buying myself a couple of seconds. When it was gone, I spoke. "It was interesting. I'm happy to be home. So, why we're you all laughing?" I wasn't ready to tell everyone about Monica's visit. And, not everyone in this room needed to hear about my new powers or the kiss in the locker room.

Jeremy, thankfully, answered the question and allowed the subject to change. "I told an embarrassing story about a date I had before I became a vampire. I tried to make a home-cooked dinner but just succeeded in making two plates full of charred meat and soggy vegetables. Let's just say she didn't want a second date."

"I made a cake," Sheena exclaimed proudly. "Alex says it's very good."

"It is," he said around the latest mouthful of dessert.

I laughed. "I'm sure it's delicious. Jeremy, Rhys and Sorin. Could I steal you for 10 minutes?" Before they could respond, I stood and left the kitchen. If the rest were curious, they didn't say anything.

I heard the men behind me as I led them to the solarium. Each one stood silently, waiting for me to say whatever I was going to say.

"I have an idea," I turned to face the waiting males. "Sheena is much older than we give her credit for. She can't spend the rest of eternity baking cakes and walking in the garden."

Jeremy turned to the other men and back to me. "Okay, so what's the idea?"

"She told me she's always wanted to be a secretary." I paused expecting comments but none came. "So, I think we should get her enrolled into a couple classes at the community college. Maybe keyboarding. It's like typing and will give her an introduction to computers. She can start in the fall."

"Oh boy," Jeremy spoke. "Will she really be ready for that?"

I raised my hands, "It's just a class. Maybe one or two nights a week. I can take her there and bring her back. It's not far from here. Rhys, could you get her some kind of ID and high school transcripts? So, we could enroll her?"

"Sure, Katie, but" he looked concerned. "What if she can't handle it?"

"Then," I shrugged "she drops out and we're right back to where we are. But, that's not it." I locked eyes with Sorin then looked at Jeremy. "While she prepares for the fall, I want you two to let her do some things to help. She wants to be an assistant and you guys need assisting. Give her some simple tasks to clear you up for bigger things. Teach her how to make simple calls, keep the calendar, write thank you cards, file, whatever."

Jeremy rubbed his chin. "I don't know. What if we overwhelm her?"

I shook my head. "Jeremy, you know all the tasks that need to be done. Plus, you're a teacher. You know exactly how to relate to her and teach her new things. You're literally the best person to do this."

Sorin nodded, looking impressed. "Actually, Katherine, I think that is a wonderful idea. Without a purpose, I have seen vampires fall into despair. This will give her something to focus on other than retrieving traumatic memories. She cannot be the lost girl forever. Someday she must find her own way and identity."

I crossed to him and kissed him. "I knew you'd get it. That's exactly what I was thinking. When can you guys start? I want to tell her the good news."

Rhys knew he'd lost. "I'll work on some papers for her soon. I have until August to get it together but it won't take that long. First, I want to wrap up my search for Bobby."

"How's that going?" Jeremy asked. "Any closer to figuring out what school she was at?"

"Unfortunately, no. I've found a solid list of places offering GEDs in the second half of the 80s. Now, I need to start digging through rosters for Sheena's name. Once I find that, I can look for a Robert or Bobby and go from there."

I left Sorin to grab Rhys' hands. "That is closer than we were a day ago. And, even if it's a dead end, at least we tried. We can tell her that." He touched his forehead to mine. "Now, let's go offer her an internship."

46

When we returned to the kitchen, I could tell that Tamela and Alex were curious but Sheena didn't appear to need to know what we'd been talking about. She looked up at us, just happy that we were back.

Sorin stepped up to her. "Sheena? I would like to ask you something."

"Okay," she answered. Alex stood but I gestured for him not to worry. He trusted me and sat back down.

"I have a great deal of work to do each night. Being a master of a city takes a team. I have Tamela, Edwin and Naseem to protect us. Jeremy helps me with office matters." She nodded. "But I need another person on my team to help Jeremy. It is very important work. Would you please be my assistant?"

She jumped up, looking from me to Jeremy to Alex and back to Sorin. "Really?" she exclaimed.

"Really," Sorin answered seriously. "Jeremy can train you but I have faith that you will be excellent and help me a great deal to stay organized."

She squealed, looking to her brother. "Can I?"

Alex cocked his head. "You don't have to ask my permission, She. If you want to do this than you're free to do so."

She jumped up and down. "Yes. I want to."

"Wonderful," Sorin responded. "After your session with Katherine tonight, if you are up to it, we will give you your first task."

"Then, I must go rest." Sheena finished her drink, gingerly placed the glass into the sink and left the room – presumably to get her beauty sleep before work.

When she was gone, Alex took his empty plate to the sink. He spoke into the water as he washed the plate and glass. "Thank you." It was all he said and all he needed to. Sorin put a hand on the man's shoulder and squeezed. "You are welcome."

Sorin took my hand and led me from the kitchen to the stairs. I could feel the night waning and knew we needed to sleep soon. There was a lot to tell him and not enough time so I had to prioritize. I spoke as we walked to the bedroom. "I have a new power." He didn't stop but I saw his muscles tense just a little and felt a tiny bit of his power flare up.

"What is it?" he asked.

"Someone at work tonight saw something. I panicked and told her to stop. She did. Then I told her to forget what she saw and she did." I said it matter-of-factly. No reason not to. We reached the bedroom and went inside, closing the door behind us.

"Interesting," he did sound interested. "Did you know how to do this?"

"Not really," I said. "I've seen Rhys glamour but I didn't know I could or even how to do it if had known. It was like an instinct, like pulling away from something hot to not be burned. I knew I was in trouble and just knew how to fix it."

I sat on the end of the bed and he stood before me. "Was she looking at you when you told her to stop?"

I had to think about it but answered. "No, she was leaving the room and had her back to me. I said stop and turn around, which she did. I was looking into her eyes when I told her to forget everything."

FATAL CURSE

"Did you tell her to forget or did you tell her what to remember?" He clarified. "I mean did you just take the memory or replace it with another?"

I wasn't sure where he was heading with this but answered. "Replaced it. I told her she'd come into the room and forgotten why she was there, that she'd been alone in the room and left to go back to work."

He nodded. "That is two powers."

"I know," I agreed. "First empathy and now this."

"No," he shook his head. "This night you displayed two separate powers. Glamouring takes eye contact. When you replaced her memory through eye contact, you were using glamour. However, when you spoke to her back and she followed," he sat next to me "that was a different power. It is called melody. It means to use your voice to command or sway or seduce. It is one of my own powers as you know. With this power, I could tell someone to forget what they saw but not replace the memory with another. I do not need to have their eyes to use it. I can do it over the phone or a recording. So long that they hear my voice, I have power over them when I choose to."

I laid my head onto his shoulder. "What is happening to me?"

He rested his head onto mine. "I do not know, Katherine, and that scares me."

Hearing him say that he was scared, scared me. The man next to me did not scare easily. "Have you ever heard of any vampire getting this much magic?"

"Not like this," he whispered. "I do not know what this means or why it is happening to you. But," he turned to kiss the top of my head. "I will find out."

Looking up, I saw that he meant it.

"What did the girl see that you needed to call power?"

"Oh," I said. "That's one of the other things I need to tell you." I stood and started to undress, preparing the bed for us to climb in, anything other than look into his eyes. "I told Alex about our talk before I went to work. I guess it was too much to just let linger so he showed

- 205 -

up at work. We were in the breakroom when Lacey came in. I can't have people at the hospital knowing how close he and I are. There's so much gossip around him. I can't get caught up in that kind of attention."

I slid under the heavy duvet and relished the sensation of the cool sheets against my naked skin. I lifted the other side as an invitation. Sorin took his place next to me. "I agree. The more of your life we keep secret, the safer you are."

"That's an understatement," I agreed. "But, it's more than that. She saw us kissing."

"I see," he said. "I expect you and Alex have spoken of your feelings to one another?"

"Kind of," I forced myself to meet his gaze and was still shocked by the way he was taking the subject of Alex and my possible love. "I don't think either one of us totally understands."

"Try to explain," he said.

"Okay," I settled into the covers on my back and looked up at the ceiling. "With you, I'm so certain. It's love – 100% total true love." I heard him settle down too. I kept talking. "With Alex, it's more like a tie. I feel like he's a part of me and I him. I want him nearby all the time. I feel protected when he's close." I turned to face Sorin, who turned to face be back. "Not that I don't feel protected by you. But, with him it's like a part of me is pulled away when he is gone."

"Was it like this when you first met him?" Sorin asked a good question. He wasn't just listening but was trying to help me understand.

"Not at all," I said. "That's what's so weird. I used to basically hate him."

"When did it change?" he asked.

"After I turned. I saw him in a bar the same night I met you and he just seemed different, more like a friend than an enemy."

Sorin reached out and brushed a piece of hair off my cheek to tuck it behind my ear. "And, when did it become love?"

I wrinkled my brow, trying desperately to pinpoint a moment. "The night in the barn, I wanted more than anything to save him. Seeing him crumpled on the floor and hearing his heart slowly quit was one of the worst things I've ever been through." My eyes slid away from Sorin and off to the side as I recalled that night. "After that, I was connected to him. I don't know when it turned to love but I know after I healed him, I never wanted him to be gone from me."

Sorin sat upright. It was so sudden that I jumped. "Dumnezeule!" He jumped out of bed, running to the couch and pulling his phone from his pants' pocket. He was dialing before I had even sat up.

I looked around for some kind of attack. "What is it?"

He was pacing and I heard someone say *yes* on the other line. He spoke quickly. "My greatest apologies, Lady. It is Lord Sorin. I know it is close to dawn but this is urgent and I would not call unless it was. Can I come to you or can you come to me? The sooner the better." He listened to something on the other end that I couldn't make out. "Yes," he responded. "I must insist and I beg of you to keep this quiet. I trust you but no one else." He listened again, nodding his head. "I thank you. Of course, I will make a room for you this night. I owe you a great debt."

When he hung up, I jumped out of bed. "What was that? Who was that?"

Crossing to me, his face was serious. "Katherine. I ask that you please trust me until I can tell you everything."

"I trust you, Sorin." He pulled me into him. "Who was that on the phone? Who's coming?"

"Lady Akila." I felt the rumble of his voice through his chest and against my cheek. "If I am correct, then she is the only one we can trust with this."

47

The first half hour after we woke was a bustle of chores and activity. Sorin had told Tamela to ready a room for Akila. She was a much better vampire than me because she didn't ask a single question, just left to go get a room ready. I wondered where the heck they were going to put the lady. The manor was getting full. I had no idea where Naseem and Edwin slept; I'd never seen their rooms. Maybe whatever part of the house they were in had extra rooms.

Sorin kissed me and told me he needed to do some research but wanted to be told before we started our next session with Sheena. I'd asked him if he needed me to get Jeremy to help with research but he'd said he only trusted this assignment to be done by himself alone. I respected his decision and didn't argue – see, I was getting better.

I ran down the stairs with the intention to find breakfast and then track down Rhys. I wanted to get some more specifics on the GED programs he'd found. I figured maybe we could split the list in half and each take one. Or, even better, get Jeremy involved and split the list in three. If we divided, we could conquer.

The front door was open. I figured in all the shuffling, someone had either forgotten to close it or was outside doing something and would be back in quickly enough that shutting the door was unnecessary. Grabbing the doorknob, I pulled the door all the way open so I could see if everyone was safely inside before I closed it. Thankfully, I looked because Alex was on the porch gazing out at the driveway. I figured he was just taking a moment to think until he took a step to the side and I could see what was drawing his attention. Or rather, who.

Monica stood at the bottom of the stairs, looking up at Alex. Both were silent. I gathered from the smell of hot tires on the air that she'd just recently pulled up. I was surprised that she hadn't tried to come during the day to avoid me and everyone else being up. I mean, she could've had Alex all to herself that way. I also wondered how she'd know he was even here.

I stepped out onto the porch, next to Alex. I promise I wasn't being territorial or anything. I wasn't marking him as mine, I was just showing solidarity.

At least, that's what I told myself.

She looked at me and back to him. "I was just asking Alex why he was here and if we could walk and talk," she said.

Alex shifted uncomfortably beside me. "Whatever you want to say, you can say in front of Kate."

Something like anger or jealously flashed across her face. It may have been both. Whatever it was, it wasn't friendly. "I'd like to talk to you in private," she snarled.

"You had no problem breaking up with me through another person," he responded dryly. "I see no reason to keep this between us now."

Ouch. I wasn't Monica's biggest fan but that was harsh. Part of me felt bad for her but another part felt she deserved that. She'd hurt him. How could she expect to not face a consequence for that?

"Okay," she shifted her feet and dropped her gaze to the ground. "I'm so sorry, Alex. The way I called it off between us was wrong and I'm a coward." She looked back up to reveal fresh tears. "I wanted to tell you to your face how sorry I am."

Alex nodded. "Thank you for that, Monica. I can't imagine that was easy. I do appreciate you coming to tell me that." He started to turn.

"Wait," she yelled, reaching out towards him. "That's not all."

He returned to his previous stance and stayed silent, allowing her to finish whatever she'd come to say. He was giving her a chance to speak but didn't look especially welcoming. I had to admit that her facing him and speaking was pretty damn brave.

"I wanted," she started and stopped, swallowing hard. "I wanted to tell you that I regret what I said. I was in a total low spot when I wrote that and sent Diana here, like super low." She rocked back and forth, tears starting to really flow now. "I'm hoping, I mean I'm asking-"

I fought the urge to grab Alex's hand. I didn't like where this was going.

She continued. "I want another chance, Alex." She took a step up to move closer to him and she had to crane her neck a little less to meet his eyes. "Please, Alex. Can we start again?"

He was frozen next to me.

She took another step up. "I've loved you since the moment I first saw you." She was so genuine that it hurt to look at her. "You didn't even notice me but for five years I dreamed of going on a date with you, calling you my boyfriend... kissing you…"

I felt like I should go inside. I didn't want to hear this. I felt sick to my stomach and wanted to vomit while simultaneously wanting to punch her square in the throat so she'd stop talking. But I knew I had to stay out of this. If Alex wanted to date Monica, it was none of my business. After all, I was engaged.

Monica was close now, only a couple steps away from him. She was smiling through her tears as she continued the speech. "And, then it happened. *You* asked *me* out. We were going on a date and my dream was coming true. I knew what it was like to kiss you and had everything I ever wanted right in front of me."

He stayed silent and unmoving as she moved closer.

"And, I blew it." She stopped, leaving some small distance between them. "I blew it, Alex. I freaked out and ran. I called the whole thing off and destroyed my chance at happily ever after. And, you know what the worst part is?"

"What?" he whispered.

She seemed emboldened by his response to her question. "I don't know why I did it. I have no clue why I would sabotage the one good thing to happen to me in a long time." She reached out her hand and Alex hesitated before laying his hand in hers. "I'm asking you if it's too late. Can I undo the damage and get a second chance with you? Please just tell me so I can be free of this misery."

It was my turn to freeze. I couldn't wrap my arm around his waist and tell her to back off. I couldn't tell him to please not give her another chance. All I could do it stand there and see what he said.

Minutes went by with no one moving or speaking. The sounds of Monica's quiet crying filled the silence and she looked expectantly but patiently at him. The spell was broken when he turned to me. "Kate," he asked. "Would you give us a moment?"

48

I can't believe I was able to speak because I was very certain that all the air had been sucked out of my lungs. "Sure," I managed and went inside. Shutting the door, I did the right thing and sat at the bottom of the stairs instead of listening at the door.

While I waited, I played the "possibilities" game in my head. He could turn her down and send her packing. He could tell her about us and she could tell the hospital. He could give her a second chance and it could not work out. He could give her a second chance and it could work out and they'd get married and live in a little house with her and Sheena and their kids and never speak to me again because she'd insisted they move away for a "fresh start."

I shook my head. "Stop," I said to the room. The last thing I needed was to make myself crazy over what was happening out there.

When he walked in, I heard her car rolling down the driveway and away from us. I stood as he shut the door behind him and walked towards me. "What did you say?" I stepped into him. "Sorry, not my business. You don't have to tell me."

"I told her that I had a lot to figure out and I just couldn't give her an answer until I sorted it all out." The blue of his eyes looked darker and there was a heaviness in them. "It wasn't a lie. I have a lot to figure out. We have a lot."

"You're right, we do." I laid a hand on his chest. "Are you okay?"

"Yeah," he answered, covering my hand with his. "It was unexpected but probably good for Monica and me that we talked."

"How did she find you?"

He smiled. "I told my neighbor I was staying with a friend from work out in the country for some down time. Since you're my only friend and Sorin's manor is in the country, she figured it out."

"Oh," I managed, dropping my eyes to the floor.

"Don't worry," he placed his finger under my chin to lift up my gaze to meet his. "I didn't tell her about Sheena or what's going on between us."

"That's good," it came from the top of the stairs. We looked up to see Sorin. Even though I'd told him everything, it was the first time he'd actual seen us acting like this together. He didn't look mad but he didn't look exactly happy. If I had to pick an emotion, I want to say he looked scared. But that didn't make sense. I fought the temptation to use my empathy. I would've hated it if he did it to me so I didn't do it to him.

Alex stepped back and broke our contact.

Sorin descended the stairs with that graceful sway of his hips that made my core start to ache for him. He slid his hand to the small of my back and used the other hand to gesture into the kitchen. "Please," he said. "You are the two people I need to speak to. Let's get breakfast and talk."

Sliding my hand around his hips, we walked side by side to the kitchen with Alex behind us. If the human was scared, he hid it well.

I found the bagels and popped one into the toaster while Sorin poured two glasses of blood. Alex sat at his usual stool with Sorin and I on the other side of the island. When the bagel bounced out of the toaster, Alex stood to silently spread cream cheese on top. Once he'd gotten a glass of orange juice from the fridge, there was no more stalling. He sat and we waited to hear what Sorin needed to say.

"Doctor," Sorin started but was cut off.

"Alex," he said, making eye contact with the vampire at my side. "I think at this point you shouldn't need to be so formal with me."

"Alex," Sorin continued. "Katherine has been honest with me about her feelings for you. I applaud this as I know it is not easy. I also know that secrets destroy a relationship and I want to be with her until I take my last breath. I do not want any secrets between us and never want her to feel like she cannot tell me something." I took his hand and squeezed it. As weird as this whole situation was, he couldn't have been any more perfect with how he handled it. He squeezed back. "I believe that she has been honest with me. So, I ask that you do the same."

Alex swallowed the bite off bagel in his mouth with an audible gulp. "Okay."

Sorin nodded. "When did you realize that you love Katherine?"

Taking a big swig of OJ, Alex set the glass down before rubbing his hands down his jeans. "I don't know. I just looked at her one day and wanted to always be around her."

Sorin seemed to be getting what he wanted but I wasn't clear yet what that was. "I find it interesting that you both have said the same thing, that you 'always want to be near each other' but neither of you is sure when this all developed. Can you tell me, was it before the barn?"

Alex shook his head. "No. Before the barn, she was a colleague. I didn't think much of her at all. I mean, I knew her and of her but she was just kind of part of my world sometimes. When she came to the bar, after being turned, she was different." He chuckled to himself. "I mean, more than just the obvious. I was more intrigued by her. But, not infatuated, you know?"

"I do," Sorin agreed, encouraging him to continue.

"And, then," Alex paused. "And, then the barn. When I woke up, you were both above me. She was radiant. I never wanted to leave her side. But Monica needed to get to the hospital and Kate asked me to please take her. I would have done anything for her."

"For Monica?" I asked.

"No," Alex looked at me. "For you."

"Please continue," Sorin coaxed.

"When I saw Kate again, that's when I think I first may have loved her a little. She came to the hospital to see Monica. She was in a black sundress in late September."

I laughed. "I remember that night vividly," I said.

Alex nodded but he was lost in a recollection and not completely in the kitchen with us. "After that, I thought of Kate often but not like I was in love, not yet. It was more like wondering if she was okay and if she needed anything. When I saw her at work, I'd be so happy. And, nights she wasn't there, I wished she was. This nurse who I'd barely noticed was suddenly like my best friend."

I didn't move. I was afraid to break whatever trance he was in. I selfishly wanted to hear everything about his feelings for me.

"It was like destiny had brought us together and I couldn't imagine how I'd ever existed without her." His gaze began to focus again and he came back to the room. When he made eye contact with Sorin again, he was apologetic. "I'm sorry, Sorin. I know this must be hard for you to hear."

Sorin gave a slight bow with his head but didn't break the eye contact or let go of my hand. "On the contrary, Alex. I asked for honesty and you gave it to me. I thank you." He looked at me for the next part. "Katherine is an extraordinary creature. It is not beyond the realm of possibility that others will love her." He returned his attention to Alex. "However, I do not think that this is an ordinary crush. If I am correct, I think we will all have answers tonight."

He stood. "Soon, a guest will arrive. She is a master, like myself, but very old and much wiser than I shall ever be. I ask that you both sit with her and I tonight. Answer her questions honestly as you have for me."

"Why?" Alex and I asked in tandem.

"Please, trust me." I knew that was all we would get from him. "Now, let's find Sheena and help her before our guest arrives. I would hate to lose another night."

He was right and we all knew it.

49

Sheena was in the garden with Tamela, just like I'd known she'd be. Sorin, Alex and I approached them to see that Sheena was chasing fireflies. I hated to ruin her fun.

"Hey, She." It was Alex that took the lead.

She squealed and ran to her brother with her hands cupped together. When she was right in front of him, she opened her hands to allow the trapped firefly to be free. Instead of making a break for it, the insect hovered in front of her face as she giggled. Then she held up her cupped palms and the little bug went right back into them. She closed her hands over top, then opened them again to let the little fly out. It flitted back and forth in front of her face. Before our eyes, we watched half a dozen more fireflies show up to dance around Sheena.

"Sheena," Sorin said stepping forward. "Do you have a lot of animals come to you?"

"Oh yes," she said joyfully. "The chipmunks are my favorite. They're so cute. But the fire flies are so pretty. They're like fairies."

I gasped. "Your power."

She looked up. "What?"

Sorin laughed. "You can call animals, Sheena. That is your power."

She didn't seem to believe us but looked around to see the little flies lighting up and dancing. Alex pointed at the tree line and we all followed his gaze. A line of small animals sat at the edge of the small forest. Chipmunks, squirrels, rabbits, a raccoon and two fawns watched Sheena expectantly. Only then did Sheena understand.

"My power?" she asked to anyone.

"Yes," Tamela exclaimed and ran to hug the girl. "Yes. You have power. I told you it would come."

"I have power," the girl said. Her and Tamela jumped up and down.

"Now," Sorin said softly. "See if you can send them away."

The girls stopped their celebrating so Sheena could face the line of animals. "Thank you, friends." She spoke to them with all the sweetness I'd grown to adore in her. "You have made me so happy. Now, you can go and do your animal things and get some sleep. I'll see you later." And, just like that the animals scampered off into the woods. Even the lightening bugs flew off.

"Incredible," Alex said.

Sheena was beaming. "When can I learn my new job?" she asked.

This was my cue. "Well, we would like to have one session tonight, if that's okay. I'd like to see what else we can learn about where you've been. Then, you will go with Jeremy to learn your new job." That reminded me of the fact I hadn't seen him all night. I looked at Sorin. "Where is Jeremy?"

"He and Rhys have split the list of colleges" he answered. "They are looking through registers. I thought if we split the task, perhaps we could find the right place faster."

I chuckled. "Great minds think alike." That bought me the eyebrow arch that I loved so much.

"Alright, kid" I said, clapping my hands and rubbing them together. "You okay with this?" I wished Jeremy was here in case she had a meltdown but knew he was right inside. I also wanted him helping Rhys more than I needed his power. If I was being honest, though, I was freaked about what I might see in Sheena's head. But it was this or give up entirely. That wasn't an option so it was best to just get it over with.

"Yes," she agreed. "I want to know."

I wrapped my arm around her shoulders. "Alright. Let's head inside." I prepared for someone to ask to stay in the lovely garden and was ready to stand my ground. I figured, if her and I saw something really bad, I wanted to be close to Jeremy and his ability to calm us both down. I didn't know how many more awful things I could take inside this girl's memories. But, if she could handle living through it, I could handle seeing it from the safety of the living room.

No one argued with me as Sheena allowed me to lead her into the house. Things were looking up.

Once in the living room, we each took a spot. Sheena sat on the couch. Alex and I took position on each side of her. Sorin and Tamela took a chair each. While they all remained very calm, I could sense an expectant energy in the room. I think all of us were afraid off what the young woman had locked away in her amnesia. All of us had been on this planet long enough to know what terrible things were possible.

Only Sheena appeared to be completely devoid of nervousness. Her sweet young face was hopeful. I actually think she was so excited to start her secretarial training that she just wanted to get the memory session over so she could learn how to send an email. My heart swelled a little with hope – hope that I didn't find anything that would break her forever.

Locking eyes with her, I started the session. "Sheena, can you try to remember another time with Bobby? I want you to close your eyes and just pull up the image of him. You know what he looks like and you remember the party with him. Think of him. Think of what he would feel like or smell like or the sound of his voice." Her eyelids dropped without hesitation and I continued. "Play it in your head like watching a movie or listening to an album."

When I stopped my instructions, I let the silence expand and fill the room. I wasn't in any rush. I just wanted to make sure she didn't feel pushed or unsafe in any way. Every muscle in the room was tensed except hers. If you didn't know any different, you'd think she was sleeping while sitting up. She was so relaxed.

A small smile appeared on her face, so I closed my eyes and slid into the darkness of her mind. With our previous sessions I was having to wait for the darkness to subside but this time it was like a flip of a switch. First it was dark and then – bam – lights.

I looked around to see where we were. The noise of people talking had a thrum of music underneath. We seemed to be inside a home, in someone's living room I thought. The high wooden ceiling met wood paneled walls which ended with a darker wood floor. The windows were dark, filled with the kind of night that only happens away from the city lights. The smell of all the wood hit my nose and mixed with cigarette smoke, beer, wine and hard liquor. Everyone around me was young. Some of the faces were recognizable from Sheena's memory of the bonfire. Some of the young adults were newer to me.

"Sheena." I looked up and saw Bobby across the room. My heart beat against my ribs. *He is so cute*, Sheena thoughts filled my head.

Moving through bodies and past clouds of smoking, I made my way to him. When he extended his hand to grab mine and pull me close, I thought my heart would actually burst from the excitement. "I'm glad you made it," he whispered into my ear. "I want you to meet someone. I told him all about you. He's upstairs."

The idea of him pulling me upstairs away from all the people was exciting. *Is there really someone to meet or does he just want me alone in a bedroom?* I didn't know which one I'd prefer. I mean, I really liked Bobby but I didn't know if I was ready to do it with him again. It had hurt the first time and I was nervous. One time, I'd heard a girl in the bathroom telling her friends that it only hurt the first time. I hoped that was true.

Before I could ask anything, Bobby was pulling me up the stairs. It was so much quieter on the second floor. The stuff around the first floor had seemed not that nice but it changed on the upper level. A table in the hallway had a vase and small statue that looked expensive. I couldn't believe that whoever owned this place would leave it out with drunk college students a floor below. Sheena figured the guy must know that no one would take or break anything. To hear Bobby talk about him, she knew that everyone here practically worshipped the dude. They made him sound like a god.

They stopped in front of a door and she could hear a man talking on the other side of it. Suddenly, she was really nervous. I mean, Bobby really like respected this guy. What if the man didn't like her? Or thought she was like too immature? Would Bobby break up with her? She'd have to go to a different school and her parents would be so pissed. But there's no way she could go back and see these guys if this went badly.

"I hear you," the man said from the other side. "Come in, Robert."

Bobby opened the door, pulling Sheena behind him and in what appeared to be an office or den. Several people sat cross-legged on the floor. Sheena saw Brian, Heather and Amanda. Like the others in the room, they were staring at the man seated in a chair in a corner. "Life is a gift," the man was saying. "But so many squander that gift. They waste it with their gossip and sit for hours watching television. They betray each other, hurt each other and for what? Greed? Power? Or worse – they slave at office jobs and enter into loveless marriages to create their 2.5 children that they raise to become the same soulless robots. They have no goals, no drive, no point; they add nothing to the universe. You need to evolve as I have. Become higher than those around you. Create a new world."

Sheena was looking at the carpet, too afraid to face him.

The past-Sheena had looked up and seen the man. But the Sheena that was reliving this memory was too afraid to see his face. I could hear her thoughts mingling with the thoughts that she'd had on that night. *Don't let him see me* was dancing around this memory like a voice being played on surround sound speakers.

He won't see you, I whispered back to her. *We aren't really here, Sheena. Look up.*

"I ask you all," the man was continuing. I watched the young audience, leaning in, eating up every word he said. "Will you join me? Can you be a higher being with me? Can we overwhelm the mediocrity and use the brainless masses for our purpose? Be warned - it will be difficult. Only the greatest of you will be asked to rise to this higher state and join me."

I felt every nerve in her body electrified. She'd been excited, enthralled by this man and his words. She'd wanted to know more, see more and join in whatever he was talking about. *Look at him, Sheena.*

I knew what I was asking her to do. I knew the man that had excited her 30 years ago was terrifying her now. I knew I had to see this man's face, knew that he was an important part of this puzzle.

Finally, her eyeline slowly began to lift. The strength it was taking her to do this was immeasurable. I begged the universe to not make this courageous act be for nothing.

But it was. Because when her eyes reached the man, all I could see was a blur. He was gesturing and talking, but his voice had become warped. He was a mass behind a dirty glass pane. And I had only a moment to try and make out an identity before she threw me from her head and the memory was gone.

50

Sheena had been taken to Tamela's room to recover. She'd apologized over and over to me, through tears of frustration. She wanted to help but her brain was protecting her from something traumatic. As much as we all wanted answers, that man's face was something that her mind was not ready to unleash. Whatever protective mechanism had caused the amnesia was strong. Just because I'd rooted around in her psyche doesn't mean her brain was going to just give up the fight.

Once we were safe behind closed doors in the office, I'd told Sorin and Alex everything I'd seen, heard and smell. I wanted so badly for it to be worth something, for me to not be re-victimizing this girl with nothing to show for it. They'd listened to me recount the memory twice and stayed silent. They were just as frustrated as I was. Since they hadn't seen it, they'd tried to get more details out of me but there was no more to give. I could only see what Sheena's brain was willing to give up. It must be how Sheena felt, wanting to be able to say the one magic thing that would solve the mystery but not knowing anything more.

"Maybe this man is our vampire," Alex said.

"Possibly," Sorin jumped in. "He is clearly someone that Sheena is afraid to remember. But, other than a living room, we know nothing about him."

"So, all this time trying to find Bobby was a waste," Alex was sounding angry and defeated.

"Not true," I said. "If we find Bobby, he can tell us who that man was. Even if Bobby's human, he's not much older than you."

"And, if he's dead?" Alex asked.

"Then we find one of the other friends in the group." I looked at both men. "Bobby is still the key. When we know the school and who he is, the rest will come out."

"Tell me about the man's voice," Sorin said. "Any accent that helps with his identity? Or could you tell age?"

I sat down, closing my eyes and replaying the voice in my head. "He was a man, not a teen or even young adult. I didn't hear any accent that I could recognize." I opened my eyes. "He was giving this speech, like he was trying to inspire these kids but under it all, he sounded cold. I don't know how to describe it. And the way everyone was looking at him, you would have thought it was a movie star or the smartest man on Earth. I imagine it's what a cult leader is like."

Shaking my head, I laid back against the couch. "This is so futile. We're looking for a needle in the biggest haystack there is. We don't know an exact place or timeline or anything. Just a normal man in some normal woods in some time in America."

"This changes nothing," Alex added. "We keep looking for Bobby. When we find him, we make him tell us everything. If the man is the one who hurt her, then we find him and make him pay. End of story."

A small rap at the door got our attention. "Come in," Sorin said.

Jeremy poked his head in. "How did it go?" he asked.

"Nothing new," I answered. "It was a bust."

He nodded but seemed as disappointed as the rest of us. "Well, if she's up to it, I was going to start teaching Sheena how to use the schedule and Rhys was going to teach her email. We both need a break."

"Anything new on your end?" I inquired but knew he would have told us immediately if they'd found something.

"No," he verified. "It's a lot to look at."

Sorin crossed to him and patted his back. "Thank you, Jeremy. Sheena is downstairs with Tamela. I'm sure she'd love to start her training. Please call me if you need anything." He retrieved a big book from the desk and handed it to Jeremy. I assumed it was the schedule.

"Oh," Jeremy said as he was leaving the office. "There is a woman here. Edwin is carrying her bags to her room. He said you were expecting her."

"Yes," Sorin said.

"Do you need me to help you with anything?" he asked.

Sorin shook his head. "No, thank you. This is private business. Please focus on Sheena the rest of the night. I will retrieve my guest."

When Jeremy was gone, Sorin faced Alex and I. He closed the distance between us and reached out his hands. Alex and I each took one. "I ask you both to trust me. Things may change this evening but I assure you that I will help you adjust."

"Sorin," I said shakily. "What does that mean?"

He stepped in to rest his forehead on mine. "Please, *regina mea.* Trust me for a few more moments and then I will answer all. I would never knowingly put you in danger."

I hated how cryptic he was being but I had to believe he was doing the right thing. I shook my head and the three of us walked out of the office and down the stairs side by side to face whatever came together.

51

Akila was in the foyer as we came down the stairs. She was exactly as I'd remembered – small. Her brown hair still had those sharp perfect bangs and tight bob. The color was a sharp contrast to the white dress she wore. When I'd met her, she'd been in the middle of a party, surrounded by vamps and we'd only spoken for a few minutes. My turning had only been a couple weeks prior to that meeting so I'd been overwhelmed easily. Looking back, I don't know why I hadn't felt her power. But, I did tonight.

Her power pushed at my chest like people pushing through a crowded room. It made it hard to breath. Having that kind of energy is such a tiny package made it even more impressive.

We reached the bottom and she looked up at the two men next to me. Sorin bowed deeply and kissed her hand. Alex looked awkwardly at me and decided to just do what he'd always do – extend his hand for a handshake. She looked at it and laughed, grabbing his hand and pumping it up and down. When she let go, his eyes were wide. I could only imagine how strong her grip felt to a mortal man. Alex may be used to vampires at this point but he had no idea the one in front of him was somewhere around 2,000 years old.

She locked her brown eyes onto mine and the smile was genuine. "Katherine, I am so happy to see you again." I bent down to hug her and she gave me one of those squeezes you save for your best girlfriends.

"We have much to discuss but I do hope you will tell me some of your medical stories." She sounded like a kid in a candy store. I'd forgotten that she'd been a healer in her time and loved the idea of hearing about modern medicine from an actual nurse.

"Of course," I said, then turned to Alex. "You know, he's a doctor."

Her eyes sparkled and she clapped her hands together. "You are?"

"I am," he answered.

Before she could start asking us questions, Sorin laid his hand on her shoulder. "Lady Akila, I cannot thank you enough for coming on such short notice. You may stay as long as you like. At the risk of being rude, I would like to insist that we postpone the talk of medicine so we may address my concerns. May we move to my office before I continue? I trust we will not be heard there."

"Of course, Lord Sorin." She nodded solemnly. "I must admit, for you to call me directly so close to dawn and sound so concerned – I was intrigued. May Amun join us?"

There was no need to ask who that was when a man came to join us. I don't know where he came from; he was just suddenly there. I saw his eyes first, which meant we shared the same height. I'd like to tell you his eyes were brown but they were too dark for that label. The irises were so dark, I couldn't tell when they ended and the pupils started. My initial thought was that he was tanned but it was the kind of brown that can only be natural. His hair was also brown and you'd think that all that brown would make him plain but it did the opposite. He was striking. The sharp nose, cheekbones and jaw line told me he was not from any European country.

"Of course," Sorin's voice pulled my gaze away from the newest addition from our group. "If you assure me that he can be trusted."

"He can," she said and it appeared to be good enough for Sorin. He gestured up the stairs. "Katherine, would you lead the way?"

I did and tried to ignore the dancing of power at my back. I was, by far, the youngest vamp in the bunch and was fighting to not be overwhelmed. I wondered if Alex could feel the power that came off of us.

Once in the office, I sat on the couch. Sorin and Alex joined on each side of me. Akila took a merlot chair and the man she'd called Amun stood behind her just off to the side. The two of them looked like a display in the ancient Egyptian wing of the museum. The only thing ruining the image was the modern clothes they wore - her a sheath dress and he in jeans and a white t-shirt. Only the sandals they both wore hinted to a different time.

She started the conversation. "Okay, Lord Sorin. You have my audience and my interest. What may I do for you?"

He lay a hand on my thigh. Instinctually, I laid mine on his – a united front.

He took a breath and let it out. "Katherine, as you know, is my chosen mate. She became vampire only six months ago and the one before her was made only 200 years ago. I know him well and his is as any other vampire." He gave a me a gentle squeeze and his voice drifted through my brain. *I love you.* "Yet, Katherine is extraordinary. As of yesterday, she has shown a dozen powers and her magic grows stronger each day."

Akila's stoicism dropped and her gaze shot to mine. The confusion, shock and disbelief were clear; she couldn't believe what she'd heard but knew Sorin wouldn't lie. He kept talking while she stared at me. "You must know how important it is that this does not leave this room"

"It cannot be," Akila whispered. "It is not possible."

"There is more," Sorin said.

Akila looked back at him. "What else?"

He stood, crossing to stand on the other side of Akila's chair, facing us. The next part he directed at Alex and I. "Please Alex, tell Akila what you have told me of your feelings for Katherine."

I didn't need to use my empathy to know how uncomfortable this made Alex. He cleared his throat. "I want to be with her all the time. Every day, the feelings are stronger. I love her and cannot imagine being without her in my life."

Sorin didn't let anything cross his face. "And when did this happen? When did it go from friendship to love?"

"It wasn't even friendship at first," Alex said bluntly. "She was just someone at the same hospital as me. I could've passed her on the street and not known she was the same nurse from work. After she turned, it was like I'd never really seen her. She was beautiful and interesting and exciting. Then the barn-"

Sorin interrupted. "Tell Lady Akila what happened in the barn."

Alex hesitated and I laid my hand on the hand that rest on the couch between us. He spoke, "I was dying. She healed me."

Akila stared at me like she was trying to understand a thing in front of her that she'd never seen before.

Alex continued. "After she healed me, I started to see her differently. She was my friend, then my best friend and then it was more."

Sorin looked at me. "Katherine, how do you feel and when did it happen?"

I didn't need to clear my throat. I knew this was coming and was prepared. "When I met him, I thought he was egotistical and rude. The other nurses were obsessed with him but I hated when he came onto our unit." I felt his hand twitch under mine. "After I turned, he was different. He was nice and I wanted to know more about him. When I saw him in the barn, heard his heart dying, I would have done anything to save him. It felt like – as he left the Earth, part of me was leaving too. After I healed him, I started to think of him more and more. He was my friend, then my best friend and then more."

Akila leaned forward. "How did you heal him?"

It was a good question but I didn't expect it and I didn't know how to put it into words. I looked to Sorin and he nodded. "May I send it to your thoughts?" I asked Akila.

Her eyebrows arched curiously and she nodded. I drew up the memory. The smell of the hay and blood and fire mixed in the air. Sorin was behind me on the floor, his arms wrapped around mine. He rested his lips onto the back of my neck to join our powers. His magic slid through my low back and into my core to meet my own power. I thrust it into Alex, willing his body to rebuild and heal. He gasped in my memory as I shot the images to Akila.

I felt it hit her the same time she reacted. She stood, slowly stepping towards me. "I thought these days were behind us" she exclaimed. "That none like you would ever exist again." She reached me and stood in front of me. Her delicate stature meant that even with her standing and me sitting, her eyes were not much higher than mine. Laying a hand on each side of my face, her touch was so light. I'd felt her strength so I knew she was being extra gentle. The awe in her eyes confused me.

"What do you mean?" I asked.

"You are something that I thought was long extinct." She urged me to stand and I did. "You, Katherine, are a maiden of Isis."

52

"What is a maiden of Isis?" I asked. "What does that mean?"

Sorin crossed to us and looked down at Akila. "So, it is what I feared? How can this be?"

She took her gaze from me to him. "I do not know, Sorin. I cannot believe it myself but there is no other explanation. I would not have thought it true if it hadn't been in front of me. You say she has a dozen powers in six months?"

"Whoa," I interrupted. "Time out. I need an explanation and fast. What is a maiden of Isis and why did you fear that I was one?"

Akila sat on the couch and pulled me down to sit. I was now between her and a very silent Alex. She shook her head as she spoke. "A maiden of Isis is what we called them. They have different names in different countries. But it is always women. They were not recognized until they became vampire but they must have always had it inside of them."

"Had what?" I asked, getting very annoyed.

"Power," she answered. "Great power. Unlike others of our kind, they would not have one or two vampiric abilities but 10 or 20. They were worshipped like Goddesses and protected the people in their village. There were tales of them in Egypt, Africa, China... and as people and nations spread and grew, the maidens would arise."

"So why did you think they were extinct?" I questioned.

"There was a time when each great nation had maidens to protect them. Humans worshipped them and vampires came to them for help. But, as long as man walks the Earth, evil and hatred and fear of what they do not understand will exist. Men started to fear these powerful women, believing that no woman should be in a place of authority. Much like your witch trials, there was a call to wipe out these magical maidens. One by one they were hunted down and destroyed. While they are harder to kill than other vampires, they can be killed. Humans were helped by vampires who envied the powerful maidens."

"Why would you think I'm one of these?" I wanted to know and still didn't believe what she was saying.

"When a maiden was turned, she would begin to show power quickly. She gained and mastered powers faster than any other of us." She looked to Sorin and he nodded that this was true of me. "She was more immune to the sun than the rest of us."

She stared at me, waiting for a response. I had been in the sun for almost an hour when I drove to save my daughters. It burned my chest but that was all. Sorin had believed I would die in the sun but I hadn't. I nodded, "Yes."

She smiled like she'd already know I'd agree. "And, lastly." She looked across me to Alex. "When a maiden is called into her power, a protector is also brought forth. He is someone close to her, someone whose life is connected to the maiden's. As she grows stronger, his connection to her grows stronger. We called them warriors of Seth. Think of it like the knights of the roundtable."

Alex stood. "Hold on," he shoved his hands in his pockets and paced. "This is crazy. I'm not a warrior and Kate is not a goddess."

Sorin took a few steps back to allow Alex some space. We could all see that the human was freaked out.

Akila stayed calm. "Doctor, think about it. All the medicine you practice today was considered magic when I was young. What you do each day takes faith, that you know what is right and real. In my time they would have called you mad. But we know now that it is science." Alex stopped his pacing and listened to her talk. "If you told other medical professionals about vampires, they would not believe you, throw you out of the hospital. But you know it to be true. Very few believe in spirits, werewolves and witches yet we know they are real."

"What does it mean for Alex?" I was trying to refocus the conversation while I could still think straight. "To be this chosen warrior? I don't want him to get hurt trying to protect me."

Amun stepped out from behind the chair. He'd been so quiet and still that I'd forgotten he was there. "I will train him."

I was too shocked to speak. I looked back and forth between Amun and Akila, trying to grasp the meaning. Akila spoke and answered what I was too afraid to ask.

"I am the last of the maidens," she explained. "And, Amun is my warrior. He was born the same year I was and called upon when my powers began to arise."

I had so many questions, I had to choose one first. "How are the warriors and maidens chosen? Why me? Why him?"

Akila laughed and it filled me with warmth. "We don't know how they are chosen and since you and I are the only two in the world, I cannot ask. As for why you two, I do not know that either."

Amun stood behind Akila and laid his hands on her shoulders. "Before she was made vampire, I knew her from our village. I saw her but did not speak to her much. Our families did not interact and I was arranged to marry another. Then, one night I saw her by the water. I was going to bathe and she was there, staring out at the moon. It was like I had never seen her until that moment. She was the most beautiful thing I'd ever witnessed. I did not approach her, just watched her until it was close to dawn and she walked away."

Akila patted one of his hands. "I knew he was there. I could smell him. But he was not threatening me and I did not want to reveal that I was no longer human."

Amun continued. "A week later a plague hit our people. I was the last in my family to contract it so, by the time they were all dead, I was ready to go too. As I lay in my bed, I saw her come to my window. The fever made it hard for me to understand what was happening. All I know is that I arose the next day, free from disease and filled with the need to be with her. We have not been apart since."

"Wait," I interrupted. "You said protectors are called from those you are connected with. You barely knew him."

"Yes," she answered. "But, to heal you must send part of your life force into them. When you healed Alex, as when I healed Amun, you became connected. And, since you are a maiden of Isis with no protector – you called forth your warrior of Seth."

Those words kicked me in the chest. I had done this to Alex. I had pulled him into something magical and now he was at risk.

Since Alex had stopped his pacing, Sorin returned to us. "Katherine, I can already feel you blaming yourself. It is not your fault."

"But," I faced Sorin. "He's human. He can't be put in danger to protect me. I won't allow it."

I felt Alex's anger before I heard it. "Hey," he snapped. "Don't talk about me like I'm not here and don't have a say in this. I don't care what she says or about whatever this magic is. I'd do anything to keep you from danger and that has nothing to do with being called or whatever." He turned to Amun. "You said you'd train me. What does that mean?"

"As a warrior you have great strength but great responsibility." Amun waved towards me. "She is to be protected. She can do amazing things for this world and that makes her a target. Other vampires will want to have her or destroy her."

"I have Sorin," I said. "He can protect me. How can I undo this thing? I don't want Alex in the middle of this."

Alex turned to face me and I saw how truly upset he was. "You don't choose for me, Kate. I want to hear what this all means and then we decide together."

He was right. I couldn't speak for him but I wasn't happy about it.

Akila took my hand and pulled me to the other side of the room, away from the men. We both knew they could hear us but I think she saw that I needed to breath. "Kate," she sounded like a mother trying to calm a child. "I know you are frightened. But I need you to understand something. You do not realize how powerful you may become and what it means for your safety. The gods and goddesses have seen fit to give you these powers and they know you must have a protector. Alex is chosen, like you. Sorin is very strong but he is vampire. Vampires cannot be warriors of Seth."

I was confused. "But, Amun?"

"He is human," she answered. "Once being called, a warrior is a mortal man who will live as long as you do."

"What?" I questioned.

"Alex can protect you. He can be in the sun, does not need to drink blood and can enter any building uninvited. He will become stronger than any human. He will never suffer disease and will not age." She patted my hand. "Please think about this. With Sorin and Alex by your side, you stand a very good chance of surviving anything. There must be a reason that you were made a maiden after a millennia of none being called forth."

I turned to look at the two men in my life. Alex was listening intently at Amun. Sorin was resting his hand on Alex's back in a show of comradery. How could this be happening? How could I be some chosen maiden of legend and these two powerful men be my protectors? Six months ago, I was just some nurse and mom, trying to figure out how to keep my checking balance from dropping into the negative. Now, I was the star of some insane movie. I half-expected Brendan Frasier to show up with a torch in his hand and insist we needed to run while music swelled dramatically.

Sadly, this was my life. No Hollywood exec had written this and I had to figure out what to do next.

53

Amun, Akila and Alex had left to give me some time and air. Alex wanted to talk to them about the reality of this new revelation before he, Sorin and I figured out what it all meant. Having them out of the room meant I could spend a few moments truly freaking out.

Sorin sat on the couch with me in his lap and just held me. I have no idea how long we stayed like that. I focused on counting his inhales and exhales while everything I'd just heard replayed in my head.

Alex could possibly live forever. But he'd have to be my guardian and I didn't understand yet what that totally meant. Would he eventually sacrifice his existence for me? Die to keep me alive?

"What are you thinking?" Sorin broke the silence and started the conversation that I knew we needed to have before Alex was back.

"What does this mean?" I asked into his chest.

"It means," he took a deep breath and let it out. "It means that you are going to be very powerful. You will do such good for this world and our kind." He ran his fingers through my hair over and over in a gesture that he knew would calm me. "It means that, if the wrong people find out, you will be in danger."

"And, I put you and Alex and everyone else I love in danger."

He stopped, grabbed my arms and pulled me away from his chest so I could see him. "Katherine," he searched my face. "Do you think any of us would ever let you run from us? To go through this alone?"

"I don't want you to have to protect me from evil mobs. I don't want Alex to have to stand between me and death all the time. Me being around you all means you're all at risk." The old Kate would be crying but I was out of tears and on a mission. "You need to get away from me, Sorin. Go back to the life you knew before me. I've already had two people try and kill me. It won't be long before another one comes along and we have no idea who or when."

He stood suddenly, my head falling to the couch. "Jesus, Katherine," he roared. "Why do we keep having this conversation?" He turned to look down at me. "I would never leave you. I would rather die. And," he pointed at the door to the hallway. "That man downstairs is ready to die for you, too."

I stood, squaring off with him. I didn't care if he was taller or bigger or older. I wasn't taking this without a fight. "I don't want that. Don't you hear me. I don't want anyone laying down their lives or dying for me."

"Too bad," he responded, not backing away from my anger. "Because this is happening. You and I are bonded. Alex and you are connected. We will be by your side until you die and then both of us go with you."

I stepped back. "What do you mean?"

He gulped and clenched his teeth. His jaw muscle flared with the stress. I could see him thinking about holding back.

I reversed my step away, closing the distance and slamming my palms against his chest. "Tell me, Sorin. What does that mean?"

He grabbed my wrists and looked down into my eyes. The storm clouds raging in his irises. It was the first time I'd seen them triggered by anything but lust. "That is part of it, Katherine. Alex will be strong and fast. He will live as long as you do. But you are tied. If you die, he dies. And if you die, I will not exist without you."

"No," I broke free from his grasp and turned from him. "Absolutely not."

Sorin wouldn't let me retreat. Instead, he grabbed my waist and pulled me back, turning me to face him. "Listen to me," he said while I struggled. "Katherine, stop and think. If he is not your protector then he dies in forty years. That's if he is not victim to an accident or cancer or any number of things." I heard the words and the horror of the thought took the fight out of me. "This way, he may live for centuries, thousands of years even. But he has none of our weaknesses."

I was still screaming but now it was out of despair and not rage. "Why him? Why me?"

He shook his head and the anger was leaving his voice too. "I don't know."

I reached my hands up to lay on his cheeks. He continued to hold my wrists but was no longer trying to restrain me, only hold me. "What does this mean for us?"

"Why won't you stop questioning me? My love for you?" His answer startled me. "Why don't you believe that no matter what is thrown at us, I will never stop loving you?" He broke free from my grasp, dropping my wrists and taking several steps back. "What do I have to say or do for you to just accept it?"

It was rare to see him this unglued. He was always so controlled and composed. I didn't know how to answer his question. "I'm scared. I'm terrified of losing it all," I yelled. "I've never been happier and I just keep waiting for it to all be taken away."

"Then, let us protect your existence. Let us fight to keep you from losing it all." He was stock still, speaking with command in his words. "Let your mate and your warrior battle by your side. Let us do what we are called to do: love you and protect you."

Those words hit me in core.

He continued. "Tell me what you truly want and it is yours."

"Fine," I screamed and felt all my walls come tumbling down. Whether it was emotional exhaustion, the power of the experience or his invitation for the truth — I stepped into him and said exactly what I wanted. "I want Rhys, Tamela and Jeremy as our army. I want Alex as my warrior." I took a breath and laid my hand flat against his chest. "I want you as my King."

"Then you shall have it."

54

The night was moving fast and we didn't have much time. I still needed to touch base with Rhys, he deserved to know what was going on. And, I had to talk to Alex. Looking at the clock, I worried I wouldn't have enough time. It was time to stop trying to do everything alone and lean on my people. It was really hard for me but better now than never.

"Sorin?" I asked. "Will you go find Rhys and give him a synopsis of what we've found out tonight? I need to find Alex. Then we can all meet up before dawn."

"Of course," he smiled. I think he was happy to be asked to help me. A brief kiss was all we needed to know we were back on the same page. Then we went our separate ways.

Akila, Amun and Alex were in the solarium. When I walked in, all three turned to me. Alex was sitting at the bar, with what looked suspiciously like liquor. I didn't know that there was alcohol in the manor and had never seen Alex drink. But I think getting dumped, finding your long-lost sister and hearing you were called by a goddess to protect a woman you barely knew half a year ago all in one week was a damn good reason to drink.

"We will give you some privacy," Amun said. "Please find us if you have any questions. We will stay a few days to make sure you are okay. And, we would like you to come to New York when you're ready for some training." He bowed and took Akila's hand. They walked out of the room to let us handle what we'd just discovered.

Alex finished his drink with one gulp and set the glass down. I went behind the bar and started to search cabinets. I found blood in the refrigerator, a rock glass and a crystal decanter of amber liquid that smelled exactly like what Alex was drinking. I poured his first before pouring mine. Then I held up my glass for the weirdest toast in history. "To being mystically connected forever."

His eyebrows arched and I thought he was going to chastise me for poor taste. Instead, he laughed, picked up his glass, clinked it against mine and said "To living forever."

Once we'd taking our sips, I decided to not let awkward silence fill the space. "So, you want this?"

He took a moment to ensure I saw how serious he was. "Yes." That was it. One word. He wanted it and that was that.

"No discussion?" I pushed back.

"No" he said. Another one-word answer.

I gave him a quick nod and finished my blood. Wiping my mouth with my hand, I slammed the glass onto the bar. "Well, that's it then. You stay young and pretty for as long as I remain breathing."

It was his turn to down his drink and slam the glass. "Not exactly," he added. "There's one more step."

"Explain, doc."

"Seems that the connection began when you turned. I was called into my destiny when you healed me. But I don't get the strength and immortality until-" he stopped, waving his hand to indicate he wanted the bottle. I pulled it up and held it just out of reach. When he grabbed for it, I pulled it back.

"Talk," I cocked my head.

"I have to drink your blood." Then he stood, reached and grabbed the decanter while I was still processing what he said. He was pouring a generous amount into his glass when I understood exactly what had just come out of his mouth.

"Excuse me?" I chimed.

He took a gulp and let out a sigh. "Gotta drink your blood to become full warrior." Then he pounded one closed fist against his chest like Tarzan.

"Nope. Not gonna happen. That'll turn you into a vampire." I wasn't actually sure that was true. I knew I'd drank Rhys' blood and turned but never fully asked the whole process.

"Wrong," he pointed a finger at me. "Because I've been called. I cannot become a vampire. So, I got two options right now. Drink your blood, complete the process and live forever." I opened my mouth to interrupt but he corrected himself. "Or as long as you live."

"Or?" I asked.

"Or, option 2." He finished what was in his glass. "I can continue to love you, be driven to protect you but die like any other human the first time I fight for you. I can't become a vampire. That option is off the table for good now."

"Is that what you wanted?" I couldn't believe it. He'd told me after the barn that he'd never want to be one of us. Rhys and I had thought about it when he was dying. When I told him we'd decided not to, he'd thanked me for not doing it.

"I've been thinking about it," he shrugged. "Doesn't matter now though."

"But you told me you didn't -"

He held up a finger to stop me. "That was before. Before the two most important people in my life were vampires." He stood. "Think about it, Kate. I'm surrounded by vampires and werewolves a lot more now. I got my ass kicked when Will got me – almost died. And that was before we were what we are to each other now. He just took me because I worked with you and was a convenient patsy. Imagine now,

now that you love me. And, Sheena -" he turned and punched the wall. "I never could have protected her – saved her. Even if I'd known she was so close, I never could've gotten her out. I'm too weak." He slammed both palms against the wall and used them to hold his weight, dropping his head low.

I smelled the blood and knew he'd busted open a knuckle or two. They'd already been torn up from his meltdown in the driveway. I couldn't imagine how much pain he was in.

I went to him, wrapping my arms under his and around his waist. Resting my cheek against this back, I spoke to the room. "I understand." His heart slammed against my face when he turned and wrapped his arms around me.

"You do?" he spoke into my hair.

I nodded. "I do. When I knew my daughters were in danger, when I saw them on the ground, when Evelyn held one up like a rag doll – I felt helpless. If Diana hadn't been there to help and I hadn't been a vampire-" I didn't want to finish the thought.

He stepped back so he could look down at me. "You'll do it? Give me your blood?"

"Can we talk to Sorin first?" I asked.

"I'm here," Sorin said from the doorway.

"Me too," it was Rhys.

Turning to see the men in the entrance to the room, I was happy to see them. I went to Rhys first, letting him pull me in for a hug. "You okay, Katie?"

I laughed. "I mean, could anyone be okay with all this going on?"

I felt him nod. "Good point, I'll rephrase. Are you as okay as you could be?"

"Yep."

I met Sorin's eyes. "He has to drink my blood to get our strength and immortality. According to Amun and Akila, he can't turn. Does that sound right?"

Sorin shook his head. "To be honest, I would not know. What I know of maidens and warriors is what I've heard in passing over the years. I always believed it to be legend until I met Akila and Amun. The first time I was near them, I felt their power. It took years for her to trust enough to tell me the truth. Only they would know for sure."

"Will it hurt?" Alex asked.

We all looked at each other but none of us knew. "I don't know Alex," I said. "The turning did but I don't know if it'll be the same for you."

He let out a sigh. "Well, doesn't matter. I'm doing it no matter what."

"When?" I asked.

Looking at his watch, he bit his lower lip. "Now," he said. "I'm buzzed and full of courage and we have an hour and a half til dawn."

55

We'd agreed that only the four of us needed to be a part of this. We didn't know what it would be like for Alex to complete his transition into a warrior of Seth. Having Sheena watch was a stupid idea. The poor girl had been through enough. Jeremy needed to stay with Sheena and Tamela was helping our guests settle into their room. We would tell each of them in our own time when we completely understood what Alex's new existence would be like.

Plus, I hate to say it but I didn't want to share any of this new information with anyone outside this tight circle yet. It's not that I didn't trust them but more that I wasn't ready to have them look at me like a freak. And, we all knew that being close to me put everyone at risk.

So, for now, it was very secret and exclusive club.

There was no better place to do this than the grove. It had inadvertently become the most important spot to us. It has witnessed some of our biggest moments and would continue to.

Alex sat on the bench with Sorin and Rhys on each side. I knelt on the ground in front of him, looking up at his eyes. At that moment, they were the familiar Caribbean blue I'd faced the night he'd strolled onto my unit and introduced himself as the "new hem-onc physician." I'd rolled my eyes at his back and wondered if anyone had ever been as important as he acted like he was.

All these years later, he'd become one of the most important people in my world and I was about to make him immortal.

"Ready?" I whispered.

"Ready," he whispered back.

Looking to Sorin for reassurance, I saw him nod slightly and put his arm around Alex's shoulder. Rhys matched Sorin's gesture and I knew the two men were ready to help Alex through whatever may happen.

Calling out my fangs, I felt them snap and asked myself again if this was a bad idea. Gazing into those blue eyes, I knew this was his choice and I had to honor it. What if Rhys had hesitated, worried about the long term and missed the window to turn me? He'd brought me over and saved me from my grave. As I drew my wrist over the tip of my fang, I felt no pain. It was only the smell of my blood that told me I'd opened a vein. I had only a minute before it would start to heal. Holding it up to Alex, he took my arm in his hands. When I rose to my knees and brought the blood to his lips, he kept his eyes on mine.

Only Sorin had ever drunk my blood and it was in moments of passion. I'd wondered if it had felt the same when not done for bonding but didn't need to wait long for the answer. Each deep pull on my vein brought a wave through me. It wasn't sexual with Alex. Instead, it was pulling power up from my center. Magic grew in my stomach, dancing up and out of my torso to my wrist. I commanded the power into Alex, willed it to enter his mouth along with my blood. From around his mouth, at first, I saw the light start to trickle out. Sliding up and around his head, the power that didn't make it into his throat found its way into his ears. On this night, my magic was purple - a mix of mine and Sorin's. It was power that we had brought together in our moments of bonding and now lived inside of me.

Suddenly, Alex pulled away from me and gasped for air. His body was thrown back against the bench in a violent spasm. I caught him in my arms as he rocketed forward. The three of us stopped him from being slammed into the ground with the force of his contractions. Rhys and Sorin followed him down as I pulled the weight of his body into my chest. Seamlessly, they adjusted so Rhys could hold his seizing legs and Sorin could be behind my back, allowing me to lean into him as the human in my embrace shook.

What started as a gasp had turned into a scream. Alex's eyes rolled back into his head and I knew we'd made a huge mistake. I thought about asking Rhys to go get Amun but the words died in my throat when Alex went limp. If Alex had just died there was nothing anyone could do. The choice had been made and there was no rewind button.

I felt for his pulse and found nothing.

He wasn't breathing and his heart was not beating.

"Sorin," I yelled. "He's not breathing." I let the body roll to the ground and pounded on his chest. "Alex, don't be dead. Please, wake up. Please." I slapped him and looked for anything – a single twitch.

"Rhys," I maneuvered, preparing to do CPR. "We have to do something." Laying my palms against Alex's sternum, I was thrown back into Sorin when Alex sat up.

I scrambled to him, throwing my arms around him. "Oh God, Alex. You were dead." That's when I felt his heart slamming against my chest. I pulled back. "Your heart. It's beating again."

He wildly looked around and laid his hand on his sternum, exactly where mine had just been. After what felt like minutes, he laughed. "It's beating. I have a heartbeat."

"Does that mean it didn't work?" I asked the group.

It was Alex that answered. "Amun said I'd still be human. I'm a strong human who can't die but still human. So, heartbeat."

We were all in disbelief. I couldn't speak for Rhys or Sorin but I knew I was not fully convinced of this whole thing until just that moment. "How do you feel?" I asked.

He thought about it. "The same actually." He did a full body stretch and shook himself out. "I mean it was painful and then I woke up on the ground. Nothing Earth-shattering."

Looking at Sorin and then Rhys I asked, "Is there some way to test it?"

Sorin shrugged. "Well, I don't recommend we try to kill him just to see if we can. Perhaps, we test his strength."

"Good idea," Alex exclaimed, jumping to his feet.

I didn't have the faintest idea what he had in mind as I watched him cross to the tree line. A crack filled the air and Alex had a tree branch in his hand that was easily a foot across at its base. He walked back to us with it in his hands and pride on his face. Then he turned and threw it into the woods as easily as he'd throw a football.

Sorin didn't look amused. "I am thrilled for you Alex but let's not kill any more trees, shall we?"

"So, what now?" Rhys asked the group.

Sorin took the lead. "We keep this to ourselves and rest. Tomorrow, Alex trains with Amun. We will continue to work on Sheena's mystery. We mustn't lose sight of that or let the others know that anything has changed."

Just as though Sorin had conjured her, I smelled orchids and lavender on the wind and heard Sheena call out her brother's name. He looked to me and I nodded. Winking, he ran off to find his sister and enjoy his new lease on life.

Rhys waited until he was gone to talk to us. "I thought he'd died."

"Me too," I agreed. "Did he? I mean did he die like we do when we turn?"

Sorin answered. "None of us knows. But I don't think it matters. He's here and we have had enough excitement for one evening. Let's enjoy this blessing and not question our luck."

"I second that," Rhys said. "I'm heading in. Gotta call Diana before bed-" he finished before Sorin could interject "- and not tell her anything about this." He dashed off to make the call.

"Are you okay?" Sorin asked once we were alone. "How do you feel about all this now?"

"I still need to process." I wrapped my arm around his waist and let him lead me towards the house.

But, let's be honest – processing was not my strong suit. I was more of the "shove it down and hope it doesn't come back" type. And, there was no manual for how to deal with being told you're a thing of legend and then turning your best friend into your eternal bodyguard. Plus, who could I talk to about it? As much as I loved Sorin and Rhys and knew that they'd both been makers – neither of them had turned a human into an immortal yet non-vampire warrior. We didn't fully understand what Alex really was or what he and I meant to each other now. We'd trusted Amun and Akila with so much. Sadly, we'd been taught a couple hard lessons about not trusting the wrong people. I threw a desperate, silent plea into the universe that we hadn't just made a huge mistake.

Not that it mattered. If we had screwed up or Alex regretted it, it was too late to turn back.

56

When I'd laid down, I was prepared for fitful tossing and turning while my brain replayed the latest episode of my very weird life but I was pleasantly surprised to snap awake the next evening. I must have gone right to sleep the second Sorin's arms were around me. It's a rare night where we don't talk before calling it a night. I didn't know if Sorin had gone right to sleep too or waited to drift off once I was out. His empty side of the bed meant I couldn't ask either.

A hot shower and new outfit improved my already good mood but I did find it strange that I hadn't run into anyone since awaking. The house was practically full so I was starting to wonder if I'd missed a party invite or something when I found Tamela in the kitchen. She was scribbling away on something that looked a lot like a journal but was instantly at alert when I walked in.

"Where is everyone?" I asked.

"Jeremy, Rhys and Sheena are in the office. Sorin and Alex are with the lady and her guard." She was sounding so business-like, like a soldier reporting to an officer. I glanced at the journal and wondered if whatever she was writing was causing the coldness.

"You okay?" I asked.

"Yes," she responded in that same tone.

A polite person would have taken the hint and left her alone but I wasn't polite and didn't give up easily. Some may even call me stubborn.

I pulled a stool closer to hers and sat down, making it clear I wasn't surrendering. "Don't lie. It's a waste of energy. What's up?"

She huffed and shook her head. "Nothing. Really. I'm fine."

I nodded and pat her back a few times for emphasis. "Okay, I'll just sit here with you then and whenever you're ready, I'll just listen." With my elbows on the island in front of us, I rested my chin on my hands and prepared for a sit in. Tamela was highly trained and could likely outlast me but I was going to give it my darndest.

She endured for roughly a minute.

Slamming her hands on the island, she stood and began to pace like a wildcat in a cage. The energy that crawled off of her tickled across my skin like electricity, making me itchy. I fought the urge to jump up and run from the sensation but was determined to sit still and listen like I had promised.

"I'm pissed, Kate." I'd never seen her be so uncontrolled. Tamela's voice had an edge to it, like her words were looking to slice someone open.

I was really glad that power wasn't directed at me.

"She was so young, so vulnerable." Her fists were clenched at her side while she repeated the march up and down the kitchen. "He turned her and then locked her up, abused her, starved her, tortured her, used her and for what? What did he get out of it?"

I wasn't sure if the question was rhetorical or if she wanted an answer but I stayed silent. First off, I said I would and secondly, I didn't have an answer.

She answered it herself. "Power, that's what. Men like him do it to control and own something they know they have no right to own. They do it to know that they hold your life in their hands. They like the fear in your eyes. They like to hear you beg for their mercy." She paused and spoke to the wall. "But, most of all, they like when they've broken you and you comply."

She whirled and stalked to me. It was an impressive sight and I had the urge to back up. Thankfully, I knew she'd wasn't angry with me, she was angry with a faceless man. She stopped in front of me and I had to look up to meet her eyes. "I want to hurt him."

"I know," I whispered. "I do too."

She shook her head in an attempt to wipe something away, then dropped heavily back down to the stool. "It's not about the memories that I have in that basement, you know? That's not the hard part for me." She took a breath and I waited for the rest. "It's that I didn't get to be the one to kill him." She slowly turned to face me with worry in her eyes. I think she wanted me to be revolted by what she said and was surprised to see agreement. "No matter how strong I get, I'll never be able to go back and make him pay."

"Sorin did," I without thinking.

"I know," she answered. "And, I'm forever grateful but I wished I'd been me."

"I get that," I assured her.

"With Sheena-" she cut herself off, afraid to say the words out loud. I froze, afraid that any movement or sound would take away her courage to speak. "-with Sheena, I have this second chance." The rest was rushed like she wanted to get it out quickly. "I don't want her to have gone through the same thing, that's not what I'm saying. But, she did. And, we've found each other and now I can be the one. I can find him and make him pay. I can do for her what Sorin did for me and maybe-" she growled in frustration. "Maybe if I kill this man, I can put it all behind me for good."

She stopped suddenly – talking, breathing, moving. Like some magician hand snapped their fingers, she just shut down and let the silence fill the air. I think she was waiting to see what I would say. I was grateful that she'd been so raw with me while being heartbroken for the tiny, young Tamela locked in a basement. My soul ached for all the young girls that had been victimized by a monster who just needed to be in complete control over something so vulnerable.

"I think," I started and was a little startled by my own voice in the air. "I think that we all want to find him and make him pay." She opened her mouth to interrupt so I held up my hand to stop her. "But," I continued. "I think you of all people should get the chance. However, T, you know we can't control when or where or who or even if this happens."

She slammed her hands on the island again. "I know. This is why I'm so angry. I know it may never come to pass and I may have to live with that." She looked at me and I saw what I thought may be the beginning of a tear in her eyes. She blinked hard and they were gone. "How would we tell Sheena that we couldn't catch him? Couldn't make him pay?"

As awful as it was, she was just saying what we'd all been thinking. Every one of us knew that there was a possibility that her captor would never be caught. It was a probability that he was long gone. I mean once he'd realized she gotten free he must have panicked and gone on the run, right?

"How did she get free?" I said with a sudden realization.

"What?" Tamela asked.

I jumped up. "Sheena! How did she get free? I mean, I saw her chained up and there was no way that she'd broken that chain. She was too weak and that was in the beginning. He had her for years." Now I was pacing but with excitement, not frustration. "We've been taking her back to the start. Maybe we need to go to the end, take her to the night she got free."

Tamela was suddenly on the same train of thought as me and on her feet to grab my hand. She was buzzing with the promise of a break through. "Yes. If she could remember something so recent, we may see something that we can find faster."

"We need to find Sorin."

57

Since Sorin and Alex were with our guests, we had to be careful about what we said. Akila and Amun didn't know anything about Sheena. I didn't see any reason to share the information with them. But there were vampire politics and manners to consider. I couldn't just yank the men away from them and leave them to entertain themselves while we played detective. It would be rude and a very poor way to repay them for their help.

On the flip side, I couldn't stand the thought of waiting until they left to follow this new trail. I wanted so badly to run my idea by Sorin and Alex then start a session with Sheena right away. It could be a dead end but the more I thought about it, the smarter it seemed. We'd been trying to track someone down from a thirty-year-old memory. For some reason I'd felt like we needed to unlock her mind in chronological order but why? There was no real rule for all this; we were basically making it up as we went. So, why not change it up and look at it from a different perspective?

And if it didn't work, we'd just be right back to where we were. No big deal.

All that enthusiasm drained out of me when we walked into the basement gym to the sight of Alex and Sorin, facing each other. Both men wore only pants and the contrast was striking. Alex was an inch or two taller than Sorin but both men seemed bigger to me in that moment, more powerful. Sorin's pale skin was made whiter by Alex's tan in front of it. While their skin was light and dark, the muscles underneath told me the same story about them – they were not unfamiliar with manual labor. I knew from my own exploration of Sorin that his torso was lean and chiseled by hard work. He'd hinted at a very difficult life before he'd been made vampire.

But it wasn't only the color of their skin that stood out as a difference. As I slowly walked around the outside of the room to experience the whole sight, I saw the scars across Alex's body and remembered what he'd said about his parents. Circular burns and long thin pale streaks marked his skin like a map of abuse.

Each man stood stock still in the middle of the large exercise mat, eyes locked on each other as Amun quietly approached Alex from his back to wrap a blindfold around his eyes. Amun was smaller than Alex and Sorin by half a foot but he too wore only loose pants, revealing the same strong musculature.

"You will fight supernatural creatures to protect her but they will underestimate you at first. It will give you an advantage," Amun spoke then soundlessly backed away from Alex and pressed his body against the wall.

Sorin was completely silent when he used vampire speed to cross the room away from Alex and press himself into a corner, almost lost in shadow.

Alex cocked his head to the side, both arms loose and relaxed. His knees were soft but I saw the tension in his legs, ready to move. I held my breath, not sure what I was watching but completely hypnotized. I felt like I was getting a peek into something I was never meant to see, a voyeur. For minutes, Amun and Sorin were frozen in the way only us vampires can – utterly motionless. Alex continued to have a calm readiness that buzzed around him.

When Sorin and Amun went for the man in the center, they were a blur.

And so was Alex as he extended each arm in different directions, strong and locked, just in time to slam each of his palms into the chest of each approaching vampire. The force threw them back against the walls they'd come from. Before they'd even responded to the blows, Alex was pulling off his blindfold to see what he'd accomplished. When he saw each man was shaking off the defensive move, he whooped in celebration. "Holy crap! I can't believe I did that. I mean, I just knew where you'd be and when to knock you back."

Sorin crossed back to Alex and slapped his back. "Indeed. That was impressive. I will be interested to see what you can do once trained."

Amun nodded in agreement. "I am in agreement and look forward to really exploring all your skills and abilities. The warrior is made by his maiden. As her powers grow, so will your skills."

Only then did I speak up to let them know I was there. "Sorry to interrupt, Amun but may I speak to my two men alone?"

My answer was a slight bow. "Of course," he answered then turned to Alex. "I will find you later."

Only once we had the room to ourselves did I let them know my idea for Sheena's next session. They both agreed it was worth a try.

58

Sheena wanted to keep learning her job as Sorin's assistant but Jeremy and Rhys were more than happy to take a break. While the young vampire was sweet as pie, she'd never seen a computer before this week and had a very long list of questions about anything remotely technical. Thankfully, according to Jeremy, she'd maintained some very lovely penmanship and was thrilled to take over his least favorite task – writing out thank you, congratulations, welcome and turning day cards to the local or new vamps when appropriate. We'd asked Tamela to take our guests on a sight-seeing, night drive around the city. She'd wanted to stay and be with Sheena during the session but her loyalty to Sorin ultimately won out.

We'd settled in the living room for the session, assuming our usual positions around the room. Sheena was eager to get back to her office lessons so she was looking into my eyes, ready for direction.

I gave it. "Close your eyes and think of the night you were found in the woods. Imagine the smell of the trees, the sounds of the animals." I let my lids fall and slid into her mind.

This time it wasn't sounds or sights or smells that hit me first but the feeling of desperation. The smell of a fire in a fireplace was next as we ran through the dark forest. My legs were so weak that I knew I wouldn't make it much further. But the fear of him finding me was too strong of a motivator to quit. Dizziness was at the edge of my mind, threatening to take my consciousness away from me. I didn't know how long it had been since I fed but it was long enough for me to be afraid I may pass out again.. Sheena's thoughts raced. She couldn't believe she'd done it, run away. She was simultaneously sure she was finally free while also being certain he was right on her heels. She knew this was her only shot. It had taken too long to gain his trust, get him to believe she was obedient enough to be given some freedom in the house. She'd thought about all those days of dusting his things, washing his clothes, cleaning the windows and being there when he'd returned. She'd shown him that she was too broken to ever fight again. And it'd paid off. He'd forgotten to lock the door this time. It was her only chance. If he caught her, realized it'd all been a show, he'd punish her worse than he'd ever had. This time it wouldn't just be the basement. He'd probably beat all her blood out of her and leave her in the sun, just liked he'd always promised.

When she heard the others in the trees, she'd panicked. Was it him? Frozen in place, she hid from the sound. The man didn't look like him but she was starting get confused, starting to feel her memories slide away. When the woman came out into the open, she'd wondered if she could trust them but knew it was this or die in the woods. She was too weak to continue on and her brain was getting fuzzy. When she fell into the lady's arms, she let the world go black.

When I pulled out of her mind, I had to let my eyes adjust to the living room again. Sheena's face was in front of me and she was talking. "Why did my memories go away?"

"I don't know, honey." And, I really didn't. If the vision was correct, her amnesia had kicked in when she'd finally gotten free. But why?

I turned to Jeremy. "Can you take her upstairs, please?"

"Wait," he and Sheena said in tandem but Jeremy continued. "What did you see?"

"It's too confusing. I don't really know what I saw yet but I need to talk to Alex and Sorin. Can you take her please?"

He looked like he was going to argue but Rhys came to his rescue. "C'mon. I'll go too. We can set up her log in ID for the computer." Rhys and Sheena left the room.

Jeremy crossed to me. "I love to teach but computers are not my area of expertise and the girl has never-ending questions. She thinks the wireless mouse is magic."

I chuckled but was unrelenting. "Sorry, J. You and Rhys are the best men for the job. Let him do the tech stuff and you just step in for the other things."

He sighed, "Fine. But I want to help with the investigation stuff too. You guys aren't the only ones that want to catch this bastard."

Once he was gone, I turned to Sorin and Alex. "It's so confusing. She was free and remembered everything right up to the moment she was rescued."

"What are you thinking?" Alex asked.

Sorin picked up my train of thought before I could answer. "She's thinking we need to talk to Justin and Beth again."

"Bingo," I agreed.

59

Before we could follow that lead, a doorbell rang through the house. I had no idea who it was but was seriously annoyed by the arrival. I couldn't believe it'd taken us this long to go back and question the couple that had found Sheena but it had. And now that the lightbulb had gone off, we couldn't act on it because someone was at the door. My impulse was to ignore it. Sadly, Sorin was the leader of the city and we couldn't just not answer the door.

Plus, he was already headed to open it while I was busy being annoyed.

I smelled them before I could reach the foyer and see who was on the porch. By the strength of the odor, I guessed there was more than one werewolf stepping onto the manor.

Diana was hugging Sorin when I turned the corner. Crossing to give her the same greeting, I saw the wolf behind her was her progeny and my ex-best friend. It stopped me in my tracks and Alex bumped into my sudden frozen form before he'd seen her. Instead of freezing though, he walked around me to go extend his hand to Diana. When she took his hand, Sorin was hugging Monica. After the greetings, the four of them turned in my direction expectantly. Only Monica looked worried; the other three were smiling.

It only took a few seconds to overcome my shock and plaster a fake smile on my face. I followed the men and gave Diana a hug since I was always happy to see her. Monica got a head nod.

"To what to we owe the pleasure?" Sorin asked.

"I'm sorry to stop by unannounced. We're getting the last of Monica's things and turning in her keys. I thought I'd swing by since we were close and give you the good news in person."

A dozen smart assed comments about Monica selling her apartment and running with her tail tucked between her legs came to mind but I bit my tongue. "What good news?" I asked.

Diana addressed Sorin. "The council was thrilled by your visit. They've been talking to the other wolves about the importance of bringing our two kinds together. Almost the whole pack agrees with us now. They want peace as much as us. Sorin, they have agreed to form a new council with us and you together. We can meet regularly to discuss issues in the area. Our first meeting will iron out the details but this is a huge step in the right direction. So, pick six vampires to represent your kind on the council and we can meet in one month."

Sorin's gaze dropped to the ground. The others saw deep thought and reflection but I knew that he was feeling overwhelmed with gratitude and relief. He'd wanted this day for so long and couldn't believe it was happening. After taking a moment to compose himself he looked up at Diana. "Your grandfather would be so proud of you. I will create my list of names and get them to you as soon as possible."

Diana smiled. "Thank you." She took a deep breath and let it out. "Do you think I could trouble you to come out one more time to address them before our first official meeting? There are others who would like to meet you. You can bring your bodyguard again and one more this time."

"It is a very delicate time, Diana." Sorin didn't hesitate but I could he was torn.

"I know," she said. "I know it's so selfish of me to ask this much time of you but I wouldn't ask if I didn't think it was really important. I know my wolves. Some believe your reputation of being merciless and exacting. Another peaceful visit from you and a couple others will go a long way. I want them to see that you are protective and just."

He looked to me, to Alex and back to Diana. I could see he was struggling so I stepped into them. "Go Sorin," I said. "Our thing can wait a little while longer but this is very sensitive. You need to keep the lines of communication open."

He kissed my forehead. "You are right, of course." Turning to Diana he relented. "I will come to you but I cannot tell you right now when I can. May we speak in private?"

Sorin opened the front door, gestured her outside and the two shut the door behind them to speak. It left Monica, Alex and I awkwardly standing in the foyer. I realized that Sorin didn't know the extent of my recent interactions with her. In all the activity, it'd slipped my mind to tell him. He probably wouldn't have left me in this situation if he'd known but it seemed trivial when compared to everything else.

Monica started to sniff the air and it reminded me how not human she was now. She locked eyes on Alex. "What happened to you? You smell different?" She stepped into him. "Did she turn you?" Rage filled her eyes as she slammed her hand onto his sternum. When she felt the thumping of his heart, the anger in the eyes slipped away to be replaced with confusion. "You're not a vampire but I know something's changed."

I'd had enough. I stepped in to push her back from Alex and stand between the two of them. "Back off, Monica. You should be the last person talking about who has changed."

She smirked. "I can smell you all over him. Didn't take you long to get over me, Alex? Does Sorin know or should I tell him?"

I felt Alex tense behind me and didn't know if my telepathy worked on him like other vamps but sent the thought anyway. *Don't show her your power. No one can know.* When I felt him relax, I figured he'd gotten the message.

"You don't know what you're talking about, Monica." He was utterly calm and all business when he spoke. "Of course, I smell like her. I've been staying here and it's her house as much as Sorin's now."

She squinted her eyes like she wasn't believing him but then decided to change tactics. She reached around me and took his hand, coaxing him over to her. "I thought you were going to think about us getting back together. What do you say? Second chance at love?"

Holding my breath, I let it play out in front of me. No matter what, we could not let Monica know that Alex was an immortal now and spiritually connected to me. It was too dangerous for everyone involved. I had to trust that he'd play this whole thing right.

"Monica," he started, laying his free hand on her cheek. "There may have been a chance for us but so much has changed."

"It's her, isn't it?" She was trying to sound cute but I heard the anger underneath. "I knew it when I saw you two that first time but you denied it."

"No, it isn't," he answered. "The truth is- " he looked back at me and then to her. "Sorin and Kate found my sister. She's back and she needs me. I need to make up for lost time. I'm sorry but she's my priority right now. I'm sure you understand."

Monica's eyes were wide. I heard her heartbeat pick up its speed. "Seriously?" She looked past him to me and I nodded. "When? Where? Oh my God, Alex. I'm so happy for you. Of course, I understand. We can postpone our date." And just like that he'd diffused the situation for now. All her anger and suspicion feel away. Ultimately, Monica - werewolf or not - loved a sappy story and Alex reuniting with his long-lost sister was her type of happy ending. "Can I meet her?" she asked.

"Not now," he answered, putting his arm around her shoulder. "She's been through so much. But I promise someday, you'll meet her." He walked her towards the front door and opened it to reveal the head of the vampires and head of the werewolves in deep discussion. They looked up and Sorin nodded.

"I will let you know tomorrow," he said and Diana looked happy.

"Come on, Monica." Diana waved her over. "We've got a lot more to do tonight."

Alex squeezed her shoulder and let her walk into the night, still trying to wrap her head around everything that'd happened in the last few minutes. She'd be half way home before she realized we'd not answered a single question for her, really.

When the wolves were gone, I asked Sorin what his plan was.

"Let's politely encourage Lady Akila and her consort to return to New York. We will assure them that we plan to come to them soon for proper training but that it is not wise for them to remain. Then, I will visit the wolves for one more night. I have made myself clear to Diana that she will have one night and one night only. I need to be with you and Sheena right now. However, you were correct that this meeting is time sensitive."

"Okay," I said.

"Then, we pay visit to Justin and Beth unannounced. I think it's best to see them when they do not know we are coming. We take Sheena to see if being out there jogs any more memories and perhaps we retrace her steps."

"Okay," I agreed but knew more was coming.

"I would like to take Rhys and Alex with me to the lycanthropes' grounds."

I stepped back. "What? Why?"

He raised both hands in surrender. "Rhys will be one of the six to be representative on the council. He would need to be introduced to them. Plus, he does not know but Diana is going to ask him to meet her family. She plans to tell them of their relationship."

I squealed - yes squealed - and Sorin shushed me. "Don't ruin the surprise for him."

I stopped. "So why Alex? Why not take Edwin or Naseem or Tamela?"

"Tamela needs to stay with Sheena. They are very good for each other right now. And, Alex," he looked at him. "You need to tell Monica very clearly that you are not interested in reconciliation. There is a wolf in the pack who is courting her and she is interested but still hoping that you two will be together. She holds onto what used to be, her last remnants of her old life. This kind of tension or ambiguity between you and her could turn sour if not handled correctly and will ruin this opportunity to bring our two sides together. Be kind and clear. Encourage her to date this wolf. According to Diana, he is a very good man and they would be a good match."

Alex nodded. "I understand."

Stepping into Alex, I had to ask. "Is that what you want, Alex? Because if you want to be with her then we can make it work."

He didn't hesitate. "No. The Alex and Monica that planned a date are both gone. She and I would never work now."

"That's the other thing," Sorin continued. "You need to break it off cleanly with her but not let anyone know that you are a warrior, tied to Kate, immortal or strong."

"No problem," Alex quipped. "We go into the pack's territory. Diana tells them that she's been secretly dating a vampire. That vampire meets the family on their turf. Then, I tell Monica that we will never date while making sure that a bunch of werewolves with really good senses don't figure out that I'm not completely human anymore. What could go wrong?"

60

Akila and Amun had loved seeing the city lit up at night but knowing they came from Manhattan, I suspected they were not as impressed as they pretended to be. It made me a little fonder of them that they made such a fuss. They followed Sorin, Alex and me to the solarium after thanking Tamela for being their tour guide. She graciously said her goodbye and went to find Sheena.

Once we were seated, Sorin began. "Lady Akila, I cannot express to you my gratitude for coming to my home and assisting us through these very perilous and unexpected turn of events. Your willingness to be so forthright with us and share your secrets with Katherine and Alex will never be forgotten. We owe you a great debt."

Akila waved her hand on the air. "Lord Sorin, you've no need to be so formal. You owe me nothing. She is a maiden and finding her means more to me than you know. I have wished so many times over the millennia that I were not the only one and now" she looked to me "I am not." We took a moment to smile at each other before she returned her gaze to Sorin. "I can only assume that you are asking us to go back to our territory but not wanting to offend. Remember that I, too, rule a city and know that there are things happening that I would not want others to know."

Sorin chuckled. "Your candor is refreshing. Indeed my lady, I must ask that you return after your sleep. However, I would like to formally ask invitation to your home soon. We still have much to discuss and I would never ask you to travel again. Additionally, given the sensitivity of our situation, it would be better for us to speak away from curious ears."

Akila reached out her hand and Sorin crossed to take it. "Lord Sorin, you, your lady and her warrior have an invitation to come into New York and visit my home. Please let us know when it will be and I will assure that I am available." Sorin laid a kiss on her hand.

I stood. "Lady, could we talk in private?" The men looked curiously at me and then each other but stayed silent.

"I would very much like that," she responded. Amun took a step to join her but she shooed him away. "I'm safe. Stay here and talk amongst yourselves. I'm sure Alex has more questions for you. I need girl time." I took her offered arm and we walked in tandem out to the yard.

The night was eerily silent and I could feel that dawn wasn't far so I didn't have time to be timid. I needed to ask my questions. "I want to apologize beforehand. I'm going to be direct but don't want to offend you."

She patted my hand. "You will not offend me, sister. Anything you say will stay between you and I unless you choose to tell your men."

My men. It was so weird to hear it said like that. I didn't have enough nighttime to start pondering what it all meant so I shoved back the thought spiral that was starting and just asked my questions. "Do warriors and maidens always fall in love?"

She let out a thoughtful "hmmm" and sighed. "The relationship between maiden and warrior is complicated and simple all at once. It is a bond unlike any other."

I was frustrated with the non-answer so I decided to be more direct. "What I mean is… are you and Amun a couple or friends?"

Akila stopped and turned to face me. "Be frank, Kate. It will save us a lot of time."

"Okay," I mustered up the 30 seconds of courage I needed and gave it to her honestly. "I love Sorin. I want to be his mate and marry him. I want him more than I have ever wanted anything. Just him walking into the room makes my body react." She let me take a pause and didn't interject. "But I also love Alex. And I think I want to be with him too. I want him here too, you know, in my life."

"And?" she asked.

"And, what? That's it. Those are my feelings."

She nodded sagely. "Is Sorin not okay with it? Or Alex?"

It took me aback but I rallied my thoughts. "Okay with what?"

She shook her. "It will never stop amazing me that people of this time have become so advanced in some areas and gone so far backwards in others." She smiled. "What I mean is are they okay with all three of you being in a relationship?"

There it was, the idea that I'd been toying with but afraid to admit to myself, let alone say out loud. "But that wouldn't be fair to them, right? For me to be with both?"

She threw her hands up in the air, exasperated. "Why? You all love each other, that is clear. And you are all bonded. Sorin to you and you to Alex. Does that not show that these men would do anything for you and each other?"

I looked down. "It feels wrong and right at the same time."

"Kate," she has taken on a softer tone. "Does it really feel wrong or have you been trained to believe that wanting two men is wrong? That you are wrong for loving two people?" I had to think about that. While I did, she kept talking. "Amun and I have shared a bed with each other since he was called. And, we have brought others into our bed over the years. It has never changed how we feel about each other. I don't know why, in the 21st century, society is so secretive about sex. It is not to be frowned upon but shared and celebrated. As long as everyone is consenting, I do not know why you would feel shame."

"So," I said. "I just need to talk to them and see what they feel?" Then a thought creeped in. "What if they aren't okay with it and I have to choose."

She took my arm and started to lead me back to the house. Dawn was close and I'd been distracted by our talk. Thankfully, she was thinking straight. "Cross that bridge if you reach it. In the meantime, I will look forward to your visit to New York."

When we came back into the solarium, we paused to take in the sight. The three men were talking and laughing like old friends. They took the breath out of my chest. Akila urged me down to lay my ear in front of her mouth. She whispered. "Try to remember how lucky we are to have such men in our lives. Stop questioning it and just enjoy it." Then she laid a kiss on my cheek and entered the room. "We have returned to break up the party. Amun, it is time for bed."

He turned to her and I was treated to the sight of love filling his eyes at the very sight of her. Like a choreographed movement, his arm came out, she took it and they glided from the room. I was left with two men, side by side, staring at me.

"Are you going to tell us what that was about?" Alex asked. Sorin's right eyebrow arched. He probably had the same question but wouldn't have just asked outright.

"I will," I answered. "Just not tonight. We need to go to bed. We have way more important things going on." I stepped between the two of them, taking one arm in each of mine and led them to the stairs.

"But we do need to talk about it soon."

61

The next night, I started by texting my daughters. We hadn't spoken much since they got to their grandparents' house. I realized that having them somewhere far from me actually gave me some relief. I loved them more than anything in the world but I was starting to really see how much danger they were in around me. As far as I knew, there were no vampires in Virginia that hated me and would use them to get to me. With my new status as ancient protector of the people or whatever, I was getting nervous that eventually a line of enemies would start and I didn't want them dragged into it.

I got texts back telling me they'd been horseback riding, hiking, to three barbeques and the beach. I told them how much I loved them and couldn't wait to see them but for them to have fun. Then, I headed for the kitchen, which had become the unofficial meeting place at the start of each night.

It was a big kitchen but with all the people tonight, it was feeling a little small and was very noisy. The whole gang was there and my heart swelled at the site. Sheena was sitting on a stool with Tamela weaving her hair into some kind of braid. Alex stood in front of her sipping on some coffee and listening to her talk about how exciting email is. Sorin was on the other side of the island, sitting next to Amun and Akila as they discussed the best way to travel from the steel city to the big apple. Rhys and Jeremy were talking to Edwin as he worked on something in a skillet at the stove.

I crossed to Sorin's back and wrapped my arms around him. He laid his head back against me and said "Good evening, darling."

I kissed his cheek. "Good evening." Then I addressed the room. "Good evening, everyone."

They all stopped to give me their greetings. Alex came around to wrap his arm around my waist. "You good?"

I smiled up at him. "I'm good." Nodding my head towards the stove, I said. "I'm guessing that's for you?"

"It is," he answered. "I'm going to be spoiled if Edwin keeps cooking for me."

Edwin didn't take his eyes off the pan. "I'm so thrilled to be able to cook again. I didn't realize how much I missed it until a hungry human was here."

"Does the smell bother you?" I inquired. "I have a hard time with some foods."

"Not at all," the bodyguard/chef assured us.

Amun and Akila stood. "We must say our goodbyes and get to the airport," the lady spoke to the room. "We have loved meeting you all. What a wonderful surprise and a very special group." She was rewarded with a chorus of voices saying their farewells and wishing safe travels.

Sorin gestured to the door. "Naseem has the car ready and will take you."

Amun and Alex embraced. They had clearly become close and I couldn't blame them. They were the only two of their kind in the world as far as we knew. Amun, Akila, Sorin and I made our way to the foyer and away from the others. Once on the porch, we spoke openly.

Sorin started. "We will come soon. Once I have wrapped up affairs here, I will let you know the exact dates."

Akila nodded. "We look forward to it. Might I speak with Kate one last time?"

Sorin and Amun headed for the car to give us privacy. She looked up at me. "Please stay in touch. Day or night, I will answer your call. I want to hear how it goes and how you are."

"Okay," I said. "I'll take you up on that."

"Whatever it is that you must attend to," she whispered. "Whatever is going on, you are more powerful than you know. But, most powerful with those two men by your side. Do you understand?"

"Not really," I answered.

"You will," was all I got from her.

As they drove away and I stood on the porch with Sorin's hand on my back, I thought about what she might have been telling me. Was my power stronger with them? I knew that Sorin and I could combine our powers. But Alex didn't have magic. Was she telling me safety in numbers? That didn't seem right. Maybe the message was about love – that we are more complete when surrounded by love or something equally cheesy.

I didn't know then but I would understand what she was saying just a few days later.

62

We called Diana from the office to let her know that Rhys, Alex and Sorin would arrive just an hour or two after sunset the next night. I could hear the gratitude in her response just by the tone of her voice.

"Who will you choose for the council?" I asked Sorin.

"I have to be very careful in my choosing," he said. "The wrong choice could undo all our hard work. Rhys will be an excellent representative. He is levelheaded, able to be trusted with sensitive information and can be an asset with his vast knowledge of technology. Jeremy is very good with people. He is able to stay calm in stressful scenarios and very adept at research when a computer does not hold the answer. Not working means he has a more flexible schedule and can go to council affairs with little notice."

I nodded. "Very good choices."

He stepped into me. "You, of course, will be on the council. As lady of the city, you will be by my side but you must have your own voice and not allow people to see you merely as an extension of me but as an equal partner. Having a seat on the council will show the vampires and werewolves that I respect your opinion. It will show the women that they are valued and honored."

Reaching up, I wound my arms around the back of his neck. "Is that a request or demand?"

His head cocked to the side. "A request, my lady. I would never demand."

"Then," I kissed him long and hard. "I accept. Who else?"

"Well," he thought. "That makes four and we have two seats open. We must choose vampires outside of my circle so as not to be accused of unfairness. I will need to look at the directory and contemplate the best choices. Someone in local politics or law enforcement would be a benefit. We have education and medicine represent with you three."

"Law enforcement?" I asked. "Seriously? There are vamps in the police force?"

He nodded. "There are. They are very solitary. I have sworn secrecy to protect them. I will approach each to determine who is willing and qualified. Once they sit on the council, they will be known to our two species."

I shook my head incredulously, thinking of the cops I knew from my days of being an officer's wife. I couldn't imagine any of them being vampires. I struggled to remember any cops that I'd never seen in the sun but it was futile. I didn't know all the cops in Pittsburgh and even if I knew the ones that were vamps, it was possible they were turned after my divorce. I mean I was a vampire now and I bet none of my old friends on the force would ever suspect.

"Alright," I agreed. "I'm sure you know best. Pick the ones you know you can trust but maybe try to have one more female. It would be hard to be the only girl vamp on the council."

"Agreed," he admitted.

Sadly, I didn't know a lot of female vampires. I seemed to be surrounded by a lot of men. And it wasn't like we got to meet a lot of vampires. The last get-together we'd had, I was playing judge. That brought on a thought. "What was the name of the female vampire who was accused of killing the cat?"

"You mean Greta?"

"Yeah," I felt like my brain was start to put some pieces together. "What's her story? I mean, I was only in her head for a minute but she felt very smart and capable."

"I believe she came here from another state," he crossed to his desk and pulled open a drawer of files. When he found the one he wanted, he brought it to the desk surface and opened it. "Moved here in 2000 from Tennessee. She was an attorney but needed to relocate when it was clear that she was not aging."

"What does she do now?"

He scanned. "She helps local vampire business and charities with contracts, set up and other legal issues."

"Maybe she would be good? I felt her and she's a good person, an honest person, with strong morals. She wants to help the helpless."

He smiled warmly at me. "I think she is an excellent choice. I will talk to her once all this settles down. Each representative should be interviewed first."

Talking about Greta reminded me of something. "Do we know if Boris has left the area? I mean, the guy is bad news and he's very pissed at me."

"Are you worried about him?" Sorin asked. "I can have Edwin follow up?"

"Yeah," I agreed. "Let's just err on the side of caution. With everything going on, I don't need anyone else wanting revenge."

Sorin stood to come to me but the doorbell stopped his movement. "I am not expecting anyone."

63

Thankfully, it was not an enemy at the door.

Jeremy was opening it as we came down the stairs and I knew by the smell that his husband was on the porch. They were sharing a kiss when I hit the bottom of the stairs and waited for my hug.

"What a pleasant surprise," I exclaimed as he pulled me into his arms and then treated Sorin to the same embrace. "Do you have the night free?"

"I do," Logan affirmed. "I missed you all and made the time. The work will be there tomorrow. I'm not imposing, am I? Jeremy says you all have a lot going on. If he's too busy tonight, I can go."

Sorin patted Logan's back. "I would never keep a couple from each other. Please," he gestured to the solarium. "Let's get some drinks and catch up."

Once seated and glasses were full, Sorin turned his attention to Jeremy and Logan at the bar. "Logan, how is the line? I hear much buzz about your teen summer options."

I clapped my hands together. "The girls are so excited to model in the show this summer. It and the wedding are all they talk about."

Logan appeared bashful. "I thank you for the compliments and allowing your daughters to be in the show. They are easy to design for, so creative and give me very useful advice about their peers' likes and dislikes." He took a sip. "Business is good but I'm here to not talk about it. I want to hear what you all have been up to."

Jeremy looked to Sorin who nodded. Then, he turned to Logan. "There's a girl here. She's a vampire and has been missing for a long time. She can't remember anything so we're trying to figure out where she's been and what happened to her."

Logan's hand flew up to cover his mouth. "Oh no. Poor thing. Do you think it was something bad or just that she was lost?"

Jeremy shook his head. "We think it was pretty bad."

Logan turned to Sorin and me. "What can I do to help?"

I stood. "Nothing for her really but I think Jeremy could use a few hours away from all of it. Maybe you guys should just go spend some time together."

Jeremy nodded. "Yes, please." They held hands. "But please call me if you're doing another session. At least I can be there if she or you need calmed."

"You got it." Then I watched them walk away and addressed Sorin. "We need to talk to Beth and Justin. Let's go out to see them the night after you're back. And, we need to have Edwin follow up on Boris."

"I will do that now," he nodded. "Then, meet me back in the office."

Half an hour later, Sorin entered to office with Rhys. "Tell her what you just told me."

Rhys sighed. "I've got nothing, Katie. Jeremy finished his list last night. I just finished mine. No record of Sheena at any of them. But you have to understand a lot of those schools don't have their records from that far back. If they do, it probably papers in boxes in some storage room."

"Oh," I said as my heart sank into my stomach. "That's okay, Rhys. We knew it was a long shot."

"Wait," he said. "There is one more idea. I was working on side stuff and I did find a few Roberts that would line up with the age, taking psychology at community colleges in the radius we were looking at. Six of them are still alive and in the area. We could visit them and just ask."

"It's unlikely," I said.

"I know," Rhys interrupted. "But it can't hurt. One even lives out in the Johnstown area."

"Now," I perked up. "That is promising. I say we start there but don't tell Sheena until we know it's something real."

"Agreed," Sorin interjected. "What about Alex?"

"From now on," I said. "We don't hold anything back from him. We're a team."

64

Alex seemed as hopeful as the rest of us when we told him about Robert, the psych student in Johnstown. He also didn't want to tell his sister but did insist he go question the man when we went.

"The pack land is only 30 minutes from that area," Sorin explained. "Since we are going there tomorrow, why not time it to meet Robert after we leave the meeting? The three of us can certainly question one human."

Alex nodded. "Yes, it would be a waste of time to be that close and not take advantage but would it mean another night away?"

Sorin met my gaze, "Alex is right. Depending on timing, we may need to stay out there to be able to do both."

I laid my hand on his cheek. "I'll be fine. I have a house full of people to protect me. The sooner we talk to this guy, the better."

"Excellent," Sorin addressed Alex and Rhys. "Pack your bag with the plan to stay, I will ask Diana to use the basement suite again. She does not need to know why. We can tell her we do not want to rush our important business."

"Did you talk to Edwin?" I asked Sorin.

"I did," he answered. "He should be back soon to let us know."

"Know what?" Alex questioned.

"I pissed off a vampire the same night your sister showed up. I just want to make sure we don't lose sight of him while dealing with all this other stuff." I felt anger flare up inside of Alex.

"You have to tell me these things," he said. "How can I protect you if I don't know everything?"

I held up my hands, "Settle down. It happened before I knew everything and it didn't seem important." Before he could get madder, I continued. "But we all agree that from now on, we tell you everything - big or small. Okay?"

He let out a breath. "Okay. Sorry, I'm on edge. I just feel like there are threats around every corner."

"Get used to that," Sorin laughed. "It's never a dull moment with Katherine around."

"Amen," Rhys joined in.

"Hey," I exclaimed, looking the three men in the room. "I don't think I like you all being friends anymore."

"Too late," Alex added and the three men walked out leaving me to wonder what I'd gotten myself into.

65

We gathered everyone in the middle of the lighted square of the yard with blankets. With the crowd growing, I didn't think a room in the house would work anymore. This way, we could spread out and I could have space to focus.

We didn't know if Logan joining was a good idea or not since we had no idea what I would see. But he hadn't seen Jeremy in so long and I just couldn't bring myself to send him off. So, he was on a blanket with his husband, facing me. The space to the right of them had Rhys and Tamela, both silently preparing for whatever may happen. To the left of the married couple was Sorin and Alex. My heart swelled with the sight of them, side by side, both sets of eyes on me and I had to force myself to look away.

Sheena had her head in my lap again, looking up at me and smiling. It was a miracle that this little thing was so unbroken by what had happened. No matter what we pulled out of her head, she dealt with it and didn't let it ruin her joy. I had a lot to learn from her and realized how fond I was becoming of her. I pictured taking her to class and proudly watching her receive her degree. I imagined her running Sorin's affairs for him, proudly having the desk she always wanted, complete with a framed picture of her brother and a cherished cactus in a brightly colored pot. I made a mental note to ask Sorin if we could carve out a little area for her to claim as her workspace.

Please, I begged the universe. *Don't let me find anything in her memories that will destroy her.*

"Sheena," I said. "Think about the time just before you escaped. You mentioned cleaning and dusting, doing laundry, washing dishes. Just imagine doing those things."

She closed her eyes and I joined her, sliding into her head to see what she saw. This one took longer to come forward. I just walked around aimlessly in the blackness, waiting for one of my senses to pick up something. She was struggling to bring this one to the front. I thought it must be awful if it was pushed so far back but when the world around me started to emerge, it was the most normal of all the memories. The first thing that I smelled was furniture polish. It was strong and her hand came into focus with a white cloth on a wooden table. She worked the polish in circles, bringing the light wood to a shine. Pulling back, I saw it was a large dining room table with eight chairs around it. As she moved into the next room, it didn't take long for me to recognize the living room from her party memory. The staircase that Bobby had led her up was off to the left but she moved to the right, into the kitchen.

She began to fill a bucket with hot water and the lemon Lysol odor filled the air when she opened the bottle to pour it into the bucket. Some splashed on her hand so she rubbed her hand down her dress. It caught in one of the tears and she wished for a needle and thread to try and save the clothing. It wasn't going to last much longer but she was hoping she'd be able to escape before she had to ask for a new dress. She knew that asking for anything always meant paying a price. Either he'd beat her for not being appreciative or he'd ask for something in return. Whatever he asked for, it wouldn't be nice and she didn't want to know how creative he'd get with his request.

Finding the mop, she dipped it into the sudsy lemon water and started to clean the kitchen floor. It was the second time she'd done it that night but her chores were done and if he stopped by to check on her and she wasn't doing something, he'd punish her for being lazy. So, she would stay busy until the sun came up. And while she cleaned, she kept herself entertained with her favorite thing - imagining what it would feel like the night he forgot to lock the door and she ran out into the open air to freedom.

Just as she was losing herself in the fantasy of finding her brother, she heard the key in the front door and prepared herself for what was to come, then I was out of her head.

I fell back. Her psychic power was getting stronger. She didn't just push me out anymore but threw me out. She sat up. "I'm sorry," she cried. "I'm sorry."

I righted myself. "Don't be, Sheena. You don't do it on purpose."

"That was incredible," Logan said. "You really saw inside her memories? What did you see?"

"Nothing," Sheena answered. "Just me cleaning. It was a waste. It told us nothing."

"That's not true," I assured her. "We know she was in the same house as her previous memory so we know the faceless man upstairs is someone we need to track down."

"How do we find him if we don't even know what he looks like?" Jeremy asked the group.

"There's another thing. It's probably nothing but I realized that the dress she was wearing when she showed up here is not the dress she was wearing when I saw her locked in the basement."

"So," Sheena said. "If I was really there for 30 years, then I'm sure I'd need more than one outfit."

"Yes," I agreed. "But, where did it come from? Did you bring it to him, pack clothes? Or, did he have to go buy it? Logan?" I asked. "If I showed you a dress, do you think you could tell me what year it would have been made?"

"Maybe," he shrugged.

"And if you can't, maybe Alex," I turned to him. "Maybe you'll recognize it as hers?"

"I don't know, Kate." He shrugged. "It was so long ago."

"It's worth a try," I turned to Tamela. "Where did you put it?"

The bodyguard stood, closed her eyes and held out her hand. Seconds later, the dress in question as in her hands. "Here."

"I didn't know you could conjure," I said and then realized I'd never asked her about her powers. I really was a terrible friend and partner. I didn't ask Sorin or Rhys about their past. I didn't ask Tamela enough about her. I had to do better.

Tamela handed the fabric to Logan. He held it up, inspected the tags and flipped it inside out. We waited with hope until he spoke. "Sorry guys. This is very standard. The design has been around for decades, being rehashed in department stores every couple of years. It could be from Penney's or Sears; it could have been bought twenty years ago or twenty days ago."

He handed it over to Alex who also didn't have much to say. "I don't remember it. But I have to say, I don't think Sheena would have chosen to buy a dress. It wasn't her style. But she did have some for church. My mother insisted on it."

Logan reached his hand out for the item. "It might not result in anything but I could take this to some fabric people I know. At least I can pin down a time when this would have been most popular?"

Sorin spoke up. "This is a very sensitive investigation."

Logan nodded. "I understand. I can tell them I am looking into a retro idea."

I tapped Sheena's arm so she'd look at me. "Do you mind if he takes the dress? He can bring it back."

She faced the item in his hands. "Take it and burn it when you're done. I never want to see it again." Something flashed in her eyes. It was a hardness that I knew well, the hardness of a survivor.

66

When Logan and Jeremy said their goodbyes, I felt bad. Were we being selfish by monopolizing my friend's time? As he watched his husband drive away, I joined his side. "You don't have to stay, J. Alex, Sorin and I are good. Rhys can take over Sheena's lessons. I can help Sorin with his work. You've done so much. We're so grateful."

He smiled down at me, wrapped his arm around my shoulder and kissed the top of my head. "That's very sweet of you but I'm going to see this through. I won't leave you here with Alex, Rhys and Sorin gone tomorrow night. I know it's sexist but I don't want you, Tamela and Sheena alone." I started to argue but he stopped me. "Plus, you know you need me if she starts to freak out. The more you pull from her brain and chip away at that mental fortress she's created, the more likely it's all gonna flood back."

I leaned my head into his chest. "You're a good friend. You inspire me to be a better person."

"Shucks," he joked. "Now, I'm blushing." Turning me towards the manor, he led me up the stairs and inside. "Let's call it a night."

We parted ways in the upstairs hallway. He went into his room and I made my way to the office. The two men I needed were in there and it was time to talk. I'd toyed with the idea of waiting until they were back but two more nights of this dancing around in my brain was going to drive me insane. Not to mention the more I found out about Sheena's past, the more I realized that tomorrow is never promised. So, I was done postponing things. If I couldn't talk to them about this, then who could I talk to?

I shut the door to the office. Alex and Sorin sat next to each other on the green couch, looking over papers on the coffee table. They both looked up when the door clicked into place. It was hard not to flash back to my first night with Sorin. He'd been looking over files on that same table while sitting on that same couch. I hadn't known when I'd walked into this room that night, that my whole existence was about to be turned onto its head.

"Hello, *regina mea*." Sorin's old-fashioned manners made him stand and I motioned for him to sit down. "We are planning our discussions for the meeting with the wolves. Do you need us?"

"I do," I said and slowly crossed to them, giving myself time to begin. I knew what I wanted to say, just needed to start the words. It was moments like this when I missed the liquid courage of a few shots. Since alcohol doesn't work on us, I had to tap into my own bravery.

While I covered the ground between us, I took in the two men. Sorin's black t-shirt fit him in the perfect way that all his clothes fit him, showing off the body that convinced you he was a dancer but was actually chiseled by hard work. His slacks were the same shade of black and both made the blue hint in his raven hair more obvious. His grey eyes shone from his alabaster face and I ached to pull out his hair tie so all that soft hair could fall. Only a foot from Sorin's gaze, blue eyes were also locked on me. The tan of Alex's skin made those irises look like they belonged to Bermuda waters. His brown hair was curled by the lack of styling products and I knew he'd just quickly towel dried it after his shower because he wanted to join his friends in the manor more than he wanted his hair to look good. When he let it curl like that, it made the hair look shorter but I was betting there was enough to run my hands through. The green t-shirt was worn from a thousand washes and laid across that broad chest like it had always belonged there. His jeans, I had noticed earlier, flattered his strong backside in all the right ways.

I was acutely aware that I may have to say goodbye to one or both of them if the next few minutes did not go the way I was hoping.

I sat on a merlot chair and put every ounce of my feelings for them into my eyes. I knew Sorin felt it by the smile that crossed his face. I wanted to be sure both men saw it, too.

"I love you both," I started with complete truth and would not hold back. "I want you both. I want you in my life and in my bed. I know I'm being selfish but I can't live without either one of you. I think a part of me would die if either of you left me." They were silent and only the arching of Sorin's eyebrow showed me that they'd heard. I waited in silence, giving them time to respond or recoil.

"So," I continued. "What do you think?" I instinctually held up my hands like I was preparing to take a blow. "This is a safe space. If you two are not okay with this, then I respect that. I mean it."

Alex cleared his throat. "I think I saw this coming but wasn't sure how the conversation would begin."

"Well," I dropped my hands and smiled. "It's begun."

"I have been a lover of men and of women," Sorin said. "Until you, Katherine, I never thought I would truly fall in love, I mean the kind of love that inspires poems and song. Yet, I find myself in that very love now." He turned to Alex. "And, when I thought I could not hold more love for anyone, you have come into our home and lives. In the beginning, you were important to her, so important to me. I respected you as a healer of humans and someone holding our secrets. Then, she admitted feelings for you and I was open to her exploring those. Once, we knew you were fated to protect her, I found relief in the knowledge that her safety would be a shared responsibility between us. Now, if we are being honest, I too do not want you to leave us but be with us."

Alex's eyes were wide, his head dancing between Sorin's face and mine. I filled the silence. "Alex, I want to be clear. You don't have to do anything you don't want to. If you aren't comfortable with this, then we remain friends. No hard feelings, I promise."

He shook his head. "I've never been with a man. I mean, I've not been with many women if we're being so candid. My whole life has been about being a doctor, finding the cure and finding my sister." His voice was getting more confident as he continued. "Then one day I looked around and had nothing, no family, no wife or girlfriend. I don't even have a goldfish. I just worked, slept and worked some more." He locked his gaze onto mine. "Then, you were there, annoying the hell out of me with your constant challenging but intriguing me at the same time. Before I knew it, you were this major part of my life. Then, you both brought Sheena back to me and treated her like the most important thing in your lives. I believed for a long time that love just wasn't a part of my story. I never thought I'd feel the way I do about you, Kate." He turned to Sorin. "And I definitely never thought I'd feel that way about you." He let out a sigh. "But I do. It's confusing and exciting at the same time. I feel like I should be grateful for one person to love. To have two feels, I don't know – greedy."

I stood, pushed the coffee table off to the side and looked down at Alex. "One thing I've learned from the vampires is this." I grabbed his hand and urged him up to do what I'd wanted for so long. I slid my hand into that hair and grabbed it, pulling his lips to mine. When I ended the kiss, I finished the thought. "As abused children, we were taught to never ask for anything. As humans, we were taught to be ashamed for wanting anything. But, it's not something to be embarrassed by and we're allowed to want things. I'm done self-sacrificing and you should be, too. The three of us are connected and it's time we own that and enjoy what the universe has given us." Sorin stood and kissed the same lips I just had. I wondered for a second if he could taste me on Alex and the thought excited me.

"I think," I whispered. "We should take this to the bedroom."

67

We didn't have much time before the sun rose but Sorin and I were both able to stay awake when we needed to... and I needed to. The following night, these men would leave me to meet with the lycans. And while I trusted Diana and she said they would be safe with the wolves, I also knew that every time we left this manor, we were all at risk. I still wasn't sure if Sorin had enemies in the pack but I knew not everyone in the city were his fans. I also knew that I had been almost murdered twice already so I was statistically sure someone somewhere was planning to come after me for something. Alex being with us meant he was in danger by proxy. If the unthinkable happened and one or both of them never came back, I wanted this moment to hold onto.

Alex and Sorin stood at the end of the bed. I think they'd unconsciously decided that I would lead this. It was sexist of them but also chivalrous. I thought we should let Alex lead since he admitted to being inexperienced and sounded nervous. But, if we were following that line of thinking, Sorin was the only one of us that had the threesome and orgy experience so maybe we should put him in charge.

I shook my head to clear the thoughts. Sorin noticed. "What is going on in that head?"

"The usual," I admitted. "Chaos and self-doubt."

Treating me to the eyebrow lift that he knew would drive me crazy, he lifted his shirt over his head and tossed it to the couch. That simple gesture brought on a rush of lust that chased all that hesitation out of my mind. Any lingering reservation disappeared when he crossed the distance between us with that hip-swaying grace that reminded me of a predatory cat approaching its meal. He undid the buttons of my dress until it fluttered to the ground. The revelation that I'd been naked under the dress all night brought a growl from Sorin and a gasp from Alex. Finding Alex's eyes showed that he shared the same hunger I'd seen in Sorin's gaze and a quick scan of his body declared that he was straining against the jeans. I mimicked the stalking gait that Sorin had just shown me, the kind of walk that only vampires can. I made sure to take my time so Alex could be prepared before I reached him. When I did, I sensed the trembling in his muscles and heard the pounding of his heart. In sync, I turned down the sound of the thumping in his chest and raised his shirt off his body, sending it to join Sorin's on the couch. Running my hands over that broad chest, the swell of his pecs hardened under my touch. Behind me, I felt Sorin press into my back and knew he was as naked and ready as I. He ran his hands over the front of me and kissed across my upper back. I leaned in to match those kisses across Alex's chest before I allowed my tongue to run over the tight ridges of his abdomen. Unbuttoning his jeans, I pulled them and his underwear down in one shift motion. Rising up to look up at him, I asked. "Are you okay with this? Say the word and it stops."

His response came out in a panting breath. "Never stop."

I reached around to urge Sorin to the front of me. "Sit on the end of the bed," I told him and he obediently sat. I met Alex's eyes. "Behind me, please." He replaced Sorin's previous spot, wrapping his hands around the front of me to take the fullness of my breast into his hands. They ached against his fingers and the feel of him squeezing them was amazing. Looking at my beautiful King, I smiled and bent over to take him into my mouth. He dragged in air as my lips slid over the length of him, sucked and pulled back. I felt Alex hard against the swell of my ass and looked back at him. "I'm yours, Alex."

The feel of him entering me and Sorin filling my mouth at the same time resulted in the first orgasm ripping through me. I pulled back from Sorin long enough to let out a cry of pleasure but resumed the greedy rhythm of my mouth as Alex began to move in and out of me. We moved like that for minutes and I was reveling in the sensations. I wanted this to last forever but was hungry for more. I stood and urged Sorin to stand with me. Alex was still inside of me, taking the moment to gather himself and stop himself from getting too close to the edge. I arched back into him and Sorin stepped into the front of me. My breasts crushed into Sorin's hard chest when he leaned in to kiss Alex over my shoulder. I was pressed between the two men: Sorin firm against my core and Alex rock hard inside of me. Sorin's power rolled out of his chest, into mine and our powers mixed. I knew the feeling well as it had become a part of our lovemaking. But tonight, it was bigger. Something fresh joined it and the smell of fresh, clean laundry hit my nose.

I knew what it was. It was Alex's power joining into mine and Sorin's. Whether he knew it or not, Alex had power now and it was growing inside of my chest as he throbbed inside my body.

They broke the kiss. I pushed Sorin away and stepped away from Alex, breaking our physical connection but allowing the men to see the dancing lights of power around us. They were lost in the sight of the magic for a moment, in awe of the show.

I climbed up the bed, resting my back against the headboard, and waggled my finger to ask the men to join. They crawled up the bed towards me and I pointed at Sorin then to the space next to me. "Lay down, please."

He did. I straddled the man, positioning myself to lower down onto the solidness of him. When our bodies met and he was sheathed by me, I leaned forward. Without being told, Alex came to my back and found the right angle to slide into my other opening. The sensation of them filling me and rubbing all the right places was almost too much. I had to breath deep and focus on not letting the orgasm consume me. I knew that the clenching of my body would push them over the edge of control and the moment would be over. We all took a few precious seconds to pull back from the precipice before slowly beginning to rock. Together we moved and the dancing of our powers matched the pace of our bodies.

When the three of us climaxed, the powers exploded in spectacular fireworks display of color. Mine red, Sorin's blue and a new sunset orange power that belong to the warrior that was now a part of us.

"Forever," I said to them.

"Forever," they echoed.

I fell asleep with my head on Sorin's chest and the feel of Alex at back.

68

I awoke first and didn't know how much time I'd have to enjoy the moment so I willed myself to mentally etch this into my mind. Alex breathed heavily, almost sighing with each expiration. His heart beat slow and steady, satiated by the night before. Sorin was under my cheek, the rise and fall of his chest like an ocean wave. I didn't need to hear his heart to know it was inside of there and capable of so much love.

What had I done in this life or a previous one to be rewarded with adoration from these two beautiful souls?

The thrill that rushed through me told me that Sorin had awakened. I lifted my head to see those wonderful eyes opened for the night. He smiled. "Good evening."

"Good evening," I whispered. I laid a soft kiss on his lips.

"What were you pondering?"

"Nothing," I fibbed. "Just so happy."

That resulted in an even bigger smile. "I share the sentiment."

"I wish you didn't have to go," I laid my head back onto his chest.

"I know," he said into my hair. "After this visit, you will go with me every time."

The second man stirred. I adjusted myself to be sitting next to Sorin, against the pillows. We both watched Alex wake. I realized that humans needed more time to rise and didn't miss that part of it. When he was done rubbing his eyes and adjusting to the darkness, he looked over at us.

"So, it wasn't a dream?" he asked.

Sorin chuckled and his voice danced along my skin. "No, warrior. It was no dream."

"Good," Alex answered. "I'm starving."

"Same," I agreed, looking back and forth between the men on each side of me. "Kitchen?"

"Kitchen," they said in tandem.

When we made it to our destination, I was shocked to see we were the first ones in there. Examining the clock, I saw that we'd risen earlier than usual and the sun was just dipping down. Pouring two glasses of blood and one glass of orange juice, I heard cereal hitting a glass bowl.

I gave each man their respective glass and sat. Alex left the milk and box of cereal next to him on the island so I assumed he was going to need more than one bowl to fill his stomach. Sorin was gulping down the glass I'd handed him.

I secretly patted myself on the back for tiring out two, strong, powerful men all by my lonesome.

When Rhys, Tamela, Jeremy and Sheena came in, they didn't seem to notice that anything was different. I had a suspicion that they knew but were being polite when I saw the twinkle in Jeremy's eyes. While vampires are normally very open about sex, no one wanted to discuss it with Sheena in the room.

"There was a weird feeling in the house last night, just before sun rise," Sheena said "Like lightening in the air."

Everyone froze and then erupted into laughter.

"What?" Sheena asked. "What did I say?"

69

Standing outside, the car doors were open and everyone was hugging. Alex lifted his sister up off the ground when he hugged her and told her to be good. Rhys hugged me and promised to be safe. Tamela hugged Sorin and asked again if he wanted her to go.

Alex set his sights on me as Rhys was shaking Jeremy's hand and telling him to take care of "the girls." Alex pulled me into him and I fought back tears. I felt like I'd just found him and now he was leaving.

"I know," he whispered into my neck. "I promise this is only the beginning of our long time together. He and I will come back."

I nodded, afraid that speaking would take away the last thread of composure I had. He pulled back, placed a hand on each side of my face and laid a soft kiss on my lips. I squeezed my eyes shut, holding those tears back where they belonged. If Shenna saw how worried I was, she'd panic. So, I mustered my strength and swallowed back the sadness.

Alex moved to Jeremy and Rhys so I could cross to Sorin. I didn't think it was possible but I loved him more today than I had yesterday. He let me fall into him and wrapped his arms around me, holding me tight until I stopped trembling. "I will return to you. We will return to you."

I nodded against his chest, wanting to believe that he was so powerful he could come through anything unharmed. I had to believe it. "I love you," was all I could manage to say as I looked up, raised onto my toes and kissed him goodbye.

"I love you," he answered.

Tamela and Sheena had gone inside when the car rolled down the driveway. Jeremy waited on the porch and watched me in the driveway. I felt like pieces of me were ripped from my body and in that retreating vehicle. I didn't move until I couldn't see or hear the car. My maker and the two men I loved most were gone and all I could do was count the minutes until I saw them all again.

Turning to face my friend, I saw a mischievous grin on his face. "So, you get both, huh? I've been dying to ask you the details but you know, not around the children."

He knew exactly how to distract me from my worries. I blushed. "It was incredible. Never in a million years did I think I'd ever do something like that."

"And, now?" he asked.

"I want to do it again and again." Just the memory of the previous night brought a wave of lust over my body.

"I think what you meant to say was 'Thank you, Jeremy for telling me to be honest with Sorin and Alex.'"

That elicited an eye roll but I knew he was right. "Thank you, Jeremy for telling me to be honest with Sorin and Alex."

"You're welcome, you lucky bitch." He threw his arm around my shoulders. "What do you want to do?" he asked.

"I say we keep up with the memory sessions. At least then my mind is on something else and we may be able to give them more information to use when they visit Robert."

70

Naseem was driving the men to the wolves' land and Edwin was still trying to find Boris. According to Tamela, peeking through Boris' windows showed that nothing was packed but both his car and he were missing. No one knew where he was. Sorin had put Greta up in a hotel until we knew that Boris wasn't a threat to her or us.

That left T, Jeremy, Sheena and I some uninterrupted time to do some memory work. Since the house was quiet, we decided to use T's room this time. It was relaxed and had plenty of beanbags. After the session, I wanted to spend some quality time with T and Sheena wanted Jeremy to teach her his filing system. Plus, she had some ideas about how to organize the schedule better. Seeing her excitement when she talked about office work made it hard for any of us to deny her. If we were lucky, the night would go quickly and we'd be one day closer to the boys coming back.

Each one of us had chosen a bean bag and were in a circle. I focused on Sheena. "Sheena, can we try to go back to the night you escaped? We saw that you were cleaning and someone came home so that wasn't the night. Try to remember the night when he didn't lock the door and you left. Imagine the feeling of grabbing a door handle and turning it."

She closed her eyes and squinched up her brow like she was thinking extra hard. I let my eyes close softly, slid into her head and was greeted to the sight of the same kitchen floor she'd been mopping earlier. I couldn't tell if this was a new memory or the same one since it was the same dress, the same floor and the same smell of lemon cleaner in the same bucket. But, once I listened to her thoughts, I knew we'd landed on something.

He didn't lock the door. I heard her thoughts racing. *I know I didn't hear the click. He forgot. He forgot to lock the door. I have to wait and be patient. Wait and see if he comes back. Maybe he'll realize and come back. How long has it been?*

She looked at the clock. It had been an hour and he hadn't returned. If he was going to come back, he would have by now, right? She had a couple hours until sunrise. If she was going to run, she needed to run now.

The sound of the mop handle dropping to the floor was a crack in the air and snapped her into motion. She ran down the stairs, throwing open the heavy door that had filled her vision for so, so long. Talking into that awful room, she held back tears. "I love you friends," she said to the scurrying of the rodents that she'd truly miss. "I will try to come back for you. Thank you for never leaving me alone." She crossed to the loose stone and pulled it from the wall. The small picture was still there. Snatching it from the hiding place, she pushed the stone back in place. Clutching the picture, she ran up the stairs for what she hoped was the last time. She knew her feet were filthy as she ran across the clean kitchen floor but she didn't care. If he caught her trying to run, a dirty floor was the least of her problems. She reached the front door and froze. This was it; she could do it. She screamed at her hand to grab the door knob and turn.

When it turned and the door popped open, the tears of relief began to pour but were quickly dried up by adrenaline.

"Run" she yelled to her feet. And they did. Down the wooden steps to the grass and then into the trees. The picture fluttered from her hand

and back. She stopped, turning back to find where the picture had fallen, seeing the cherub face and a smile with two front teeth missing. The crack of a branch filled the air and she gasped. Looking up at the house she'd been held in, she waited for a sign that he was back and looking for her.

The fear propelled her into the trees where she would run into a vampire couple and be reunited with her brother. Risking only one more glance back, she saw the cabin disappear.

It was me who ended the session this time. Instead of being pushed out by her, I pulled myself out.

I knew that cabin. I'd seen it before in someone else's thoughts.

Opening my eyes, I found Jeremy.

"Shit," he whispered and the world went black.

71

It was the scurrying that cleared my head. I was back in Sheena's memories, seeing the stone wall and hearing the rats. She'd called them her friends. The chain was back on her foot but it looked different, newer. And her feet looked different. I hadn't remembered her toes being painted. Was this a different time?

My thoughts were foggy, like they were there but I couldn't reach them.

I knew the red nail polish on her toes. It was called "I'm Not Really a Waitress." It was one of my go-to shades. Sorin loved that I walked around barefoot and liked when my toes were painted. That's why I had painted them a few nights ago.

Sliding my gaze up the leg, I saw the purple flowers against the white dress and the pieces fell into place. It was my dress on my body and the red toes were mine. That meant that the chain was on my ankle not Sheena's.

I knew it was real but didn't really mind the chain. I mean everything was okay. I wasn't in danger. It was just a basement.

To my right, I heard a moan and saw the lump on the ground – no not a lump – Sheena. It was Sheena. She was here, too. A quick scan of her body showed the same shiny chain around her ankle.

Oh, thank goodness. I wasn't alone. See? It was all okay and there was nothing to worry about.

She stirred but wasn't awake, not yet. She was still safely asleep. And wasn't that nice.

On the other side of her, I was glad to see Tamela had come too. I didn't think she was breathing but that was fine. We were all together in the basement and all chained. It was all okay and there was nothing to worry about. It was just a basement.

I let my neck give into the weight of my head and let it fall back against the wall. The muscles of my shoulders were spasming. How long had I been here? How had we gotten here?

Sheena moaned and rolled onto her back. I watched her eyes flutter open and go wide. "No," she whispered. "No, no, no, no, no." She bolted upright, grabbing at the chain on her ankle and pulling. I followed the chain to see it disappear into the ground. I didn't know what it was attached to but was pretty sure it wasn't budging. She yanked at the chain as she continued to pant "no, no, no, no."

"Why are you so upset, Sheena?" I asked. "It's just a basement. We're all together and everything's okay."

She looked at me wildly. I think it was the first moment she'd even realized I was there. Crawling to me she said "Kate. Oh my God. You're here. How did we get here? What's going on? Please tell me we're in a memory."

I sighed. "I don't know how we got here, Sheena. It's not a memory but I don't think you should worry." I couldn't understand why she was so upset. We were all together and it was going to be fine. I was sure of it.

She scanned the room, seeing Tamela and scrambling over to her friend. Shaking the sleeping women, Sheena screamed. "Tamela. Wake up, please. Please, wake up. We have to get out of here. Wake up, wake up."

"Sheena," I said. "Honey, you need to calm down. Everything is okay."

"What is wrong with you?" she yelled angrily over her shoulder at me. "We are not fine, Kate. We are very fucking not fine. We have to get out of here, now!" She slapped Tamela's cheek. "T. You have to wake up. I need you." She lifted the woman up to sitting and let go. Tamela fell loosely back down to the dirt floor.

The door opened and Sheena threw herself back against the wall like she thought she could go through it to the other side. She screamed. "No! I remember now, you prick. I remember it all and I won't be yours again. I'll kill myself first."

"You remember," he said. "Because I let you."

He faced me. "How you doing, doll?"

"Good, Jeremy. You?"

72

"What did you do to them?" Sheena asked in a voice that dripped with disdain. "Why bring them here? You aren't man enough for three."

He snarled at the girl and she shrunk back, losing her temporary courage. Pleased with the reaction, he turned his attention back to me. Closing the distance, he bent his knees to crouch down and level his eyes with mine. He was careful to not get dirt on his slacks. "Sorry about this Kate. This was supposed to be like Plan D or E. I never wanted to pull you into this part of it." He tapped his finger into my forehead to emphasis each word in the next sentence. "But you just had to poke around in her brain, didn't you? Couldn't leave it alone."

I giggled. He was so funny and I was so glad he was my friend.

He cocked his head to the side and seemed to examine me for a moment. "I may have used a little too much of the waking dream on you. Sorry about that. But I needed you guys out cold so I could get you all to the car. I'm strong but, damn, that one," he cocked his head towards Tamela. "She's big. That height makes her just awkward to handle." He glanced at the bodyguard like she was just something that he was mad he had to carry, like a heavy bookcase and not a person. "I really knocked her out. Had to," he looked back at me. "She's the one that I think may actually give me a fight."

He grabbed a handful of my hair. "I'm gonna pull back on the power, all right? Give you a minute to think. I want to be able to talk to you but if you scream or fight." He slammed my head into the wall behind me and I saw stars for a second. "I knock you out, kill the tall one and disappear with the girl. You'll starve to death with the rats to eat your body. Got it?"

I giggled. I didn't know what game he was playing but I did like games. I gave him the thumbs up. "Got it, buddy."

Something like warm water poured over the top of my head to roll down my torso and limbs. The world around me became sharper and I drew in a breath. Everything was very *not* okay. This bastard in front of me had not only kidnapped me and two other women, but had been under our noses the whole time.

And, it was impossible to count the number of lies he'd told.

He watched the tendrils of revelation snake through my brain and fill my eyes with a sick amusement. "There it is," he smiled. "Man, that's worth it."

"Why?" I asked, battling back the words I wanted to say. I knew that he had all the cards and I had to play this right.

He stood, held up a finger and without a word, left the basement. Seconds later, he returned with a chair in his hand and slammed it down in front me. With something that looked like pride in his face, he sat. "This is gonna take a while, my dear. I've been hoping for this moment and I don't want to rush it. I mean how many times do you get a villain's monologue and a captive audience, am I right?" He laced his fingers, extend his arms to crack his knuckles and laid his hands on his thighs. "Why, huh? That's the question you want to start with? Can you be a little more specific."

"Why did you kidnap Sheena thirty years ago?" He wanted specific? I could give him specific.

"Well," he leaned back, kicking out his legs in utter relaxation. "That was sort of a fluke. I mean I didn't plan it. You see, I had this brilliant idea to start a new community of sorts. I wanted to make a group of vampires that lived together in peace. We are higher individuals, evolution at its finest. But, instead of being revered and honored, we hide in the shadows." He threw his hands up in the air. "I mean, how is *that* fair? Hiding from humans, the things we feed on. It's like humans hiding from cows. Ridiculous. So, I was going to find the brightest and most deserving, turn them and grow a family. Place them in important positions around the city until we could rise and take over. Under my guidance and teaching, I would make them the superior race that we are."

"So," I said dryly. "A cult?"

He leaned forward before I could react, grabbed my hair and treated the back of my head to another slam against the wall. "I can do this all night, Kate. You'll just keep healing so it'll be a fresh blow each time. You asked me a question and I'm answering. I'm the teacher and you're the student. I'll tell you when it's time for another question. Got it?"

"You might as well do what he says," Sheena said. "He can get inventive when he wants to teach you a lesson."

He nodded at Sheena. "Thank you, Sheena." Meeting my eyes, he continued. "I'd listen to her if I were you. Learn from her mistakes. She was such a good protege. So bright and full of life. I loved that fight in her. That's why I picked her. And, why it was so much fun to break her. When someone like that stops fighting, I mean there's no bigger high."

I gulped back my words. He paused, waiting to see if I'd be obedient and stay quiet or if I needed another lesson.

"But a missing girl can draw a lot of attention, attention that I didn't see coming. Back then, missing teen girls were labeled runaways, especially trouble makers like our little Sheena. Unfortunately, that burnout Bobby and his half-wit friends wouldn't let it go. They brought a lot of heat down on our little college. I had to finish the semester and resign. But he showed up here one night, insisting that I had something to do with his girlfriend disappearing. Once I killed him, it was time to scrap my plans." Sheena let out a wail and I was afraid he'd punish her but I think he wanted that reaction. "I figured I'd wait a year or so, then move and start fresh somewhere else. But I met Logan and well, you know, he made me a better man."

I allowed him to stop, sitting still in the silence and wondered what reactions he'd hoped to get from me. Whatever it was, I refused to give it to him. I stayed frozen and made my face as blank as possible.

"I give you permission to ask another question," he stated.

"Why didn't Rhys find her or you in the school records? Did we miss the school on our list?"

"Good question," he smiled. "And very simple. I took the list with our school on it. Wrote down that it was a dead end and moved on. Easy one. Next question."

I cleared my throat in an attempt to not say what I wanted to. I reminded myself that two women were relying on me to not piss of the psycho killer. "Why be my friend? When I met you, we all thought that Sheena was living a fabulous life overseas."

He stood and clapped in a mock standing ovation. "Oh, good. I was hoping you'd ask this one." He sat. "Ready?"

I nodded and the ache in my head was subsiding. The wounds were already healing. How much damage had Sheena had to heal in thirty years of this?

"So, it's a funny story. I had *no idea* who you were in the beginning. You, Kate, were a lucky accident." He waited anxiously for a response but I didn't know what he was expecting.

"I don't understand," I said and played to his ego. "I need you to explain."

"I apologize, of course you do. You have no clue, do you?" He rubbed his hands together like a man about to tell you some very good news. "I was trying to ruin Sorin."

73

"**I** must admit that I'm a little embarrassed by how very simple my motive is," he continued. "I want power. That's what I've always wanted – what I deserve. Being ruler of the city brings power – new powers and a boost in your existing power. It means wealth and respect. I realized that I'd been wasting my time with small plans – small groups of even smaller people. I needed to think bigger. Being master of Pittsburgh will open doors to bigger cities and bigger opportunities."

He stood and started to pace the floor animatedly. "But, Sorin would wipe the floor clean with me if I came up against him in a challenge. I needed him to be sent packing by the people. It was actually a news broadcast that gave me the inspiration." He clapped his hands once and the crack of it sent chills down my spine. I didn't like how excited he was. "What I needed was a scandal. How many human politicians have we seen ruined by the right piece of dirt? So, I spent months trying to dig up something juicy on the man." He growled in frustration. "I couldn't find anything on him before he arrived in the city. Your man was a ghost prior to the 1970s. The years he's been here have been clean. Either he's actually a good person or he's good at wiping records. I talked to everyone, tried to find a scorned lover or two that would talk some shit on him but no luck. Everyone loves him. So, I had to think bigger, you know, outside of the box. If past lovers wouldn't spill than who would?"

He turned to face me with absolute giddiness on his face, like a kid on Christmas morning. "Staff. I needed someone close to him and who better than his assistant? It was too perfect. Will was so desperate for attention; everyone ignored him. When I started to seek him out at parties and talk to him, he was so excited for a friend that he spilled. And I mean spilled! The man loved to brag about how smart he was and the things he'd done in the war."

Heat was rushing up my throat and my ears were on fire with dread. I didn't like where this was going.

He didn't notice or didn't care, he just kept talking. "Whispering in his ear couldn't have been any easier. The man's brain was already so far in left field. He was a classic narcissist and an absolute nutjob. Convincing him to start murdering girls wasn't that hard. All I needed was for him to get caught and everyone to realize that Sorin had a rogue vamp under his nose and didn't know." He stopped and sighed. "I see you want to interrupt, go ahead."

"Are you the reason Sorin never knew Will was the killer?" I asked, trying to keep any emotion out of my voice.

He applauded again. "Oh Kate, this is why we're friends. You're so damn quick on the uptake. Yes! I wiped Will of his memory after the kills so Sorin wouldn't feel it on him. Will basically had to be led to the girls and told what to do. He thought he was a genius mastermind but I can tell you," he clapped for each next word. "He. Was. Not."

I shook my head. "You led him to me?"

"To my defense, that was supposed to be a lot quicker and easier than it went. I knew that for him to get caught, we had to stop going after nobodies and kill someone that would get more police attention. Who better than a nurse? We waited across the street and when he saw you, he freaked. He started to rant about how you looked like the vampire that turned him. The man was so cracked. I looked into his head and saw the girl. Sure, she was similar to you but you guys weren't twins or anything. But it was a good opportunity. I convinced him that you were her and that he had to kill you to stop the ghost from haunting him. I think it worked a little too good because holy shit, was he savage with you. I mean, even I was a little grossed out." He hissed like he was seeing something disgusting then turned to me. "We took off and I waited for the news to break." He ran his hand across the air like he was reading a headline. "Local beloved RN and mother slaughtered outside the hospital."

He shook his head and dropped down to his knees in front of me. "Who could have fucking seen that nerd turning you into a vampire?" He laughed. "The plan was so perfect and he ruined it." Jeremy threw his head back and raged at the frustration of his plan not working. Sheena scurried over to me and I wrapped my arms around her. He stood up. "But, then a whole new area of opportunity presented itself. Sorin, the man with zero weakness," Jeremy looked down at me. "Had fallen in love with the nobody nurse who was supposed to be his downfall."

He laughed, took his place on the chair and ran his hands through his hair. "So, I took a step back and reformulated the plan. I told Will he needed to get close to you and find out how you survived, that figuring it out would be the key to breaking the curse that the gypsy vampire had put on him back in Germany. I told him to plant seeds of doubt in you about your maker. Then, I told him to kidnap you, Rhys and Alex. Told him how to make it look like Rhys was the killer and had murdered you and Alex in a jealous rage. I unlocked the memories of what he had done to those girls and convinced him that he would be cleared of all the murders, gaining Sorin's respect at the same time. I knew it would destroy Sorin to lose you. She'll never remember it but I even sent Monica to your house when I knew Will was there. I made it so God-damned easy for him and he still screwed it up. He was beaten by *you*." He shook his head like he was amused. "I mean when it all came out, I thought I *have to get to know this girl*. The girl who grabbed

Sorin's heart and killed a vamp 70 years older than her! Who wouldn't be intrigued?"

"So, I waited for a party and introduced myself," he chuckled. "I don't need to tell you that part, you were there. I'm curious, what did you think when you met me?" I thought carefully about how to answer and he didn't like the hesitation. He leaned forward. "Truth, Kate. I'm being honest with you; I deserve the same."

No point in lying. "I thought you were handsome and smart and nice. I thought you were safe and I instantly wanted to be your friend."

He seemed pleased with the answer and leaned back. "You weren't a little gun shy? After having Will turn on you and being kidnapped and all that?"

"A little," I admitted. "But I also knew I needed to move on and not everyone was a psycho." I wanted to say *I was obviously wrong* but decided against it.

"That's what I was hoping," he said. "I thought it would be a tad harder to earn your trust but you we're in from the first meeting and I appreciated that. Sometimes it nice for things to be easy, you know?"

I nodded. Sheena shook in my arms. Tamela was still motionless on the floor.

"When I first met you, I didn't see what all the fuss was about, no offense. You didn't feel particularly powerful. You're pretty but not like some of the women Sorin's been with. You were smart and witty but I couldn't figure out why Sorin was willing to die for you and how you were able to kill Will. You were like this puzzle I needed to figure out." He shook his finger at me. "You did, however, really piss off Evelyn and I loved that. I'd been trying to figure out how to get rid of her for years. That party was when I figured out how to get Sorin's position and Logan's business back with one idea. Two bird, one stone, you know?"

Now I was shaking. Not in fear but with pent up rage.

"Evelyn was very easy to turn against you. That woman was crazier than Will. I'd been on the frontlines of her Sorin obsession for years and she was a couple crayons short of a box. I think the really hot ones are always looney toons. And let me tell you, she hated you at first sight."

"Same," I said and that sent him into the kind of laughter that comes from the stomach.

"I do love a good cat fight," said when she stopped guffawing. "At least with you and Evelyn, it was entertaining. She'd rant about you at our house, the store, on the phone. Poor Logan got the brunt of it but I heard my fair share and for all her elegance, Evelyn had the mouth of a sailor. I had to get you in the fight though. I felt bad for the damage but a simple word scratched in the side of a car can really spark some fires."

The monologue was having the effect I think he was going for. Hearing him talk about my life like it was a play, blow after blow and the realization that my closest friend had been behind my worst moments was almost too much. I felt my brain threatening to shut down, wanting to protect me from what was to come by knocking me out. I tapped into my years of locking down my feelings at work, being able to get through a bad shift without letting it destroy me. I slammed that wall into place and felt myself dying inside, turning off the emotions.

"Let me be transparent, Kate. This is something I've been dying to get off my chest. I did not tell her to kidnap your kids." He held up his hands in defense. "I told her she needed to do something to get you out of the way. It was my idea for her to offer you money to leave. I never could have foreseen Sorin cutting her off and her jumping off the deep end. I knew she was nuts but I didn't know she was that level of nuts." He put his hand on his chest. "For that, I am truly sorry. I never would've told her to go after your daughters. I'm not a monster."

He waited for a sign of forgiveness from me but he wasn't getting one so he moved on. "How lucky was it that you called me to help you get rid of her? It was too perfect. You actually did me a *huge* favor. I think she was about to tell Sorin everything to try and take the heat off of her and put it onto me. She was so desperate to win him back. Killing her was good for both of us. And, listen, no judgement. She deserved it. We really are a good team, Kate." He leaned into me, forearms on his thighs. "I was contemplating dropping my whole campaign to ruin Sorin. I did like you. And the more I found out about your powers, the more I realized that I should have you on my side not against me. When you were at my house that first time and looked in my head and saw this cabin, I almost snapped your neck. I couldn't have you asking about it or talking to Logan about it. Thankfully, I didn't panic and you believed my story. When a few weeks had gone by and you didn't ask again and no one showed up here, I knew I'd dodged a bullet."

He sighed. "Then," he cocked his head towards Sheena. "She got out and everything fell apart. The night of your party, the one she showed up at? I had driven out here to check on her. When I saw that door open, holy shit Kate, I just about died." He tapped the side of his head. "Thankfully, I had her so brainwashed that she was programmed to forget everything if she ever set foot out of this house. My powers really are wasted out here among you all. All you care about is me making you feel happy. I can do so much more."

"You're getting off track," I said and immediately regretted the comment. I braced for another blow to the head but he didn't appear to be mad.

"Am I. Thank you, Kate. Where was I? Ah, yes, the night of the party. When you texted me, I was cleaning up all evidence of her. Then, I was searching the woods and nearby homes. Nothing. I was hoping she was still outside when the sun came up and there was nothing left." He stood and paced again. "Who could have ever predicted that she was at *your house*. Are you freaking kidding me? Of all the places for her to show up? When I heard that she'd been dropped off with Sorin, I wanted to slaughter Beth and Justin in their sleep." He rubbed his chin and I could see the wheels in his head turning. "I still may."

I wanted to keep him on track. The more he talked, the more I learned about him and the better chance I had to get us out of here. "And we welcomed you right into the investigation. How helpful of us."

"Yes, you did." He beamed. "I got to be right on the front row of every memory session. I was standing outside the room when she had the vision of my party. I made sure to blur my face when she was going to see me. I kept her calm and happy. I was planning to have to distract you but," he smirked at me. "Sorin and Alex did that for me. You were so focused on them you wouldn't have noticed if I carried around a sign that said 'it was me'." He laughed and clapped his hands together. The sound made Sheena jump in my arms. "I have to say that I *never* pegged you for a swinger. Good for you, I have no issues with it but I definitely had you marked as an uptight, missionary position type in the beginning. When you and Sorin marked each other, well color me shocked. Did not see that one coming so quickly. You must be something in the bedroom." He dropped down in front of me and leaned in. "Tell me, who put what where last night?"

We were not friends. I was not interested in his opinion of my sex life and was absolutely not giving him details. "Why did you let her roam the house?"

He sighed, stood up and brushed off his slacks. "In hindsight, that was not smart. I was so sure I'd broken her. She hadn't fought me in so long. She was weak. I allowed her upstairs to clean when I was watching. Then, I allowed her to do it when I wasn't home but kept everything locked. She went years like this, cleaning all night and going to the basement at sunrise. In exchange, I brought her blood from the butcher. Enough to keep her alive and without powers. If you start them young, you can pretty much train them to do and believe anything. She was an experiment at first but I grew fond of her. A hundred times I thought about sending her out into the dawn and being done with the sneaking around but I couldn't bring myself to do it. And, she hadn't shown any signs of rebellion in decades." He moved to her and snatched her out of my hands before I could stop him. She was in the air, her little feet slack. She'd learned not to fight him and her instinct was to allow him to do whatever he wanted. She'd reverted back from the bright, happy girl I knew to the shattered doll I'd first met. He shook her as her spoke. "But she was plotting all along, weren't you?"

She nodded her head in agreement. "I'm sorry," she squeaked out. "I won't do it again."

He dropped her and she lay limp next to me. I didn't dare reach for her with him so close. "You're right," he said. "Because I've learned my lesson. And you, my dear piece of evidence, will be greeting the sun as soon as possible."

She whimpered in response.

I stood to face him, squaring my shoulders. "What about Tamela and me? We can't just disappear. Sorin knows that you were with us. Don't you think he'll notice if all of us are gone?"

He leaned in so close that his nose was almost touching mine. "I know, Kate. But I will figure out what to do with you. Don't worry. I already have a plan. It buys me just enough time to get rid of you and be gone before anyone knows you're missing."

I locked eyes with him. I knew in a one-on-one fight, I would win. He only knew a fraction of my power. "Unchain me and let's see how strong you are. What are you waiting for?"

"He's waiting for me," it was Logan and we were officially fucked.

74

I turned to the man entering the room, battling between rage and utter heartbreak. "No," I said. "Not you."

"Why not me?" Logan asked.

I didn't know how to answer that. Why not him? If Jeremy could pretend to be my friend for six months and I never had an inkling, why couldn't Logan also be lying? Someone once said if you see two people in a relationship, they were more similar than you realized, one just may be better at hiding it.

I thought of him checking on me when Jeremy was "handling an emergency." I thought of him telling me how sorry he was that Evelyn was a psycho and how he had no idea she'd take it all so far. I thought of my daughters in their fashion show, so close to the two men that had almost gotten them killed. All the while, they had a girl not much older than Ellie and Olivia locked up in a basement.

I looked down at the little girl on the ground and rage filled me. "So, which one of you forced yourself on her? Or was it both of you?"

Logan gave me a *tsk, tsk* in disapproval. "There's no reason to bring up such unpleasantness. Jeremy is a changed man. When I met him, we mated, vowed to only be with each other and understood there were better ways to get someone to listen to you. Right?"

Jeremy had the audacity to look embarrassed. "Like I said Kate. I've done some terrible things in the past but I grew and evolved. I haven't touched her that way in decades. I'm not that man anymore."

I spat at his feet. "You disgust me." It was now or never. I needed to end these two and figure out how to free us later. With them dead, I could far-see to Sorin or Rhys. I dropped to my knees and called on the power in me that brought fire. The power bubbled inside of me and then went cold as a sense of calm came over me. I didn't know why I'd wanted to killed Logan and Jeremy. They were my friends and had brought me to this lovely cabin. "Thank you for having me over," I said.

Logan turned to Jeremy. "How did she figure it out?"

Jeremy sighed, "She saw it in the girl's head. I had to act fast."

"How many times did I tell you to get rid of her?" Logan was trying to stay calm but was speaking in the angry whispers we've all used. "How many times did I beg you to end this? To sell the cabin?"

"I know," Jeremy ran his hand through his hair. "I know Logan, but I didn't and we can't change what happened. We have to deal with this and argue later."

"Why would you take all three?" Logan asked. "Why didn't you wipe Kate and Tamela's memory and grab Sheena?"

"I had to make a decision in the moment," Jeremy said. "You weren't there. I was. You were at work like you always are."

Logan threw up his hands. "I came and got the dress, didn't I? Got the one piece of evidence that you hadn't managed to get in days of being there. If they had tied that dress to me, we would've been in deep shit."

"I get it," Jeremy responded. "You can tell me a hundred different ways that I messed up but it doesn't change that this is the situation we're in. I got us out of the Will mess and the Evelyn mess. I can get us out of this one, too." He pulled out a phone from his back pocket and I saw it was mine. "Can you do it, please?"

Logan sighed and grabbed the phone from his husband. Within seconds, he had the phone to his ear and I heard the ringing. Sorin answered and the sound of his voice had no effect on me. I was too relaxed to be excited. "Hello, my love," Logan said but it wasn't his voice it was mine. He sounded just like me and I shook my head. He was so cool. "Don't be alarmed but I'm on my way to Virginia. I'm almost to the girls. A small accident. They'll be okay but I had to go. Tamela is driving me and Sheena, well, I figured it was safest for us to stay together." Logan paused and listened. "No, please. Don't worry about us. You handle what you need to and I'll handle the girls." Logan's mouth moved but my voice came out. How was he doing it? "I'll keep you updated through texts. I love you." He clicked it off and tossed it to Jeremy. When he spoke, he was back to using his voice. "He said something in his language so I had to end the call. No clue what he was saying."

I felt giddy. "I love when he speaks Romanian."

"Good for you," Logan snapped then addressed Jeremy. "We have a few days to clean this all up and then we need a very good story. You brought the BMW?"

"Yes," Jeremy answered. "If you take me back to the manor, I'll get my car."

Both men turned to the door and the next few seconds were a blur of events. Tamela stood with the broken chain in her outstretched left hand, as the chain fell to the ground, a large butcher's knife materialized in the same palm. She charged for the men. Logan dodged the knife as she lunged. Jeremy grabbed her arm and bent backwards. I heard the snap of a bone and saw the knife fall to the ground. Tamela fell to her knees, screaming in pain or defiance, I couldn't tell. Her left arm lay loose at her side, longer than before. Logan stepped behind her, grabbed her right arm with one hand and roughly pulled it behind her. With the other hand he held her hair at the scalp and pulled her head back as far as it would go. My mind fought against the calmness that filled me but it couldn't work fast enough to stop what happened next. Jeremy retrieved the knife from its resting place on the ground and with one motion drove it into her neck. As he forced it across, Logan pulled and neither stopped until Tamela's body fell to the ground and her head remained in Logan's grasp. He threw it off to the side of the room.

"Great," Jeremy said. "What a mess. And, this knife is probably ruined. It's very expensive."

"No one cares," Logan scoffed. "We don't cook anyways. It doesn't even make sense to have these things around."

They continued the conversation as they walked out of the room. I heard Jeremy say, "It's the presentation. If people come over and we don't have food or ways to cook it, it's going to raise some suspicions." Then the door was shut and the sound outside of this room was muffled.

Sheena crawled to Tamela, wails and moans escaping her as she struggled against the weight of the chain. "No," she cried and threw herself over the headless body. "No, please. I'm sorry, T. I'm so sorry. I never should've escaped. Never should have left. It's my fault." Her voice was harsh with sobs. "Please be okay. Please don't die."

I knew I was supposed to be upset, knew that something was wrong but couldn't figure it out. I was too relaxed to be worried. "Can't come back from that, Sheena. Can't grow back a head."

Sheena lifted herself off of Tamela and turned very angry eyes on me. "What the fuck is wrong with you? I thought you were some all-powerful Queen? You can't fight off his stupid power? My brother said you can do anything but he lied. You're weak."

She returned to the woman in front of her and rubbed her hand up and down the back, stopping just before she touched the base of the now empty neck. I watched this and couldn't figure out why I was supposed to be upset. We were okay, right? This was all okay. Jeremy and Logan knew what was best for us.

Then, the darkness took me over.

75

The whispering was all I heard at first. It took a minute to understand where I was and what the sound was. Rolling over to face Sheena, I saw her laying on her stomach. Inches from her eyes was a rat, nodding its head and listening to her talk. Its little nose shook, making his whiskers dance. Several squeaks came out and it ran. "Thank you," she said to the retreating rodent then faced me. "You're awake," she said.

"I am," I answered.

"He said that Logan and Jeremy are gone, left last night when they were done cleaning up and have been away all day. I think they knocked you out so you wouldn't try anything." She looked away from me. "I guess they don't think I'm a threat."

"Is it night?" I asked.

"Yes," she answered. "Sun just set."

I sat up, trying to recall the previous night. When I did, I glanced around the room to see that Tamela wasn't actually there. I breathed a sigh of relief. Was it a vision? Did Jeremy put her death in my head to mess with me?

"They took her," Sheena said and my heart sank. "After you were out, they took her outside and dropped her onto the driveway before they left. The rats sat next to her so she wouldn't be alone when the sun came up. It would've destroyed any evidence. When they get back, they'll probably just hose away the dust and no one will ever know what happened to her. They certainly won't let use live to talk."

As she told the story, I struggled to clear the fog in my brain. I knew she was telling the truth, knew I should feel something but I didn't.

She kept talking and I held onto her words like an anchor. "I hope they kill me next and quick. I don't want to see what they do to you. I don't think I could take it. Kate?"

"Yes," I mumbled.

"I'm so sorry about what I said to you. It was so mean. You've been like a big sister to me and I was so mean to you. It isn't your fault. None of this is."

Those words were having some kind of effect, pulling at something inside of me. "Keep talking," I said.

"Alex loves you, you know. He looks so happy when he talks about you and Sorin. It makes me happy to see him happy. He was so excited to see what the future was going to bring us and now, it'll never happen. He won't just lose me again, now he'll lose you too. And I think that will kill him." She sighed. "I should have stayed gone."

The fog was clearing in my mind as she spoke. A bubbling heat in my stomach started slow and almost unnoticeable but it was there.

"I think about my mom and what she was going through when I went missing. I don't think she was sad. I think she was probably thrilled to be rid of me. I bet she got all the attention and sympathy she always wanted." She rolled onto her back and looked up. "But your daughters will be so sad. They'll cry for you because you're a good mom. I wish I could've met them at the wedding, could've seen you walk down the aisle."

The image of my wedding and my daughters at the end of the aisle, standing as my maidens of honor dissolved into the image of them crying and asking their dad why I never came back. I heard Tom on the phone, telling officers to keep looking. I pictured Sorin punching a wall, furiously demanding that the vampires of the city to never stop searching. I thought of Alex, who'd die when I died.

I thought of brave, wonderful Tamela. She'd survived so much and was so strong that I'd believed nothing would ever take her down. How could someone live so long and their death be so quick? How could someone be there and then just not be there?

I thought of Jeremy and every lie that he'd told me with words, smiles and hugs.

The bubbling in my stomach rose to a rapid boil and the power slid up my throat. "We're getting out of here," I said and heard the power in my voice.

Sheena sat up. "What is that?"

"It's magic," I said. "My magic."

76

Standing wasn't as easy as it should've been. Whatever Jeremy had done to me hovered just on the periphery of my brain. I'd felt my power pushing it back and then his power resisting and seeping in. It was a magical tug of war, a battle to be in charge of my muscles, my thoughts and my reality.

When I thought my legs would obey me and hold my weight, I raised my hand from the floor to find the stone wall for balance and stood. Sheena watched my struggles to get and remain upright with wide eyes. "What are you doing?" she asked.

"I'm trying to figure out how to get us out of here," I answered, trying to sound confident.

She shook her head. "I've been here for thirty years. I know every inch. There's no way out of here and the chains on us now are even thicker than the ones he used before."

I heard the words but had to check for myself. Bending over, I wrapped my hands around the thick links, pulling with everything I could. It was no use. We were vampires held by vampires. They knew what to do and what it would take to keep us captive.

Righting myself, I squared my shoulders, flipped my hair out of my face and started to scan our surroundings. It was the kind of cellar you've seen in the movies and the very sight of it makes you certain that the captive is done for. A dirt floor met a stone wall and a stone ceiling that wasn't much more than six feet high. As I'd already mentioned, the chains around our legs disappeared into the dirt. More than likely, they went deep and ended on some very secure concrete hold. The only way to get out of here, was to get someone to us. A sick realization came over me. Jeremy had said he was done with this type of behavior, that he was a changed man. If so, why would he have more chains put in?

I knew in that moment that if we didn't stop Jeremy, someone else would end up in this basement.

Closing my eyes, I focused on Sorin. I tried to conjure his smell and far-see to him. But the woodsy smell that I knew so well with replaced with a sudden calm and I completely forgot why I'd even wanted to leave here.

Weakness overcame my legs, bringing me back to my butt on the dirt.

Sheena was next to me in a second. "No, he won't win." She whispered in my ear. "Your daughters love you. I love you. Rhys loves you. Alex and Sorin love you. Tamela loved you." Her forehead rested on my temple. "Please don't slip away again, Kate."

The scream that ripped from my throat was savage. I squeezed my hands into fists, letting the feel of my nails digging into my palms bring me back. Pushing at Jeremy's power, I cleared my head again. Slamming my fist into the ground, I was reminded of the night Alex had found out his sister's fate and raged. I drew on that, standing for the second time.

"New plan," I said to Sheena. "If I use my focus to try and reach Sorin, I drop my defenses and Jeremy's mind control comes back. So, that's no longer an option." Searching the room again, I tried to conjure up a new idea. I spoke aloud. "I can call fire but that doesn't help." I was no longer worried about if someone knew all my powers. "I can read minds, see memories, heal, glamour, fly and use my voice." Sighing, I ran my hands through my hair. "None of those can help us."

"You have all those abilities?" Sheena sounded awe-struck. "Wow."

"I also get visions of the future but didn't see this coming so basically all my magic is," I screamed, "useless."

"Not all your powers," a new voice said.

My eyes grew wide and I followed the sound off to my right.

"You can also see ghosts." It was Tamela, here to help.

77

Attempting to blink the tears back so I could see her clearly, I took a step in her direction, around Sheena. "T?"

Sheena gasped. "What do you mean?"

Turning to her, I chuckled through the edge of crying. "Oh, I can see spirits, too. Tamela is here."

The sound that broke from Sheena was a mix of a laugh and a sob. "You can see her?"

"I can," I answered and returned my gaze to my lost friend. In case this didn't last, I wanted to say something before the moment was gone. "Tamela, I'm so, so sorry." That broke my hold, releasing the flood of red tears that I'd suppressed. She crossed the room. I'd expected like a floating or something ethereal but she just walked like she'd always had. When she reached me, she'd stopped. Unbeknownst to Sheena, T was right in front of her.

Tamela smiled. "Don't you dare apologize. This is not your fault, Katherine. Nor is it hers." She gestured to the shaken girl. "This is the fault of the men who killed me. No one else." She looked at me. "I would do it again. I would always have fought to protect you and her. We must stick together, us women. So, I ask this."

I waited and gave her time to be ready.

She finished. "Get out of here. Kill those men. Live a life of love and joy. For me."

I nodded because I didn't know what to say. Then, the reality of our situation came back to me. "But I don't know how."

Tamela smiled. "I cannot tell you much. But I can tell you that I marked the way."

"Okay," I said, confused.

"And," she winked. "You will see it when you need it."

"What?" I asked, "See what?"

"You're ready," she answered. I didn't need to see her start to shimmer before my eyes to know that this gift from the universe was only meant for a matter of seconds. "Tell Sorin I will love him forever." As Tamela faded, her fist came to her sternum in a salute and my friend disappeared from the basement she had died in.

I would not let her death be for nothing.

"Is she still here? What did she say?" Sheena was tugging on my sleeve in a way that felt childish but was enough to bring me back to reality.

"She's gone," I said. "She told me she marked the way and I'll see it when I need it."

"See what?" Sheena asked.

"I don't know," I answered, trying to not let her hear my frustration.

Whether it was the constant metaphysical battle between my magic and Jeremy's in my head or the loss of Tamela or the scared girl at my side who reminded me of my daughters or all if it – I was close to giving into the crushing weight of everything.

I was getting real freaking tired of being in life-or-death situations and having all eyes on me.

But this was not my first time being held captive and I was starting to think I needed to get used to this. Looking around, I begged my eyes to see whatever Tamela was trying to show me, what she'd said I would need. There was nowhere to hide anything. If there was, Sheena would have found it in her decades down here.

The loose brick, I thought just as I sensed Jeremy entering the cabin above me.

Wheeling around, I ran my hands over the wall. "Sheena, where is the loose stone? Quick."

She dropped to her knees, counting out loud and she tapped each stone in an order only she knew. "One, two, three."

I heard them hit the top of the steps. "Hurry," I whispered.

"Six, seven." She slipped the tips if her fingers into spaces that she knew well, pulling the stone from the rest with a scraping sound. Peering into the dark space, she looked up at me in horror. "It's empty."

And, the cellar door opened.

78

"Lovely," Logan said into the room when he saw the missing rock and a shiver ran through Sheena. "Did you know about this?"

"I did not," Jeremy answered. Crossing the room, he snatched the stone from the girl's hand and threw it to his left. The image of Tamela's head being tossed in the same direction threatened to take me over but I ignored it.

"It's empty," he said over his shoulder to his husband. Then grabbed Sheena by her hair. "What were you going to put in there or what was in there?"

"Nothing," she said.

"I don't believe you," he responded with a hard yank that pulled her neck back at an unnatural angle.

"There's nothing in there and nothing on us," I growled. "So why don't you believe her?" I had nastier words on my tongue but knew it wasn't the way to approach this. When all else fails, apply logic.

He threw her to the ground and turned his attention to me. "I see you fought off my power." That was it. No anger really, more fascination.

That was when I cursed myself for not pretending to still be under his spell. I could have used it to my advantage but had let my temper get the better of me – again. Too late now. I might as well play another hand.

"I did," fighting to manage a coy smile. "I'm much more powerful than you realize." I ran my options through my head. I could hint at more magic. I could tell him that his power was weaker than he thought. I could threaten.

None of those felt right. I had to remember that this was the Jeremy who'd been my best friend for half a year. What did I know about him that was possibly real? I knew he was a teacher and loved to learn.

Yes… that was it.

"Ever heard of a maiden of Isis?" I leaned back against the wall, attempting to look calm.

Logan moved in a blur to Jeremy's side. Jeremy arched his eyebrow. "Legend. It's an old wives' tale. Is this how you're going to buy time? Tell me stories like Scheherazade."

"Wrong," I chuckled. "It's true and I'm a maiden."

"What's a maiden of Isis?" Logan asked.

Jeremy's head continued to shake back and forth. "They're supposedly these powerful women called forth, like chosen ones. They get all our vampire powers. It's complete bullshit."

Standing up straight, I squared my shoulders and lifted my chin. "Not bullshit. I'm a maiden and Alex is my warrior. Why do you think he, Sorin and I made the kind of power in the manor that we did? When we came together?" I tapped my temple. "Think about it, Professor. You're not dumb. You and I both know that I'm not your usual vamp. You said so yourself. I'm different."

With the last phrase, I willed my voice to make he and Logan feel special. Watching their faces change, I knew it had worked. I used the momentum. Holding up my hand, I pulled from the magic in my core, felt the heat slide up and then down my arm to erupt into flame on my palm.

I was certain that Jeremy's eyeballs were about to fall out of his head. Unfortunately, Logan was looking angrier by the second. I extinguished the fire, dropping my hand to my side.

"What does it matter?" Logan asked and each word dripped with fury. "Parlor tricks."

"Maybe," I laughed, dryly. "But not all my powers are for show. For example," I locked eyes with him. "I know that you're seriously pissed right now. But, not with me or the situation." I let my gaze slither to his partner. "With Jeremy." I let my stare remain on my ex-friend but spoke to Logan. "You're so sick of cleaning up his messes. He's fucked up one too many times. You think you're the brains of the operation and you're getting really tired of having to carry his weight."

I was pretty sure that Jeremy just paled a little.

Logan guffawed and everyone in the room knew it was a forced reaction. "Please," he snapped. "Your tricks aren't going to work on me. You aren't going to win by splitting us up."

Logan's words brought Jeremy's confidence back and I couldn't let that happen. I opened up my empathy and my psychic ability to pull anything I could. I hoped I wasn't too frantic to use my powers.

Inspiration struck.

"You feel like you bound yourself to an anchor, not someone that will move with you." Logan's face told me I was onto something but I knew I needed more. "For a while, you were madly in love. Then, something happened." I felt Logan trying to lock me out of his thoughts. He was humming in his mind and it filled my thoughts but I pushed through. "When Jeremy attacked the actor – that's when you knew."

Both men faced each other, in shock. "Did you tell her?" Logan asked his husband.

"No," Jeremy insisted. "Why would I?"

I kept going. "You took him to see a show downtown and let him wait to meet the actor on the street, outside the side door. But, instead of just taking a selfie, Jeremy attacked him."

Jeremy held up his hands in the face of Logan's rage. "Logan, I didn't tell her. I swore I never would."

Logan vehemence turned towards me. I didn't like seeing that level of hatred in anyone's gaze but there was no reason to end this.

"Killing someone in Pittsburgh would get you punished by Sorin. You were so scared when Jeremy befriended me," I continued. "You were certain that he was actually starting to think of me as a confidant and would spill the beans. You never really believed he could pull this off."

Now, it was Logan's turn to lose all the color in his face. I was getting to him and I could use this to my advantage. If they were distracted, I had a chance.

"Nice try," Jeremy interjected. "I have to hand it to you, that was very impressive and also intriguing. But joke's on you. You can't live with someone as long as we've lived with each other and not be able to read them. I already knew he thought all of that."

Pretty sure it was my time to go ghost white with shock.

Jeremy shook his head and reached behind his back. A *ting* hit my ears as the long, shiny blade was withdrawn from his back and shown to me. I don't know if you'd call it a sword or a knife or something else. All I knew was - in the hands of the men who decapitated my friend with a kitchen knife - this thing was a problem. As Jeremy was revealing the weapon, Logan had crossed to retrieve something in the doorway of the cellar. When he returned, I wrenched my gaze from the blade to Logan's new toy - bolt cutters.

I didn't want to know what their plan was for either one of those items.

"Here's how this goes," Logan's anger was definitely all for me now. "I will break both chains. You *will* both listen to what we tell you or the rebel can watch the other die." He locked his eyes on Sheena. "I'm looking at you, honey. Pretty sure, Kate is the one who'll fight so you'll be the one to go first."

Looking down at Sheena, all I could see was Alex's beloved sister. In an instant, several flashes went through me. I saw Alex talking about his sister in the bar on the night I turned. I saw her broken, beaten and scared in Sorin's bathroom the night I met her. I saw Alex's joy when he was reunited with her, his anguish and bloody knuckles when he knew she'd been abused and him sleeping on her floor. Then, I saw him and Sorin looking at me with love in their eyes.

We both had to survive this. There was no other option.

I raised both hands. "I won't fight you."

The next phrase came across like he was more annoyed than anything. "Great. Let's do this then."

"Do what?" I asked, knowing I was pushing it.

While he spoke, Logan used the tool to snap each chain off of my and Sheena's ankles. I made a show of rubbing the spot, even though we all knew it didn't hurt vampire skin. "Moving you both to a different location. We need you far away from Sorin until we can get into another country."

Jeremy went behind Sheena, dramatically sliding his arm around her waist and holding the sharp metal to her throat. "You and I go first up the stairs, then Kate with Logan behind her." He hissed in her ears and the vehemence poured off of him. "I know you know your way to the front door and outside."

And so the parade started, out of the cellar and towards our fate.

79

Walking through the kitchen that I'd seen in Sheena's memories was almost disorienting. It was like walking through a dream come to life. Entering the living room brought on that same surreal feeling of walking through a vision. In my periphery were the same stairs that Sheena had walked up to see Jeremy for the first time.

And in front of me, was the door Sheena had crossed through in the desperate attempt to be free after thirty years of captivity. She never could have foreseen what that decision would set in motion and I could only imagine the amount of bravery it had taken. Sadly, she had ended up back in this cabin and her living nightmare. What would this door hold for us tonight?

I watched Jeremy shove her through the open door and down the stairs. She stumbled but didn't fall to the ground. I silently applauded her for her enormous strength. After everything she'd been through, she still fought to hold herself upright.

As I crossed the same threshold, I saw the car that Sorin had given me. As silly as it seemed, it saddened me that it'd been pulled into this. I wanted it to be safe in the manor's garage and not the vehicle that would take Sheena and I further away from the people we loved so much.

When all four of us were at the bottom of the wooden steps and on the same gravel that I'd seen in Sheena's memory, I was horrified to see the ashes. They were in the undeniable shape of a headless body. The sight of it filled me with rage. My chest ached with the knowledge that these men hadn't even bothered to sweep up the remnants of my friend and Sorin's progeny. My respirations involuntarily spiked. I could see my ribs expand and fall with the painful breathing that accompanies unreleased screams.

Through the blinding rage, I felt the emotions around me change. Sheena's resignation to her death was the same. Logan's annoyance and sheer frustration were steady. But, Jeremy – Jeremy was wavering. He hated me, that was for sure. Why, I wasn't certain. But, part of him was so interested in me and wanted to have me as an ally. He fully believed now that I was a maiden of Isis and the professor in him wanted to learn so much more about what it meant and what I could do. I was a thing of legend and his ego wanted to be a part of it.

I shot him a thought. *You can still get out of this. We can get rid of Logan, wash Sheena's brain and you could be on my right hand as I rule this city with Sorin. Continue to be his assistant and my confidant.* It was a long shot. However, all of my options ended in death, so I might as well try.

Every muscle in Jeremy's body tensed and he froze. In slow motion, he turned to face me. I knew he'd heard my thought and was considering it, weighing his options.

Logan wrapped his arm around my waist and squeezed hard enough to make me groan. "Whatever she's doing," he growled, "don't fall for it, Jeremy. We're almost out of this."

Damn. The downside to mates is that they know each other – for better or for worse. Logan knew I was talking to his partner and Jeremy would choose his husband every time. I was out of ideas.

"Where are you taking us?" Sheena asked. I was so happy to hear that she could put together a sentence. It was killing me that I didn't know how to save us.

"Far," Jeremy barked. "We'll drive 'til the sun forces us into some motel. Then, when it's gone, we drive some more."

"I'm thinking North," Logan said like he was telling us we are going to Disney World. "Ditch you in some Maine wilderness to meet the sun, then Jeremy and I cross the border and get on a plane heading away from the sun."

Jeremy picked up the master plan where Logan left off. "By the time your men know you're not in Virginia, we'll be long gone and they'll be looking south." Logan punctuated the end of the plan by driving his knee into the back of mine, forcing me to the ground. Jeremy handed the blade back to his mate like they'd choreographed it. I felt it on the front of my throat before I even accepted that it was no longer with Sheena. She looked back at me, pleading and I saw the single blood drop roll down her cheek.

We only had that fraction of a second to say what we needed to with our eyes before Jeremy used his favorite move to grab a handful of her hair and yank her head back. Walking her toward the BMW, he shoved his free hand in his pocket and I saw the trunk pop open.

Shit. How many times am I going to be thrown in a trunk in my undead time on Earth? Twice in six months has to be a record.

Sheena didn't even seem to fight. The resignation was obvious in the way she walked over and climbed in.

I could fight but for what? They'd kill me and take Sheena to the wilderness. If I got in the trunk, at least we'd be together and have some more time.

Logan took the blade from my throat, grabbed my arm and yanked me up to standing. Dropping my head and looking down at my feet, I willed them to take steps towards the car. I felt the joy rolling off of both men. They were awfully proud of themselves and felt like real bad-asses and I hated it.

Revenge later, I thought to myself.

The trunk came into my downward gaze. Was I really going to do this? Was I going to voluntarily get into a trunk? I'd told my daughters

1,000 times that you fared better when you ran away than when you got into the stranger's vehicle. But here I was, getting into the bad guys' car.

Sheena looked up at me from her fetal position. Her eyes were full of hope – hope that I had an idea.

I didn't need one.

I heard the tires on the gravel as Logan yanked me back against him and the knife found its way back to my throat. Campfire and laundry detergent hit my nose.

Alex and Sorin were here.

80

Jeremy's top half disappeared into the open passenger's side window and reappeared with a twin of the blade resting on my trachea.

You had to be kidding me. Two swords?

He yanked Sheena from the trunk and met his partner at the bottom the stairs. The men stood side by side, each with a murder weapon and a captive, watching the rescuers race to save their loved ones.

The car came to a skidding stop. The cloud of gravel dust was still hanging in the air when both front doors opened. I heard Sorin's voice before I saw him and Alex. "Do not hurt them."

His voice cracked through the air, greater than the strongest thunder clap. If I hadn't been afraid to move, I would have put my hands over my ears. Instead, I let the power of those words hit me, knowing that Jeremy and Logan felt it, too.

Alex and Sorin came to stand side by side, directly in front of us. Heroes facing villains, like two sides of a mirror. One side was hope, the other side was my death. I refused to believe I'd survived all of this just to die this way but had seen how quickly Tamela was ended and knew it was a possibility.

It was a showdown and only one side was walking away from this.

"Leave us," I said to Sorin and Alex. "Let them run."

"Please," Sheena echoed next to me. "Alex, please. Just go. I don't care if I die but I do care if you die."

"It's not going to happen," Alex answered without a beat.

"We're taking you home," Sorin added.

"I doubt that." This came from behind me. Logan's voice rumbled against my back and hit my ears. "I'd say we have the upper hand so we're making the decisions."

I watched Sorin pull back his rage and put on his politician face. "Then, what do you ask?"

Jeremy was the one to respond. "Let us take them tonight. We'll have them somewhere that you can come get them later, closer to the border. And, you don't look for us." I saw him look over at me in my peripheral vision. "I don't want to hurt her but I will." Turning back to Sorin, he finished. "This is the only way that they live. The other option is that we slit their throats in front of you, you try to kill us and exist forever without them."

What Jeremy didn't know is that my death would bring on Alex's death since we were tied now. So, Sorin would lose Sheena, Alex and me in a matter of seconds if he fought and lost. I saw the calculations happening in his brain. Even I knew it was bad odds. Maybe I could level the field.

I slid into Jeremy's thoughts and back out, sending the information to Sorin and Alex. *He's lying. They plan to kill us before you'd ever get to us.*

Sorin met my eyes and nodded. I found Alex's gaze. He shook his head and his eyes filled with pleading. He didn't want this to be the reality – didn't want to lose so much. Strength overtook his desperation as he accepted that this was the right choice. I sent both men my feelings – let them feel my love for them before I made my move. Then, with a thought, I called out to Sorin and Alex's power and felt it hit me – the three of us merged and all that magic filled my chest.

Before Jeremy and Logan could react to us calling power, I wrapped my arms behind me to grab Logan and shot upwards into the air with a new found speed, strength and confidence.

His shock gave me the moment I needed. He pulled the knife from my throat and I looked down. Jeremy was gazing upward where I'd taken his husband, which gave Sheena the second she needed to run into the woods. Logan attempted to wriggle free but he was fighting the power of three now. I blasted magic out of my back and felt Logan lose his grip on me. So, I lost my grip on him and let him plummet to the driveway below.

As my feet gently returned to the ground, Sorin and Alex were already on Logan. Alex had gotten the blade from Logan, just in time for Sorin to grab each side of his opponent's face. I expected to hear the snap of Logan's neck but instead he lurched forward to fight. I didn't have time to see how it turned out.

I was already chasing Jeremy and Sheena into the woods, leaving the sounds of the battle at my back. Not knowing which way to run, I stopped by a tree and focused my hearing. A whimper ahead and to my right sent me racing.

The woodsy-citrus scent of Jeremy was on the wind. I tried to lock in on it and was sure he was nearby when a crack filled the air. A thick branch filled my vision, crashing into my chest and throwing me back. Before I could recover from the blow, dozens of rocks joined behind the branch, slamming into every part of me. The one that connected with my forehead rocked me off balance, taking me onto my back on the ground.

Scrambling behind a fallen log, I found shelter from the onslaught.

Two could play at the telekinesis game. I hadn't manifested it yet but it didn't hurt to try. Jumping up to my feet, I spread my stance just as the next round of forest debris was sailing into my direction. Raising up both hands, I screamed and push power from my palms. Every item headed my way, hit an invisible wall and rushed backwards away from my body, only to drop to the ground when my opponent's magic pulled back.

"Nice," I heard from somewhere unseen. "You really are a maiden, huh?"

"Yep," I said into the trees, in response to my ex-friend's comment.

"Probably shouldn't have made you my enemy," he said and I couldn't help but laugh as I looked for any sign of where he was.

"Probably not," I answered, starting my creep towards the place I'd heard the whimpering. "You out there, Sheena?" I waited for anything to let me know she was okay but heard nothing.

"She was the warm-up," he said. "Now, I'm ready for you."

I expected him to charge me and was ready. Instead, I heard the sounds of him running away from me, deeper into the forest. I didn't even consider not following him. Instinctually, I propelled myself after him and away from Sorin and Alex. Moving through trees, over logs and rocks, I chased the scent of him for what felt like a mile until the smell was suddenly gone. I froze and let my senses refocus. I'd definitely lost the trail and was pretty sure I knew why. The roar of a waterfall slammed against my ear drums.

Stepping gingerly, I followed the sound until I found the thing I needed.

The waterfall was beautiful in the darkness of the night but there was no time to enjoy it. All I was interested in was the obvious space behind the cascading water – the only place that a vampire could hide his sounds and smells from another of his kind.

Lifting up and above the trees, I floated to the spot where the small river fell over the Earth and down. Following its pathway, I descended with the water so close to my face, that the mist off the waterfall soaked my dress. When my feet were just about to touch the river below, I pushed through the falls to enter the cave behind it and face the shocked man on the other side.

The wet soil took the weight of my soft landing and I stood stock-still in front of my would-be killer, the man who'd caused my mortal death and actively tried to ruin my afterlife. What do you say in this moment?

"I hate you," my statement would've been lost to human ears, thanks to the roar of the water behind me but I knew he heard me.

Jeremy's face should've given me sorrow or fear or pain. I would've taken any of those options. But he gave me amusement. "At the end of all of this, with all your power." He spread his arms. "You're still just a chick with hurt feelings. How disappointing."

He didn't deserve a response, that so I changed the subject. "Just let me take you to Sorin. He might go easy on you, exile you."

He cocked his head. "C'mon. You don't believe that and neither do I." That was when I realized that blood was streaking his face. "He killed Logan. I felt it happen." I had a spilt second of remorse or grief. "So, no, you won't be taking me to Sorin. I'll be leaving."

I focused my energy in my belly and felt it start to boil. There was no way I was letting him run again. Pulling my power into my core, it cooled and I forgot why I was so mad.

"Ah, ah, ah," Jeremy scolded, wagging his finger. "Try to pull power on me, toots, and I'll just shower you with bliss." I felt his power recede, leaving me empty. "I'm happy to continue this as equals but I will not allow you to use your powers. Thanks for displaying them all, by the way. It helps me hold them back."

That was going to limit my options. I couldn't throw flame at him without calling it forth and he'd stop it before it started. Farseeing to Sorin meant leaving my vulnerable body behind. Flying wasn't going to help me either. I could use my voice to try and control him but had the feeling it was going to be futile. One look at his eyes told me he was insane with grief and frantic to escape. That was a dangerous mixture.

I may not have been able to use magic to get through to him but I'd spent over a decade talking to people in the worst moments of their life - long before I was a creature of myth. Two things break though: compassion and the hard truth.

"Since this is the last time we'll ever talk, can I say something?" I kept all emotion out of my voice.

He was suspicious but also curious. "Okay."

I drew in a breath and let it out. "I've been though some fucked up things. Dad left, Mom abused me, assaulted in college... you know, the usual." Jeremy didn't look the least bit empathetic. I wasn't surprised so I kept going. "Murdered outside my workplace, then became undead, have to live off blood. Then, kidnapped by a Nazi. Then, kids almost murdered in front of me. But, you-" I took a step toward him and he didn't move away. He was cocky. "Your betrayal is the most screwed up thing that's ever happened."

This got me a slight reaction; something passed over his eyes.

I used the crack in his resolve. "My parents were trash. The guy in college was garbage. Will and Evelyn were insane. But you knew exactly what you were doing. You were purposefully trying to destroy someone for your own gain. You assualted and tortured a girl so you could feel powerful, not because you deserved more than you have." Rage replaced the directionless grief he'd had before. Maybe I was playing this wrong.

It was too late now. "You pretended to be my friend for months and it was all a lie. You're not a genius." I stepped closer. "You're a delusional psychopath."

His fist connected to my jaw before I knew what had happened. I was on my back looking up at the cave ceiling. He stepped over me, foot on each side, filling my vision - but not before I saw the red handle in the rock and knew for a fact that I would be the one making it out of this cave.

Triumph filled his face as he looked down onto me. I scrambled backwards and jumped to my feet, taking on the fighting stance that Tamela had taught be over 100 sessions. Jeremy didn't advance, he threw his head back and laughed.

"Man to man? Really, Kate?" he said through guffaws. "We're going to duke it out?"

Outstretching my hand, I willed the item embedded in the cave rock above his head to my palm and closed my hand around it when I felt the weight of the sword. Jeremy's eyes grew wide and the rage was replaced with shock and awe.

"No, Jeremy. This was never going to end in a fair fight." I brought the sword up across me to my left, holding it up with both hands, ready to swing when the moment was right. "I believe Tamela left a gift for you. She may not be able to kill you, but she made sure her sword and I would."

I watched him relax. All laughter, grief, rage…. gone. For a few moments, we stood like that, eyes locked. Then, he shrugged his shoulders. It was such a simple gesture, something a child does when they're busted stealing the cookies before dinner. "You can't fault me for trying," he said before he bent down and charged like a linebacker.

I side-stepped, pivoted and swung the blade down on Jeremy's neck as he expected to ram into my core. His body was still running through the waterfall and into the river below as his head hit the cave floor. I ended the fluid movement on a knee, one arm raised high and the other was angled down, holding the sword that Tamela had left for me exactly where she knew I would need it.

When I looked up, to the back of the cave, I saw her there, smiling. She pressed both hands to her mouth and sent me a kiss before disappearing.

81

I almost ran into Sorin as I reach the edge of the woods. He was running in to save me or find me or both. He slid to a stop – taking in the sight of me. Tamela's sword was still clutched in my hand, pointed to the ground and at my side. I was soaking wet, barefoot and held a head in my other hand.

Sorin slowly stepped towards me, reaching forward to take the sword from my grasp. I let him take that but I wasn't ready to let go of the head. I needed to hold onto it to know that this was all really over. I think he knew that and only slid his free arm around my waist to lead me out and to the driveway.

Alex had Sheena in a hug. The sight brought a wail of relief from my lips and I dropped to my knees, the head rolling off to the side as every muscle in me grew weak. Sorin came to the ground with me. Alex and his sister joined us and eight arms enclosed the tiny circle of trauma.

The men shushed rhythmically, trying to assure Sheena and I that it was safe, that we were safe. Sheena and I found each other and held on, shaking with the release of fear.

To Alex and Sorin's credit, they gave us the time we needed to deal before they got to business. "We have to burn the bodies," Alex said. "And get you all home before sunrise. We need to move fast."

He was right. We had to handle things and could try to process all this later.

Alex and Sheena built the bonfire while I looked for gasoline and matches. When I came out of the little shed in the back with my items and reached the driveway, I saw Sorin staring down at the ashes of his progeny.

We only had minutes left before we needed to move on but I'd already prepared for this. I set the gas can and matches at his feet, then handed him the rusty tin I'd found. "Put her in here so we can take her home."

He looked at me, a single blood tear creeping down, and nodded. I left him to transfer our much-loved T into the container. Pouring the gas over the pile of sticks and branches, I flicked the match and threw the tiny flame into the heap. Flames burst from the dry wood, engulfing the sticks and looking for more to feed off of. Alex threw Logan's lifeless body onto the pyre. I saw the angle of his neck before the fire took him and knew how he'd met his end. Sorin came to join us with the last offering – a head.

"What about the body," I asked, staring into the flames.

"I will ask the wolves to come find it and burn it along with this cabin," Sorin answered. "We do not have time before the dawn."

"Can we trust them?" I worried.

"Yes," Alex and Sorin said in tandem before turning to walk over to the cars.

As I took in the fire for one last moment and remembered it held a person who'd been my dearest friend for half a year, I wanted to feel sad. But, I didn't.

As I'd told Alex. Some people haven't earned your tears when they go.

82

Sorin drove me home in the BMW. Alex was ahead of us with Sheena in the car they'd used for our rescue. The last time Sorin had driven me to the manor after being kidnapped and having to kill someone, I'd curled up in the back seat. This time, I sat in the passenger seat with one hand in his and the other hand holding a precious tin. The world speed past us as we raced against the sun. It was so weird that everyone else was going to start this new day like any other day but to us, unimaginable tragedy had just struck.

My heart was so broken that I thought I may never recover. I thought of all the nights I should have hung out with Tamela but hadn't. I thought of all the places she'd never see. I thought of the hairstyle scrapbook she'd compiled for my wedding and the joy in her face when I'd asked her to be a bridesmaid. I thought of all the years she'd existed before I'd met her and how much I wished I could've had more time.

I thought of the little girl in the basement, praying her mom and dad would come save her.

I thought of the man at my side who would mourn her like the only child she was to him and that he'd never be the same.

We pulled into the garage, behind Alex and Sheena, with only minutes to spare.

Once in the kitchen, we stood silently. None of us knew what to say.

A note on the island from Edwin simply said "Naseem & Rhys - safe with wolves - will be back tonight. Boris has left town. Tamela has not checked in."

"What will we tell everyone?" Sheena's question broke the silence of the room.

"We'll tell them that she died a hero, protecting us and giving her life for ours." It was the last of my energy for the night and I knew I couldn't speak or move anymore tonight.

Sorin sensed what everyone needed. He silently handed the tin to Sheena. "She will protect you while you sleep today. Tonight, we will put her to rest."

Sheena nodded, gently took the container, pressed it against her chest and left the kitchen to rest. Alex turned to us. "I think I need to sleep on her floor for just one more night."

"Of course," Sorin said and we watched Alex follow his sister.

Wordlessly, I turned into the chest that had been comfort in my worst moments. While I knew I should be comforting him, I had no more to give. My arms found his neck and he lifted me up to cradle my exhausted body. I asked the universe to please make this the last time he carried me up the stairs after a night of battle and near death.

When we were safe in our room, he sat me on the end of the bed and lovingly removed my clothes. I never wanted to see that dress again.

While he disrobed, I found my spot in our bed and under the heavy comforter. When he joined me at my side, I laid against him.

"I'm so sorry, Sorin."

He was still, not giving away his thoughts or feelings. "I know, *regina mea*. I know." He kissed the top of my head. "It is not your fault." He responded to a thought I hadn't said out loud. "And, as sad as I am. I know that dying for someone she loves is exactly how she would want to leave this world."

I nodded, burying my face into his chest. I expected a flood of tears but had no more left for the night.

As I drifted off, I heard his quiet sobs and knew he was crying enough for both of us.

83

I rose the next night with Sorin thankfully still under me. I knew he was awake, just as I knew he felt me awake. A light tapping at the door, made us sit up together. The door cracked open and I saw Alex.

"Please come in," Sorin called.

Alex closed the door behind him, crossed the room and joined my side, putting me in the middle. His arms around me were comforting, like a warm blanket when you're shivering. "I'm not much of a guardian, abandoning you this morning to sleep on my sister's floor."

"Stop," I teased. "First of, you're new at this whole thing. Second, she needed you and I had Sorin. But lastly, I don't always need a protector. I do fine for myself."

"I saw the proof of that in your hands," Sorin added.

Something occurred to me. I pulled out from the middle of them, crawled a foot or two and turned to face them. "How did you guys find us? I mean, for all you knew, we were down South."

Sorin and Alex exchanged glances. "I knew something was wrong with that call. You sounded off and didn't ask about Alex. Additionally, you didn't try to respond to my Romanian. I know how proud you've been of what you've learned."

Alex added. "He mentioned to me that he thought something was weird but we thought maybe you'd had a bad session in Sheena's head and didn't want to tell us until we were back."

Sorin sighed. "And, then I felt the death of my progeny." He licked his lips to buy himself a moment before continuing. "I felt her die and felt nothing from you. That is when I knew you were in trouble, knew that it was very bad."

Alex picked up the story. "We left Rhys and Naseem with the pack, left without saying a word to anyone. But, had no idea where you could be. Sorin called Tom and he told us the girls were fine, that there was no reason for you to go to Virginia. He wanted to come up here to look for you but we told him to stay put until we knew more. We came back here to look for clues. The call gave us nothing, really. I assume they forced you to make that call?"

Both men were looking at me, expectantly. "You didn't talk to me," I answered. "You talked to Logan. He made his voice sound like mine."

"I see," Sorin responded. "I did not know he possessed that power. He never told me."

"Well, that was the least of his bad behaviors," I said.

Sorin nodded. "We had to rest for the day. I was awakened by a voice in my ear, telling me to head to Justin's land. It was Tamela's voice." He shook his head like he was trying to convince himself. "I thought perhaps there had been a mistake, that she was alive and psychically sending me a message."

Alex took over. "When we were only a few miles from Justin's, we saw her."

"Who? Beth?" I asked.

"No," Sorin answered. "Tamela. She was in the middle of a crossroads, pointing us to the west. I stopped to get her but," he looked to Alex. "She vanished." He turned back to me. "I knew then that she was a spirit."

"She marked the way," I said, more to myself than them. Then I explained, "she showed up in the basement. She told me that she'd marked the way and I would see it when I needed it."

"Her sword?" Sorin asked.

"Yeah," I was still trying to wrap my head around it all. "Showing up in the road, I get. But, how did she bring her sword from here to there and know where I would need it?"

"I don't know." Sorin rarely had to say that phrase. It added to the mystery of the whole event. We'd have to ponder it all later.

I leaned forward, taking each man into one arm. "I don't know how or why but I know I never thought I'd see you both again and I'm never going to take this for granted. We owe her that."

84

A few hours later, a group stood around the rose bushes that Tamela loved so much. Edwin and Naseem had taken the news of her passing with stoicism. They'd expressed Sorin's own sentiments – that Tamela would be honored to give her life for those she protected.

Rhys and Diana had arrived two hours after sunset. A nod from the wolf told us that the evidence was now gone.

Sheena held the tiny tin in her hands. At her feet, just under the most flowery of the bushes, a deep hole had been dug. Alex was next to her with his hand on her back. His other hand was on my back. My arm was around Sorin, who stood at my other side. Both men had been extra touchy-feely since I'd risen and I think they just needed to feel me to know I was really okay. I understood the need and wasn't complaining.

"Do we all want to say something?" Rhys said. "Before you lay the tin down?"

Sheena nodded.

Rhys continued. "Tamela was someone you'd be lucky to have in your corner and we did. She never looked frustrated or impatient. She treated everyone who came here with the same level of respect. I always admired that in her and want to be more like her."

Diana picked up. "Tamela scared the heck out of me when I first met her. She was protecting her boss and to be fair, I wasn't so honest in the beginning." We all chuckled. "But, as she got to know me, I was lucky enough to call her friend. And when I took over the pack, she helped me learn how to be strong but fair. I watched her command respect without saying a word and took that into my own leadership." The next was for Tamela only because Diana changed to Spanish. "También te estaré agradecido, amigo mío."

Sheena joined in. "She was my best friend. I wanted to be her friend forever. I wanted to tell her about college and for her to teach me how to fight like her. She made me feel safe. I never want to forget her."

Alex went next. "Tamela. I hope you can hear me because I need to say this. You took my sister in when she was broken. When she didn't trust anyone, she trusted you. You brushed her hair. You slept next to her. You protected her like she was your own sister," his voice broke and he took a moment to regain composure. "Then, when I just got her back, I almost lost her for good. But you gave your life for hers so I wouldn't have to say goodbye again. I'll always love you for that. Thank you, Tamela."

I sucked in a breath and let it out, shakily. "You died for me, my friend. You protected me even as a spirit. I don't know many people who would do that for another. You held on after death to get me to safety and I'll never be able to repay you. We killed the men who took you from us. And, I promise you this. We'll live every second to its fullest and I will never lose sight of the extra time you gave me on this Earth with your sacrifice." I looked over to Sorin as I said the last. "I will love your father for the rest of time and make him as happy as possible." Then, I looked back down at the tin. "Please be at peace."

Sorin's voice was monotone and I knew he had to control himself so he didn't leak his sorrow onto everyone else with his words. He was the Master of the city. He didn't have the luxury of falling apart in public, even in this small group. It didn't take away from the power of his words. "You saved the love of my life and that alone would be enough to mourn you. But you are more. You are my child." I felt him tremble and sent him some of my strength. He straightened and continued. "I will always be grateful that I descended those stairs and found you. I would have killed a thousand men to save you but you were the one who saved me. You made me a father and I will cherish our time. I will carry you in my heart until I take my last breath. I hope you are reunited with your human parents and know nothing but joy."

Sheena slowly sank to the ground and laid the tin in its resting place. Sorin laid her ruby necklace on top of it. Each one of us played a part in covering the hole with dirt, whispering our final goodbyes and walking away until only Sorin stood in front of the small gravesite.

We let him have his time to grieve freely without having to be lord of the city. We let him be a dad saying farewell to his little girl.

And, my car was never started for me again.

85

Two weeks later, I stood in front of a small gathering, not far from those roses. Unlike human weddings, a mating ceremony doesn't start with me walking down the aisle or anything. It's very simple. Sorin and I stood in front of our bench, holding hands and facing each other. Around us were Alex, Diana, Rhys and Sheena. Akila and Amun had come back for this occasion. Akila had even agreed to be the one to officiate.

"A mating amongst our kind is special," Akila began. "Unlike mortals, we can live for millennia so promising to be with no other is momentous. And, unlike mortals, we do not split once united. So, to mate is to commit to working on and through everything."

"But, to make this an even more special mating," she held her hand out to Alex. "Sorin and Katherine will not only mate each other but in front of these witnesses, declare that this man is to treated as their third mate. They hold the same promise to him as they do to each other - to never part." He stepped forward to meet us and took each one of our hands in his, forming a triangle.

Akila continued. "You will all serve as witnesses to this and hold these mates to their promises for each other. You will support them in their mating, becoming protectors of their love and devotion for each other."

Everyone clapped around us as I was treated to a kiss from Alex and then Sorin. Looking up into the sky, I watched a star shoot across the darkness. "I see you, T."

86

Today

So, there you have it. Not what you were expecting? Yeah, me neither. But I've learned some important things thanks to the very dangerous afterlife I seem to have.

First, time is precious. Even if you're an immortal, every time you wake for a new day is a gift. A sharp blade or unexpected sunbeam can end it all. So, don't waste it. Tell people you love them. Enjoy the moments and don't rush from one thing to the next. Don't give your time to people who don't appreciate it.

Second, real friends are hard to find. If you find them, don't take them for granted. Love them exactly as they are and celebrate the crap out of each other. On the rare occasion that one of them turns out to be a psycho who was secretly trying to kill you or ruin your life, don't let it make you afraid to make new friends. Even if it happens to you twice in one year.

Third, love is wonderful but you can't just wait for it to find you. You're going to have to put yourself out there and be open. Sometimes, love will surprise you. You may meet a hot but obnoxious man who you think you hate but then realize you love. It may even happen twice. Who knows? The point is, love comes in all shapes and sizes. Don't be afraid to follow your heart and see where it leads you. And also, don't judge someone else's love. That's not cool or your business.

So, this is my last journal entry for a little while. I'm following my own advice and not wasting anymore time. I'm putting the diary away and existing in the moment........right after I turn in this resignation and walk out of the hospital for good.

Okay, I don't know if I'll really stay away for good but I do know I need my time.

I have a wedding to plan, need to get Sheena to and from classes soon, need to spend more time with my daughters and need to help bring the new Interspecies Council into fruition so vampires and wolves can be united. Plus, I have two men in my bed every night. My plate is full without being pulled into the hospital all the time.

When I find myself with some free time or the need to work through something traumatic, I'll write another journal and send it in to the publishers. In the meantime, you guys have much less time than I do. I urge you to look around and ask yourself – am I giving my precious hours and energy to something or someone that doesn't deserve it?

The End.

Afterwards

To the fans of the Eternal Night Shift Series,
This is not the end of Kate's story but it is goodbye for now.
The next three books will bring you the back
stories of Rhys, Alex and Sorin.
I want you to get to really know them, see what
led up to the moment we meet them in
Bite Shift. There is more to those men than you get to see
from Kate's perspective. They deserve to be known.

After those three books – if you want it – Kate's story will continue.

Wicked Hugs & Bloody Kisses,
Lena

www.ingramcontent.com/pod-product-compliance
Lightning Source LLC
Chambersburg PA
CBHW030232120726
47903CB00005B/1453